PRAISE FOR AM

'Everything a pony-mad girl wants and needs in a fabulous series of pony stories. Every time I read the latest book I think it's the best but Amanda has done it again.'

— AMAZON FIVE STAR REVIEW

'These books are timeless and yet perfectly modern. Highly recommended.'

— AMAZON FIVE STAR REVIEW

'A pony classic for the future.'

— AMAZON FIVE STAR REVIEW

THE RIVERDALE PONY STORIES

BOOKS 4 - 6

AMANDA WILLS

Cherry Tree
Publishing

THE RIVERDALE PONY STORIES

Redhall Riders
The Secret of Witch Cottage
Missing on the Moor

REDHALL RIDERS

1

———————

Poppy McKeever knew that the haunting cry of the curlew would forever remind her of the accident. *Coor-lee, coor-lee, coor-lee* called the bird into the vast Dartmoor sky as Cloud thundered across the moor towards the isolated farm they had passed an hour earlier. Poppy crouched low over the saddle, urging her pony faster. Cloud, his ears flat and his nostrils flared, responded by lengthening his stride until they were galloping flat out. Poppy wound her hands through his silver mane and chanced a look back, but the others were already tiny specks on the horizon. An old stone wall loomed ahead and she eased Cloud back into a canter. Seeing a stride she squeezed her calves and he soared over the wall with a foot to spare, landing nimbly on the spongey grass on the far side. They turned right, following the steam as it dipped and curved towards the farm, Poppy's heart crashing in time with Cloud's pounding hooves.

Coor-lee, coor-lee, coor-lee cried the curlew from the marshland between the stream and a belt of emerald green conifers. A dark stain of sweat was seeping across Cloud's grey flanks and Poppy could feel him beginning to tire.

'Not far now,' she whispered, running a hand across his neck. He flicked an ear back at the sound of her voice. 'Look, I can see the farm.'

With every stride the farmhouse grew bigger. Poppy remembered the rosy-cheeked woman in a red and white checked shirt who'd been picking runner beans as they'd ridden past earlier. Balancing a trug on her hip, she'd called a cheery greeting and they'd waved back. Poppy hoped with all her heart that she was still at home.

They clattered up a stony track to the farmyard. Poppy slithered to the ground and looped her pony's reins over a fence post. Bella would be horrified but there was no time to waste. Cloud watched her, his ears pricked, as she ran into the farmyard, scattering a handful of chickens pecking about in the dirt. Their indignant squawking woke an elderly collie curled up on a rug by the back door. He raised his head and gave a low woof before settling back to sleep.

'Please be in,' Poppy muttered, tugging at the brass door knocker. She almost wept with relief when the door swung open and the woman in the checked shirt stepped out, brushing flour from her hands.

'There's been an accident. I need to use your phone,' Poppy croaked, her mouth dry.

The woman glanced briefly at Cloud standing patiently by the fence and ushered Poppy into a shabby hallway that smelt of freshly-baked scones.

'Whatever's happened? Are you hurt?'

'Not me. One of the other riders. Her pony fell.' Poppy pictured Niamh lying motionless on the ground and Merry standing next to her, the bay mare's hind leg hanging uselessly from her hock. She felt the prickle of tears. 'There was no phone signal. I need to call an ambulance.'

The woman handed her a phone and a tissue and watched as Poppy dialled 999. As she waited for the call to connect Poppy looked wildly around. 'I don't know where we are!'

'Tell them to head for Pegworthy Farm and we can take them from here. I'll write down the postcode.'

Poppy took the scrap of paper and gave the woman a grateful smile. 'Thank-you.'

'That's alright.' She laid a hand on Poppy's arm, leaving a faint floury imprint. 'Don't worry. I expect they'll send the air ambulance. Everything will be OK.'

Poppy nodded. But inside her heart she knew the woman was wrong. Everything was not going to be OK.

THE DAY HAD STARTED SO WELL. When Poppy's battered Mickey Mouse alarm clock pulled her out of a deep slumber with a persistent ringing that had bordered on impolite, she groaned, pulled the duvet over her head and almost went back to sleep. Until she remembered with a delicious jolt that it was the first day of the summer holidays. No school, no homework, no interminable talk of coursework and options for a whole six glorious weeks. And as if that wasn't exciting enough, the day she and Scarlett had been looking forward to for weeks had finally arrived.

Poppy jumped out of bed and crossed her room in a couple of strides, picking up a pair of jodhpurs from the end of her bed on the way. She flung open her bedroom window and whistled. Cloud looked up from where he was grazing in the paddock and whinnied. Chester gave an echoing heehaw. Poppy narrowed her eyes and scrutinised her pony. The Connemara had a grass stain on his dappled grey rump, a patch of mud running down his shoulder and a tangled mane. She glanced at the alarm clock. Seven o'clock. Two hours before Scarlett's dad Bill was due to arrive with the trailer to take Cloud and Scarlett's Dartmoor pony Blaze to Redhall Manor Equestrian Centre. Two hours to transform the muddy vision in front of her into a beautifully turned out pony. She knew she was lucky to be invited to Redhall for the week. The least she could do was to meet the exacting standards of Bella Thompson, Redhall's owner.

A bucket of warm water in one hand and a carrot in the other, Poppy headed out of the back door. Wisps of mist that had settled in dips and hollows the night before were already evaporating under the strong midsummer sun. Cloud and Chester stood at the gate flicking flies away with their tails. Poppy measured out their breakfasts and let them into the small area of crumbling concrete in front of the stables and barn that she ambitiously called the yard. While they ate she squirted horse shampoo into the bucket and set to work on Cloud, using a sponge to rub the shampoo into his coat and her fingers to work suds into his mane and tail. She gently hosed him down and used a sweat scraper to squeeze out the excess water. Chester nudged her, as if to remind her it was his turn. Poppy kissed his nose.

'I'm sorry, Chester. You're staying at home with Caroline and Dad.'

At five past nine Bill's Land Rover bounced up the Riverdale drive, the trailer swaying gently behind it. Scarlett leapt out and slammed the door.

'Poppy! We're here!'

'I heard you,' grinned Poppy, emerging from the tack room with Cloud's saddle on one arm and his grooming kit in the other.

'I'll take that. You load Cloud. I've done a haynet for him.' Scarlett opened the door of the Land Rover, propped the saddle alongside her own and squeezed the grooming kit into a space between a sack of sheep pellets and a metal feeding trough. 'I'll get your bridle. Where's your bag?'

'Here,' said Caroline, appearing from the house with Poppy's battered holdall. 'The place is going to feel a bit empty with you off for the week and Charlie at Cub camp.'

'Least Dad's at home,' said Poppy.

Caroline nodded. 'I've got a list of jobs for him, starting with clearing the guttering. He's going to wish he was at work.'

Cloud safely loaded, they said goodbye and Bill nosed the Land Rover back down the drive. Soon they were on the Okehampton road heading towards Redhall Manor.

'So you're going to be guinea pigs for the week?' said Bill.

'That's right. Bella wants to start offering pony camps in the holidays. She's put together an itinerary but wanted to have a trial run before she starts,' said Poppy.

'So we're getting a whole week at Redhall absolutely free.' Scarlett jiggled in her seat. 'I can't wait.'

Once they'd pulled into Redhall's immaculately-swept yard Poppy and Scarlett unclipped their seatbelts and went in search of Bella. They found her in the office, staring in exasperation at Harvey Smith, the tabby stable cat named after the famous showjumper, who was stretched across the keyboard of her laptop purring loudly.

'Damn cat. How am I supposed to finish the accounts?' Bella tutted. 'Let's get these ponies settled and I'll tell you my plans.'

Half an hour later Cloud and Blaze were happily munching hay in their borrowed stables and Poppy and Scarlett had joined their fellow guinea pigs around Bella's large kitchen table.

'I think you all know each other,' Bella said, looking at the five expectant faces before her.

The children nodded. Joining Poppy and Scarlett for the week were Bella's grandson, Sam, and two girls from Poppy and Scarlett's school, who also had weekly lessons at Redhall Manor. Tia had brought along her own pony, a chestnut gelding with a white blaze called Rufus, and Niamh would be riding one of the Redhall ponies, a bay mare called Merry. Sam would ride his black Connemara mare Star.

'As you know, some of the children on the pony camps we'll be running will be bringing their own ponies and some will be using ours, so it's a good mix. We'll be hacking out on the moor every morning and having group lessons in the afternoons, tackling a different theme each day, from pole work and jumping to dressage. I'll also be giving lessons on stable management in the evenings. With me so far?'

The children nodded. Bella looked at her watch.

'Today's hack is a six mile circular ride around the base of Barrow Tor. We'll leave at half past ten.'

A WARM WESTERLY breeze ruffled the ponies' manes and tails as they clip-clopped out of the yard, crossed the road and set off down a rutted track onto the moor. Bella led the way on her liver chestnut Welsh cob Floyd. Tia and Niamh rode two abreast behind her and

Poppy, Scarlett and Sam brought up the rear. Cloud jogged down the track, his neck arched and his tail high.

'He's full of beans,' said Bella, looking back. 'A blast on the moor will do him good.'

Poppy nodded. She could feel excitement zipping through her pony like an electric current. She relaxed into the saddle and kept the lightest touch on his reins until he took her cue and broke into a walk. Bella nodded approvingly.

They followed the track as it climbed steadily, Dartmoor ponies and black-faced sheep watching as they passed. Falling into single file they crossed through a gate onto a rough lane which led past a remote farmhouse, waving to a woman picking runner beans in the garden. Eventually they came to a wide grassy ribbon of a track. Bella pulled Floyd up.

'All OK for a canter?'

'You bet,' said Scarlett. Cloud danced on the spot and Poppy tightened her reins.

Bella kicked Floyd on and the cob broke into a canter. Tia and Niamh followed.

'You two go next. I'll bring up the rear,' said Sam. Poppy squeezed her legs and Cloud sprang forwards into an easy canter, Blaze following close behind.

'Yee-hah!' shouted Scarlett, waving an imaginary lasso. She was getting so tall she joked that she would soon need roller skates to ride Blaze. This would probably be her last summer riding the big-hearted Dartmoor pony that she'd had since she was five and she was planning to make the most of it. Poppy felt giddy with exhilaration as they sped on.

'Pony camp rocks!' she cried, pushing Cloud faster. She was so focused on Cloud's grey pricked ears that she didn't see the rabbit hole ahead. Neither did Merry. The bay pony's near hind leg shot down the hole and she pitched forwards. There was a gut-wrenching crack and Merry span into a somersault, throwing Niamh into the path of Tia's pony Rufus. Poppy watched with horror as Tia yanked the reins to the right. But it was too late. There was nothing the chestnut gelding could do to avoid Niamh and his hoof landed squarely on the small of her back as she lay face down in the grass.

In the seconds before Scarlett screamed Poppy heard the plaintiff cry of a curlew echo across the moor. *Coor-lee, coor-lee, coor-lee.* And then there was silence.

2

oppy, Scarlett and Sam sat on upturned bales of straw outside the tack room listening to Bella's one-sided phone call with growing horror.

'Injured her spine? Are they sure?'

A pause.

'And there's nothing they can do? She could be in a wheelchair for life?'

Scarlett clutched Poppy's hand. They could hear an angry buzz from the other end of the phone.

'Yes, I understand that. But it was an accident. The pony fell down a rabbit hole. There was nothing anyone could have done.'

More enraged buzzing, like a mosquito was trapped in the handset.

'I'm so very sorry.' Poppy was sure she could detect a catch in Bella's voice. She gripped Scarlett's hand back.

'If there's anything I can do please let me -' Before Bella could finish there was a click. Conversation over, she tramped out of the office, her normally ramrod-straight shoulders stooped, muttering about it being the final straw.

When she saw the three children she cocked her head towards the office. 'I expect you heard all that.'

They nodded.

'Who was it, Gran?' Sam asked.

'Gordon Cooper.'

They looked at her blankly.

'Niamh's dad,' Bella said. 'He's threatening to sue. Says it should never have happened. I tried to explain it was an accident but he wasn't having any of it. Apparently I should have inspected the route and carried out a risk assessment.'

'That's ridiculous!' exploded Scarlett. 'Perhaps he'd like to sue the rabbit, too.'

'Poor Niamh,' said Poppy. 'Will she be in hospital for long?'

'A few weeks. And then she'll be transferred to a specialist spinal unit, according to her father. Rufus's hoof damaged her spinal cord. It's unlikely she'll ever walk again.'

Scarlett stifled a sob and Poppy put her arm around her shoulders. 'We should keep busy. Keep our minds off it. We'll do evening stables tonight, Bella.'

Bella rubbed a hand across her face. 'That would be a real help, Poppy. There's a million and one things I need to do. Sam'll show you where everything is.'

'Do you think your gran'll be alright?' Poppy asked Sam, trying not to look at Merry's empty stable. The police had radioed for a vet once the air ambulance had taken off, its whirring propellers flattening the wiry moorland grasses. The vet slammed the door of his 4x4, strode over to Merry, took one look at her broken leg and shook his head.

'There's nothing I can do. I'm sorry,' he told Bella.

She nodded. 'Just make it as comfortable for her as possible.'

Poppy couldn't bear to watch as the vet sedated the pony.

'Take the horses to the farm. It'll only upset them. I'll come as soon as we're done,' Bella said.

Sam took Floyd's reins from his grandmother and they started walking. Poppy glanced back to see Bella rubbing the bay mare's ears, talking to her in a low murmur as the vet reached inside his bag. They were half a mile away when a single gunshot rang out over the moor. Poppy gasped and clung to Cloud's neck. She could hear Scarlett sobbing. Sam's face was like granite.

'She'll be OK. She's as tough as they come,' he said now, handing Poppy a pitchfork.

'What did she mean about it being the final straw?'

'A new livery yard opened at Claydon Manor a couple of months ago. State-of-the-art facilities. The horses are stabled in luxury loose boxes and they've got indoor and outdoor schools, a cross country course and a horse walker. They've even got a horse solarium. Gran's already lost two of her best liveries to Claydon and she's worried they won't be the last. That's why she wanted to start the pony camps. She needed the extra income.'

'Did you say Claydon Manor?' said Scarlett, poking her head over Floyd's stable door.

Sam nodded.

'But that's -'

'Georgia Canning's home,' he said. 'According to Gran, they've spent their way through their lottery win and are now having to make the place pay. Georgia's trainer has been promoted to livery yard manager and Georgia's had to sell most of her jumping string to make way for liveries.'

'Ouch. I don't suppose that went down too well,' said Poppy, remembering Georgia's supercilious smile as she'd beaten Sam and Star in the open class at Redhall's affiliated show the previous autumn.

'And Angela Snell seems intent on poaching Gran's liveries.' Sam kicked the bale of hay outside Floyd's stable.

'Who's Angela Snell?' asked Poppy.

'Georgia's trainer. She's a nasty piece of work. She knows she'll be out of a job if the yard isn't a success. And knowing Angela she won't let anything or anybody stand in her way.'

~

THAT EVENING, as Poppy cleared the kitchen table and Scarlett began attacking their dirty plates with a soapy washing up brush, Bella asked them if they wanted to leave.

'I've decided to postpone the launch of the pony camps in light of Niamh's accident,' she said heavily. 'Tia's gone home. I quite understand if you want to go too.'

'Are you kidding? We've been looking forward to our week at Redhall for ages,' said Scarlett.

'We don't mind that the camp is cancelled. But we'd like to stay and help. That's if you want us to,' said Poppy shyly.

Bella looked at Sam, who was flicking through a tattered copy of Horse and Hound.

'It's fine by me. What do you think, Sam?'

He looked up from the magazine and glanced at Poppy. She found her cheeks growing hot.

'Makes sense, now they're here,' he said. 'We could probably use the help.'

'That's settled then.' Bella smiled briefly. 'You ought to be making a move, Sam. Otherwise your mum'll be moaning about child labour again.'

Sam nodded, plucked his cycling helmet from the detritus on the Welsh dresser and headed out of the back door with a casual 'See you in the morning'. Poppy picked up a tea towel and started drying up, trying to ignore the knowing smile on Scarlett's face.

The phone rang.

'That'll be my insurance broker. I've been trying to reach him all afternoon.' Bella picked up the phone, listened for a moment and replaced the handset.

'No luck?' said Poppy.

Bella shook her head. 'Wrong number. It's the second one this evening. Leave the rest of the washing up. I'll show you where you're sleeping.'

Bella led the two girls to a double bedroom at the front of the house, overlooking the drive. The walls were painted the colour of ripe corn and a reproduction Munnings had been given pride of place above the fireplace. The room was simply furnished - two single beds, a large pine chest of drawers and an old pine door in the wall, which Poppy presumed led to a built-in cupboard - but Bella had added brightly coloured patchwork quilts, scatter cushions and a pile of pony magazines on the chest of drawers.

'What a lovely room,' Poppy said.

'The other bedroom is along the landing. I've painted that moss green and there's a Stubbs over the fireplace. That's where Tia and Niamh should have been staying.' A look of anguish crossed Bella's face and she sat down on one of the beds. 'I can't stop thinking about poor Niamh. If only we'd gone a different way.'

Poppy looked at Scarlett helplessly. Bella was usually so indomitable, although Poppy knew her brusque exterior was misleading. She cared deeply about her ponies and riders.

'You mustn't blame yourself. It was an accident,' she said. 'Niamh's dad'll realise that once he's had a chance to think.'

Bella shook her head. 'You didn't hear him, Poppy. He was incandescent. And he holds me wholly responsible.' She cocked her ear. 'And the blasted phone is ringing again. I suppose I'd better get it.'

Once Poppy and Scarlett had unpacked they went down to find Bella. She was sitting at the kitchen table with her head in her hands.

'What's the matter?' said Scarlett.

Bella exhaled slowly. 'And there I was thinking that today couldn't get any worse. My Auntie Margaret's had a fall and broken her hip. I need to go and see her.'

'That's alright,' said Poppy. 'You can go in the morning. We'll look after everything here, won't we Scar? Sam can help us.'

Scarlett nodded. 'Where's she in hospital? Plymouth?'

Bella shook her head. 'Inverness.'

Poppy and Scarlett were watching an old episode of *Friends* when Bella found them half an hour later.

'It's all sorted,' she said. 'My godson Scott is going to come and stay for a few days. He's a working pupil at a showjumping yard in Exeter. He used to have a Saturday job here when he was younger and knows the place inside out. I'd cancelled all lessons anyway because of the pony camp, so it's just a matter of looking after the liveries and the riding school ponies. My daughter Sarah - Sam's mum - is also going to move in until I'm back. She's hopeless with horses but she's a wonderful cook and she'll look after you all.' Bella paused. 'Do you think you'll be able to cope?'

The two friends nodded.

Bella smiled. 'Thank you, girls. I know Redhall will be in good hands.'

THE NEXT MORNING Bella lifted her suitcase into the boot of her car, slammed it shut and turned to face Poppy, Scarlett and Sam.

'I've phoned around the liveries and told them what's happening. A couple of them weren't too happy but there's not much I can do about that. The only one I couldn't get hold of is Vivienne. She'll probably be up this afternoon anyway. You'll have to tell her then. Sarah's on her way and Scott said he'd be here by eleven. You've got my number, haven't you Sam?'

He patted the mobile phone in his pocket.

They watched Bella's car disappear down the drive. Poppy was puzzled. Sam had gone quiet the minute Bella had mentioned her godson.

'What's Scott like,' she asked.

'He's OK. If you like that sort of thing,' he muttered, sweeping his blond fringe out of his eyes.

Scarlett's ears pricked. 'And you don't, by the sound of it.'

'Let's just say we don't always see eye to eye. But other people seem to like him. Especially girls,' he said darkly.

Scarlett raised her eyebrows and winked at Poppy. 'He sounds interesting.'

3

Poppy unfolded the list of instructions Bella had pressed into her hand before she'd left. 'What should we do first?'

Sam peered over her shoulder. 'I'll start on poo-picking if you two can muck out. Do the liveries first, just in case they turn up.'

Poppy nodded. Bella's five liveries were all stabled in the newest loose boxes on the south facing side of the yard. She and Scarlett had helped Bella turn them out before breakfast. Two nervy thorough-breds, one chestnut, one bay. A skewbald, a palomino and a showy Danish warmblood.

Poppy followed Scarlett over to the wheelbarrows, which were propped along the side of the barn, and picked up a pitchfork and broom. They worked together, forking out the muck and wet straw and banking the clean, dry straw around the sides of the stable. While the floors dried they filled the hayracks and water buckets and emptied the wheelbarrows onto Bella's towering muckheap. Poppy was balancing two bales of straw precariously on the wheelbarrow when she heard a car turn into the yard and the sound of a door slam-ming. As she looked up to see who it was the top bale toppled over and knocked over a bucket of water.

A tall, thin woman wearing pristine white jodhpurs and black leather riding boots strode over and looked down her aquiline nose at Poppy.

'Where's Bella?' she asked in clipped tones.

'I'm sorry, she's not here. Can I help?'

The woman eyed Poppy with disdain. 'I don't suppose so for a minute.'

'Bella's had to go away for a couple of days,' said Scarlett, emerging from the stable behind them.

'Who's running the yard?'

'We are,' said Poppy. 'With help from Sam and Bella's godson Scott. He works in a showjumping yard in Exeter. He'll be here soon.'

The woman's lips grew thin. 'I see.' She tapped her thigh impatiently. 'I wanted to check the farrier's coming this afternoon.'

Poppy consulted Bella's instructions.

'John the farrier is due at three o'clock to shoe three of the liveries,' she read. 'Cherry, Otto and Ariel.'

'Make sure he does Ariel first. We have the National Dressage Championships qualifier tomorrow and if my horse hasn't been shod in time there'll be consequences.' She looked from Poppy to Scarlett and back again, her eyes narrowed. 'Understood?'

Poppy and Scarlett watched the woman stalk back to her car.

'What an old bag,' whispered Scarlett, sticking her tongue out at the woman's bony back. Poppy stifled a snort of laughter, quickly disguising it as a cough when she stopped in her tracks and turned back to face them.

'And leave him in the stable in the morning. We've got an early start and the last thing I need is to be traipsing halfway across the paddocks to catch him,' she said.

'It'll be a pleasure,' Poppy said, hoping the woman didn't detect the irony in her voice.

'That must be Vile Vivienne. Sam warned me about her earlier. He said she orders him about like he's her personal slave,' said Scarlett as the woman drove off.

'Which one's Ariel?' Poppy asked.

'The black Danish warmblood that shares a paddock with Paint the skewbald. He's a real sweetie apparently.'

'Nothing like his owner then.' Poppy blew her fringe out of her eyes. 'Let's get this straw down and we'll see how Sam's getting on.'

Scarlett produced a penknife from her pocket and cut open the first bale of straw. 'What time is Scott supposed to be here?'

Poppy checked her watch.

'Half an hour ago,' she said drily.

POPPY AND SCARLETT were shaking out the last of the straw when a second car pulled into the yard.

'Perhaps that's Scott,' said Scarlett hopefully.

But a pretty woman in shorts and a vest top was emerging from the car. Judging by her honey blonde hair she was Sam's mum, Sarah. She saw the two girls and smiled.

'Are you ready for some lunch?'

'Am I ever,' said Scarlett.

'Good. I've made a mountain of sandwiches. Mum made me promise to keep you both fed and watered, like you were two of her riding school ponies.'

'I'll fetch Sam,' Poppy said, heading for the top paddock where she could see the quad bike and trailer Bella used for poo-picking. Sam was in the far corner.

'Your mum's here,' she said.

'That's good timing. I've just finished. Want a ride back?' he said. 'I'm as safe as houses, honest.'

'I guess,' said Poppy, looking at the seat of the quad bike dubiously. It didn't look very big.

Sam climbed on and looked around to see where she was. 'C'mon then, I'm famished,' he said, patting the padded seat behind him.

Poppy gave a tiny shrug and climbed behind him. He turned on the ignition.

'Hold on then,' he said, revving the engine. Poppy held on as loosely as she could and soon they were off, bumping along the field towards the yard. The quad bike hit a rut and lurched sideways. Poppy shrieked, her arms instinctively tightening around Sam. She could feel the muscles in his back flexing as he steered the bike onto more even ground.

'I'll just get rid of this lot on the muck-heap,' Sam shouted over his shoulder. He stopped at the gate to the yard and Poppy leapt off like a scalded cat. But not before Scarlett had seen them and had given her a knowing wink.

'Don't,' Poppy said. 'It was quicker than walking, that's all.'

Scarlett smirked. 'I'll take your word for it.'

THEY WERE FINISHING the last of Sarah's homemade chocolate brownies when the throaty growl of a motorbike cut through the warm afternoon air. Sam checked the time on his phone.

'Only an hour late,' he said.

Scarlett rammed the last piece of brownie into her mouth, stood up and ran her hands through her hair. She was already halfway across the yard when a black and silver motorbike roared in. The rider turned off the engine, kicked down the side stand and pulled off his helmet.

'Are you Scott?' said Scarlett, holding out a hand. Instead of shaking it the visitor handed her his helmet.

'I certainly am. And which one of my lovely helpers are you, Poppy or Scarlett?'

'I'm Scarlett,' Scarlett said breathlessly. 'We've already mucked out and done the liveries' hay and water and we'll do the riding school ponies after lunch so the only thing you need to do is make sure the farrier does Ariel first because Vile Vivienne's got a dressage qualifier in the morning and she said if he isn't shod there'll be consequences and Bella's had enough consequences this week to last her all year, so we really don't want any more.'

Scott threw his head back and laughed loudly. One of his front teeth was chipped, the only flaw in an otherwise perfect smile. 'Slow down Scarlett. I have absolutely no idea what you're talking about. Let me have a cup of tea first, eh?'

'Sorry Scott,' Scarlett said, bobbing her head. 'I'll go and stick the kettle on.'

'White, strong and sweet please,' he called after her. He gave Sarah a hug and pinched the half-eaten brownie on the paper plate on her lap. She smiled indulgently and batted him on the arm. Sam returned his high-five with about as much enthusiasm as a turkey invited to be guest of honour at lunch on December the twenty-fifth. Poppy allowed herself a small smile. Assuming it was meant for him Scott grinned back.

'And you must be Poppy,' he said, his muddy brown eyes assessing her.

She nodded and fled to the kitchen. Scarlett was stirring a mug of builder's tea, a dreamy expression on her face.

'He's so hot,' she said. 'He looks like Benedict Cumberbatch.'

Poppy raised her eyebrows. 'D'you think?'

'No, you're right. He's even better looking.' Scarlett picked up the mug and headed for the yard. Poppy sighed and followed her.

Scott was lounging against the door to Ariel's stable. Curls of damp hair were stuck to his head and tickled the collar of his battered black leather jacket. When he pulled off his leather gloves to take the tea from Scarlett Poppy noticed his nails were bitten to the quick.

Harvey Smith, woken from his cat bed in the tack room by the roar of the motorbike, padded out, saw Scott and made a beeline for him, rubbing his tabby cheek against Scott's skinny jeans. Scott took a slurp and looked around him.

'It's good to be back,' he said.

SCOTT DISAPPEARED INSIDE to unpack and Sarah began tidying away lunch.

'We'd better make a start on the other stables before the farrier gets here,' said Sam. 'I'll muck out if you two do the hay and water.'

Sam worked sparingly and methodically down the line of stables while Poppy and Scarlett emptied wheelbarrows, scrubbed out and filled water buckets and replenished hayracks. Soon the eight stables used by the riding school ponies were finished and it was time to catch the three liveries.

'You bring Ariel and Scarlett and I'll get Cherry and Otto,' Sam said, handing Poppy a brand-new leather headcollar. 'Just mind Paint because he has a habit of following Ariel out of the gate if you're not careful.'

Poppy and Scarlett followed Sam down the dusty track that led to the paddocks. Halfway along he stopped and pointed to a bay mare and a chestnut gelding who were standing nose to tail under an apple tree.

'That's Cherry and Otto,' he said. 'They've only been with us a few months. They're owned by a husband and wife, Debbie and Tim. They're both a bit highly-strung.'

'Cherry and Otto, or Debbie and Tim?' Poppy asked, admiring the two thoroughbreds' fine build and handsome heads.

'They all are actually,' said Sam. 'Not a good combination. Debbie and Tim are both over-horsed really. They'd only been having lessons for a few months when they bought these two from a yard in York-shire that produces top competition horses. They have lessons with Gran but they're both a bit neurotic and worry about absolutely every little thing. They treat Cherry and Otto like their children. There's Ariel, over there.'

The big Danish warmblood was watching them from the next paddock. He was a glossy jet black apart from four white socks.

'He's beautiful,' Poppy said.

'Much too nice for Vile Vivienne,' agreed Scarlett.

Grazing in the far corner of the paddock with his rump towards them was a hogged skewbald cob. Poppy's heart lurched. Paint was a dead ringer for Beau, the horse she'd fallen in love with during her trekking holiday in the Forest of Dean. She opened the gate and walked over to Ariel, offering him a Polo. He lowered his head and took the mint from her palm. She was standing on tiptoes buckling his head strap when she felt a nudge and warm breath on her back. Paint was standing behind her, eying her expectantly.

'Where did you spring from?' she laughed, peeling off a mint for him. He snatched it greedily and nibbled her pocket. 'Alright then, just one more. I was saving these for Cloud,' she told him.

Poppy clicked her tongue and started leading Ariel towards the gate. Paint pricked his ears and followed. They reached the gate and Poppy looked back. The skewbald cob was so close to Ariel that there was no way she would be able to lead him out without Paint following. She looked around for help but Cherry and Otto's rumps were already disappearing around the corner into the yard. She pushed Paint gently on the shoulder but the sturdy cob simply leant his bulk towards her.

'You're more like Beau than I thought,' she told him. 'Luckily I know something you won't be able to resist.' She peeled off the remaining Polos and dropped the first onto the grass under Paint's nose. Ariel followed her patiently while, one by one, she laid a trail of mints leading away from the gate. As the cob sniffed his way along the trail, snaffling the mints up, Poppy opened the gate and led Ariel through.

'Job done!' she said, patting the black gelding's muscular neck.

By ten to three all three liveries were in their stables ready for the farrier. Poppy picked up a broom and began sweeping the yard. Three o'clock came and went with no sign of John. By a quarter past Sam was anxiously checking the time.

'It's not like him to be late,' he said.

'He's probably been held up at his last job. He's not even half an hour late yet,' reasoned Poppy.

By half past three Sam's forehead was creased with worry. 'It wouldn't normally matter, but if Ariel's not shod today Vivienne will have a nervous breakdown,' he said. 'Gran must have John's number somewhere. I'll phone him.'

As Sam disappeared into Bella's office the phone started ringing.

'That'll be John, letting us know he's running late,' said Scarlett.

'What's up?' Poppy asked, as Sam came out shaking his head.

'It was another wrong number. So I tried phoning John, and he said he had a call from Gran cancelling his visit this morning. He's on the other side of Okehampton and won't make it today.'

'Why would Bella have cancelled him and not told us? It doesn't make sense,' said Scarlett.

'Maybe she forgot about tomorrow's dressage test and thought the farrier would be one less thing for us to worry about,' Sam shrugged.

'But he's on the list,' said Poppy, pulling it out of her back pocket. 'John the farrier at three o'clock to shoe Cherry, Otto and Ariel. Was it definitely Bella who called?'

'That's what John says and he wouldn't have any reason to lie. He's usually really reliable. That's why Gran always has him.'

Ariel leant over his stable door and nibbled at Poppy's pony tail. Her face paled.

'Oh God. Who's going to break the news to Vile Vivienne?'

4

———

S cott drew the short straw.
'On account of him not being here,' said Poppy. 'Come on
Scar, let's go and tell him the good news.'

They found Sarah peeling potatoes in the kitchen.

'Have you seen Scott?' Scarlett asked.

'I've made a bed up for him in Sam's room. He went upstairs to
unpack,' she said.

As they climbed the stairs they became aware of a soft whistling
sound coming from the back of the house.

'Someone's snoring,' said Poppy.

'It sounds as if it's coming from Sam's room,' whispered Scarlett.
'What should we do?'

They stood outside the room and looked at each other uncertainly.
The door was ajar. Poppy pushed it open with her index finger and
peered around it. There was Scott, fast asleep on top of the duvet in
the bed furthest from the door, his shoes still on and his rucksack
beside him.

'Dead to the world while we've been hard at it. I thought he was
supposed to be here to help,' fumed Poppy.

'But we can't wake him. He looks so peaceful,' protested Scarlett.

'Too right we can,' said Poppy. She coughed loudly. Scott didn't stir. She shoved open the door, letting it hit the wall with a satisfying bang. They watched as Scott opened first one eye, then the other, before yawning so widely they were given an unrivalled view of his tonsils. Puppy pulled a face.

'Sorry to wake you, Scott, but we've got some bad news,' said Scarlett.

He sat up, ran a hand through his hair and eyed them blearily.

'Must have just nodded off. Had a late one last night,' he said. 'What's happened?'

'I'll leave you to fill Scott in,' Poppy told Scarlett. 'I'm going to see if I can find Vile Vivienne's number. It must be in Bella's office somewhere.'

Sam was sitting in Bella's swivel chair with his head in his hands. Poppy stood at the door watching him for a moment. He looked as though he was carrying the weight of the world on his shoulders.

She cleared her throat. Sam looked up and gave her a fleeting smile.

'I'm after Vivienne's phone number. Perhaps Scott can go on a charm offensive and smooth things over,' she said brightly.

Sam reached for a blue ledger buried under a pile of Horse and Hound magazines. He flicked through to the back page, copied a phone number on an old envelope and handed it to Poppy.

The phone rang. Sam stared at it as if it was contagious.

'Aren't you going to answer it?' said Poppy.

'What if it's Vile Vivienne? I don't know what to say to her,' he said.

Poppy crossed the room and picked up the handset, bracing herself for Vivienne's clipped tones.

'Redhall Manor Equestrian Centre. Can I help?'

But there was nothing but silence on the other end of the line.

'Can I help you?' she repeated.

Poppy held her breath and listened really carefully. Was that static on the line or the sound of someone breathing? A shiver ran down her spine and she stabbed the end call button with her finger. She realised Sam was watching her.

'Wrong number again?' he asked.

'I guess. They didn't actually have the courtesy to say,' said Poppy.

'We've had a few this weekend. I'll have to get Gran to call out the engineers when she gets back. She's obviously got a crossed line.'

Scott appeared with Scarlett at his heels. Poppy handed him the phone and Vivienne's number.

'Just explain there's been a misunderstanding and that the farrier has promised to come out first thing tomorrow,' said Sam.

Scott nodded at the door. 'Clear off you lot. I don't want an audience. There must be plenty of jobs that need doing.'

Sam shot Scott a filthy look and Poppy rolled her eyes. Only Scarlett seemed happy to do his bidding.

'I'll go and make you another cup of tea,' she said, virtually skipping across the yard. Sam shut the door and beckoned Poppy to follow him down the side of the office to an old window at the end.

'I've got to hear this,' he said.

They crouched down under the window and listened as Scott dialled.

'Hello, can I speak to Vivienne Montague? It's Scott from Redhall. I'm afraid I have some bad news. No, Ariel's absolutely fine. It's the farrier. He crashed his van on the way here and won't make it tonight.'

Sam shook his head at the bare-faced lie.

'He says he's really sorry and he'll be here at seven tomorrow to shoe Ariel. Will that be in time for your dressage test?'

Poppy held her breath as Vivienne squawked down the line.

'No, there's no point you phoning him. He said he won't be able to get here any earlier. I'll make sure Ariel's groomed and plaited before the farrier arrives if that's any -'

There was a thud. Poppy presumed it was the phone being flung onto the desk. It was followed by the sound of the swivel chair scraping along the flagstone floor and Scott muttering under his breath. Poppy strained to hear. She thought she caught the words 'Bloody woman.'

Scott threw open the door. Scarlett scampered across the yard and handed him his tea.

'How did it go?' she asked.

'As well as can be expected,' he said. 'Are you any good at plaiting?'

～

POPPY CHECKED HER WATCH. Half past four. The stables were mucked out and the hay and water had all been done. The horses had been groomed and were grazing peacefully in their paddocks. There was a natural lull before evening stables. Sam was schooling Star in the indoor school. Scarlett had offered to help Sarah with a supermarket shop and Scott had zoomed off on his motorbike, muttering about needing some down time. Poppy found a sunny corner of the yard and sat down, Harvey Smith purring beside her.

She was texting Caroline when a lorry with a postbox-red cab turned into the Redhall drive, easing its way through the gateposts into the yard with millimetres to spare. The ruddy-faced driver climbed down from the cab, a clipboard in his hands. Poppy slipped her phone into her pocket, hauled herself to her feet and walked over.

'I've got Mrs T's delivery,' he said.

Poppy noticed the embroidered logo above the pocket of his red overalls. *Baxters' Country Store.* Bella hadn't mentioned a delivery on her list.

'Oh, we didn't know you were coming today. I'm not sure where it's supposed to go.'

'It's OK, I usually unload it outside the tack room,' said the driver. He walked around to the back of the lorry, slid open the doors and reached for a mustard-yellow sack barrow.

'The old girl's really pushed the boat out this week, hasn't she? Enough food to feed the flippin' cavalry and all them fancy supplements. They cost a bleedin' bomb. Has she won the lottery or summat?'

'Er, no.' Poppy joined the driver at the back of the lorry and peered inside. 'Crikey, is that all for Redhall?'

'Yup.'

'Are you sure there hasn't been a mistake?'

The driver whipped a stubby pencil from behind his ear and tapped his clipboard. 'It's all on the order form. Just sign here.'

Poppy scrawled her signature and the driver began pulling sacks of expensive-looking horse feed onto the sack barrow and wheeling it over to the tack room. Poppy picked up a couple of cartons of liquid pro-biotics and followed him. For the next ten minutes she helped him unload the lorry. Supplements for healthy bones and joints, strong hooves and glossy coats. Antioxidants and draughts to aid gastric health and digestion. Herbal tinctures promising vitality. Who knew all this stuff even existed? And since when had Bella, an old-school equestrian, had her head turned by all the marketing hype?

Once they had finished unloading the lorry Poppy sat on a tub of herbs for hormonal mares and watched it reverse slowly out of the drive. She was just finishing her text to Caroline when Sam led Star out of the indoor school and did a double take.

'What on earth's all that?'

'It's Bella's delivery from Baxters'. The driver said he usually leaves it outside the tack room.'

'It can't be. This is way too much. Gran has about a fifth of this. And none of this expensive stuff.' He picked up a tub and read the label. "Electrolyte supplement for the performance horse.' I don't even know what it is. And look at the price - nearly twenty quid! Gran hasn't ordered this.'

Poppy felt the colour drain from her face. 'But it was all on the order form, Sam. The man from Baxters' showed me before I signed for it. Bella must have changed the order.'

'You signed for it?' Sam's eyebrows shot up. 'This is going to cost hundreds of pounds. There's no way Gran can afford it, especially at the moment.'

'I'm sorry,' Poppy said in a small voice. 'I thought I was doing the right thing. I should have come and found you.'

'It's not your fault. I'll phone Baxters' now. Explain there's been some sort of a mix-up. I'm sure they'll sort it out.'

'I'll do Star,' she offered.

Sam handed her Star's reins and Poppy led the mare over to the tie ring outside her stable.

'I feel terrible,' she whispered as she untacked Star and ran a body brush over her gleaming coat. The mare whickered as Sam tramped over from Bella's office.

'Any luck?' Poppy asked.

He shook his head. 'They have an exchange policy on tack and rugs, but not on food.' He rested his head on Star's flank and stared at the mountainous pile of feed and supplements. 'Looks like we're stuck with it.'

AFTER DINNER POPPY took a mug of hot chocolate and a carrot out to the yard, her eyes on Cloud's borrowed stable. She whistled softly and his head appeared over the stable door. He watched her cross the yard, his silver grey ears pricked. She offered him the carrot and he crunched it noisily while she opened the stable door and settled in the straw to drink her hot chocolate.

She still felt bad about the Baxters' order, although Sam had told her not to blame herself. If only she had checked with him before she'd signed the order form. She had offered to use her savings to buy half a dozen of the tubs of supplements, joking that she would have the shiniest, calmest, least hormonal gelding with the healthiest digestive system and hooves ever seen. But Sam had told her not to be silly and that Bella would sort it all out when she was back.

'And I haven't spent any time with you today, have I Cloud?' she said, kissing his nose. 'It's just been manic.' It was true. She had hardly stopped. Her back and shoulders ached from hefting bales of straw and wheelbarrows of muck and despite five minutes spent scrubbing with a nail brush until the tips of her fingers were pink her nails were still black with grime. And tomorrow it would start all over again.

'Whoever says that working with horses is easy should give it a try for a few days. It's like painting the Forth Bridge.' Cloud nuzzled Poppy's hand, which still smelt enticingly of carrots. She scratched his forehead. 'It takes so long that by the time you've finished you have to start all over again.'

Realising Poppy didn't have any more titbits, Cloud sank to the floor and lay down in the straw. Poppy snuggled up close and sighed contentedly.

'We'll try and get out for a ride tomorrow,' she promised him. 'Just you and me.'

POPPY WAS LETTING herself in the back door when the phone started ringing. When no-one answered she picked up the extension in the kitchen, expecting another wrong number. She almost jumped out of her skin when Vile Vivienne began screeching down the phone.

'I phoned the farrier and there was no crash! He said Bella cancelled his visit. Well, she had no right. I have been working towards tomorrow's qualifier for the last six months. Six months! And she's ruined my chances. But worse than that, I have been lied to. I will put up with a lot, but I will not tolerate lying. I shall be removing Ariel from the yard.'

'But -' began Poppy.

'And in the light of what's happened I consider my contract with Redhall to be null and void. I will not be giving one month's notice. Please have him ready at ten o'clock in the morning.'

The line went dead. With a sinking heart Poppy headed for the lounge to break the bad news.

5

---

oppy woke early to the chatter of magpies. She squinted at her watch. Ten to five. She closed her eyes and tried to empty her brain so she could drift back into unconsciousness. But a shaft of sunlight that had slunk through a crack in the curtains like a cat burglar flitting through a heavily-alarmed art gallery played on her eyelids, banishing any chance of sleep.

Sighing, Poppy threw off her duvet and grabbed a clean teeshirt and pair of jodhpurs from her case. As she did she glanced at Scarlett. Her best friend's auburn hair was fanned around her face, her duvet was tucked under her chin and she was breathing deeply. She didn't look like she would be waking up anytime soon.

Poppy picked an apple from the fruit bowl and scribbled a note on an old envelope. *Gone for a ride. Will be back by seven.* She found her jodhpur boots in the tangle of wellies and riding boots by the back door and went in search of her pony.

Cloud must have had a sixth sense. When Poppy burst out of the back door, the apple between her teeth, he was watching over his stable door as if he'd been expecting her. He whickered and she scratched behind his ear, took a last bite of apple and gave him the rest.

Poppy reached under the flowerpot brimming with pale pink geraniums for the key to the tack room, plonked her hat on her head and carried Cloud's saddle and bridle to his stable. He shook his head impatiently as she tacked him up. Blaze, Star, the riding school ponies and the liveries all watched with interest as she led the Connemara over to the mounting block, tightened his girth, pulled down his stirrups and swung into the saddle. Soon they were turning out of the yard towards the moor.

They crossed the road outside the riding school and followed the rutted track they'd ridden along on Bella's first fateful trek to Barrow Tor. So much had happened since the accident it seemed like another life, yet it was only two days ago. An unwelcome memory of Merry pitching forwards as her hind leg disappeared down the rabbit hole swam in front of Poppy's eyes and she shook it away. The last thing she wanted to do was re-live that terrible morning. Instead she fixed her eyes on Cloud's pricked grey ears and tried to forget.

Ahead an orange sun smouldered behind the purple and grey horizon. Behind her the moon was fading in the early morning sky like a footprint in wet sand. The air smelt fresh, cold and clean and Poppy breathed deeply. Gradually she felt the tension of the last forty-eight hours ease from her shoulders. Her thoughts turned to Scott. Scarlett seemed in awe of Bella's godson but Poppy had been relieved to discover within minutes of meeting him that she was totally immune to his charms. He was way too smooth for her liking. And his laidback attitude to his new responsibilities irritated her. He was supposed to be helping, yet he'd barely lifted a finger while the rest of them worked their socks off to keep the yard running like clockwork. And she hated the way he belittled Sam.

Sam had got his own back the night before. As they'd sat down to eat Sarah's legendary fish pie, Scarlett had asked Scott how he'd chipped his front tooth.

Scott had run his tongue along the offending tooth and given them a rueful smile.

'An argument with a feisty gelding,' he said mysteriously.

'At the showjumping yard in Exeter?' Scarlett asked, impressed.

Sam snorted with laughter and Scott shot him a filthy look.

'Not exactly. He fell off Treacle,' Sam smirked.

'Our Treacle?' said Poppy. She couldn't imagine Scott atop the diminutive Welsh pony that Bella used for Redhall's beginners, despite his uncanny knack of dumping most of them in the nearest puddle while they were out on a hack. With a stomach the size of a barrel and an evil glint in his eye, the chestnut Section A gelding shared more than a passing resemblance to a Thelwell pony and was definitely not as sweet as his name suggested. It was a wonder the beginners came back for more.

'I was eight at the time,' Scott clarified. 'I learnt to ride on him. And he can buck like a bronco when he's in the mood, you know.'

'That's funny, I never had a problem with him,' said Sam, looking more cheerful than he had all day.

Cloud reached the gate at the top of the track. Ahead was the lane that led to the farmhouse where Poppy had called for help. A bridleway to the right led back down to the riding school. Poppy's stomach rumbled and she checked her watch. Half past six. She turned him right.

'Come on Cloud, let's go and get some breakfast.'

Poppy fed Cloud and Blaze and followed the smell of bacon that was wafting from the open kitchen window. As she heeled off her jodhpur boots by the back door a white van pulled into the yard. A woman wearing a royal blue apron let herself out of the driver's side and went around to the back of the van. Poppy pulled her boots back on and wandered over. Painted on the side in a curly script decorated with denim blue forget-me-nots were the words *Fern's Flowers*.

The woman in the apron appeared holding a huge bouquet of white lilies.

'These are for Bella Thompson,' she said.

'They're beautiful,' said Poppy. 'She's not here at the moment but I can take them.'

The woman handed Poppy the bouquet. The scent they gave was cloying and Poppy rubbed her nose with the back of her hand to head off a sneeze.

'There's a card in with them,' said the woman, pointing to a small white envelope tucked between the stalks. She smiled sympathetically. 'I'm sorry for your loss.'

What a strange thing to say, Poppy thought, as she carried the flowers into the kitchen. Sarah was standing by Bella's massive range cooker frying bacon.

'Flowers?' she asked, surprised.

'They're for Bella,' Poppy said. She fished around for the envelope and handed it to Sarah.

'Perhaps Mum's got an admirer,' Sarah joked. 'I'm sure she won't mind me having a look to see who they're from.'

She used the bread knife to open the envelope and took out a card with a dove on the front. The knife slipped through her fingers and clattered to the floor. Her hand flew to her mouth.

'What's wrong?'

'It can't be right. They must have delivered them to the wrong address,' she said.

'The *Ferns Flowers* woman definitely said it was for Bella. Why, what does the card say?'

'RIP,' said Sarah faintly.

Poppy's mind went blank. 'What does that stand for?'

'Rest in Peace,' said Sarah with a shiver.

'THAT'S what people say when someone's died, isn't it?' said Scarlett, as they waited for Vile Vivienne to arrive to take Ariel to his new home.

Poppy nodded. 'Sarah was a bit freaked out at first, and then she wondered if someone in the village had heard about her Great Auntie Margaret's fall and jumped to the wrong conclusion.'

Scarlett looked sceptical. 'What, like Chinese whispers? Sounds unlikely to me.'

'That's what I thought, too,' said Poppy.

At ten o'clock on the dot a familiar-looking smart sky blue lorry pulled into the yard.

Poppy watched glumly from Paint's stable as Vile Vivienne jumped out of the passenger door and strode over to the office, her lips pursed. Another woman let herself out of the driver's side and began letting down the ramp. Poppy wracked her brains, trying to remember where she'd seen the lorry before. And then she noticed a small navy logo on the passenger door and groaned.

Vivienne emerged from the office with Scott trailing behind her.

'Are you sure I can't persuade you to stay?' he said half-heartedly.

Vivienne waved him away with her hand. 'My mind is made up. I've been considering a move to Claydon Manor for a while. The facilities there put this place to shame. I only stayed out of misguided loyalty to Bella. But I will not be lied to. Fortunately Angela was more than happy to offer me a place.'

I bet she was, thought Poppy, watching Georgia Canning's former instructor fix partitions in the horse lorry. She walked down the ramp and looked around, unimpressed. She had cold grey eyes and a contemptuous look on her face, as if she had a permanent bad smell under her nose.

'Where's the horse?' she asked, looking around disdainfully.

Vile Vivienne pointed to Ariel's stable. His noble head appeared over the stable door and Vivienne's normally arch expression softened. She may be an old dragon but she does love him, Poppy realised.

Sam appeared with Ariel's tack and grooming kit while Scarlett ran into the tack room to find his rugs. Soon the big black gelding had been loaded onto the lorry and it had pulled onto the Okehampton road bound for Tavistock.

'Good riddance,' said Scott. 'That woman was as mad as a box of frogs if you ask me.'

'She also paid through the nose for Gran's deluxe bespoke livery package. And now she's gone. And to Claydon Manor of all places,' said Sam.

'Chill out Samantha,' mocked Scott.

'Vivienne may have been vile, but she and Ariel have been here for years. Perhaps you'd like to phone Gran and let her know her oldest livery has gone.' He shoved his hands into his pockets. 'Actually don't bother. I'd rather break the news to her myself when she gets back from Great Auntie Margaret's. Just try not to lose us any more liveries will you?'

'I don't know why he's so uptight,' said Scott as Sam stomped over to the trailer, hooked it onto the quad bike and roared off towards the top paddocks.

Poppy stared at him in disbelief. 'Because he's worried about Redhall's future!' she spluttered. 'Angela Snell has poached so many of Bella's liveries she's struggling to keep the place afloat. That's why she decided to start trekking holidays. But that's on hold after Niamh's accident. No wonder Sam's upset.'

Was that a glimmer of uncertainty flickering across Scott's face? Poppy wasn't convinced. But as she pushed the wheelbarrow towards the hay barn she hoped he might have finally got the message that all was not well at Redhall.

6

P oppy and Scarlett were fluffing up the straw bed in Paint's
stable when Sam appeared with three headcollars.
'Where's Scott?' he asked.
'He went in to make us a cup of tea,' said Scarlett.
'Really? I don't think I've ever known him to make a drink for
anyone other than himself,' said Sam.
'Yes, but he did disappear about half an hour ago. He's probably
fast asleep on the sofa by now,' said Poppy.
'It's hardly surprising. He must work so hard at that showjumping
yard,' said Scarlett.
Poppy and Sam exchanged a look.
'I could do with some help exercising the liveries. Fancy coming
with me?'
Scarlett's eyes lit up. 'You get to ride the liveries?'
Sam nodded. 'Debbie and Tim pay extra for Cherry and Otto to be
exercised a couple of times a week. So does Kim, Ellie's owner. Some-
times Gran lunges them, sometimes I school them, but I reckon we
deserve an hour off to go for a hack, don't you?'
'Bags I ride Cherry,' said Scarlett.

'I'd better take Otto. He can be a bit unpredictable.' Sam held out a navy headcollar for Poppy. 'Are you OK with Ellie?'

Poppy nodded. Ellie was a showy palomino mare with four white socks and an extravagantly long mane and forelock. At 15.2hh she was a hand taller than Cloud but more finely-built.

'Her name's actually Elidi, which means gift of the sun in Greek,' said Sam as Poppy tied Ellie up next to Otto. 'She's not a novice ride, but I reckon you can handle her.'

The mare fidgeted while Poppy set to work brushing the dust from her butterscotch-coloured coat. She tossed her head as Poppy combed her mane and pawed the ground impatiently when Poppy appeared with her tack.

Poppy placed the saddle on the mare's back, buckled the girth loosely, looped the headcollar around Ellie's neck and put the bridle on. As she fastened the noseband Harvey Smith darted out of the tack room door and flashed across the yard with his tabby tail as bushy as a fox's, sending an empty bucket flying. Ellie leapt about a foot in the air, her hooves jangling on the concrete yard.

'Easy girl,' Poppy murmured, running her hand along Ellie's neck. She felt a flutter in her stomach at the thought of riding the flighty mare.

Scarlett was already leading Cherry over to the mounting block. Poppy re-tied her ponytail, put on her hat, unfastened Ellie's head-collar and waited while Scarlett mounted the towering thoroughbred.

'It's about two degrees cooler up here,' Scarlett grinned. 'Blaze is going to feel like a Shetland pony after Cherry.'

Poppy tightened Ellie's girth, adjusted the stirrup leathers and led her over to the mounting block. She climbed the steps, gathered the reins in her left hand and was just about to put her left foot in the stirrup when the mare swung her quarters away, leaving a yawning gap between them. Poppy got back down, circled the mare and led her back to the mounting block. But she did exactly the same again, swinging away just as Poppy was about to get on.

'Having a spot of bother?' said a voice. Poppy turned to see Scott lounging against the post and rail fence around the school, his hands curled around a mug of tea.

Poppy felt her face grow hot. 'Third time lucky,' she muttered, circling Ellie again. This time the mare backed away from the mounting block before Poppy had even climbed onto it.

'I'll hold her for you if you like,' Scott said, not waiting for an answer. He took Ellie's reins and pushed her rump firmly towards the mounting block. He scratched the mare's poll and she lowered her head demurely and stood perfectly still while Poppy jumped on and gathered her reins.

Ellie nibbled Scott's pockets and sniffed at the dregs of his tea. Poppy wouldn't have been surprised if she'd fluttered her long eyelashes at him. The palomino mare had obviously fallen for his charms, too.

'Thanks,' she said.

'Anytime. Enjoy your ride.'

'The buckets and water troughs need filling,' Sam said as they rode out of the yard. Scott pulled a face and disappeared into Bella's office.

'If they're done by the time we get back I'll eat my hat,' Sam sighed.

ELLIE JOGGED up the road behind Otto and Cherry, her nostrils flared as she spooked at the tattered remains of a plastic carrier bag caught on a barbed wire fence. Poppy grabbed a handful of her long mane and held on tight.

'It's alright, you silly horse. It's a bag, not a bogeyman. It won't hurt you.'

In the year since she'd learnt to ride on Flynn, Scarlett's brother Alex's rotund Dartmoor pony, Poppy had only ever ridden four other horses. Cloud, Bella's New Forest mare Rosie, Sam's Connemara Star and Beau, the big, hairy piebald cob she'd fallen in love with during their week at Oaklands Trekking Centre in the Forest of Dean. Ellie was nothing like any of them. She felt like an active volcano, ready to erupt at any minute.

Sam pulled Otto alongside her.

'Alright?' he asked.

Poppy licked her lips. The roof of her mouth was sandpaper dry. 'She's quite, er, lively,' she said, as Ellie shied at a sheep, cannoning into Otto before Poppy could stop her.

'She's always a bit spooky when she hasn't been out for a few days. She'll settle down in a minute,' he said.

'I'll take your word for it,' Poppy muttered, tightening her reins.

Instead of turning onto the track Poppy and Cloud had followed that morning, Sam took a right into a narrow lane that ran parallel to a stream. A clutch of fluffy yellow mallard ducklings glided gracefully after their parents. Poppy imagined their tiny feet paddling furiously under the water and smiled.

'OK for a trot?' Sam called.

'You bet!' cried Scarlett.

Ellie needed no encouragement either and sprang into the floatiest trot Poppy had ever experienced. It felt as though they were trotting on air.

They reached a T-junction and turned right over an old stone bridge. Ellie spooked, boggle-eyed, at a yellow salt bin, but this time Poppy was ready for her and sat relaxed in the saddle.

'We usually have a canter through the woods,' said Sam, turning Otto down a bridleway. Ellie snatched at her bit and crabbed sideways down the track, but Poppy was unperturbed. She'd realised that nothing the mare did was malicious, she was just fresh. And Poppy had to admit her canter was as amazing as her trot. They cantered through the woods, one after the other, the horses' pounding hooves sending pheasants scurrying for cover.

Too soon they'd reached the end of the bridleway and turned for home.

'This road brings us out at the back of Gran's. We can ride through the fields back to the yard,' said Sam.

Ten minutes later they came to a five bar gate.

Ellie gawked at a puddle of water.

'That's funny,' Poppy said.

'What is?' asked Scarlett.

'Look at that massive puddle. But I can't remember the last time it rained, can you?'

Scarlett shrugged. 'Perhaps it rained last night.'

They rode past the field Cloud was sharing with Blaze and Treacle. Poppy held her hand over her face.

'What on earth are you doing?' said Sam.

'Hiding from Cloud. I don't want him to see me riding another horse,' Poppy whispered. At that moment Cloud lifted his grey head and whinnied. 'Oh no, he's seen me!' she cried.

Scarlett howled with laughter. 'What, are you worried he'll be jealous? He's a *horse!*'

Scott was sitting on a bale of hay texting on his phone when they arrived back in the yard, a row of empty water buckets at his feet.

'I might have known,' muttered Sam, jumping off Otto.

Scott shoved his phone in his back pocket. 'Good ride?'

'It was great. Cherry's just brilliant. I've decided I want my next pony to be a 16.2hh thoroughbred. I'm going to skip the 14.2hh stage,' said Scarlett.

Scott noticed Sam scowling at the empty water buckets. 'Before you say anything, Samantha, I did try and fill them, but there's no water.'

'What do you mean?'

Scott sauntered across to the tap outside the tack room and turned the handle. The tap coughed, gurgled and spluttered out a few paltry drops of water.

'See? I've told your mum. She doesn't know where the stopcock is so she's trying to get through to Bella, but it's just going straight to answerphone at the moment.'

Poppy tied Ellie up and began untacking her. 'It might be a leak. Remember that puddle we passed on the way in? I could phone the water board. They might send someone out to have a look.'

'In the meantime where on earth are we going to get water for the horses?' said Scarlett.

She had a point, thought Poppy. The nearest neighbour was probably a quarter of a mile away. She remembered the family of mallards.

'What about the stream? It's a bit of a trek but if we do it together it shouldn't be too bad. At least the water is clean and fresh.'

'Sounds like our only option,' said Sam. 'I'll turn Ellie out if you phone the water board, Poppy. There should be a number in the office somewhere.'

Harvey Smith was sprawled over Bella's dog-eared phone book. Poppy tickled his chin and deposited him on the floor. He immediately jumped onto her lap and began kneading her thighs, purring loudly. Poppy flicked through the phone book to W and there was the number she was looking for in Bella's precise handwriting.

She was just about to pick up the phone and dial when it rang, making her jump. Harvey Smith mewed crossly and sprang off her lap.

'Hello?'

Poppy listened for an answer but all she could hear was static.

'Can I help you?'

Still no answer. Poppy felt irritation rise. This wasn't crossed lines. Someone was deliberately phoning Redhall and giving them the silent treatment, she was sure of it.

'Look, if you're the person who keeps calling, I think you've got the wrong number. You need to check it and stop phoning this one. It's getting really annoying,' she said.

She nearly jumped out of her skin when a bark of bitter laughter rang in her ear.

'Who *is* this?' she said.

But the laughter had been replaced by the drone of the ring tone. Whoever it was had hung up.

~

Poppy found the others stacking buckets ready to carry them down to the stream.

'The water board is going to send someone out in the morning. They say if no-one has turned off the stopcock it's probably a leak. And since none of us know where the stopcock is, they're probably right,' she said. 'Oh, and there was another nuisance call, though this time I heard someone laughing. And when I dialled 1471 it was number withheld.'

'I took one before breakfast,' said Scarlett. 'It's a bit creepy, isn't it? Do you think someone's trying to freak us out?'

Scott's face was scornful. 'They'll have to try harder than that.'

7

Poppy collapsed in an exhausted heap in the shade of an apple tree. Opposite her a pink-faced Scarlett was grimacing as she stretched out her back.

'I'm so sweaty,' she moaned.

'Horses sweat,' Poppy corrected her. 'Men perspire and ladies *glow*.'

'Well, I'm glowing like a lightbulb at the moment. I'm shattered.'

It had taken the four of them a solid two hours of back-breaking work to fill all the water troughs and buckets. The stream had seemed a lot closer when they'd ridden past it. In fact it was a ten minute walk there and even longer on the way back with heavy buckets bumping against their shins and water sloshing all over their feet.

While Poppy had hefted buckets she'd mulled over the last couple of days and she had come to the conclusion that the series of unfortunate events to befall Redhall was no coincidence.

'Scar, I think someone's trying to sabotage the riding school,' she blurted out.

'What do you mean?'

'I know it sounds far-fetched but think about it. The nuisance calls. The delivery from Baxters' that no-one ordered. The lilies. Someone called the farrier to tell him not to come and it wasn't Bella.'

'I think your imagination's gone into overdrive. Who on earth would want to harm the riding school?'

'It's obvious isn't it? Who's in direct competition with Redhall? Who's going to benefit if Bella goes out of business?'

Scarlett gawped at her. 'You don't mean -?'

'Yes, I do,' said Poppy. 'Angela Snell.'

They heard the click of a gate. Sam was walking towards them with a couple of cans of lemonade.

'Don't say anything yet,' Poppy whispered to Scarlett. 'We need to get some hard evidence before we accuse her of anything.'

'How on earth are we going to do that?'

Poppy grinned. 'Fancy a trip to Claydon Manor?'

'But how will we get there?'

'There are a couple of old bikes at the back of the hay barn. We'll ask Sarah if we can borrow them. And we'll go this evening.'

Poppy found Sarah in the kitchen stirring a huge saucepan of bolognese sauce. She glanced at the clock above the sink. 'It'll only be another twenty minutes,' she said.

'It smells yummy. Sarah, you know those two old bikes in the barn?'

Sarah smiled. 'I certainly do. They were mine and my brother's. Why?'

'Scarlett and I wondered if we could go on a bike ride on them after dinner.'

Sarah dipped a teaspoon into the sauce, tasted it and added a pinch of oregano. 'You don't have any cycling helmets.'

'We could wear our riding hats,' Poppy said.

'Alright. As long as you promise to stick to the lanes and be back before it gets dark.'

'I KNEW I shouldn't have had seconds, but Sarah's such a good cook. Her spaghetti was to die for. And now I'm absolutely stuffed,' groaned Scarlett.

They pushed the two mountain bikes out of the barn. Poppy wheeled hers past Cloud's stable and peered in. He was pulling wisps of hay from his hayrack.

'Hey baby,' she called softly. He abandoned the hay and came over to say hello. She breathed in his familiar scent and sighed.

'I wish I could stay here with you all evening, Cloud, but I've got to go. Things to do, people to see,' she told him, kissing his nose. He nudged her and returned to his hay.

'I used to pretend my first bike was a pony,' she told Scarlett. 'I used to practice my rising trot as I cycled round and round the park near our house. And when we got home I would poke handfuls of grass into the handlebars and offer it a bucket of water.'

Scarlett hooted with laughter. She looked down at Sarah's rusted pink Raleigh. 'Let's pretend these are famous horses. It'll make the ride much more fun. Bags mine is Red Rum.'

'Hello Black Beauty,' Poppy said, patting the coal black frame of her bike. She clicked her tongue and pedalled off, Scarlett in close pursuit.

'Trot on,' Poppy shouted in her best riding instructor's voice. 'On the left diagonal please, Scarlett. That's it. Up down, up down.'

The two friends circled the yard, their bikes wobbling dangerously as they bobbed up and down. Horses heads appeared over stable doors as they careered past. Poppy was giggling so hard her insides ached.

'Come on Beauty,' she cried, pedalling as fast as she could. 'Let's race Red Rum to Claydon Manor!'

TWENTY MINUTES later the two girls pulled onto the verge opposite a pair of grand wrought iron gates set in an imposing stone wall. To the right was a keypad on a metal post and set into the stone was a slate sign saying *Claydon Manor*.

'Electronic gates,' said Scarlett.

'And CCTV,' said Poppy, nodding towards a small camera on top of one of the huge gate posts.

'How are we going to get in?'

Poppy reached into her backpack and pulled out a royal blue book.

'I found Ariel's equine passport in Bella's office. I'm amazed Angela Snell didn't ask for it when they picked him up. Perhaps she's not quite as efficient as we think. We'll say Sam sent us over with it.'

Scarlett looked impressed. 'Ingenious. Perhaps I'd better let you do the talking.'

'There's a first time for everything,' Poppy teased. 'C'mon, let's press the buzzer.'

They wheeled their bikes across the road and Poppy studied the keypad. 'I guess it's the one with the bell on,' she said, jabbing it with her index finger.

A tinny voice made them jump. 'Who is this?'

Poppy cleared her throat. 'It's, um, Poppy and Scarlett from Redhall. Sam sent us over. We've got Ariel's passport.'

An exasperated sigh emanated from the keypad and the gates clicked and began to swing open.

'You'd better come in,' said the voice.

Poppy and Scarlett pushed their bikes towards a beautiful grey stone Georgian manor house. Poppy's eyes were on stalks as she took in the sleek thoroughbreds grazing in immaculate paddocks on either side of the sweeping gravelled drive.

'Wow,' she said. 'This is some place.'

'Don't forget it was all down to a winning lottery ticket,' said Scarlett, waving her hand dismissively. 'They didn't earn it. They just got lucky.'

A figure was beckoning them from a stable block to the right of the house. Even from this distance Poppy recognised the prickly demeanour of Angela Snell.

'So what are we looking for?' Scarlett asked.

Poppy shrugged. 'I'm not really sure. Anything that might link Snell or the Cannings to what's been happening at Redhall, I suppose.'

They set their bikes against a granite wall and walked over to

Angela Snell. The livery yard manager held her hand out. Poppy gave her the passport.

'Thanks,' said Angela curtly. 'I thought Vivienne had it.'

A whinny rang out across the cobbled yard.

'It's Ariel,' said Poppy. 'Can we say a quick hello?'

Angela Snell sighed. 'Just a quick one. I have work to do.'

The black gelding seemed pleased to see them and delicately ate the Polo Scarlett offered him.

'Nice loose box,' said Poppy, noticing the rubber matting, automatic water drinker and thick bed of shavings. 'There's even a smoke alarm. No wonder Vile Vivienne wanted to move him here.'

Angela strode across the yard, checking her watch. 'All done?'

'Is Georgia around?' asked Scarlett.

'Why, are you friends?' said Angela, surprised. Her eyes travelled over Scarlett's dishevelled appearance with barely disguised contempt.

'Not friends exactly,' said Scarlett, unperturbed. 'We used to go to the same school. When Georgia and her mum and dad still lived in a three bedroomed semi in Tavistock and the family car was a clapped out hatchback.'

Poppy's eyes were drawn to the pristine white Range Rover parked in the furthest corner of the yard next to a silver Bentley. It was impossible to imagine the family who owned all this ever having to make do with a clapped out hatchback.

'She's schooling Barley in the indoor arena,' Angela said.

'I'm sure she won't mind us watching,' said Scarlett, dragging Poppy towards the huge wooden-slatted building behind the row of loose boxes before Angela could stop her.

'Trust Georgia to have an indoor *arena*,' she muttered.

Poppy recognised the palomino gelding Georgia was cantering in perfect twenty metre circles at the far end of the arena.

'He's the one Georgia beat Sam on, isn't he?' she said.

Scarlett nodded. 'He's her top jumping pony. Her mum paid over ten thousand pounds for him. He's a demon against the clock.'

'Not as fast as Star though,' said Poppy, remembering how Sam had only lost to Georgia because Barley had rattled a pole which had fallen during Sam's round.

Georgia changed reins and the palomino executed a flawless flying change. As she cantered towards them she noticed them watching and eased Barley into a trot. She stared at them with china blue eyes.

'I recognise you. You were at the Redhall affiliated show last summer. You're Sam's fan club. What are you doing here?' she said.

Scarlett scowled and was about to say something but Poppy cut across her. 'Angela told us to come and say hello. We've just dropped off Ariel's passport.'

Georgia patted her pony's neck and slid off. She was wearing a crimson polo shirt, cream jodhpurs and expensive-looking leather boots the same shade of bitumen black as her plaited hair. Her high cheekbones and English rose complexion made Poppy think of Snow White. Without the seven dwarfs of course. Although Angela would make a convincing Evil Queen.

'Nice place you've got here, Georgia. It puts Redhall to shame,' Poppy said.

Scarlett's eyes widened but Poppy winked at her and she took the hint.

'It's amazing,' she agreed. 'We'd love a guided tour. If you've got time.'

Georgia looked at them warily. Poppy held her breath. They needed evidence that Angela Snell was trying to sabotage Redhall and if being nice to stuck-up Georgia Canning was the only way they were going to get it, it was a price worth paying. She smiled at Georgia hopefully.

'OK,' Georgia shrugged. 'I'll just put Barley away first.' She led the palomino gelding to a row of looseboxes opposite Ariel's.

'How many liveries do you have?' asked Poppy.

'Ten with Ariel. Plus my ponies, Barley and Fizz.'

'You used to have way more than two didn't you?' said Scarlett.

Georgia gave a brief nod and began untacking Barley. Poppy studied the girl's expression for clues but her face gave nothing away. Yet something about her was different. Poppy thought back to the day of the Redhall show. When Georgia had ridden past Poppy had been struck by her hooked Roman nose, the only imperfection in an otherwise flawless face. But as she watched Georgia undo Barley's girth and run up the stirrup leathers she realised the Roman nose had gone, smoothed away by a surgeon's knife.

Georgia led them to the largest tack room Poppy had seen in her life. It looked like a high-end tack shop, with rows of gleaming saddles and bridles and piles of neatly-folded day rugs, night rugs and New Zealand rugs. The room smelt of saddle soap and hoof oil.

'Each livery has their own storage trunk where they keep their grooming kits. Every horse has a daily groom as part of the service,' said Georgia. 'And this is the feed room.'

Poppy and Scarlett followed her into an adjoining room which contained huge bins of food.

'You must get through tons of feed with twelve horses. Where do you get it from,' asked Scarlett conversationally.

'Baxters',' said Georgia. 'They do a monthly delivery.'

Poppy gasped as Scarlett elbowed her sharply in the ribs. Fortunately Georgia had already turned away.

'This is the solarium,' she said, opening the double doors of a high-ceilinged barn. 'We have two heat lamps so two horses can use it at once.'

Poppy cricked her neck to examine the space-age bulbs set in curved units above two empty stalls. 'What do they do that the sun can't?' she asked, genuinely curious.

'The lamps have infra-red rays that help increase blood circulation and muscle elasticity, which can help reduce healing time for injuries. We also use them for drying horses after a bath, especially in the winter.' Georgia sounded as if she was reading from a brochure. She flicked a switch on the wall and the lamps in the solarium nearest to them glowed orange. 'And they're nice and warm to sit under when you're cleaning your tack.'

'You clean your own tack?' asked Scarlett in disbelief.

Georgia shot her a scornful look. 'Who else do you think does it?'

She switched off the solarium and stalked over to a huge metal contraption which reminded Poppy of an industrial-sized rotary washing line.

'This is the horse walker. All the horses have weekly solariums and are exercised daily, either by Angela or me or on the horse walker.'

'Wouldn't they prefer to go out for a hack?' said Scarlett. Poppy gave her a warning look. They were supposed to be keeping Georgia on side after all.

Georgia shrugged. 'Probably. But owners expect us to have one for the price they're paying.'

'Do you have any vacancies at the moment?' asked Poppy.

'Why? Think you can afford it here?'

Poppy shook her head and kept her face neutral, although inside she was seething. 'I prefer to keep my pony at home, thanks. I just wondered.'

'Whatever,' said Georgia. 'We have two at the moment. The two looseboxes next to Ariel. Though Angela is confident they'll be filled very shortly.'

They walked back to the yard. Behind the palatial Georgian mansion the sun was setting.

'Thanks for showing us around. It was very *interesting*, although I don't think my pony Blaze would like it here,' said Scarlett.

Georgia stared at her. 'I used to know a pony called Blaze. She was the first pony I ever rode. She was owned by the daughter of a friend of my mother's. They lived on a ramshackle farm in Waterby.'

'We still do,' Scarlett said quietly.

'I *thought* I recognised you at the Redhall show but you said we'd never met before.' Georgia's cut-glass accent sounded unnecessarily loud.

'We used to go to the same school a long time ago. Before you had all *this*,' Scarlett said, with a sweep of her arm.

There was an awkward silence. Poppy could feel Scarlett bristling beside her and gave her a nudge.

'Come on Scar, we'd better make a move. There aren't any lights on the bikes and we promised Sarah we'd be home before it gets dark.'

Scarlett nodded, turned on her heels and headed for the bikes without a word. Poppy gave Georgia an apologetic look and went to follow her but stopped when the older girl started speaking.

'Your friend Scarlett won't believe me but I was insanely jealous of her and her brother, growing up on a farm like Ashworthy. I know it was tatty and tumbledown, but I used to love spending time there. It seemed like the perfect life to me.'

'And this isn't?' said Poppy, perplexed, thinking of the solariums, the horse walker and the huge indoor arena.

Georgia looked at her feet. 'Some things are more important than money.'

8

'That's easy enough to say when you've got millions in the bank,' said Scarlett scathingly as they pedalled back to Redhall.

'Sam says they've spent all their money, remember. That's why they had to sell most of Georgia's ponies and take on all the liveries.' Poppy swerved to avoid a pothole, almost colliding with Scarlett. 'Sorry Red Rum.'

But Scarlett wasn't in the mood for make believe any more and they rode the rest of the way in silence. It was only that night as they lay in bed that Poppy decided to tackle the subject again.

'So do you think Angela and Georgia are behind all this?'

Scarlett looked at Poppy as though she was mad. 'You bet I do! Look at the evidence. They use Baxters'. They have vacancies. And, most importantly, they have a motive.'

'Do they,' asked Poppy faintly. It all seemed a bit circumstantial to her.

'Money!' Scarlett declared triumphantly. 'Isn't that what everything comes down to in the end?'

A MAN in a white van pulled into the yard as Poppy was grooming Cloud the next morning. He showed her an identity card on a lanyard around his neck.

'I'm from the water board. I've come to see what the problem is with your supply,' he said.

Poppy jogged across to the house and called Sarah, who showed him the stopcock. He scratched his head.

'There's no problem this end. It must be further down the line.'

'There's a water leak in one of the fields. I can show you if you like. I was just about to turn Cloud out anyway,' said Poppy.

He grabbed a tool kit from the back of his van and followed her to the paddock they'd ridden through the day before. The puddle was even bigger.

'Hmm, this looks serious,' he said, pulling out a mobile phone and calling for reinforcements.

Poppy, Scarlett and Sam had finished morning stables and were about to start the weary trudge to the river for water when the engineer reappeared, a satisfied smile on his face. He walked over to the outside tap and turned it on. The three children cheered when a jet of water gushed out.

'Well, I've solved the mystery,' he said, showing them two short lengths of blue plastic pipe. 'But I can't explain why it happened.'

'What do you mean?' asked Poppy.

'Pipes like this are buried about a foot underground and should last for decades,' he told them. 'But someone had dug down and cut this one clean through.'

POPPY, Scarlett and Sam watched in silence as the van disappeared down the Redhall drive.

'I don't understand. Why would anyone want to cut our pipe?' said Sam.

Poppy looked at Scarlett, who nodded and mouthed, 'Tell him.'

'We think someone's got it in for Redhall, Sam,' Poppy said. 'That all the stuff that's been happening - the mixed-up order from Baxters', the nuisance calls, the flowers, the water leak - is being done deliberately to sabotage Bella's business.'

'That's ludicrous,' said Sam. 'Why would anyone want to do that?'

'Why do you think?' cried Scarlett. 'Use your brain for goodness' sake. They want to steal her liveries.'

'But who would want to do that?' he said with a frown.

'Angela Snell and Georgia La-Di-Da Canning, that's who,' hissed Scarlett.

'Well, we're not one hundred per cent sure,' said Poppy. 'But it's certainly looking like it might be.'

Sam looked at each of them in turn. Scarlett glared back and Poppy held her hands up helplessly. 'We can't think who else it might be,' she said.

'I suppose I ought to tell Scott,' he said. 'Any idea where he is?'

'He's popped into Tavistock. He said he'd be back before lunch,' said Scarlett.

'That's another morning stables he's conveniently missed. I don't know why Gran bothered to ask him to come. He's been about as much use as a chocolate teapot.'

Poppy silently agreed but Scarlett leapt to his defence. 'He did help get the water yesterday. And I'm sure he'll help with evening stables.'

'There's a first time for everything,' Sam grumbled.

Hoping to head off an argument, Poppy clapped her hands.

'Hey you two, I've had a brilliant idea! Now we don't have to spend an hour fetching water let's take the ponies out for a ride.'

THAT NIGHT POPPY lay in bed mulling everything over. Should they phone Bella and tell her what was happening? Poppy didn't think so. Not yet. She had enough on her plate looking after her Auntie Margaret. Should they call the police? Poppy pictured portly Inspector Bill Pearson and his penchant for digestive biscuits. When Poppy and her friend Hope Taylor had turned up at Tavistock Police

Station with what must have seemed a dubious account of deceit and duplicity he had listened to everything they had to say - and had believed them. But all Poppy would be able to report this time was a series of events that could be linked but could also be totally unrelated.

Poppy tried to see it through Inspector Pearson's eyes. John the farrier could have misunderstood a call from Bella confirming his visit to shoe Ariel. All it needed was a crackly line and, after all, the phone reception out here was patchy at best. Sarah's theory about someone in the village hearing about Margaret's fall and jumping to the wrong conclusions might be right after all. Perhaps Baxters' had made a genuine mistake and accidentally mixed their order up with someone else's. No matter how hard she tried Poppy couldn't explain away the nuisance calls and the damaged water pipe, but she could see they didn't exactly amount to a vendetta.

And if it was some kind of hate campaign, who was behind it all, anyway? Scarlett was convinced that it was Georgia Canning and her hard-nosed livery yard manager. Poppy wasn't about to rule the pair out either. But they hadn't exactly found any incriminating evidence during their visit to Claydon Manor. And there had been something about Georgia Canning that evening that didn't fit with the win-at-all-costs spoilt little rich girl Poppy had always assumed she was. Although there had been flashes of her trademark snootiness she'd also seemed subdued. If Poppy had been pushed to describe her she'd have said she was lonely.

Poppy checked the time on her phone. Half past twelve. She was physically exhausted yet sleep seemed tantalisingly out of reach. The room was uncomfortably hot. She threw off her covers, padded across the room to the window and pulled open the curtains. The moon was large and low, almost but not quite a full moon. Poppy opened the catches of the Victorian sash window and was just about to heave it open when a movement on the driveway caught her eye.

A hooded figure was creeping along the side of the hedge towards the road. For a moment Poppy was rooted to the spot, paralysed by indecision. The figure stopped and glanced back towards the house. It must have seen her pale face at the window because it turned, crouched down and ran towards a vehicle parked haphazardly on the verge on the other side of the road. The sight of the fleeing intruder galvanised Poppy into action. She tugged at the sash window, but years of neglect had left it stuck fast. Instead she banged on the glass with her fist as hard as she dared. But it was too late. The car was disappearing down the road. Poppy watched with resignation until the tail lights were tiny red pinpricks in the dark and then disappeared altogether.

Her nerves were so taut that when she heard a sound behind her she almost jumped out of her skin.

'Wha's goin' on?' her best friend mumbled. Scarlett sat up and rubbed her eyes. She saw Poppy at the window. 'What on earth are you *doing*?'

Poppy started pulling on jeans and a jumper. 'I've just seen an intruder. We need to go and check everything's OK. You get dressed and I'll go and wake Sam and Scott. I'll meet you in the kitchen.'

Before Scarlett had a chance to answer Poppy legged it out of their room and turned down the hallway towards the bedroom Sam and Scott were sharing. She tapped on the door and let herself in. Sam was asleep in the nearest bed, the frown he'd worn since Scott's arrival softened by sleep. Poppy shook his shoulder. His eyes snapped open.

'What's wrong?'

Poppy told him about the intruder. 'We need to check on the horses. I'll wake Scott.'

But Scott's bed was empty.

'He's still not back?' Poppy said in exasperation.

Sam shook his head. 'I'll text him.'

They met in the kitchen. Poppy handed them each a torch and unlocked the back door. They looked at each other, their faces grave.

'I'll check the stables and barn if you two look over the paddocks,' said Sam. 'Stick together, just in case. And shout if you need me.'

Poppy and Scarlett nodded and let themselves out. But when Poppy headed for the yard instead of the fields Scarlett grabbed her arm.

'Where are you going?'

'I have to check on Cloud first, Scar.'

She ran across to her pony's stable and slid open the bolt. Training the torch on the straw bed so she didn't blind him with its powerful beam she whispered his name. Cloud opened an eye and whickered. Poppy balanced the torch on the narrow window ledge and threw her arms around his neck in relief.

Scarlett's tousled head appeared over the stable door.

'All OK?'

Poppy nodded.

'Blaze too. Come on, let's go and check on the riding school ponies.'

Poppy kissed Cloud's nose and joined her friend. On the other side of the yard they could see the beam of Sam's torch as he looked in each stable.

'How many are out?' Poppy asked. Her brain felt scrambled and she couldn't remember who was stabled and who wasn't.

'Rosie and Buster are in the first paddock,' said Scarlett, counting on her fingers. 'Salt and Pepper are in the next and Treacle's in the top paddock on his own.'

Poppy exhaled with relief when her torch picked out Rosie. The strawberry roan mare was standing in a field shelter with Buster, the chestnut Dartmoor pony Poppy's friend Hope had learnt to ride on.

'We should check them over,' said Poppy. The two girls climbed the gate and crossed the field to the shelter. The ponies watched them sleepily as they ran their hands along them and lifted their feet.

'They're fine,' said Scarlett. 'Let's check on Salt and Pepper.'

The two fleabitten grey New Forest geldings were brothers, bred by Bella out of Rosie's dam, an elderly mare called Conker who was stabled overnight. Salt and Pepper had inherited their dam's easy-going nature and none of Rosie's occasional stroppiness and were the most popular ponies with the more experienced riders at Redhall.

Woken by the sound of voices, the two geldings stood by the gate watching them, their grey ears pricked. Their breath was warm in the chill of the night and they nibbled at the girls' pockets for treats as they were checked over.

'They're OK, too,' said Scarlett. She paused. 'Are you sure it was a man you saw Poppy?'

'Yes!' Poppy replied hotly, though she was actually beginning to doubt herself. Her eyes couldn't have been playing tricks on her in the moonlight, could they? But no, she had definitely seen the figure and heard the car engine splutter into life.

'Don't get your knickers in a twist, I was only asking,' said Scarlett mildly.

'I know it sounds far-fetched. But I definitely saw someone, Scar.'

In the distance they heard the rumble of a motorbike.

'Sounds like Scott's back at last,' said Poppy. She climbed the gate into Treacle's paddock and shone the torch in front of her, zigzagging the beam to and fro as though she was waving a sparkler on Bonfire night.

'I can't see him, can you?' said Scarlett, who was searching the other side of the paddock.

'Perhaps he's in his field shelter,' Poppy said. She directed the torch into the wooden shelter. It was empty. 'Perhaps not,' she said, half to herself.

'I've checked the rest of the field. He's not here,' said Scarlett, her voice rising a level. 'Do you think he could have got out?'

Poppy pictured the solid post and rail fences that bordered the Redhall paddocks. Bella was meticulous about maintenance and they were kept in perfect condition. She doubted that even the wayward Treacle could stage an escape. Even so, it was worth checking.

'You check the fences and I'll look behind the shelter. Poppy remembered there was a gap of about a metre between the back wall of the weather-boarded shelter and the fence. Bella used it to store wheelbarrows and the skip and rake for poo-picking. She shone her torch down the gap. The light settled on a perfectly round chestnut rump.

'There you are, you little monkey.'

'Any luck?' Scarlett called.

'I've found him!' Poppy shouted. She walked over to him. 'Come on little man, let's get you back in the field.' She gave him a gentle push. Treacle took a step forward and squealed in pain. 'What's wrong?' Poppy cried, shining the torch down. Her blood began pounding in her ears. Rusty barbed wire clung to the pony's back legs like ivy strangling a sapling.

9

———————

P oppy could see beads of blood where the barbs had pierced
Treacle's skin. He tried to free his legs but as he struggled the
wire twisted tighter.

'Steady boy,' Poppy murmured. 'You're making it worse.'

Another beam of light appeared around the far end of the shelter.
Behind it was Scarlett's familiar silhouette.

'He's caught in barbed wire, Scar. You need to get Sam to call the
vet. And see if Bella has any wire cutters. I'll stay with Treacle.'

Scarlett shone her torch at the little chestnut gelding's back legs
and gasped. 'How did it happen?'

'That's not important right now. We need the vet Scar. Just go!'

Scarlett turned on her heels and began running towards the house.
Poppy moved carefully up to Treacle's head and stroked his neck,
talking to him quietly. Every now and then the gelding tugged at the
wires and Poppy pictured the barbs sinking their rusty teeth even
deeper into the thin skin around his cannon bones.

'Hurry up,' she whispered into the dark, willing Scarlett to arrive
with help. What seemed like hours later she heard voices crossing the
field.

'Where is he?' Scott asked urgently. Poppy was sure she could detect a catch in his voice.

'Behind the shelter,' panted Scarlett.

Scott appeared with Sam at his shoulder. When he saw Treacle he dropped to his knees and ran his hand along the gelding's back. Poppy could sense Treacle relaxing to his touch.

'Shine your torch on his back legs Poppy,' Scott said.

Poppy did as she was told. Scott swore under his breath as he took in the torn skin on Treacle's poor legs. He looked up at Sam, his face ashen. 'Pass me the wire cutters. We need to cut the wire before it does any more damage.'

Sam handed the solid metal wire cutters to Scott and joined Scarlett and Poppy. He slipped a headcollar onto the gelding. Treacle offered no resistance. His head was low and his normally mischievous eyes were dull with exhaustion. Poppy kept her torch trained on Treacle and they talked in low whispers as Scott snipped away at the barbed wire.

'The vet's on his way. Mum'll bring him straight over the minute he gets here. It's the same one who came out to put Merry down.'

Scarlett gave a small cry. Poppy put her arm around her.

'He'll be OK Scar. Though he's going to need a lot of stitches.'

'Good job Gran keeps up to date with all their injections,' said Sam, looking at the lengths of rusty wire.

Scott stood up and stretched his back. 'That's the wire cut,' he said.

'Should we walk him back to the yard?' asked Poppy.

'Let's see what the vet says,' said Scott.

They all breathed a sigh of relief when they saw the beams of two torches approaching from the direction of the house. Sarah had pulled on some leggings and a fleecy jumper, though she hadn't realised in her haste that she was wearing it back to front. The vet also looked bleary-eyed and his dark auburn hair was dishevelled. But he'd probably been dragged from his bed by the emergency call too, Poppy realised.

'Bella's not having a very good week, is she?' he said, dropping his medicine bag on the floor and stooping to look at Treacle's legs. They watched in silence as he examined the cuts, one by one, under the beam of Poppy's torch.

'He's going to need a few stitches, but it's not as bad as it looks,' he said finally, sitting back on his heels. 'I'll wash out the wounds with a saline solution and give him a course of antibiotics to prevent an infection. I'll also give him something to ease the pain. But I think he's probably had a lucky escape. If those cuts had been deep enough to damage his joints or tendons it could have been a whole different story.'

Poppy felt a wave of relief wash over her.

'Let's get him back to the yard. It'll be easier to do the stitches there.' The vet closed his medicine bag and set off with Sarah towards the stables. Scott took Treacle's lead rope from Sam and the gelding hobbled slowly back.

'Let's pick up those bits of barbed wire. The last thing we need is for another of the horses to cut themselves,' Poppy said.

They picked up as many pieces as they could see.

'That'll do for now. We'll have another look in the morning,' said Sam.

By the time they reached the yard the vet had washed out Treacle's cuts and was stitching the flaps of torn skin back together, a look of deep concentration on his face. After half an hour Treacle's two white socks resembled a jagged patchwork of black stiches. The vet peeled off his pair of blue surgical gloves and ran a hand through his rumpled hair.

'That's him done. He's had a shot of antibiotics and I'll give you some painkillers to add to his feed for the next couple of days. Keep him stabled and I'll pop by in a couple of days' time to see how he's doing.'

'We'll put him in Ariel's stable,' said Scott, handing Treacle's lead-rope to Scarlett. 'I'll make it ready for him.' He shook the vet's hand. 'Thanks for coming so quickly. We really appreciate it.'

The vet nodded, climbed into his Land Rover and gave them a brief wave as he drove away into the night. Scott disappeared into the barn, emerging with a bale of straw. He filled the hayrack with a couple of sections of meadow hay and filled two water buckets. Soon Treacle was settled in Ariel's stable, pulling wisps of hay from the rack. Satisfied the pony was comfortable Scott bolted the door and kicked over the bottom door latch.

'Come on, let's go,' he said.

Poppy followed the others into the kitchen and accepted a mug of hot chocolate from Sarah with a grateful smile. They sat at the kitchen table cradling the mugs in their hands, deep in their own thoughts.

Sarah broke the silence. 'I'll phone Mum in the morning to tell her what's happened.' She glanced at the clock above the range cooker. It was a quarter to three. 'Well, later this morning,' she corrected herself. She drained the rest of her hot chocolate and stood up. 'I'm going up. Don't be too late.'

They shook their heads. Once they heard Sarah's footsteps on the landing Scott turned to Poppy and said, 'Sam told me you saw someone driving away. Tell me what happened.'

Poppy described the shadowy figure, dredging up any details she could think of that might help identify their intruder.

'He was wearing a coat with the hood up rather than a hoodie. It was dark grey or black. And he was wearing dark navy jeans,' she said.

'He?' asked Scarlett sharply.

Poppy shrugged. 'I wouldn't swear on it. But I just got the feeling it was a man by the way he walked.'

'And you checked the other horses and the rest of the yard?'

'Everything else was OK,' said Sam.

Scott pushed his mug away, as if he suddenly didn't have the appetite for it. 'And you think this was deliberate?'

Sam nodded. 'Gran hates barbed wire. That's why all the fences are post and rail. You know how careful she is, Scott. I bet there wasn't a single strand of barbed wire in the whole place.'

'And yet Treacle was trapped in coils of the stuff. Why would someone want to hurt him? It doesn't make sense.'

'They weren't trying to hurt Treacle,' said Poppy. 'They were targeting Redhall. They want to hurt Bella.'

10

Poppy felt as though she'd been asleep for a nanosecond when the unwelcome buzz of the alarm on her mobile phone dragged her from her dreams. They'd agreed to put morning stables back until half past seven, an hour later than usual, because they'd been so late the night before. Scarlett groaned and pulled her duvet over her head but Poppy climbed stiffly out of bed, picked up her towel and headed for the bathroom.

By the time she'd showered Scarlett had at least got out of bed and was staring out of the window.

'It's too dry for footprints and tyre marks,' she said glumly.

'Who are you, Sherlock Holmes?' Poppy teased.

'I wonder what car Angela Snell drives,' said Scarlett, ignoring her.

Poppy raised her eyes to the ceiling and headed downstairs. To her surprise Scott was already at the table, working his way through a mountain of scrambled eggs on toast.

'Scrambled or poached?' said Sarah, waving a wooden spoon at Poppy. She realised she was starving.

'Poached please,' she said, pouring a glass of orange juice. 'Did you manage to get through to Bella?'

Sarah shook her head. 'I couldn't work out why her mobile wasn't working. And then I found this.' She pulled a mobile phone charger from a kitchen drawer. 'She's only forgotten to take her charger.'

'If her phone's dead, how did she phone the farrier?' Poppy pondered.

'Have you tried Great Auntie Margaret's home phone?' asked Sam from the doorway.

'Yes. It just rings and rings and there's no answerphone so I can't leave a message. I suppose Mum's spending each day at the hospital with her. I'll try again tonight.'

Scott wiped his last piece of toast around his plate.

'I'll change Treacle's dressings and then give you a hand with the liveries,' he said.

He must have caught the look of surprise that flashed across Poppy's face because he added sheepishly, 'I know I haven't been much help since I arrived, but that's going to change, I promise.'

Scott was as good as his word and once he'd seen to Treacle he began mucking out Cherry and Otto's stables. Poppy had to hand it to him, once he'd made up his mind to help he worked like a demon, finishing both stables before Poppy was even halfway through Paint's. Little beads of perspiration dotted his forehead like raindrops on a car windscreen. He wiped them off with the back of his hand and grinned at Scarlett, who had wandered across the yard with a broom, still looking half asleep.

'Afternoon,' he teased. Scarlett yawned and grinned back.

'I just can't wake up,' she said. 'I reckon we only had about three hours' sleep last night.' She glanced over to the drive. 'Oh, I wonder who that is.'

Poppy pushed the laden wheelbarrow out of Paint's stable and joined her. A red people carrier was crawling up the drive. The sun was glinting off the windscreen making it impossible to see who was driving. The car came to a stop and a slight figure in jeans and a teeshirt flung open the door and jumped out.

'Tia!' cried Scarlett, dropping the broom she was carrying and running over to give her a hug. 'It's great to see you, but what are you doing here? There aren't any lessons this week.'

'I know. I was going mad at home on my own. I persuaded Mum to give me a lift up,' she said. She looked over to the car. Her mum wound down the window, tapped her watch and called out, 'I'll see you in an hour.'

Tia nodded and turned back to Poppy and Scarlett, her face suddenly serious. 'I just wanted to be with people who were there when it happened. Mum and Dad have been trying to talk to me about it but they don't really understand.'

Poppy knew exactly what she meant. No matter how hard she tried not to think about it during the day, at night, when she finally succumbed to sleep, her dreams were filled with images of the accident. Merry somersaulting forwards. Rufus landing on Niamh's back. Scarlett's eyes wide with shock as she screamed. Sometimes Poppy wondered if her dreams would be haunted forever.

Poppy stuck her head over Cherry's stable door. 'Is it OK if we finish the stables after lunch, Scott?'

He nodded. 'Sure.'

'Sam's in the barn,' said Scarlett, linking arms with Tia. 'Let's go and find him.'

Poppy loved Bella's hay barn. From the outside the timber-framed weather-boarded building was nondescript, but inside the feeling of space and timelessness reminded her of a cathedral. Shafts of light danced from floor to ceiling like swirling sprites and although the intense smell of newly-cut hay made her sneeze, Poppy swore it captured the very essence of summer.

As they walked through the big double doors there was a shout - 'TIMBEERRR!!' - and a bale of hay bounced down from the top of the stack and landed at their feet. They looked up to see Sam grinning at them from the small space between the tightly-stacked hay and the roof.

Scarlett, who had been playing in hay barns since she could walk, scaled the bales as nimbly as a mountain goat. Tia and Poppy looked at the near vertical wall of hay and then at each other.

'You go first,' Tia said.

'Thanks.' Poppy stuck a toe between two bales as if she were mounting a horse and pulled herself up. Bale by bale she clambered up the hay, eventually reaching the top. She heaved herself over the last bale and sat down with relief. Seconds later Tia joined her.

Poppy studied Tia's face as she caught her breath. A year older than her and Scarlett, Tia wasn't textbook pretty, but she had thick, wavy dark blonde hair which framed delicate features. Today her eyes were puffy, as if she'd been crying. Which, Poppy imagined, she probably had.

Scarlett was the first to speak. 'So, how's Niamh?'

Tia shook her head and bit her bottom lip. 'Not good. Mum spoke to her mum last night. She's bruised her spine. She can't move from the waist down.'

'Bruised, not broken?' said Poppy, hope flooding through her.

Tia nodded. 'At first they thought she might have fractured it but she had another scan yesterday morning and it's just bruised.'

'So she'll be able to walk again, once the bruise has healed?' said Scarlett.

'That's the million dollar question, Mum says. She might, she might not.' Tia took a deep breath. 'It depends how much damage the swelling has done to her spinal cord and they might not know that for weeks. Even months.'

'Poor Niamh,' said Sam.

A single tear ran down Tia's cheek. 'And it's all my fault.'

'No it isn't,' cried Poppy.

'Yes it is! If I'd reacted quicker I could have stopped Roof in time. If I'd pulled him left and not right he would have missed Niamh altogether. If I hadn't been there, she would have been fine. Maybe a bit winded, but that's all. Don't you see, I was to blame!'

'You can't think like that, otherwise you'd spend your whole life thinking what if,' said Poppy. 'Anyway, what if we hadn't cantered? Merry would probably have missed the rabbit hole altogether. What if I'd been riding behind Niamh instead of you? It would have been Cloud's hoof in her back, not Rufus's.'

'What if Claydon Manor had never opened a livery yard?' spat Scarlett. 'Bella wouldn't have lost any liveries, she wouldn't have had to start holding riding camps, we wouldn't have been her guinea pigs and Merry and Niamh would never have even been on that ride, that's what. I blame Angela Snell.'

Tia looked at Scarlett in confusion. 'Who's Angela Snell?'

'Doesn't matter,' said Sam.

Poppy felt the beginnings of a sneeze fizzing up her nostrils. She pinched the bridge of her nose. 'Do you know if Niamh's dad is still planning to sue Bella?'

Tia looked shocked. 'I didn't know he was going to. Mum didn't mention that. Anyway, he thinks it's my fault, too.'

'What do you mean?' said Sam.

'I wanted to go and see Niamh in hospital to say sorry. Her mum didn't mind but her dad said over his dead body. Mum said she could hear him yelling at Niamh's mum while they were on the phone. She reckons he's probably having some kind of breakdown.'

11

_____

Tia left just before lunch.

'Let us know if you hear any news about Niamh,' said Scarlett.

Tia nodded. 'And tell Bella to give me a ring once everything is back to normal.'

They waved as the red people carrier drove off.

'I don't think it ever will be,' said Poppy.

'Will be what?' said Scott, appearing from the barn with a bale of hay in each hand.

'Normal,' said Poppy. 'I don't think it'll ever be normal again.'

Scott dropped the bales, sat down on one and motioned Poppy, Scarlett and Sam to do the same.

'We need to talk about that,' he said. 'After I mucked out I searched the fields for barbed wire. I checked every fence and hedge. And do you know what?'

'There isn't any,' said Sam.

'That's right, Samantha. There isn't any. So how did Treacle end up with barbed wire wrapped around his legs?'

The other three were silent.

'Anyway,' said Scott, 'it got me thinking about everything else that's been happening since Bella went up to Inverness. And I reckon it's too much of a fluke for it not to be connected.' He paused for effect. 'I think someone has a vendetta against Redhall.'

Poppy exhaled loudly. Sam raised his eyes to the sky. Even Scarlett, for whom Scott could do no wrong, tutted loudly. He looked at them all in turn, confusion in his muddy brown eyes.

'What is it?'

Sam jumped to his feet. 'We worked that out ages ago, super sleuth. The question is, what are we going to do about it?'

'We need to put some simple security measures in place. I want to chain and padlock the field gates, make sure the office, tack room and barn are locked at all times - even if we're around - and I want us to take it in turns to check on the horses every couple of hours during the night.'

Scarlett groaned. 'You're kidding. I'm already shattered! Look at the size of the bags under my eyes! You could do a weekly super-market shop with them, and I'm not joking.'

'Sam and I'll do checks at midnight and two o'clock, and you two can do the four o'clock one. We're all up at six anyway.'

Before Scarlett could reply the phone in Bella's office began ringing.

'I'm not getting it,' she said. 'It'll be another one of those nuisance calls and they freak me out.'

Poppy was about to get up and answer it when Scott jumped to his feet and headed for the office. But before he was halfway across the yard the ringing stopped. Seconds later Sarah appeared with a bag of carrots in one hand and the phone in the other.

'It's a man called Stanley Smith from the Tavistock Herald,' she said. 'He wants to talk to someone about the riding school, so I suggested he speak to you, Scott.' She held out the carrots.

'I don't think that's going to work,' he said.

Sarah looked down and laughed. 'Sorry. Try the phone.'

Scott sat back down on the bale of hay and held the handset close to his ear. Poppy nudged Scarlett, who was grumbling about another broken night's sleep, pointed at Scott and held a finger to her lips.

Stanley Smith, nicknamed Sniffer because of his nose for a good story, had once interviewed Poppy and her brother Charlie when they'd seen a big cat on the moor. Sniffer loved a bad news story above all else. Why did he want to speak to someone at Redhall? It didn't bode well.

Scott chewed on a nail as he listened to Sniffer, his expression turning from curiosity to disbelief and then to outrage.

'You've heard *what*? Who on earth told you that? No, it's not true! Yes, the vet was here, but that was to see one of the riding school ponies. No, he hasn't got strangles! He was cut by barbed wire. You need to get your facts straight before you start throwing around accusations like that, mate.'

Scott shot up and began pacing across the yard. 'What d'you think I mean? Someone's been feeding you a pack of lies. The yard isn't on shut down. We don't have strangles. And if you publish anything to suggest we have I will sue you. And that's not a threat, it's a promise.'

Scott ended the call with an angry jab of his index finger and turned to face them. 'Someone emailed the Herald this morning to say the yard was on shutdown after two of the ponies were diagnosed with strangles.'

He sat down heavily on the hay bale and ran his hands through his hair.

Sarah looked puzzled. 'What's strangles?'

'It's a super-contagious disease that affects horses' upper respiratory tracts, Mum,' said Sam. 'It can cause these really nasty pus-filled abscesses on the sides of their heads and their throats.'

Sarah pulled a face. 'Not sure I needed quite that much detail, thank you Sam. But none of the horses have strangles, do they?'

Scott shook his head.

'So what's the problem?'

'Don't you see? All it needs is for a rumour to get out that there's a confirmed case and Redhall's future is on the line. The liveries Bella does have left will be out of here like a shot. People will be worried about coming here for shows. The place will be stigmatised. I know a livery yard that had an actual outbreak. The horses were quarantined and eventually all recovered. But the yard never did. It went out of business shortly after,' said Scott.

'Did Sniffer say who told him?' Poppy asked.

'An anonymous email was sent to the newsroom from a Hotmail account.'

'No way of tracing it, I suppose,' said Sam. 'Is there anything we can do?'

Poppy thought hard. They needed to be upfront and quash any rumours before they reached the liveries. 'We should phone everyone and tell them what's happened before they hear anything themselves. If they need reassuring they can phone the vet. He'll be able to tell them why he was here last night.'

Scott spent the next half an hour on the phone talking to Bella's few remaining liveries.

'How did it go?' asked Scarlett when he finally finished.

'Debbie virtually had a meltdown and was threatening to pull Cherry and Otto from the yard. I did point out that if the rumour was true no other yard would touch her horses with a bargepole until we were clear of strangles anyway. And if it wasn't true there was no reason not to stay. She's going to phone the vet to check, but I think she'll probably stay. Ellie and Paint's owners were both fine. They've kept horses here for years and were more worried about who could be starting the rumour.'

'Join the club,' said Sam morosely.

Poppy looked around at their worried faces. 'Come on, let's go for a ride. Otherwise we'll end up going stir crazy, staying here and worrying about everything.'

Scarlett's face brightened. 'Can I ride Cherry?'

SCARLETT WAS ALREADY SITTING on Cherry by the time Poppy led Cloud over to the mounting block. Scott was riding Otto and Sam was on Star. The two Connemaras, one as black as night, the other dappled grey, followed the bay and chestnut thoroughbreds out of the yard.

Scarlett swung around in the saddle. 'Let's head over towards Claydon Manor,' she called.

'She's obsessed,' Poppy muttered to Sam.

'There is a nice ride that goes past the manor house. It takes a couple of hours but we've got time,' he said.

'Perfect,' said Scarlett. Soon she was chatting to Scott about his job at the showjumping yard. He was a great rider, Poppy had to admit. He sat tall and deeply in the saddle and had the lightest contact on Otto's reins. The big chestnut gelding's long, loping gait was relaxed as he strode out next to his stablemate.

They turned off the road onto the moor and followed a dusty farm track. Cloud felt fresh and full of energy and every so often he snatched at his bit and broke into a jog. Cherry swished her black tail irritably whenever he came too close for comfort. They clattered along the track until they reached a farmyard. Cloud spooked at a rusty plough half buried by brambles and almost collided with Star.

'Sorry,' said Poppy. 'He's a bit full of himself today.'

'There's a great place for a gallop in a minute,' said Sam. The track cut through two fields of barley, which shimmered silver green in the sun. Scott looked back.

'Ready?' he asked.

'Yes,' said Sam, tightening his reins. Even the perfectly-schooled Star was now jogging sideways up the path. Poppy nodded.

The two thoroughbreds broke into a canter, Cloud and Star hot on their heels. Soon Cherry and Otto were galloping, their hooves thundering like racehorses in the Derby. Cloud lengthened his stride and Poppy crouched low over his neck as he raced to catch up with them. Star matched him stride for stride, their necks outstretched and their manes rippling in the wind. Cloud was strong and surefooted and Poppy felt a bolt of total euphoria that pasted a grin to her face and cancelled out all the worry of the last few days.

The track cut through the barley and climbed the side of the valley. The four horses galloped up the hill, their tails flying.

'Horse ahead!' called Scott. He pulled Otto back into a canter and the others followed suit. Poppy looked up to see a palomino pony standing as still as a sentry on the brow of the hill. A girl in a candy pink teeshirt with matching silk was watching them intently, a hand to her forehead to shield the sun from her eyes. The four Redhall horses slowed to a walk. The girl spun her pony around and shrieked, 'Stay away from us!'

Poppy would have recognised that voice anywhere. 'It's Georgia Canning!'

'Why's she screaming at us?' said Scarlett.

Georgia and her pony were now only metres away. 'I said stay away! You shouldn't even be out. It's totally irresponsible!'

'What do you mean?' said Scott.

Suddenly Poppy realised. 'She thinks we've got strangles!'

Scarlett was shocked. 'But how can she? Only the person who emailed the Herald and that reporter know. Unless -'

'-she or Angela were the ones who sent that email,' finished Poppy.

Georgia was still screeching at Scott, who was trying to get close enough to tell her that there was no strangles at Redhall.

'I've had enough of this,' said Scarlett. She cleared her throat and bellowed, 'There's no strangles at Redhall!' Cherry leapt about three feet into the air. Scarlett didn't bat an eyelid. Poppy wished yet again that she was half as good a rider as her best friend.

Georgia narrowed her eyes and looked Scarlett up and down. 'Why should I believe you?'

'Do you really think we'd be mad enough to take the horses out if the yard was on shut down?' Sam said scathingly.

Georgia looked uncertain. Her pony stepped forward and whick-ered softly to Cloud. She caught Poppy's eye.

'It really is true,' said Poppy quietly. 'The horses are all fine. But who told you?'

Georgia shrugged. 'I can't remember.'

Scarlett tutted loudly.

'Please tell us, Georgia. It's really important we find out who's spreading these rumours,' Poppy said.

Georgia stared down the valley towards Redhall. Something tugged at Poppy's memory. Something Bella had said about Georgia the day of the affiliated show, when Georgia had beaten Sam to second place.

'Hey, I remember. You used to ride at Redhall, didn't you?'

Georgia glanced at Poppy and gave a faint nod.

'Gran taught you to ride, didn't she Georgia?' said Sam. 'Before your family came into all that money. She was always singing your praises. She loved that you were so single-minded and ambitious. In fact she didn't charge your mum for your lessons half the time, did she?'

Poppy saw indecision behind Georgia's eyes and took advantage.

'Redhall's in serious trouble. Someone's trying to put Bella out of business and we need to stop them before it's too late. Who told you about the strangles, Georgia?'

'Angela,' said Georgia finally. 'She told me while I was tacking up Barley. She sounded -'

'What did she sound?' said Scarlett sharply.

'She sounded *pleased.*'

12

'I knew it!' said Scarlett. 'We need to ride straight to Claydon and have it out with her, right now.'

'There's no point,' said Georgia.

Scarlett's eyes narrowed. 'What do you mean?'

'She isn't there. It's her day off. She always drives down to Cornwall to see her parents. She passed me as I rode down the drive. She won't be back until late tonight.'

The horses were growing impatient.

'Which way are you going?' Sam asked Georgia.

'Home,' she said, pointing to the track in front of them. 'Mum helps me do the horses on Angela's day off but she needs me there to tell her what to do.'

'Mind if we join you for a bit?' Sam said.

'I suppose not.'

Poppy rode Cloud alongside Barley and began telling Georgia about all the things that had happened at Redhall since Bella had left for Inverness. Her china blue eyes widened when she heard about the wire around Treacle's legs.

'I remember Treacle! He bucked me off into a puddle once. Is he OK?'

'He'll be fine, but it could easily have been much worse. That's why we need to find out who's behind all this, so we can stop anything else happening.' Poppy paused. 'What's she like?'

'Who, Angela?'

Poppy nodded.

'Driven, strict, demanding and really competitive. She's a perfectionist and she hates failure.'

'So she would hate it if Claydon's livery yard wasn't a success?'

Georgia nodded. 'But there's one thing wrong with your theory. She may play to win, but she loves horses. She would never have hurt Treacle.'

'Perhaps she didn't mean to. Perhaps she just left the barbed wire in the field as a warning? Perhaps the wire was already there and what happened to Treacle was a genuine accident and we've just assumed it was part of the vendetta.'

'Perhaps,' agreed Georgia. 'But you won't be able to ask her until the morning.'

They rode on in silence until they reached the far boundary of Claydon Manor's huge estate.

'Please don't say anything to Angela. We'll come over in the morning,' said Poppy.

Georgia nodded briefly and turned Barley for home.

'You two seem to have hit it off,' said Scarlett. Poppy thought she could detect a touch of resentment in her best friend's voice, though Scarlett had tried to disguise it.

'Not really. I was just pumping her for information,' she said. She didn't add that she thought Georgia's haughty exterior was probably shielding a less confident person underneath and that the older girl had looked genuinely shocked when she'd told her about all the things happening at Redhall. If Angela Snell was behind the plot to bring down Bella's yard, Poppy was convinced Georgia Canning knew nothing about it.

THE YARD WAS quiet when they finally arrived back an hour later.

'All OK?' Scott asked Sarah as she ladled spoonfuls of tomato soup into bowls and passed them around the kitchen table.

'Not a hint of trouble,' she confirmed.

'Well, there wouldn't be, would there?' said Scarlett. 'That Snell woman's in Cornwall.'

'We'll still padlock the gates and do the checks tonight, just to be on the safe side,' said Scott.

As Poppy did afternoon stables she could feel wave after wave of exhaustion sweeping over her. Her eyes felt gritty with tiredness and her limbs were sluggish. She longed to find a quiet corner in the hay barn and sleep for a week. When they sat down to eat Sarah's home-made cottage pie she couldn't stop yawning and after she'd helped Scarlett wash and dry up she announced that she was heading up to bed.

'There's no point me staying to watch TV. I'll only fall asleep. I'll set the alarm on my phone for four o'clock, Scar.'

'It doesn't need to take long,' said Scott. 'Just a quick check on the paddocks and stables to make sure everyone's where they should be and that the gates are locked and then you can go back to bed.'

POPPY SANK GRATEFULLY into bed and pulled the duvet under her chin. She had never felt so bone-tired in her life. She switched off her bedside lamp, curled up in a ball and was just drifting off to sleep when she realised with a start that she'd forgotten to set her alarm. She sat up abruptly, grabbed her phone from the bedside table and stared blearily at the screen.

'Is it even light at four o'clock?' she muttered to herself, tapping the tiny alarm clock icon and scrolling down until she'd reached 0400 hours. She turned the volume up as high as it would go and set the snooze button just in case. Satisfied the alarm was set, she placed her phone back on the bedside table and snuggled back down under the duvet. Seconds later she was asleep.

THAT NIGHT POPPY dreamt she was riding Cloud bareback and without a headcollar across the moonlit moor. She wound her fingers around his mane, gripped with her knees and crouched low as he galloped through valleys and past tors towards Claydon Manor. As they grew close to the boundary of the manor house Poppy saw a huge yew hedge looming in front of her. Cloud lengthened his stride.

'You can't jump it, it's too high!' she cried, tugging his mane, terrified he was going to attempt to hurl himself over. At the last minute she saw a narrow opening the size of a doorway in the wall of yew. Cloud galloped through it without hesitating. They were flanked each side by walls of dark green foliage so high they blocked out the moonlight. Cloud slowed to a trot, and then to a walk. Poppy stared around wildly and shivered as the green walls seemed to close in around her.

In a moment of clarity she realised they were in a giant maze. 'We need to head for the centre,' Poppy said. She knew it was vital they found the heart of the maze, although she had no idea why.

She used her heels to guide Cloud left and right. They twisted and turned, hitting dead end after dead end. Soon they were completely lost and Poppy could feel panic rising.

Just when she thought she couldn't stand any more Cloud stood stock still, sniffed the air and neighed. An answering whinny echoed around the walls of the maze. Poppy felt a shiver run down her spine. Cloud walked forwards purposefully and she sat quietly, letting him choose his route. Poppy became aware of a pearly glow ahead, like moonlight reflected on water. As they came closer the light became stronger, until it glowed as bright as magnesium. Poppy shielded her eyes. She knew they had almost reached the centre of the maze.

Cloud turned the final corner and whickered. Poppy gasped. Standing in front of them, lit by the ghostly glow, was Merry, with Niamh sat astride her. The bay mare whickered and Cloud stepped forward and blew softly into her nostrils.

Niamh jumped down from Merry and smiled.

'We've been waiting for you, haven't we, Merry?' she said.

Poppy could feel tears welling behind her eyes. 'We just kept hitting dead end after dead end.'

'But you found us in the end.'

Poppy nodded. She slid off Cloud's back and tried to peer around Niamh and Merry. 'What's in the centre of the maze?'

Niamh stepped forward, obscuring the source of the light. 'The truth,' she said simply.

'I need to see it!' cried Poppy. 'I need answers!'

'The answers are there, Poppy. You just need to know where to look.'

As Poppy leant forward Niamh grabbed her shoulder and started shaking it. 'No, Poppy, no!'

'Get off!' Poppy cried. But the shaking wouldn't stop. Poppy felt herself swim back to consciousness. She opened her eyes groggily. Scarlett was standing over her, shaking her shoulder.

'Oh no, Poppy! No! We've slept through the alarm!'

The image of the dream was still so powerful it took a moment for Poppy to register what Scarlett was saying.

'Wake *up*, Poppy!' Scarlett flung Poppy's jeans and sweatshirt at her. 'We need to check on the horses!'

Poppy sat up slowly. Scarlett was already dressed and had pulled the curtains. The bedroom was flooded with light. Poppy checked the time on her phone. Twenty five past six.

'But I don't understand,' she gabbled. 'I set the alarm last night. I remember doing it.'

'You set it for two o'clock this afternoon,' said Scarlett, pointing. 'Look.'

Poppy scanned the screen. Scarlett was right. The alarm was due to go off at 1400 not 0400. She must have accidentally pressed one instead of nought. What an idiot. She grabbed her jeans and pulled them on, trying to ignore the knot of fear tightening in her stomach.

'They'll be OK. It's all padlocked,' she said, more to convince herself than Scarlett.

They had reached the bottom of the stairs when Sam bowled in like a tornado. He skidded to a halt on Bella's oak floor when he saw them and looked at Poppy. His face was leached of all colour.

Poppy knew then that something had happened to Cloud. It was her punishment for not setting the alarm properly. She felt light-headed with fear and grabbed hold of the newel post to steady herself.

'What is it? What's happened to him?' she whispered.

Sam shot a desperate look at Scarlett, who put her arm around Poppy's trembling shoulders.

'I'm so sorry, Poppy. He's gone.'

13

Poppy's legs buckled under her and she sat down on the bottom stair with a thump.

'Gone? What do you mean, gone?'

'He was there when we checked at two o'clock. I woke up at six and thought I might as well check on them. Someone had cut through the chain around the gate and it was swinging open.'

'Are any of the others missing?' Scarlett asked, her face pale.

Sam shook his head. 'Cloud's stable door was the only one that was open. I've spent the last half an hour checking all the fields but I can't find him anywhere. I'm sorry Poppy. He's gone.'

'This is all my fault!' Poppy wailed.

'What do you mean?' Sam asked, frowning.

'I set the wrong time on the alarm. We didn't do the four o'clock check. Oh Scarlett, what am I going to do?'

Scarlett sat down beside Poppy. 'It's alright. We'll find him, I promise.'

'He lived wild on the moor for *five years*, Scar. I couldn't catch him last time. What makes you think this time'll be any different?'

'We don't know he's on the moor,' Scarlett reasoned.

Poppy jumped to her feet. 'You're right. I need to check the fields again.' She marched over to the back door and pulled on her jodhpur boots, Scarlett and Sam trailing behind her.

'Did you check behind the shelter in Treacle's field?' she asked Sam.

He shook his head.

'Well then, that's where we'll start.' Poppy set off at a jog towards Treacle's paddock. She scanned the fields for any sign of Cloud, but the only grey ponies in sight were Salt and Pepper, who lifted their heads and watched as she ran past.

Poppy paused at the open gate to Treacle's paddock. Her heart was thudding painfully in her chest. She puffed out her cheeks and blew. Her mouth was so dry it took three attempts before she could muster a half-decent whistle. Poppy held her breath. Normally there would be an answering whinny and Cloud would appear in search of a titbit and a welcome scratch behind his ear. But today all she could hear was the blood pounding in her head.

She raced across the field to the shelter, trying not to think about poor Treacle's shredded skin. She crossed her fingers and peered around the back wall. But the only thing there was a green wheelbarrow.

She became aware of Scarlett and Sam behind her and spun around.

'I'm going to double-check the other fields too,' she panted. She knew she sounded slightly hysterical but she didn't care. If Cloud felt even a fraction of the love for Poppy that she felt for him he wouldn't have run away, would he?

She spent the next half an hour checking and re-checking the paddocks, running to and fro like a kid with a sugar rush. Eventually Sam grabbed her arm and pulled her to a stop.

'He's not here, Poppy,' he said.

Poppy knew in her heart that he was right. She looked at him, her face streaked with tears.

'Come on,' said Scarlett gently. 'Let's go back to the house.'

Scott was by the gate inspecting the chain when they tramped back. He beckoned them over.

'Whoever did this must have had a really heavy duty set of bolt croppers,' he said, showing them where the metal had been cut cleanly through.

'But why was Cloud's the only stable he opened?' wailed Poppy.

'It's the closest one to the drive. Perhaps he was intending to let all the horses out but got spooked and legged it,' said Sam.

Poppy knew he was probably right but it didn't make it any easier to bear. If only she'd put Cloud in Merry's stable. If only she'd set her alarm properly. If only they hadn't come to Redhall in the first place none of this would have happened. Cloud would be safely tucked up in his stable with Chester, waiting for his breakfast. As it was, he could be miles away, frightened and alone.

Scarlett guessed what she was thinking. 'Remember what you told Tia, Poppy. You've got to forget the what ifs. What we need to do is decide what we're going to do next.'

'I'll do morning stables so you three can look for Cloud,' said Scott.

Poppy ran her hands through her hair. 'But where do we start?'

'We'll phone the police and all the local vets and animal sanctuaries,' said Sam. 'Have you got a photo of Cloud we can send them?'

Poppy thought of her phone, lying on her bedside table. 'Hundreds,' she said.

'Good. Mum can start phoning around while we go up onto the moor.'

ONE OF THE things Poppy loved most about Dartmoor was the vastness of it. She loved the sense of freedom and adventure the huge landscapes and sweeping panoramas promised. But this morning, as she trudged down the Redhall drive with Cloud's headcollar on her shoulder and a bucket of pony nuts in her hand, the sheer size of the moor only served to remind her of the enormity of the task ahead. Sometimes, when they hacked out alone on the moor, Cloud would stand stock still, lift his head, sniff the air and Poppy would feel him quivering with excitement. She often wondered if he pined for the freedom he'd once taken for granted. Poppy knew that by bringing him home to Riverdale she'd taken his freedom away and replaced it with a life of captivity and routine, dependence and predictability. What if he hated her for it and longed to be free?

Where would he go? Would he head for Riverdale, pulled by an unconscious force back to the safety of home, the companionship of his stablemate Chester and the promise of a bucketful of breakfast? Or would his flight instinct take over, send him galloping for the horizon, the lure of rediscovered freedom erasing Poppy and Riverdale from his memory?

'We'll check the routes we've ridden on first,' said Sam, interrupting Poppy's spiralling thoughts.

She automatically glanced left and right as they reached the road. An image of mangled metal and Cloud's lifeless body pushed its way into her mind's eye like a mirage.

'What if he's been hit by a car?' she cried. Her mum Isobel was killed in a car crash when Poppy was four. Surely fate wouldn't be so cruel?

Scarlett shook her head. 'He'll be fine, Poppy. I know he will.'

They set off down the rutted track onto the moor, their shoulders hunched and their heads bowed as the track climbed steadily. Soon they were passing the farmhouse where Poppy had called for help. The woman in the red-checked shirt was pegging out a line of washing. She waved when she saw them.

Scarlett waved back. 'You haven't seen a grey pony, have you?' she called.

The woman dropped her bag of pegs into the basket of wet washing and walked over.

'A Dartmoor pony?'

'No, he's a dappled grey Connemara, about so high,' Scarlett said, holding her hand above her shoulder. 'He escaped from Redhall last night.'

The woman shook her head. 'Sorry, I haven't.' She noticed Poppy, who was standing behind Scarlett. 'You're the girl who asked to use the phone after the riding accident the other day.'

Poppy nodded.

'How is your friend? I've been thinking about her.'

'Not good. And her pony had to be put to sleep,' said Scarlett.

'I did wonder when I saw the vet's Land Rover. What an awful thing to have happened. And now you've lost a pony, too.' She turned to Poppy. 'Is it the one you were riding when you came for help?'

'Yes.' Poppy swallowed the lump in her throat. 'If you see him, please will you phone me?'

'Of course. I'll get a pen and paper and you can write your number down. I'll tell my husband to keep a look out while he's checking on the sheep. And I can pass the word to our neighbours, too, if you like.'

'Thank you, that's really kind,' Poppy said, smiling feebly.

They asked everyone they passed that morning but no-one had seen Cloud. Poppy's hopes were raised when a couple walking their chocolate Labrador said they'd seen a grey pony drinking from a nearby stream. She raced over, her heart in her mouth, only to find the pony was an iron grey Dartmoor mare with a bay filly foal at foot. She could have wept.

At one o'clock, when there was still no sign of the Connemara, Sam suggested they went back to Redhall.

'We can ride out this afternoon. We'll be able to cover much more ground than we can on foot. We'll head over to Claydon Manor to see if he went that way,' he said.

'OK,' said Poppy dully, though she knew it was a waste of time. Cloud was gone. And he was never coming back.

SARAH WAS WAITING by the back door and ushered them in.

'I've phoned the three nearest vets, two local animal sanctuaries and the police. There haven't been any accidents and no injured ponies have been brought in. So that's good, isn't it?' she said brightly.

'But no-one's seen him,' Poppy said flatly.

The smile slipped from Sarah's face. 'No, they haven't. But I've left our number with everyone. He's bound to show up sooner or later.'

Poppy's nerves, already stretched to breaking point, suddenly snapped. 'Horses aren't like homing pigeons, Sarah. He's not going to suddenly turn up on the doorstep.'

Sarah flushed. 'I'm sorry. I didn't mean to upset you.'

Poppy hadn't thought it possible she could feel any worse. But when she saw the hurt on Sarah's face she knew she was wrong.

'No, I'm sorry. I shouldn't have snapped. It's not your fault. And I do appreciate your help, I really do.'

Scarlett banged her forehead with the heel of her hand. 'Talk about homing pigeons, you have phoned Caroline to check he hasn't gone home, haven't you?'

Poppy shook her head numbly. In all the panic she had completely forgotten. How stupid. If Cloud was going to go anywhere, surely it would be Riverdale?

Sam passed her the phone and as Poppy dialled she felt a tiny glimmer of hope flare in her heart. Caroline answered on the fourth ring.

'It's me,' Poppy gabbled. 'Is Cloud with you?'

The glimmer of hope was snuffed out like a candle the second she heard Caroline's sharp intake of breath.

'What do you mean is Cloud here? He's with you, isn't he? What's happened, Poppy?'

Poppy looked at Scarlett, Sam and Sarah's expectant faces and shook her head. She held the phone close to her ear.

'It's a long story.'

THEY SET OFF AFTER LUNCH, Poppy on Rosie, Scarlett riding Blaze and Sam on Star. Poppy rode ahead, her eyes swivelling left and right as she scanned the horizon for Cloud. Rosie, who was infamous at Redhall for being highly temperamental, had picked up on her mood and she walked meekly as they rode up the dusty track, through the farmyard and into the field of barley.

Poppy's thoughts slipped back to the day Cloud had arrived at

Riverdale in Bella's horsebox, his coat matted with blood and his ribs standing out like the wooden bars of a xylophone. She had promised him then that she would always look out for him. And she had broken that promise. It was unforgivable.

The tight ball of fear in Poppy's stomach was morphing into a knot of anger, directed solely at the shadowy figure who'd let her beloved pony out of his stable and in doing so had broken her heart. Life without Cloud didn't bear thinking about. She kicked Rosie into a canter without even telling the others and soon she was crouched over the roan mare's neck as they thundered through the barley.

By the time Scarlett and Sam caught up with her at the top of the hill Poppy had made up her mind.

'I'm going to go and have it out with Angela Snell,' she said.

Sam looked at her in consternation. 'We don't know she's behind all this.'

Scarlett gave him a scathing look. 'She has the motive, the means and the know-how. And anyway, who else could it be?'

'She knew about the strangles,' Poppy reminded Sam.

'I know, but -'

But Poppy didn't hear any more. She had already turned Rosie towards Claydon Manor.

ANGELA SNELL WAS STRAPPING a big chestnut thoroughbred when they clattered into the yard. She greeted them with a steely gaze.

'I hope for all your sakes that Georgia was right when she said there's no strangles at Redhall. Otherwise you'll be hearing from our solicitors.'

Poppy jumped off Rosie and marched over to Angela. 'Our horses are perfectly healthy. Who told you the yard was on shutdown?'

Angela frowned. 'I had an email.'

'I need you to show me,' Poppy said, handing Rosie's reins to Scarlett. She eyed Angela defiantly, challenging her to refuse. Angela nodded slightly.

'Follow me.'

She beckoned Poppy inside the airy office next to the tack room, flipped open an expensive-looking laptop and opened her email account.

'It was sent the day before yesterday,' Angela said, pointing to the screen. 'There's no name on it.'

Poppy read the brief email over her shoulder:

'WARNING: A case of highly-infectious strangles has been diagnosed at Redhall Manor Equestrian Centre. Please help everyone keep their horses safe and spread the word. Redhall is a no-go area.'

Poppy checked the sender's address. It was a Hotmail account she didn't recognise.

'Probably the same account used to email the Herald.' She glared at Angela Snell. 'And you didn't bother checking this was true before you started telling people Redhall was on shutdown? What if someone was spreading lies about Claydon Manor? How would you feel?'

'Alright, you've made your point. Anyway, I only mentioned it to Georgia. I've been down in Cornwall with my parents. I didn't get back until nine.'

'Nine last night?' Poppy said sharply, thinking of Cloud.

Angela gave her a black look. 'No, nine this morning. I decided to stay the night. Why?'

Poppy felt her throat constrict. 'Someone let my pony out of his stable at Redhall last night. He escaped onto the moor. We've been looking for him all day.'

Angela studied Poppy's face. 'That's tough, and I'm very sorry. But if you think I'd stoop so low you are very wrong. Redhall might be in competition with Claydon but I never play dirty. It's not my style.'

14

oppy lay in bed staring at the ceiling. In the bed beside her Scarlett's breathing grew slow and regular. Once she knew her best friend was definitely asleep she flung back the duvet, pulled on thick socks, jeans and a fleece and slipped out of the room. After less than a week at Redhall she was already familiar with the creaky floorboards and she stepped over them lightly and headed down the stairs, her hand trailing down the polished mahogany banister. In the kitchen she made herself a cup of tea and carried it carefully out into the yard. The moon was full and heavy and it gleamed in the sky like an illustration in a children's storybook. Blaze's chestnut head appeared over her stable door and she whinnied when she saw Poppy.

'Shush, you'll wake the others,' Poppy said. She found a couple of pony nuts in the pocket of her jeans and held out her palm. Blaze whickered her thanks and Poppy laid her head against the mare's soft head. 'Oh Blaze, do you think he'll be OK?'

Blaze regarded Poppy with limpid eyes. Poppy gave her one last stroke and headed for Cloud's empty stable. She leant on the door, her chin resting on her folded arms. Scott had mucked out while they'd been on the moor. He'd even filled the hayrack and water buckets. She slid the bolt across and tugged the door open. Moonlight flooded into the empty stable. Poppy left the door open wide and sat down in the straw, her hands clasped around her mug of tea. She wondered where Cloud was, what he was doing. Closing her eyes, she pictured his face, as familiar to her as her own. She literally could not bear the thought that she would never see him again.

Perhaps she could try sending him a telepathic message. Poppy didn't believe in that type of thing but surely anything was worth a try?

'Come back to me, Cloud,' she whispered, willing her thoughts to span the wide expanse of Dartmoor between her and her beloved Connemara. She sent message after message, pleading with him to hear.

But there was no clatter of hooves on the concrete, no whicker of recognition. She knew she was wasting her time. Cloud had gone and he wasn't coming back.

She thought about their visit to Claydon Manor that afternoon. Poppy felt bad that she'd ever blamed Angela Snell for the vendetta against Redhall. As they'd left Claydon they'd bumped into Georgia, who confirmed that the livery yard manager had arrived home just after nine o'clock. The pair were either telling the truth or they deserved Oscars for their performances. Poppy believed them, anyway. That hadn't stopped Scarlett's lips curling in disbelief when she'd told Scarlett and Sam as they'd ridden home. Scarlett was still convinced of their guilt.

Poppy took a sip of her tea and listened to the sounds of the yard. Horses shifting in their stables, the rustle of straw, the steady breathing of Blaze next door as the mare settled down to sleep. The sounds were soporific and Poppy felt her own eyelids grow heavy. Before long she had nodded off.

POPPY AWOKE to the oddest sensation that someone was in the stable with her. She froze. What if it was the intruder, come to finish what he'd started? What if he was towering over her right now, his bulk obscuring the shafts of moonlight that had cast a friendly glow over Cloud's stable? Poppy realised her best option was to pretend to still be asleep. At least she would have the element of surprise. She kept her eyes squeezed tight and tried to marshal her groggy thoughts. Stupidly she'd left her phone on her bedside table and the nearest pitchfork was in the barn, which was no use at all. She inched her hand towards the mug in the straw beside her. It was the only thing she had at her disposal. She decided to throw it at the intruder and make a run for it.

Poppy was so focused on her escape plan that at first she didn't notice the draught of warm breath on her cold cheek. She didn't register the feather-like tickle of whiskers against her earlobe. Her fingers curled around the handle of the mug and she drew it close to her chest. And then, in the silence of the stable, a pony whickered softly. Her eyes snapped open.

There, standing in front of her, his face centimetres from her own, was Cloud. Poppy wondered if he was an apparition, an image conjured up by her deep longing for him. She reached out to touch him, half-convinced he would disappear, wraith-like, in a puff of smoke. But the tips of her fingers met warm horse. He stepped forward and gave her the gentlest of nudges. Finally allowing herself to believe he really was there, Poppy jumped to her feet and threw her arms around his neck as tears streamed down her face.

'Oh Cloud, I thought I was never going to see you again. But you came back.'

He nibbled the pocket of her fleece and Poppy rested her face against his, delighting in the feel of his soft coat against her skin. She realised she should never have questioned the bond between them. Cloud must love her as much as she loved him.

She gazed into his deep brown eyes. 'You could have gone back to Riverdale. But you didn't. You came back to me.'

THE NEXT MORNING Poppy and Scarlett free-wheeled into the Baxters' car park and propped their bikes against a green bottle bank. Normally Poppy loved wasting half an hour in the cavernous shop, drinking in the smell of new leather and inspecting the displays of riding gear and equipment, but today her stomach was churning.

'What's the plan? Shall I cause a diversion while you try and slip behind the counter?' whispered Scarlett.

Poppy shrugged helplessly. 'I guess. Although I'm not sure what I'm supposed to be looking for.'

'All Dad's invoices from Baxters' have his contact phone number on. See if you can log into the computer, open Redhall's account and find Monday's invoice.'

Poppy swallowed. 'You make it sound easy, Scar. What if I get caught?'

'Look,' she said, waving her arm. 'The car park's deserted. They only ever have one member of staff on at this time of the afternoon. If it's Tanya we'll be fine. She can talk for England. I'll keep her busy while you do the business. And if anyone sees you behind the counter just pretend you dropped your phone or something.'

Poppy frowned. It didn't sound like much of a plan. But, she realised, it was the only one they had.

'Alright, here goes.'

She pushed open the double doors and stepped in. Scarlett nodded towards the dark-haired girl sitting behind the counter and gave Poppy a surreptitious thumbs up.

'Tanya!' she cried. 'Haven't seen you for ages. How's things?'

'Hi Scarlett. What brings you here?'

'Mum and Dad sent me over to choose a new hat for my birthday. Dad said to stick it on his account.'

Poppy raised her eyebrows. Scarlett's birthday was in May, a cool ten months away.

'Sure,' said Tanya. 'Let me just finish this and I'll come over and measure you up.'

Tanya tapped away at the computer keyboard in front of her and, with a couple of clicks of the mouse, the printer chugged into life, spewing out an invoice. She tore it off and opened the middle drawer of a metal filing cabinet behind her. Poppy watched as Tanya's fingers walked along the files until she found the one she was looking for. She pulled the cardboard folder out, slid the invoice inside, replaced the folder and pushed the drawer closed with her backside.

'Right,' said Tanya, lifting the hinged counter open. 'The hats are over there.' She pointed to the far corner of the shop, where a couple of dozen hats were on display on wooden shelving units.

'I'm just going to have a look for a card for Caroline's birthday,' said Poppy, edging over to a wire carousel beside the counter.

'Help yourself,' smiled Tanya. 'So Scarlett, do you want a hat for hacking or are you going to be using it for competitions as well?'

Poppy pretended to scan the arty horse cards and Thelwell cartoons while Tanya and Scarlett disappeared to the back of the shop. After a couple of minutes she glanced up. Tanya was standing with her back to Poppy, holding a tape measure around Scarlett's head. Scarlett caught Poppy watching and winked.

Poppy realised this could be her only chance. She darted behind the counter and stared at the computer screen. It was on the Baxters' home page. Poppy pressed enter and groaned inwardly when she was asked for a password. She tried 1234 and 4321 and then Baxters1234 and Baxters4321, but the computer stubbornly refused her entry. She could hear Tanya murmuring about the new regulations governing riding hats. Poppy abandoned the computer and turned to the filing cabinet. Four drawers, the first marked A-G, the second H-M. Poppy eased open the third, marked N-S, and looked wildly for Redhall. But there was no folder for the riding school. Sure she must have missed it, Poppy checked again. Still nothing.

She thought hard. Maybe the invoices were kept under Bella's name. She slid the third drawer closed and opened the bottom one, marked T-Z. There were five files marked Thompson and Poppy cursed Bella for having such a popular name. Adrenalin coursed through her veins as she pulled out each file and checked inside.

As Poppy pulled out the second to last file she risked a look over her shoulder. Tanya and Scarlett were still deep in conversation,

Tanya holding a mirror as Scarlett modelled a skullcap with an emerald green silk. Poppy opened the file.

Bella Thompson
Redhall Manor Equestrian Centre

Bingo.

'So you found the latest invoice?' Scarlett whispered as they pushed their bikes across the car park.

Poppy nodded.

'And there was a mobile number on it?'

Poppy waved her hand in Scarlett's face. 'I couldn't find a piece of paper so I wrote it on my hand. It's definitely not Bella's number. I've just checked.'

'Don't forget it's there and go and wash your hands,' Scarlett cautioned.

'Do I look stupid?' said Poppy hotly. The adrenalin that had helped her through her spying mission was now threatening to bubble into ill temper.

'No need to bite my head off.'

'Sorry.' Poppy gave her best friend a brief smile. 'What did you tell Tanya?'

'That I couldn't make my mind up and that I would come back next time Dad's over. She seemed to buy it. Shall we try the number now?'

Poppy checked her phone. 'No signal.'

They jumped on their bikes and began pedalling slowly towards Redhall. At the top of a particularly steep climb Poppy called Scarlett to stop.

'I've got two bars. Shall we give it a go?'

They collapsed on the verge and Scarlett grabbed Poppy's hand.

'I'll read you the number.' She screwed up her face. 'Is that a seven or a nine?'

Poppy squinted at the smudged biro scrawl on the back of her hand. She'd scribbled it down so quickly it was almost illegible.

'Um, a nine I think.'

Poppy dialled as Scarlett read out the number. She felt a flutter of nerves as she waited for the call to connect.

'Put it on speakerphone,' Scarlett said urgently. Poppy nodded and pressed the speakerphone icon.

A woman's robotic voice cut through the summer afternoon. *'Your call cannot be completed as dialled. Please check the number and try again.'*

Poppy groaned. 'I must have written the number down wrong.'

'Try a seven instead,' Scarlett said.

Poppy re-dialled.

This time the call connected. Time slowed down as the phone rang. Poppy realised she was clutching Scarlett's arm in a vice-like grip. On the fourth ring, just as she was beginning to lose hope, someone picked up.

A gruff voice. 'Hello?'

The two girls were silent.

'Who is this?' The voice sounded irritated. 'I said, who's calling?'

Poppy panicked. 'Er, sorry. Wrong number,' she cried, and ended the call.

BACK AT REDHALL they found Sam mucking out Treacle's stable. He listened in silence as they relayed what had happened.

'So we're no nearer to finding out who phoned in that order,' Poppy said glumly.

Sam stared into the middle distance. 'I've had an idea. It might not work, but it's worth a try. Follow me.'

He crossed the yard to Bella's office, tipped Harvey Smith gently off the office chair and booted up the laptop.

'What was the number?' he said.

Poppy checked her call log and read out the eleven digit number. 'What are you going to do,' she asked.

'Put it into Google and see if it comes up with anything. You never know.'

They watched as Sam tapped in the number and pressed search. He hit the top result. A website for a building firm slowly opened.

'Another dead end,' sighed Scarlett.

Sam's hand hovered over the mouse, ready to click away from the page.

But Poppy had seen something the other two had missed. She pointed to the bottom right hand corner of the screen.

'Of course,' she muttered, replaying the events of the past week in her mind's eye. 'It's completely obvious. How can we have been so blind?'

15

The door to the office swung open and the silhouette of a man appeared. Poppy jumped out of her skin and Scarlett smothered a small scream.

'Three guilty faces if ever I saw some,' said Scott, perching on Bella's desk. 'What's up?'

'You wouldn't believe us if we told you,' said Poppy.

'Try me.' Scott yawned widely, showing his chipped tooth. 'But you'd better be quick. I was going to sneak forty winks before evening stables.'

'Some things never change,' said Sam drily. 'Poppy and Scarlett went over to Baxters' this afternoon and managed to get the mobile number of the person who made that massive order. And it's him.'

Scott studied the computer screen and looked back at them.

'Am I missing something here?'

'It's a building company. Owned by Gordon Cooper,' said Scarlett.

Scott shook his head. 'Er, still none the wiser.'

'Gordon Cooper,' said Poppy patiently. 'Owner of Cooper Construction.'

Scott shrugged.

'Never heard of him.'

'He's Niamh's dad.'

SCOTT GRABBED his helmet and was threatening to race over to the offices of Cooper Construction to confront Gordon Cooper.

'We know that he made that order, but we can't prove he did anything else, Scott. Not yet, anyway,' said Poppy.

'You were sure the intruder you saw was a man, weren't you?' said Scarlett. 'Even though I didn't want to believe you at the time.'

'And cutting through the water pipe wouldn't be a problem for a builder, would it?' said Sam.

'All circumstantial though, isn't it?' said Poppy. 'We need proof.'

'But how are we going to get that?' Scarlett asked.

Poppy gave a helpless shrug of her shoulders. 'I don't know.'

THE DINNER TABLE was quiet that night, everyone lost in their own thoughts. They'd decided not to tell Sarah about their discovery - not until they had some concrete proof that Gordon Cooper was behind the vendetta. When the phone rang half way through Sarah's mouthwatering apple pie they held their breath as Sarah picked up the phone in the lounge, wondering if it was yet another nuisance call. Poppy felt her shoulders relax when Sarah walked in, a smile on her face.

'That was Mum. Great Auntie Margaret's settled in a nursing home for some respite care until she's back on her feet and Mum's decided to come home. She's setting off shortly and is going to drive through the night. I told her to wait until tomorrow but she insisted. She should be home just after breakfast.'

'Did you tell her about all the things that have been happening?' said Sam.

Sarah shook her head. 'I decided there was no point worrying her. We'll fill her in when she's back. Anyone for seconds?'

Later, when Sarah had gone to bed, they discussed what to do.

'I vote we do hourly checks tonight. I'll pair up with Scarlett and you two can go together,' said Scott.

Scarlett's face flushed with pleasure. 'That's a great idea.'

But Poppy wasn't going to rely on hourly checks while Gordon Cooper was still at large. 'There's no way I'm leaving Cloud tonight, after everything that's happened. I'm sleeping in his stable,' she announced.

Sam nodded. 'I'm with Poppy on this. I'll bring my duvet down and sleep in Star's stable.'

Scott looked at them both in amusement. 'You are more than welcome to hunker down with your horses. I, however, need my beauty sleep so I'm afraid I won't be joining you. And if you two are spending the night in the yard you won't need me and Scarlett to do our rounds, will you?' He rubbed his hands together in satisfaction.

Poppy could see the indecision in her best friend's hazel eyes. Scarlett loved her sleep and she idolised Scott but would she risk anything happening to Blaze? Poppy didn't think so.

She was proved right when Scarlett finally stood up and said: 'Looks like it's a night in the stable then.'

THE HORSES LOOKED on with curiosity as Poppy, Scarlett and Sam dragged their duvets and pillows across the yard and into the three stables. Cloud was the only one who wasn't surprised - at home Poppy often slipped down to his stable in the early hours if she'd been woken by a nightmare and couldn't get back to sleep.

They inspected each other's makeshift beds.

'Looks cosy,' said Sam. 'So, have you both got torches and your mobile phones?'

'Yes sir!' said Poppy, saluting. Scarlett giggled.

Sam sighed. 'I'm just trying to be practical. And we'll text each other if we hear or see anything?'

The girls nodded.

'Is there anything else we should do?' said Poppy.

Scarlett clapped her hands. 'I know! We could set some booby traps.'

Sam looked at her as if she was mad, but Poppy's mind was whirring.

'You're right. You know that roll of electric fence wire in the hay barn?' The other two nodded. 'Why don't we lay it along the front gate so when he goes to open it he gets an electric shock?'

Scarlett grinned evilly. 'Oh yes, I'm loving that idea. And we could arrange those bits of barbed wire he so kindly left on the driveway so he gets a puncture.'

'Neat,' Poppy said. 'What about tying together baler twine to make a trip wire? We could fix it just inside the gate.'

Scarlett nodded vigorously. 'And I could do the old Tom and Jerry classic and leave a couple of rakes on the ground. With any luck he'll stand on one and whack himself on the head.'

Sam's eyebrows were raised as he looked from one girl to the other. 'Remind me never to get on the wrong side of you two. You're reprobates.'

'He won't be getting anything more than he deserves,' said Poppy grimly.

HALF AN HOUR later their traps were laid. After Sam had positioned the strands of barbed wire Scott had cut from Treacle's legs across the drive like a police stinger device, he'd wrapped the electric wire tightly around the latch and top bar of the five bar gate and plugged it in. Poppy had tied together a dozen lengths of baler twine and fixed them between two fence posts a few paces into the yard. When she gave the taut orange twine a tug it gave a satisfying twang. Scarlett spent ages arranging and re-arranging the three rusty rakes she'd found languishing in the back of the hay barn.

The last glimmer of dusk was fading into blackness as they inspected their work.

'Good job,' said Scarlett, shining her torch at the electrified gate and Poppy's tripwire. 'He's going to wish he never picked on Redhall.'

'We'd better make sure we get up early enough to take it all down before Gran gets home,' said Sam.

Scarlett chuckled. 'Good point. We should all set the alarms on our phones for five o'clock.'

Poppy yawned, wondering if she would ever enjoy a lie-in again. 'Let's try and get some sleep while we can. It could be a long night.'

Cloud blew in her hair as she let herself into his stable and she kissed his nose. She wrapped herself in her duvet and wriggled around in the straw until she was comfortable. She closed her eyes and listened to her pony chewing hay. Scarlett was murmuring to Blaze in the stable next door.

"Night Scar,' Poppy called, her voice already drowsy.

"Night Poppy.'

Poppy's limbs grew heavy and her breathing deepened. Soon she was asleep.

POPPY WOKE with a start and she sat up, looking around her groggily. It was dark. Too dark to see her hand in front of her face. She felt a fizz of fear pulse down her spine. Cloud stirred beside her and she relaxed. He was safe. And then she heard someone tapping gently on the stable wall.

'Scar, is that you?' she whispered.

'I thought I heard a car,' Scarlett whispered back. 'It's either driven off or stopped, I can't tell which.'

Poppy cocked her head and listened. 'I can't hear anything.'

'Nor can I now. But I'm telling you, I'm sure I heard a car's engine a minute ago.'

'I'll text Sam,' whispered Poppy, groping in the straw for her mobile. She tapped out a text.

This is a Code Red. I repeat, this is a Code Red. Stand by your stations.

A few seconds later her phone vibrated.

Copy that. I am standing by. Over and out.

Poppy slipped her phone into the back pocket of her jeans, picked up her torch and edged out of the duvet, trying to make as little noise as possible, but every time she moved the rustle of straw seemed to reverberate around the walls. Cloud was staring out of the stable, his nostrils flared as he sniffed the wind. Suddenly he gave a snort and wheeled around, almost knocking Poppy off her feet. She ran her hand along his flank, trying to calm him, even though her own heart was thudding.

'It's OK baby. I won't let him hurt you,' she whispered.

She stiffened as she heard the unmistakable sound of a car door clunking shut. She crept over to the stable door and peered into the yard. But the moon was veiled by thick cloud and she couldn't see a thing.

Was that the crunch of gravel? Poppy strained her ears to hear but it was impossible to tell. She jumped out of her skin when one of the thoroughbreds whinnied loudly, the sound slicing through the still night air like a speedboat through water.

Her phone vibrated in her pocket. She was just reaching for it when a guttural cry and a string of expletives rang out. Scarlett gasped in the stable next door and Poppy's fingers tightened around her torch. She stared into the dark, willing her eyes to distinguish between shadow and shade. As she stared the outline of a hunched figure began to take shape, like a drawing in one of Charlie's dot-to-dot picture books.

It was the same man Poppy had seen the night Treacle was hurt, Poppy would have bet her life on it. And he was heading straight for them.

16

---

oppy narrowed her eyes and watched the hooded figure
stumble over the tripwire and curse again. She braced herself
for a confrontation as he approached Cloud's stable. But he
strode straight past, heading for the padlocked barn. As he walked by
Poppy noticed he was carrying a pair of bolt croppers and a red
plastic petrol can. It took her a moment to grasp the significance of
the can but when she did white-hot anger began bubbling up inside
her, giving her courage.

'Oh my God, he's going to burn down the barn!' she cried, sotto
voce.

'What do we do?' Scarlett hissed through the wall.

'Call the police. Tell them there's an intruder and they'll send out a
patrol car. I need to stop him.'

She laid her face against Cloud's cheek as if to draw strength and
let herself out of the stable. As she did she saw Star's stable door swing
slowly open and Sam appeared, his finger on his lips. He pointed his
thumb towards the intruder. Poppy joined him and they crossed the
yard in silence. The man had reached the barn doors and had lifted
the bolt croppers to the heavy-duty padlock when Sam whispered.

'Ready? On the count of three. One, two, THREE!'

Sam yelled, 'Stop right there!' And they simultaneously switched on both their torches. The man dropped the bolt croppers and his hand shot to his forehead as he tried to shield his eyes from the glare of the two torch beams.

'What the -?' he roared, lunging towards Sam.

'Not so fast! The police are on their way,' shrieked Poppy, hoping with all her heart that they were.

'You've called the police?' he asked in such a menacing voice that Poppy's blood froze. 'Now why would you want to be doing that?'

Poppy watched in horror as he turned his back on them and began unscrewing the top of the plastic can. The noxious smell of petrol filled her nostrils.

'In an ideal world I'd have got inside the barn. But needs must,' he muttered to himself, splashing petrol up the huge double doors of the barn.

'What are you doing?' Poppy cried. 'You'll destroy everything!'

He turned to Poppy. She kept the torch trained on his face, though the dancing beam gave away her trembling fingers. She lifted her chin and met his gaze. Under a deeply-lined forehead his eyes were emotionless.

'Bella Thompson deserves to lose everything.'

He turned back to the barn, reached into his pocket and pulled out a box of matches. 'Why don't you children run along and leave me to it?'

Poppy heard Sam move away but her feet were rooted to the ground. She had to keep him talking to stop him setting fire to the barn.

'It wasn't Bella's fault Niamh fell off. I was there. I saw what happened. It was an accident!'

He turned to face her again. 'So you know who I am?'

'Gordon Cooper,' she whispered. 'Niamh's dad.'

'My beautiful Niamh is lying in a hospital bed unable to walk because of Bella Thompson,' he spat. 'She's ruined my daughter's life. And I'm going to make her pay.'

Gordon Cooper's mouth stretched into a rictus grin and he pulled a match out of the box, his dead eyes never leaving Poppy's face. He struck the match against the box once, twice. On the third attempt the match splintered in two and he flung it on the floor at his feet. He took out another and struck it viciously.

For a split second the smell of burning sulphur dioxide as the match ignited masked the petrol fumes. And then there was a whoosh as the sleeve of Gordon Cooper's coat caught fire. Poppy screamed as flames darted up his arm and set his coat alight. Within seconds he was engulfed in flames.

Suddenly Sam was at her side, pointing the yard hose at the human fireball in front of them.

'Scarlett, bring one of the duvets!'

Poppy ran to Cloud's stable and grabbed his two buckets of water. As she ran back Scarlett joined her, holding the duvet in her outstretched arms.

'Hold the hose,' Sam shouted to Poppy. She took it from him and spurted it at Niamh's dad. Sam took the duvet from Scarlett and threw it over him.

'Now roll on the floor!' he yelled.

Gordon Cooper's dead eyes were now filled with panic. He dropped to the floor and began rolling around on the ground by their feet.

'The police are on their way,' Scarlett said, just as the back door slammed and Sarah and Scott came running out.

'What on earth's going on?' Sarah shouted.

Scott took one look at Cooper. The duvet had smothered the flames but he was still writhing around on the concrete, his soot-blackened face twisted in fear.

'Is this him?' Scott asked.

The children nodded.

Scott hauled Cooper to his feet.

'Are you burnt?' he said.

Cooper rubbed his arms gingerly and shook his head. Scott marched him across the yard, flung him in Merry's empty stable and bolted both doors.

'You can stay in there until the police arrive,' he said.

The adrenalin that had given Poppy the courage to confront Cooper was seeping away and her legs had turned to jelly. She stumbled over to Cloud's stable, sank to the floor and listened as Sam and Scarlett told Sarah and Scott what had happened.

'Some of the petrol must have splashed back onto him when he was dousing the barn doors,' said Sam.

'He's lucky he was wearing such a thick coat,' Sarah said.

'And that Sam knew what to do,' Scarlett added.

Sam shook his head. 'I can't take credit for the booby traps.'

'Booby traps?' said Sarah faintly.

'Speaking of which, I'd better switch off the electric fence and move the barbed wire before the police arrive, otherwise they'll be arresting me as well as Niamh's dad.' Scarlett headed for the gate, reappearing a few minutes later with a wide grin on her face and lengths of barbed wire, like a deadly bouquet, in her hand.

'Our homemade stinger worked like a dream,' she told them with satisfaction. 'He had three punctures. Three! He'd never have got away in a million years.'

THE REASSURING SOUND of sirens grew louder and soon a police patrol car, its blue lights flashing, pulled up behind Gordon Cooper's old van. Poppy hauled herself to her feet and joined the others by the gate. A female police officer emerged from the driver's side, followed shortly by an older male colleague who was talking into his radio. Poppy recognised the female officer immediately. It was PC Claire Bodiam, the kind and capable officer she and her friend Hope Taylor had met at Tavistock Police Station the previous year.

PC Bodiam recognised her, too. 'Hello Poppy! What on earth are you doing here?'

'It's a long story,' Poppy said.

PC Bodiam took in the petrol can, the abandoned duvet and the strong reek of petrol. 'So, who would like to tell me what's been going on?'

She listened in silence as between them Poppy, Scarlett and Sam explained the events of the last week, Scott interjecting every so often.

Soon the two police officers were leading Gordon Cooper away in handcuffs. His head was bowed and he looked utterly defeated, as if all the fight in him had gone. Perhaps he had finally realised Niamh's accident wasn't Bella's fault. Poppy hoped so, for Redhall's sake.

Once he was safely in the car PC Bodiam walked back over.

'He's been arrested on suspicion of criminal damage and attempted arson, although there may well be other offences. We'll know more when we've taken statements from you all,' she said. 'In the meantime I've just called out our crime scene investigators who'll be here first thing to take photos of the petrol can, matches and bolt croppers, and to examine the barn doors, so please don't touch anything until they've been.'

'OK,' Sarah nodded. 'Thank you.'

'No problem,' said PC Bodiam. She smiled at Poppy, Scarlett and Sam. 'You did exactly the right thing back there. If you hadn't stopped the fire Mr Cooper could easily have died. And Niamh would have lost her dad, just when she needed him most.'

'I don't suppose he's going to see it like that,' said Sam bitterly. 'He hates Gran's guts.'

'Oh, I don't know. I think some time down at the station will give him a chance to reflect. I don't think he'll be giving your gran any more trouble. And if he does, you're to let us know immediately,' she said.

'What shall we do about his van?' Sarah asked.

'We'll push it out of the way for now and let his wife know she needs to arrange a recovery truck to come and collect it,' said PC Bodiam's colleague.

They watched the patrol car accelerate away towards Tavistock. Although the sky was still inky blue a lone blackbird had begun a fluty warble from the hawthorn hedge that bordered the Redhall drive, sounding the first mellow notes of the dawn chorus.

'I can't believe Niamh's dad hates Mum so much that he was prepared to burn down the yard,' said Sarah.

'Tia did say she thought he was having some sort of a breakdown,' said Sam.

Scott scowled. 'That's no excuse for putting the horses' lives in danger.'

'I was wrong, wasn't I?' said Scarlett. 'I blamed Georgia Canning and Angela Snell. I thought the motive was money. But it wasn't. Gordon Cooper's motivation was revenge, pure and simple.'

17

Everyone was bleary-eyed but cheerful at breakfast. The nameless threat that had cast its menacing shadow over the riding school for the past week had evaporated the minute Gordon Cooper had been led away in handcuffs. Sun streamed through the kitchen windows as Sarah made pancakes drizzled with maple syrup and freshly-squeezed lemon juice. Poppy wolfed hers down, suddenly ravenously hungry. She was going to miss Sarah's cooking.

They whizzed through morning stables in record time and the horses had all been groomed and turned out by the time the crime scene investigator sent by PC Bodiam arrived in her white van and started dusting for fingerprints.

They showed her the barbed wire and the two pieces of cut water pipe and she photographed the abandoned petrol can, the bolt croppers, the box of matches and the petrol stains on the door of the barn. Poppy carefully undid the dressings on Treacle's legs and held the Welsh pony so she could take pictures of the wounds. The thin skin around Treacle's cannon bones was beginning to heal and there were no signs of an infection but Poppy knew that he would always bear the scars of the barbed wire.

The crime scene investigator was reversing out of the drive when Bella pulled up in her dusty estate car. Poppy ran over and opened the gate so she could park in the yard.

Bella yanked the handbrake up and wound down the window.

'What was a police crime scene investigation van doing here?' she asked, mystified.

'How was the journey?' Poppy asked brightly, hoping to deflect the questions until Sarah arrived. She didn't think Bella was the type to shoot the messenger, but you never knew. She could be a formidable character at times.

Bella heaved herself out of the driver's side and slammed the door so firmly the whole car shuddered. She scanned the yard, her razor-sharp eyes falling on the petrol can. Treacle chose that moment to poke his head over the stable door and give a high-pitched whinny.

'Never mind the journey. Why's Treacle in? Why is there a can of petrol by the barn doors?' She fixed Poppy with a penetrating gaze. 'And what was that crime scene investigation van doing here?'

Poppy held up her hands in surrender. 'The important thing is, everything is fine now.' She lifted Bella's case out of the boot and gave her what she hoped was a beatific smile. 'Why don't we go and find Sarah and she can fill you in.'

ONCE POPPY HAD DELIVERED Bella to the kitchen she wandered over to the paddock Cloud shared with Blaze. She leant on the gate for a while and watched the two ponies grazing side by side. Vaulting the gate, she gave the ponies a Polo each and sat down with her back against the knotty stump of an apple tree and turned her face to the sun. An introvert by nature, Poppy was beginning to crave some time on her own, so she could recharge her batteries. She let her mind drift aimlessly through the events of the past week. She couldn't believe the morning they'd turned up as Bella's pony camp guinea pigs was only seven days ago. It didn't seem possible. This was their last day at Redhall and Bill was due to pick them up at six o'clock. Poppy knew she would be sad to leave after everything that had happened, but she was looking forward to going home. And she and Scarlett still had five whole weeks of the summer holidays left to enjoy. It wasn't so bad.

Scarlett found her in the paddock half an hour later. She waved her mobile phone in Poppy's face.

'Tia's just called. She'd heard about Niamh's dad being arrested and wanted all the gory details. She said it's the talk of their village. But she also had some good news about Niamh. She wiggled her toes this morning.' Scarlett collapsed in a heap beside Poppy.

'Does that mean she'll be able to walk again?'

'Not sure, but it's a good sign, isn't it?'

Poppy picked a daisy and began pulling the petals off, one by one. 'Pity her dad didn't wait a week before he completely lost it. He might have thought twice about waging war on Bella if he'd known Niamh was on the mend.'

'Tia said that according to village gossip his marriage is on the rocks and his building company is about to go bust. There was a fire in his warehouse a couple of weeks ago and the police hauled him in for questioning. Apparently they suspect he started it because he wanted to claim the insurance money. Niamh's mum packed his bags and chucked him out. He's been living in his van ever since. Sounds like Niamh's accident tipped him over the edge.'

'That would make sense,' Poppy said. 'How did Bella take it?'

'I think she's just relieved he's been caught and everyone is alright.'

'Is she cross about losing Vile Vivienne?'

Scarlett grinned. 'Nope. She said she and Angela Snell deserved each other.'

Poppy giggled. 'It's a match made in heaven.'

The two girls watched their ponies companionably. Poppy twirled the petal-less daisy between her thumb and forefinger.

'We should go for a ride this afternoon. All of us. And we should go on the Barrow Tor ride. Finish what we started.'

'Blimey, that's a bit deep.' Scarlett picked a blade of grass and chewed it thoughtfully. 'But it's an excellent idea. Let's go and tell the others.'

~

ONCE AGAIN BELLA led the way on Floyd. Sam and Scott, on Star and Otto, rode two abreast behind her. Scott was winding Sam up as usual, but they were both laughing - these days Sam gave as good as he got. Poppy and Scarlett rode side-by-side behind them on Cloud and Blaze.

The track onto the moor was bone dry and the horses' hooves sparked little puffs of dust every time they hit the ground. They passed a herd of solemn-faced black and white belted Galloway cattle.

'They always remind me of zebra crossings,' Poppy said inconsequentially.

'If you say so,' said Scarlett.

Soon they reached the gate to the lane which led past the farmhouse where Poppy had called the ambulance. The farmer's wife must have heard them coming, because an upstairs window was thrown open and she leant out.

'You found him then?' she called.

Poppy ran her hand along Cloud's neck and smiled back.

'Actually, he found me.'

They reached the wide grassy ribbon of a track where it had all gone wrong. Bella pulled Floyd up.

'I don't think we'd better canter today,' she said.

'I do,' said Sam.

'But what about the rabbit hole?'

'It's not there any more. I brought the quad bike up the day after the accident and filled it in.'

'Nice work, Samantha,' Scott said.

Sam rolled his eyes and tightened his reins. Star tossed her ebony head and crabbed sideways but he sat easily in the saddle.

'So are we going to lay those ghosts to rest or not?' he asked.

'Yep,' said Scarlett. Poppy nodded.

'If you're sure,' said Bella, kicking Floyd into a canter. Sam and Scott followed suit, still riding side by side. Poppy clicked her tongue but Cloud needed no encouragement. He cantered behind the others, his neck arched proudly and his mane rippling. She crouched low over the saddle as Cloud lengthened his stride and soon they were galloping as one across the moor towards the distant horizon.

Poppy glanced over to Scarlett and was shocked to see a single tear sliding down her best friend's cheek.

'You OK?' she called.

Scarlett nodded. 'Just thinking about Niamh.'

'Niamh's going to be OK, Scar. I know she is,' Poppy said.

And in that moment, as she and her friends galloped across their beloved Dartmoor, the wind in their ears and their horses' hooves thrumming on the springy grass like a beating heart, Poppy knew with absolute certainty that she was right.

THE SECRET OF WITCH COTTAGE

1

P oppy McKeever squinted into the sun, her eyes never leaving her best friend Scarlett as she cantered off towards the horizon. Scarlett's shoulders were stiff and unyielding, in contrast to her loose ponytail of auburn curls, which bounced jauntily on her back with every stride. Her Dartmoor pony Blaze was growing smaller by the minute. Which was ironic, Poppy thought wryly, as that had been the catalyst for their row. Cloud stamped an impatient foot, desperate to gallop after them, but she ran a hand down his neck and shook her head.

'Let them go. She'll come round once she's had a chance to cool off. Drama queen,' she added under her breath.

Cloud gave a tremulous whinny.

'She'll be fine. All I did was tell her that she looked like a drum on a pea when she rode Blaze these days. It was meant to be a joke and she totally over-reacted. Ridiculous.'

Poppy sighed. On reflection, it had sounded pretty mean. And she felt a small sliver of remorse as she remembered Scarlett's last words before she'd taken flight.

'I know I'm too big for Blaze, Poppy. You don't have to rub it in. It's alright for you. You've got Cloud. Mum and Dad have already told me they can't afford another pony. It's Blaze or nothing.'

Poppy had tried to backtrack but Scarlett, her eyes shining with unshed tears, had held her hand up to silence her.

'Save your breath. I'm not interested. I'm going home.' And she had wheeled Blaze around and kicked her into a canter, leaving Poppy gaping at her retreating back, completely lost for words. It was only when Blaze had disappeared that Poppy realised she didn't know the way home. Bored with their usual rides, Scarlett had taken them on a new route across the high, open moorland towards Princetown. Poppy loved the bleak, windswept panoramas they had crossed, but landmarks were few and far between and one craggy tor looked much like another. She patted the pocket in which she kept her mobile but pride stopped her from phoning Scarlett.

'We can find our way home, can't we Cloud?' The Connemara flicked an ear back and stamped his foot again. Poppy gathered his reins and clicked her tongue. 'Come on, let's go.'

∾

BEFORE LONG THE WIDE, stony path split in two. The first track was deeply rutted and lined with a gorse hedge and veered off sharply to the left. The second path was narrower and less well trodden and led in arrow-like precision towards a cluster of conifers straight ahead.

Poppy glanced over her shoulder. She could just make out the high granite walls of HMP Dartmoor. The impenetrable building, constructed two centuries before to hold prisoners of the Napoleonic Wars, dominated the skyline on this part of the moor. Her brother Charlie was fixated with the prison and had a ghoulish fascination for stories about the many convicts who'd escaped over the years.

'If Princetown is behind us, we must be facing east, so I think we need to follow the farm track,' Poppy said. Cloud was sniffing the wind, his nostrils flared and his eyes fixed on the conifers. He whin-nied again, the tremors shuddering along his dappled grey body like a mini earthquake. Perhaps he'd caught the faintest scent of Blaze and the chestnut mare was ahead, hidden from sight in the trees. Poppy trusted her pony implicitly. After all, he had roamed wild on the moor for years. If he couldn't lead her home to Riverdale, no-one could.

She gave him his head and he stepped onto the narrow path. It was a gloriously sunny afternoon in the middle of August yet the ground was still boggy in places. Poppy admired the way Cloud instinctively avoided the squelching peat by sticking to the grassy tussocks. At the edge of the band of trees the grass gave way to a carpet of rust-coloured pine needles and pine cones and when the path petered out Cloud kept walking, his ears pricked and his eyes still fixed ahead.

The deeper they walked into the trees the more the light leached away like sand in an hourglass. It was as if someone had pressed fast-forward to dusk. Charlie would say the shadowy forest was a perfect place for escaped prisoners to hide. Poppy shivered in her thin cotton tee-shirt.

They skirted a fallen tree and a clump of acid-green forest ferns. Poppy twiddled with a length of Cloud's silver mane.

'Are you *sure* this is the right way?' she said. But Cloud ploughed on through the towering conifers. Scratchy branches grazed Poppy's bare arms and the scent of pine needles filled her nostrils.

'Scarlett!' she yelled. 'Are you there?' Poppy cocked her head to listen for an answering shout, but the only sound was the static-like crackle of Cloud's hooves hitting the forest floor. 'Ridiculous!' she muttered again, as a branch caught her cheek. She was sure Scarlett would never have ridden this way home. But they had come so far she was curious to see what lay beyond the trees, and why Cloud was so intent on leading her there.

Gradually the gaps between the conifers widened and the sunlight streamed through the green canopy once again. Cloud stepped out onto open moorland, sniffed the wind and whickered softly. Poppy gazed around in astonishment.

'This is *beautiful*,' she breathed.

The small forest of evergreens concealed a teardrop-shaped tarn, on the banks of which stood a tumbledown cottage. A dry stone wall circled the cottage like a granite necklace. Poppy slithered to the ground and laced her fingers in Cloud's mane. He whickered again and began walking resolutely ahead.

'Wait! We don't know who lives here,' she whispered, tugging his reins. She stared at the cottage, looking for signs of life, aware they could be trespassing on private property. What if it was the home of a terse old hill farmer, with a distrust of strangers and a shotgun under the bed? Poppy's eyes travelled over the building, taking in the gaping hole in the catslide roof, the front door hanging off its ancient hinges and the rotting wooden window frames. She realised that the cottage must have been abandoned decades ago. Cloud strained forwards and Poppy finally relented.

'You win,' she told him. 'We'll go and explore.'

THE COTTAGE WAS TINY, as small as a shepherd's croft. A battalion of nettles, heavy with tiny white flowers, guarded the front door. Poppy looped Cloud's reins over an old fence post, edged past the nettles and gave the door a tentative push. It swung inwards, hitting the wall with a clatter. She took a deep breath and stepped over the threshold.

The front door led straight into a small, empty square room that Poppy supposed must once have been the parlour. The air smelt fusty, as if it hadn't been disturbed in years, and when she ran her fingers along the windowsill they picked up a layer of fine, sooty dust. Blackened beams intersected the low ceiling and the uneven floor was laid with cracked and stained quarry tiles in shades of sienna and ochre. On the outside wall was a fireplace with a granite hearth and a simple wooden mantelpiece. Opposite the fireplace was another door. Poppy tugged at the tarnished brass handle.

The kitchen was even smaller than the parlour and was also empty apart from a stone sink under the window and a rusty range. A creaky narrow staircase led to two tiny rooms in the eaves. Poppy inched her way across the woodworm-ridden floorboards in the larger of the two bedrooms to the window to check Cloud was still happy nibbling grass where she'd left him. A movement in the corner of her eye made her jump, but it was only a swallow, swooping out of a gap in the roof towards the still waters of the tarn. Hearing high-pitched cheeping, Poppy craned her neck and saw four baby swallows peeking out of their mud nest tucked under the eaves.

An old hessian sack had been tossed into one corner and two wooden crates were arranged in the middle of the floor facing the window. Almost like chairs, it occurred to Poppy. The silence in the old cottage was absolute. She wondered what kind of person would choose to live such a remote and lonely life so high on the moor. She gazed at the sloping ceilings and uneven walls, but the cottage wasn't giving away any of its secrets.

Feeling a sneeze looming, Poppy tramped back down the stairs. Cloud lifted his head as she emerged into the sunlight and she unhooked his reins and led him to the water's edge. He grazed while she threw stones into the dark water of the tarn, enjoying the ripples they made as they sank out of sight. Cloud seemed so at ease Poppy was sure it wasn't the first time he had been to the cottage.

'This place is so cool. Charlie and Scarlett will love it,' she said, before remembering that Scarlett wasn't talking to her. Poppy's earlier irritation had waned, to be replaced by an anxious knot in her stomach. She hated conflict and usually avoided it at all costs. She knew Scarlett was devastated that she had almost outgrown her beloved Blaze and was gutted that her parents couldn't afford another pony. It was hardly surprising she'd had a serious sense of humour failure. Poppy wished she could turn back the clock. Falling out with her best friend in the middle of the summer holidays was the last thing she wanted to do. She reached for her mobile and tapped out a quick text.

Sorry Scar, didn't mean to upset you. Still BFF???

But the screen remained stubbornly blank. After half an hour of checking and re-checking her phone she admitted defeat, dragged herself to her feet and swung back into the saddle. She and Cloud retraced their steps back through the conifers.

'This time we'll go my way,' she said, turning him down the gorse-lined farm track to their right. 'These tractor tracks must lead somewhere.'

The track climbed steadily until Poppy could see over the band of conifers to the cottage and lake below. After a couple of miles the track became even more rutted. The gorse bushes were replaced by an old stone wall, which they followed for another mile or so to a farm tucked in the hollow between two tors. The farmyard was deserted, save for a couple of bantams scratching around in the dirt. When the track merged with a tarmac lane Poppy squeezed Cloud into a trot. Eventually they reached a staggered crossroads and a lichen-covered sign. *Waterby four miles*.

Poppy wondered if Scarlett was still seething at her thoughtless jibe. She could kick herself for being so insensitive. As she turned Cloud towards home one thing dominated her thoughts. How could she make amends?

2

___

The next morning Poppy found Charlie helping Caroline stick labels onto dozens of jars of homemade raspberry and strawberry jam.

'You haven't forgotten it's the fete today?' Caroline mumbled, a pen between her teeth.

Poppy groaned. 'Do I have to come?'

'You promised to do pony rides, remember? Cloud's one of the star attractions. You can't let all those children down,' her stepmother said.

Poppy pulled a face. 'He's not a novice ride. Some awful screaming toddler is bound to fall off and end up with concussion. And then I'll be sued. I don't think I should go.'

'No-one is going to fall off. Cloud will be on the lead rope and the children will be wearing hats. You never know, you might even enjoy it,' Caroline said.

Charlie licked a label and smoothed it onto a jar of strawberry jam.

'Charlie, that's disgusting!' Poppy shrieked.

'Someone got out of bed the wrong side this morning,' said Charlie, smoothing out the air bubbles with his thumbs.

Poppy shot him a filthy look and slammed two pieces of bread in the toaster. She had woken up grumpy and her mood hadn't improved when there was still no text or missed call from Scarlett. At least her best friend had agreed to help with the pony rides, giving Poppy a chance to apologise face to face.

The phone rang. Caroline stuck the pen behind her ear and answered it.

'Hello Pat! Yes, the tombola's done and we've almost finished the jam. We just need to load the car and we're ready. Poppy will ride Cloud over and meet us there.' There was a pause. Caroline frowned. 'Oh, that's a shame. I hope she feels better soon. Give her our love, won't you?'

'What's happened?' Poppy demanded.

'Scarlett's not feeling too well. She's decided not to come.'

Poppy gouged a piece of butter from the tub and began attacking her toast. 'Just brilliant,' she grumbled.

'Why *are* you in such a bad mood?' said Charlie, who had finished packing the jam into cardboard boxes and was counting the float.

'I. Am. Not. In. A. Bad. Mood,' Poppy growled. But Charlie wasn't listening. His eyes had taken on a faraway look and a smile was tugging at the corners of his mouth.

'Mum, do we have any brown wool?'

'I expect so. Have a look in the dresser.'

Charlie scrabbled around in a drawer and pulled out a ball of soft, mocha-brown wool.

'Perfect,' he said.

Despite herself, Poppy was curious. 'What do you want it for?'

'You know I'm doing pin a tail on the donkey for the Canvas Challenge?'

Poppy nodded. Charlie's Cub pack had launched an appeal to raise money to buy new camping equipment to replace its leaky tents. Charlie had spent the last week tracing out and colouring in a huge, lop-sided donkey which he'd pinned to a cork board and planned to set up on an old easel Caroline had found in the loft. Blindfolded fete-goers would be invited to try their hand at pinning the tail on the donkey for fifty pence a go, and anyone who managed to pin the tail anywhere near its backside would win a plastic cup of sweets.

'I'm going to do a 3D version,' he announced.

Now Charlie was a dab hand with Lego but Poppy sincerely doubted that even he could knock up a donkey in the hour they had before they had to set off for the fete.

'I just need to make a tail out of this,' he said, waving the wool in Poppy's face, 'and check Chester's nice and clean and we're in business.'

Poppy almost choked on a mouthful of toast.

'You are *not* using Chester for pin the tail on the donkey!' she screeched. 'Are you *mad?*'

'Why not? Chester loves children and he's too old for donkey rides.'

'You can't have people sticking drawing pins into him. It's animal cruelty!'

Charlie gave her a withering look. 'I wouldn't use drawing pins, grumpy-pants. I'm not that stupid. We've got some double-sided sticky tape in the craft box. I'll use that instead.'

Caroline held up her hands. 'That's enough, you two. How about a compromise? We bring Chester along to the fete so children can make a fuss of him, but we use Charlie's lovely picture to pin the tail on. I can still make you a wool tail if you want, Charlie?'

Appeased, Charlie nodded.

'We'll leave at nine. That'll give us plenty of time to set the stall up before the fete opens at ten,' said Caroline.

THE ANNUAL WATERBY SUMMER FETE, held on the third Saturday in August, was one of the highlights of the village's social calendar, eclipsed only by the Christmas Eve nativity service, which drew people from far and wide. The nativity boasted real animals in a lovingly re-created Bethlehem stable at the front of the church. More impressive still, the youngest babe-in-arms in the parish was always given the honour of playing Jesus. One especially memorable year, when there had been a shortage of babies, the job had been given to a wilful eighteen-month-old toddler called Isaac, who had thrown his swaddling cloth off just as the Three Kings arrived, climbed out of the manger, pointed at Mary and bawled, 'That's not my mummy!' It had made headlines in the Tavistock Herald.

Every group in the village ran a stall at the summer fete to raise funds for their own organisation and the competition to outdo each other was fierce. Caroline had been roped into running the tombola for Charlie's school's PTA, and had, through a combination of cajoling and coercion, amassed a vast array of prizes, from cans of fizzy drink and bottles of bubble bath to food hampers and, the star prize, a digital camera.

When Caroline had first asked Poppy if she and Scarlett would like to organise the pony rides it had seemed like a good idea. Poppy had been obsessed with horses all her life and it wasn't so long ago that she would have happily traded the clothes on her back for five minutes on someone else's pony. It would be good to let other pony-mad kids have a ride on Cloud. She and Scarlett would have a laugh. But running the pony rides on her own wasn't going to be half as much fun.

She tied Cloud and Chester to the fence behind their car and gave them the haynets she'd filled earlier. Satisfied they were happy chomping away, she helped Caroline put the finishing touches to their stall.

'Have you decided who you're raising money for yet?' Caroline asked.

'Either the PTA or Charlie's tent fund, I suppose,' she said, although she had little interest in either. She'd never attended Waterby Primary as they'd moved to Dartmoor when she was eleven. Her old primary school was miles away in Twickenham. And she would rather pull out her own fingernails one by one than join Charlie and his fellow Cubs for a night under canvas, even if the tent didn't leak.

She gave the handle of the tombola drum a hefty crank, imagining all the folded raffle tickets somersaulting inside like popcorn in a microwave. Her gaze wandered to the empty space next to their stall.

'Who's supposed to be there?'

'Some animal rescue charity, according to Pat.' Caroline checked her watch. 'But they need to get a shift on. The fete opens in fifteen minutes.'

As she spoke an ancient Land Rover came flying into the field. It narrowly missed the Methodist ladies' cake stand and drove straight over a couple of the guy ropes on the bunting-clad tea tent. It finally came to an abrupt halt in front of the McKeevers' stall. A blonde girl in her early twenties in cut-off denim shorts and a red tee-shirt leapt out and slammed the door shut behind her.

'Is that for me?' she said without preamble, pointing to the space beside them.

Caroline stepped forward, a smile on her face. 'Yes. Do you need a hand setting up? Poppy and I can help, can't we Poppy?'

Poppy, who had picked up a box of after dinner mints and was pretending to read the list of ingredients, shot her stepmother a mutinous look. 'I need to go and get ready.'

'Nonsense. You can spare ten minutes.'

Inside the back of the Land Rover was a long trestle table and several tall display panels.

'Pat said you're from an animal rescue charity,' said Caroline.

'Nethercote Horse Rescue,' corrected the girl, pointing at the logo on her tee-shirt.

'We'll help you unload,' Caroline told her. But the girl shook her head.

'I can manage.'

Ignoring her, Caroline nodded to Poppy to take one end of the top display panel. As they opened it up Poppy almost dropped it in shock. A huge photograph pinned to the royal blue panel showed a skeletal skewbald mare. She was so thin Poppy could count every rib. Her sunken flanks were covered in angry red sores, her head drooped listlessly and her eyes were dull. She looked hours away from death.

'That's Kirsty. She was skin and bone when she came to us. She was riddled with worms and had infections in both her eyes. Our vet said she'd never pull through.' The blonde girl's voice was matter-of-fact. She opened another fold of the display panel. 'That photo was taken last week.'

Poppy shook her head. She couldn't believe the plump mare standing proudly in a field, her skewbald coat glossy and her eyes bright with life, was the same horse.

'That's incredible.'

The girl dipped her head in acknowledgement. 'I think so.'

Charlie appeared, his face painted like a Ninja warrior, the woollen donkey tail clutched in his hand. He looked the blonde girl up and down. 'Who are you?'

'Jodie Morgan. Who are you?'

'Charlie McKeever. And that's my sister Poppy. But be very careful. She got out of bed the wrong side this morning.'

Poppy glared at Charlie, who raced back out of their gazebo holding the tail in the air like a pennant. Sometimes he was so embarrassing.

She helped Jodie unload the rest of the panels. Before and after photos of horses and ponies were pinned to each section, with handwritten stories alongside each one. In one of the pictures a horse had overgrown hooves so long they curled up like Aladdin's slippers. Others had matted coats, hollow necks and bony rumps. Poppy had a sick feeling in the pit of her stomach. How could anyone treat an animal so badly? It was beyond belief.

'Some people complain our photos are too graphic and say we shouldn't use them because they upset people.' Jodie gave a derisory snort. 'I don't care. You can't sweep cruelty and neglect under the carpet. These pictures need to be seen. What do you think?'

Taken aback by her directness, Poppy glanced towards Caroline. But her stepmum was deep in conversation with the woman running the face-painting stand.

'They are shocking,' she said. 'But I agree with you. People should know it goes on. And maybe it'll help with donations.'

Jodie's lips thinned. 'If only. People have absolutely no idea how much it costs to run Nethercote. They seem to think I can feed the horses on thin air.'

Charlie re-appeared. 'It's one minute to ten, Poppy!' he cried. 'You need to start the pony rides.'

'Pony rides?' Jodie asked.

'My pony Cloud is over there with our donkey Chester.'

Chester's long brown ears had flopped forward as he dozed but Cloud was looking around with interest as fete-goers began streaming into the field.

'Did you say Cloud?' Jodie said.

Poppy nodded, wondering why the older girl was staring at the Connemara as if she'd seen a ghost. Then she had an idea. 'I was going to raise money for new tents but I'd much rather give the money to help your horses. It might not be much, but anything is better than nothing, right?'

Jodie dragged her eyes away from Cloud. 'Yes,' she echoed faintly. 'Anything is better than nothing.'

THE NEXT TWO hours passed in a blur of shortening and lengthening stirrup leathers, giving leg-ups and leading young riders up and down the length of the field as proud parents snapped away on their mobile phones. Poppy had been worried how Cloud would react to the swarms of people but he was basking in all the attention, standing patiently as he was stroked and petted, taking the Polos and tufts of grass proffered on countless sticky palms so gently that Poppy's heart swelled with love. Chester was an old hand at village events and when Poppy hit on the idea of charging fifty pence for the privilege of having a selfie with the donkey an orderly queue quickly formed.

Halfway through the morning Jodie appeared with a plastic cup of lukewarm orange squash.

'Your mum sent me over with a drink. And you can put this on if you like,' Jodie said, handing Poppy a red tee-shirt that matched her own.

Poppy pulled the tee-shirt over her head and smiled. 'I reckon I've made about fifty pounds already.'

'Wish I could say the same. People are so tight they won't even fork out the price of a cup of coffee.' Jodie rubbed Cloud's forehead and he snuffled at the pocket of her shorts. She looked as if she was about to say something else, then thought better of it. She patted him on the neck and smiled briefly at Poppy. 'Anyway, gotta go.'

By two o'clock the queue of children waiting for a ride had dwindled to nothing. Poppy left Cloud tied up next to Chester and went in search of Caroline. Charlie charged through the crowd towards her, shaking an old biscuit tin heavy with loose change.

'I've made millions!' he said. 'Enough to buy ten tents, I reckon.'

'I've made lots, too. I was going to have a count up and give the money to Jodie before I take Cloud and Chester home.'

'She's gone.'

'You're joking.'

'Nope. She told us it was a waste of time and she'd have been better off staying at home.'

Poppy jiggled the coins in her pocket. 'How am I supposed to get all this money to her?'

Charlie shrugged. 'Ask Mum.'

Poppy found Caroline at their stall wrestling with the trestle table.

'I was just about to come and find you. Are you all done?'

'Done in, more like. I'm shattered. You have no idea how tiring giving pony rides is.' Poppy collapsed on the ground. 'And Charlie said Jodie's already gone.'

'She had to get back for the horses. I said we'd drive over tomorrow. There's a map on the back of the leaflet she was giving out.' Caroline pulled a crumpled piece of paper from the pocket of her jeans. On the front was a picture of Kirsty the pretty skewbald mare looking inquisitively over her stable door. Inside were some of the before and after photos Jodie had used on her display board and on the back of the leaflet was a map.

'It's really close,' Poppy said, surprised. Nethercote was half way between Waterby and Princetown. In fact she and Cloud must have ridden pretty close the day before. And yet until today she'd had no idea the horse rescue sanctuary even existed.

3

The sanctuary was at the end of a long and windy track flanked by fields of black-faced sheep. Nethercote itself was a squat stone farmhouse with a slate roof and incongruously tall chimneys. Ivy crept up the walls and net curtains blocked the view into every window, giving the house a shuttered look. As Caroline parked the car Poppy noticed a small sign pointing around the side of the house.

'It says the rescue centre is this way.'

Poppy led Caroline and Charlie through a gate and into a wide strip of concrete sandwiched between two long rows of whitewashed stables that looked as if they had once been cow byres. On the wall by a door to what Poppy presumed was the feed room was a bell with a sign above, *Please ring for attention.* She gave the bell pull a tentative tug and jumped a foot in the air when Jodie appeared over the nearest stable door and barked, 'Who is it?'

'Only us,' Caroline said.

The scowl on the older girl's face lifted fractionally. 'Sorry,' she said, pushing the stable door open. 'People think that because we're an animal sanctuary they have the right to just turn up on the doorstep any time they like.'

Poppy fingered the small brown envelope in her pocket. 'We've brought the money we raised yesterday,' she said.

Jodie wiped her hands on her shorts. 'Thanks.'

Charlie, who had been walking up the line of empty stables peering into each one, fixed his cerulean blue eyes on Jodie and said, 'Can we have a tour?'

Caroline smiled apologetically. 'I'm sorry about my son. He has no manners. We can see you're busy. Perhaps we'll pop by another day.'

Jodie checked her watch. 'No, you're OK. I've got time to give you a quick tour. Show you where your money will go.'

'I'd love to meet Kirsty,' Poppy said shyly.

'Kirsty's gone, I'm afraid,' Jodie said.

'Oh, no! What happened to her?'

'Not *gone* gone. I mean gone from here. She was put up for adoption in the spring. She's gone to live with a family near Taunton. She's settled in really well.'

'That's good,' Poppy said, relieved that the skewbald mare was still enjoying life after the cruelty and neglect she'd endured.

'We run an adoption scheme, otherwise we'd never be able to take on any more horses,' Jodie said.

'How does that work?' Charlie asked, looking around with interest.

Caroline sighed. 'Don't get any ideas, Charlie. We haven't got room for any more animals.'

'I was just asking,' Charlie said indignantly, then flashed a grin at Jodie. 'We've already rescued our dog Freddie. We gave Chester a home when Tory couldn't look after him any more. And I suppose we sort of rescued Cloud. Dad says Riverdale's turning into a home for waifs and strays.'

Jodie finally smiled. 'Good for you. Why buy an animal when so many desperately need new homes?' She beckoned them to follow her to the fields at the end of the two rows of stables, where more than a dozen horses and ponies grazed, dozed in the sun or stood head to tail, swishing flies.

'Once a horse or pony has fully recovered they go up for adoption and I put their details on our website. New homes are vetted and if everything is OK they have the horse on permanent loan, with the understanding that should the horse need to come back for any reason, they'll always have a place at Nethercote.'

Poppy gazed at the horses. An idea was forming in her mind. 'Who's up for adoption at the moment,' she asked.

'Percy. He's the Welsh Section A over there,' said Jodie, pointing to a cheeky-looking grey gelding with a bushy mane and a pink nose. 'He's available as a companion. And Mr Darcy. I called him that because he's tall, dark and handsome.' They followed Jodie's gaze to a dark bay thoroughbred gelding who was grazing next to a sway-backed chestnut mare. 'He has a touch of arthritis so can only do light work.'

'You haven't got any between fourteen and fifteen hands?' Poppy said hopefully.

Charlie gaped at her. 'You don't need another pony. You've got Cloud!'

'Not for me, you twit. I was thinking of Scarlett. She's my best friend,' Poppy explained, ignoring the fact that Scarlett hadn't spoken to her for a whole forty eight hours, the longest time they'd ever fallen out. 'She lives on the farm next door to us. She's almost outgrown her pony but her parents can't afford to buy her a new one. I was wondering if you had anything that she could adopt.'

Jodie leant on the fence and stared at her disparate herd of horses and ponies. 'Is she a good rider?'

'Really good. She's been riding since she was two.'

'She lives on a farm, you say?'

Poppy nodded. 'They've got loads of lovely grazing and a spare stable and whoever came would have two Dartmoor ponies for company.'

'There is someone who might fit the bill.'

Jodie whistled and a rangy chestnut gelding lifted his head and trotted over. He gave Jodie a gentle butt and she scratched his ear affectionately.

'This is Red. He was born at Nethercote. We didn't realise his dam was in foal at first. Unfortunately we lost her the night he was born and I had to hand rear him. I started breaking him this spring. He's coming on well but he needs to go to a really experienced home.'

Poppy knew Scarlett would fall in love with the chestnut gelding the minute she saw him. He was a couple of inches bigger than Cloud and had a flaxen mane and tail, four white socks, an extra daub of white on his nose and kind eyes. Poppy imagined Red and Cloud cantering along a moorland track together, matching each other stride for stride. He was absolutely perfect.

'She would have to come and see him first,' said Jodie. 'I only let horses go if I'm satisfied they are a good match with their new guardian.'

'That won't be a problem,' Poppy said. 'I'll speak to her when I get home.'

'Do you get upset when the horses go to their new homes?' Charlie asked.

'Can't afford to. A job like this toughens you up.'

'He's sweet,' said Caroline, pointing to an appaloosa pony who was lying down in the sun.

'He looks like he's been out in a snowstorm,' said Charlie.

He was right, Poppy thought. The white spots on the pony's chestnut back looked like snowflakes.

'That's Biscuit. All the horses here have a story to tell, but his is probably the most incredible. If you read about it in a book you wouldn't believe it,' said Jodie. 'He was found by the RSPCA tethered to railings on top of a tower block of flats in the Midlands.'

'I remember that!' Caroline said. 'I saw it on the news. They had to airlift him down by helicopter, didn't they?'

'That's right. The lift was broken and they thought it would be less traumatic for him to be winched down by helicopter than to be carried down the twenty seven flights of stairs.'

Charlie was staring at Biscuit with his mouth open. 'He lived on top of the building?'

Jodie nodded. 'No-one knows for sure how long he'd been up

there. And no-one was ever prosecuted. Neither the RSPCA nor the police could prove who he belonged to. He'd been kept alive on vegetable peelings, scraps of bread and rainwater. He was pretty thin and had terrible rain scald when he came to us.'

Poppy couldn't imagine what life must have been like for Biscuit, living on his own on top of a tower block, with sheer drops in every direction, at the mercy of the elements.

'That's awful. How was he found?'

'A new tenant moved in and tipped off the RSPCA. The inspector told me their call centre didn't believe him at first and they almost dismissed it as a prank call. Luckily for Biscuit someone decided to check it out.'

'He looks pretty content now,' said Caroline. Biscuit yawned, showing a row of yellow teeth, and collapsed, asleep, in the daisies.

Jodie smiled. 'He is the most chilled out pony I have ever known. Sometimes, when things get on top of me and I fantasise about walking away from it all, I look at Biscuit and remember what all the blood, sweat and tears are for. He keeps me going.'

'Do you run the centre on your own?' Poppy asked.

Jodie gazed at Biscuit's snowflake-splotched flanks gently rising and falling. Poppy was shocked to see a look of bitterness darken her features, but the expression was so fleeting she wondered if she'd imagined it.

'This is my dad's dream, not mine,' Jodie said eventually.

'So he helps you with the horses?'

'He would if he could,' Jodie conceded. 'But he's away at the moment.'

'Our dad's always away, too. He works for the BBC,' said Charlie. 'What does your dad do?'

Jodie bent down to pick a handful of grass for a bay mare who had wandered over to say hello. 'He runs a small import business. Mobile phones, mainly.'

Caroline looked impressed. 'Mobiles are big business. He must be doing well.'

'Not really. It's a very confined market where he is. In more ways than one,' she muttered.

Poppy remembered the envelope in her pocket.

'Here's the money we made yesterday. I hope it helps a little bit.'

The older girl gave the ghost of a smile. 'It'll keep the wolf from the door for a few days.'

4

———

Caroline had barely pulled up the handbrake before Poppy had unclipped her seatbelt and jumped out of the passenger door.

'I'm going to tell Scarlett about Red,' Poppy said.

She'd taken a dozen photos of the chestnut gelding on her phone and scrolled through them as she crossed the field of sheep that separated Riverdale and Ashworthy, the farm where Scarlett lived with her older brother Alex and their parents Bill and Pat. Red was the same shade of burnt umber as both Blaze and Scarlett's own auburn hair. It was fate, Poppy told herself, as she climbed over the gate onto the roughshod Ashworthy drive. All she had to do was convince Scarlett to see her.

Pat was kneading a huge ball of dough in the farm's shabby but cosy kitchen when Poppy poked her head around the door.

'I wondered if Scarlett wanted some company.'

Pat pushed the dough down and out with the heel of her hand, pulled it back into a ball and sprinkled it with flour. She nodded in the direction of the lounge. 'Your guess is as good as mine. She's been moping around the house since Friday. I don't know what's up with her.'

'Caroline said she wasn't very well and that's why she didn't come to the fete yesterday.'

Pat dropped the dough into a bowl to prove on top of the Rayburn. 'That's what she says, but I'm not convinced. She hasn't got a temperature. She hasn't been sick. She just seems to be down in the dumps. Perhaps you can cheer her up.'

'I'll do my best. But before I do, can I talk to you about something?'

POPPY TOOK a deep breath and pushed open the door to the lounge. Scarlett, wearing faded My Little Pony pyjamas and a glowering expression, was curled up on the sofa with Meg, the family's border collie. The dog gave a welcoming woof and jumped down to see Poppy, her tail wagging.

'At least someone's pleased to see me,' joked Poppy. She stroked Meg's silky ears and chanced another look at Scarlett. On closer inspection she realised her best friend was clutching a tissue and her eyes were red-rimmed.

'Hey, are you OK?'

Scarlett waved the remote control at the television. They watched together as a beautiful bay gelding galloped in blind panic through No Man's Land, shells exploding all around him and barbed wire tearing his chest. War Horse was one of Poppy's all-time favourite films - it was right up there with International Velvet - but it was so sad it was enough to make a statue weep. No wonder Scarlett was crying.

'Turn it off before Joey gets caught in the barbed wire. I can't stand that bit,' Poppy said, plonking herself down on the sofa beside Scarlett. 'I know you're really cross with me, and I don't blame you, but I've got some really exciting news I promise you'll want to hear.'

Scarlett blew her noise noisily and glared at Poppy, who ignored her and reached in her back pocket for her phone.

'This is Red. He's fifteen hands and four years old. Gorgeous, isn't he?'

Scarlett glanced at the screen and looked away. 'Are you getting another horse?' she said dully.

'No, you idiot, he's for you!'

A damson-dark flush was inching its way up Scarlett's neck. 'How many times do I have to spell it out, Poppy? Mum and Dad can't afford another horse.'

'Red's not for sale.'

'So why are you showing me his picture?' Scarlett uncurled her legs and swung her feet to the floor. 'I'm going upstairs.'

'Blimey, Scarlett, you can be a stroppy mare sometimes. Just listen for a minute, will you? Red is a rescue horse. He lives at Nethercote Horse Rescue. He's about to go up for adoption. I've had a word with the girl who runs the place. He's as good as yours if you pass the home visit and you and he get on.'

Eyes wide, Scarlett gawped at Poppy. 'Are you serious?'

'Absolutely. We met Jodie, the girl who runs the rescue centre, at the fete yesterday. She's -'

But Scarlett wasn't listening. She was two steps ahead and her voice was resigned. 'It won't work. Mum and Dad are bound to say no. It's another mouth to feed, isn't it? Another horse to shoe. More vet's bills. Tack we can't afford.'

The door opened and Pat appeared with two mugs of tea. 'What can't we afford?' she asked, winking at Poppy.

'Nothing,' said Scarlett, sliding Poppy's phone down the side of the sofa.

'Poppy's just been showing me the photos of Red. He's a handsome lad, isn't he?' Pat set the mugs on the coffee table. 'Are you going to go and see him?'

'There's no point, is there? We can't afford to keep him.'

Pat smiled at her daughter. 'Barney was only asking me the other day if you might be interested in a Saturday job at the shop. If you take him up on his offer and use your wages towards Red's keep, I'll make sure we find the rest. It's been a good year for lambing and the pigs are doing really well. You'll have to make do with second-hand tack, but you're used to hand-me-downs, aren't you?'

Scarlett nodded, a smile creeping across her freckled face at last. She sprang up from the sofa and threw her arms around her mum.

'You have Poppy to thank. It was all her idea,' Pat said.

Poppy caught Scarlett's eye. 'Am I forgiven?'

Scarlett's forehead creased in a frown and she tilted her head to one side and rubbed her chin thoughtfully. Poppy's heart sank. If finding Scarlett a new horse wasn't enough to win her over she didn't know what was. Then Scarlett broke free from her mum and hugged Poppy.

'Of course you are, you twit! I had already forgiven you really. I should know by now that tact isn't one of your strong points. I was just feeling sorry for myself. And now I feel like Christmas has come early and Santa has promised me the best present ever!'

Friends again, the two girls decided to celebrate with a ride. Feeling magnanimous, Poppy asked Charlie if he wanted to tag along on his bike. 'As long as you only speak when spoken to and promise not to be annoying,' she told him sternly.

Charlie smiled his sweetest smile. 'I'm *never* annoying.'

'Ha! That's open for debate.'

Back at Ashworthy Scarlett was zinging with excitement. 'Mum's phoned Jodie. We're going to see Red in the morning. Want to come, too?'

'You bet.'

'Never mind tomorrow. Where are we going today?' Charlie asked.

'Follow me,' Poppy said mysteriously. 'I know exactly where I want to go.'

CLOUD'S EARS were pricked as they approached the band of conifers that cloaked the tumbledown cottage. The ground was so squelchy Charlie had to push his mountain bike. 'My feet are soaking,' he grumbled. 'Where exactly are we supposed to be going?'

'Stop whingeing and keep walking, little brother. It's worth the wait, I promise.'

They plunged into the conifers. Poppy grinned at the other two. 'Almost there.'

Scarlett gasped when she saw the dilapidated building and the dark waters of the tarn.

'It's Witch Cottage! We can't go there!'

Poppy jumped off Cloud and gave Scarlett a puzzled look.

'It's fine. Cloud and I explored it the other day. No-one lives there any more. I reckon it's been empty for years.'

'You don't understand! It's haunted!'

Charlie propped his bike against a tree and stared at Scarlett agog.

'The pool's in the shape of a tear, isn't it?' Scarlett said.

Poppy nodded. 'Why?'

'My Granny Martha used to say the pool came from a single teardrop wept by an old woman whose only son was killed in a tin mining accident like about five hundred years ago. Granny said it's bottomless, and anyone who gazes into the waters at midnight on Midsummer's Eve will see a reflection of the next person in the parish to die.'

Scarlett's voice had taken on a low, chilling tone. 'People thought the old crone was a witch and one full moon a group of villagers crept into her cottage, dragged her from her bed and burnt her and her familiar at the stake.'

Charlie frowned. 'Her familiar what?'

'A familiar is another name for a witch's animal companion, Charlie. In this case it was a cat.'

Poppy tutted. What a cliché. 'Was it black, by any chance?'

'No, it was ginger, actually. He was called Marmaduke. That's what the legend says, anyway. And now the witch can be seen gliding around the banks of the pool on the night of every full moon, with Marmaduke riding on her withered old shoulders and the ends of her tattered cloak on fire.'

By this time they had reached the stone wall surrounding the cottage and tarn.

'*And,*' said Scarlett, pointing to a small wooden cross Poppy hadn't noticed before. 'About five years ago a group of wild swimmers were crossing the pool when one of them got into difficulties and drowned. And do you know what?'

'What?' breathed Charlie, who was hanging onto her every word.

'The swimmer who died was *exactly* the same age as the old woman's son when he was killed in the tin mine.' Scarlett drew her hand across her neck in a cut-throat gesture. Poppy rolled her eyes.

'But that's not all,' Scarlett said dramatically. 'Sometimes at night lights can be seen in the windows of the cottage. Some people say it's the old crone lighting candles in memory of her son.'

'Some people talk a load of absolute rubbish,' said Poppy. 'Are you going to come and have a look around or what?'

Scarlett was aghast. 'Haven't you heard a word of what I've been saying? There's no way you're dragging me into that house of horrors. I'll stay and look after the ponies, thanks.'

Charlie had no such reservations. He sprinted to the crooked front door and heaved it open, beckoning Poppy to follow. She handed Cloud's reins to Scarlett and ran after him.

Charlie was already disappearing up the creaky staircase.

'Be careful, some of the floorboards are a bit rotten,' she called.

'No need to worry, sis. I can look after myself,' he shouted back.

'Famous last words,' Poppy muttered, inspecting the decrepit remains of the kitchen. Someone must have lived in the cottage since the old crone in Scarlett's dubious legend, although Poppy guessed the house must have been empty for at least half a century. A corroded black kettle sat atop the rusty range. A couple of tarnished knives and forks gathered dust on some woodworm-infested shelves. Poppy pulled open a couple of cupboards, but there was nothing inside apart from ancient cobwebs and a couple of dead bluebottles. Upstairs she could hear Charlie exclaiming with delight as he thundered between the two bedrooms like a baby elephant with a sugar rush.

She was prising open the door of the range when there was a shout and the ceiling above her head shook ominously, sprinkling her with a layer of dust as fine as icing sugar. She raced up the stairs, two at a time. Charlie was sitting with his back to her, hugging his right knee.

'What on earth's happened?'

Charlie looked over his shoulder. 'My foot's stuck,' he said sheepishly.

'In one of those rotten floorboards I warned you about?' Poppy knelt down next to him. Charlie's foot had broken clean-through the crumbling plank and was wedged between two joists. She slipped her hand into the gap and felt for his shoe. 'I think it's your trainer that's stuck. If I undo your laces you should be able to wiggle your foot out. We'll give it a try.'

Poppy began picking at the double knot but the gap was so small that every time she moved her hand she grazed her knuckles on the rough underside of the floorboards. Eventually she felt the laces slither undone. She sat back on her haunches and Charlie wiggled out his foot.

'You're lucky you didn't break your ankle,' Poppy told him, reaching back into the gap for his trainer. As she did her fingers brushed against a hard edge. It didn't feel like a joist. It was more like the cover of a book. Poppy leant on her elbows and slid her hand further in. It was definitely a book. But who would hide a book beneath the floorboards of an abandoned croft where an old woman who may or may not have been a witch had once lived? The hairs on the back of her neck stood up.

'Have you got my shoe yet?' Charlie asked. He had a cobweb in his hair and his knees were filthy.

'No, it's caught on something' she lied, keen to keep this discovery to herself. 'Go over to the window. There's a swallow's nest under the eaves. See if you can see the babies.'

Once Poppy was sure his attention was diverted she swivelled around on her heels so her back was facing him and pulled out the book. It was long and slim with a black cover and the year embossed in silver leaf on the front. A diary. Poppy flicked through it, as furtive as a pickpocket stealing a wallet. Pages and pages were crammed with tiny writing. Her heart was hammering in her ribcage as she tried to decipher the loops and curls.

'What are you doing?' Charlie asked.

'Nothing,' said Poppy, tucking the diary in her waistband and reaching back into the hole in the floorboards. 'Here's your shoe,' she said, tossing him the white and navy trainer. She checked her watch. 'We'd better go or Scarlett will have a fit. She hates it here.'

'I think it's awesome. It could be our secret den where we plan all our adventures.'

'Maybe we'll come over on the next full moon. See if Scarlett's right about the place being haunted,' said Poppy, half-joking.

But if she thought her brother would be fazed by any ghostly goings-on she was wrong. His eyes were sparkling.

'Cool idea!' he said, grinning at Poppy. 'Why didn't I think of that?'

THE DIARY PRESSED UNCOMFORTABLY into Poppy's back all the way home. As they cantered across the moor, Charlie pedalling furiously to keep up, she wondered why she hadn't shared her discovery with Scarlett. Perhaps it was because her best friend had showed no desire to have anything to do with the tumbledown cottage. She'd flung Cloud's reins at Poppy and jumped on Blaze the second they'd re-appeared, muttering about bad vibes and negative energy. Scarlett was one of the most superstitious people Poppy knew. She shrieked with horror if Poppy spilled salt and forgot to hurl a pinch of it over her left shoulder, and if Poppy dared dice with death by walking under a ladder she virtually went into meltdown. Poppy didn't hold any truck with superstitions - she supposed it was having a cynical journalist as a dad. As far as she was concerned Scarlett's tale of supernatural happenings was utter nonsense.

'We're leaving at ten tomorrow,' Scarlett said, as they clip-clopped down the Ashworthy drive.

'I'll be there,' Poppy said, grimacing as she surreptitiously shifted the diary further down her jodhpurs.

'Why are you pulling a face? Don't you want to come?'

"Course I do. I'm just trying to scratch a mosquito bite,' Poppy lied.

Back home, once she'd turned Cloud out with Chester, Poppy raced upstairs to her bedroom, closed the door, and propped her old wicker chair under the door handle. It wouldn't stop Charlie coming in, but it would buy her enough time to hide her find. She sat cross-legged on her bed and opened the diary with trembling fingers.

5

The first two pages were covered in doodles. Circles and spirals, squares and triangles, stars and flowers. So many squiggles and scribbles that at first Poppy didn't see the three words in the middle of the facing page. When she did, she blinked and looked again, in case the loopy, slanting script somehow untangled itself and snaked into three completely different words. It didn't. The words were there in black and white. *Caitlyn Jones's Diary.*

Poppy realised she was gripping the book so tightly she was in danger of breaking the spine. She closed it, drummed her fingers on the black leather cover and wondered what to do. Caitlyn Jones had always been a complete enigma to Poppy. Someone she had obsessed about and felt inferior to ever since the McKeevers had moved to Riverdale. Someone who, if ghosts did actually exist, came as close to haunting Poppy's subconscious as anyone ever would.

Caitlyn was the other girl in Cloud's life. Poppy corrected herself. *Had been* the other girl in his life. Not any more.

There was a photo of Caitlyn and Cloud in Tory's flat, taken at the Brambleton Horse Show the same year Poppy's mum Isobel died. Poppy scrutinised it every time she visited, battling the jealousy and inadequacy it inevitably stirred, feelings that were as invasive as goosegrass, no matter how hard she tried to suppress them.

Poppy loved Cloud with all her heart. She would walk over burning coals for him, no question. And she knew her pony loved her. After all, he'd found her when he'd been let loose on the moor during their stay at Redhall Manor Equestrian Centre, hadn't he? But did he love her as much as he'd loved Caitlyn? Poppy had no answer to that.

And yet here, in her hands, was the key to unlock Caitlyn's innermost thoughts. A window to her dreams and fears. A chance for Poppy to see the world through Cait's eyes.

Poppy gazed at the diary almost reverently, her fingers flicking through the pages as if it was a kids' flip book. She itched to read it. And yet the diary held secrets and thoughts Caitlyn had scribbled down never imagining that anyone else would ever see them. It was private property. Poppy had kept a diary ever since Caroline had bought her one for Christmas the previous year. She hated the thought of anyone reading it. It would be so embarrassing. More than that, it would make her feel exposed, vulnerable. Poppy slammed the book shut. If she felt like that about her own diary, it would be hypocritical for her to read someone else's, wouldn't it?

Poppy shoved the diary under her pillow and stood up. She was halfway across her room when she stopped, as if glued to the floor. The desire to read the diary was overwhelming. Caitlyn was dead, killed seven years ago when Cloud fell at a fence during a hunter trial. What harm could reading it do? Poppy would never divulge what she'd read. It would be their secret, a bond between them as strong as the one they each shared with Cloud. With a certainty she couldn't explain, Poppy knew Caitlyn wouldn't mind. She spun on her heels, jumped back on her bed and pulled out the diary before she could change her mind.

A slip of folded paper fluttered out of the pages and settled between her crossed legs like a sycamore seed on a blustery autumn day. It was an old newspaper cutting, brittle and flaking. Poppy smoothed it out, tucked a strand of hair behind her ear and began to read.

Friends and rivals compete for showjumping glory

Best friends Jodie Morgan and Caitlyn Jones were the only two young riders to make it through to the jump-off in the final class at the South Devon Open Showjumping Competition on Saturday.

Fourteen-year-old Jodie and her pony Nethercote Nero jumped first, giving a textbook performance with a fast, clean round, piling on the pressure for her thirteen-year-old friend and fellow Pony Club showjumping team member Caitlyn.

Caitlyn and her pony Cloud Nine looked like they were in with a chance, but knocked a pole in the double to collect four faults and second place.

Earlier this year Jodie, a rising showjumping talent, was selected to represent Great Britain in the British Showjumping Pony European Championships squad.

'Both Nero and Cloud have been jumping out of their skin all season so winning the open jumping class against such stiff competition was pretty special,' said Jodie.

'Hopefully we can keep up the momentum for the European Championships in Malmo, Sweden, in August.'

Jodie and Caitlyn had been best friends! Poppy studied the photo next to the story, the diary forgotten. Cloud stood proudly, his neck arched and his mane neatly plaited, an enormous blue rosette fixed to his browband. Caitlyn sat gracefully astride him, holding the reins with one hand, her head turned towards the girl next to her, who was riding an eye-catching light bay gelding, her hand clasped around the stem of a silver trophy. Jodie was winking at Caitlyn and laughing. She looked younger, more carefree, less spiky, but it was definitely her. Poppy checked the date. Seven years ago. She squinted at Nero, trying to remember if she'd seen him when they'd visited Nethercote. She didn't think so. She was sure she'd have remembered him.

Poppy supposed it was no fluke that the two girls had known each other. They must have been in the same school year and they were both talented riders. They had a lot in common. It was inevitable they'd been friends. Suddenly Jodie's reaction to Cloud made sense. Poppy shivered. Poor Jodie. Coming face to face with her old friend's pony must have been a shock.

A thump, thump, thump on the stairs caught her attention and the handle on her bedroom door turned. Poppy shoved the newspaper cutting back in the diary and slipped it under her mattress. She streaked across the room and whipped the wicker chair away as the door creaked and swung open.

Charlie eyed her suspiciously. 'Why are you holding your chair?'

'Just re-arranging my room. Felt like a change,' Poppy said airily.

Charlie raised his eyebrows. 'Mum sent me up. Dinner's nearly ready. You need to come down and lay the table.'

POPPY DIDN'T GET another chance to look at the diary until she'd gone to bed. Her lamp cast a pool of sallow light over the crackly pages as she scoured the tiny loopy handwriting, looking for mentions of Cloud. She found the first on the fifth of January.

Mum finally agreed to drive me up to Gran's this morning. I was getting desperate. I hadn't seen Cloud since New Year's Eve. That's five whole days ago! I think he was pleased to see me. But not as pleased as I was to see him! It was freezing, but we managed a quick ride around the lanes. I'm never going to get his fitness up for competing if I can only ride a couple of times a week. Gran said she would've lunged him but the fields were too waterlogged. But I shouldn't have to rely on her to exercise my pony. Mum just doesn't get it. I wish, wish, wish she was into horses like Jodie's dad is. She doesn't know how lucky she is.

Poppy realised she was lucky, too. Imagine only seeing Cloud a couple of times a week! It would be torture. She could see him first thing every morning and last thing at night. She could ride him whenever she wanted. She could even watch him from her bedroom window. They spent every spare second together. For the first time in her life Poppy felt stirrings of sympathy for Caitlyn.

She scanned through the weekday entries, which seemed to consist mainly of Caitlyn moaning about school and the amount of homework she'd been given. The bits that fascinated her were the references to Cloud and Jodie. One entry on the twentieth of May caught her attention.

What a fantastic weekend! The Annoying Parents had some boring wedding to go to in Somerset. They were going to take me until I suggested I stayed at Gran's. So they dropped me off at eight yesterday morning and didn't pick me up until six tonight. It was brilliant, having a whole two days with Cloud. And Chester and Gran of course. Jodie's dad brought Nero over in their box yesterday and we went on this amazingly long ride. We were gone for hours. Mum would have been panicking, thinking we'd been kidnapped by aliens or something, but Gran's so chilled. She always says she trusts Cloud to look after me. Anyway, we found this awesome place. It's an old abandoned cottage over towards Princetown way. You have to ride through a forest to reach it. There's even a small lake for the ponies to drink from. We decided we'd hang out there whenever we can. It's so cool.

And then a couple of weeks later:

No shows this weekend so Jodie and I rode over to the cottage. We took a picnic this time, which we ate on the banks of the lake. I brought along an article I'd printed from the internet about how to teach your horse tricks. It was so funny. Honestly, we were in stitches. Cloud was a quick learner, and by the end of the afternoon he was giving me a kiss for a pony nut. Nero was hopeless. But secretly I didn't mind. It was nice to be better at something than Jodie for once!

Poppy yawned and checked the time. Five to eleven. She closed the diary, slid it back under her mattress and turned off her bedside lamp. It's funny, she thought sleepily, as she wiggled under the duvet trying to get comfortable. She'd spent two years feeling inferior to Caitlyn. But, as she'd flicked through pages and pages peppered with the insights and insecurities of any teenage girl, she realised they were not so very different after all.

6

A fine drizzle as soft as a whisper had settled on the moor overnight and, despite promises by the weathermen that the afternoon would be hot and sunny, the mizzle seemed as stubborn to linger as an unwelcome houseguest reluctant to pack their bags and go home. Poppy's hair had frizzed by the time she had fed Cloud and Chester, cleaned and re-filled their water trough and poo-picked their field.

She was changing into a pair of marginally-cleaner jodhpurs when she heard the toot of a horn and saw Bill's Land Rover bump to a halt outside the front door. Scarlett slid across the bench seat to make room for her.

'Excited?' Poppy said, fixing her seatbelt.

'I feel a bit sick, actually.'

Poppy was surprised. Scarlett usually took everything in her stride. Things that would make Poppy's knees knock with fear, like meeting new people or talking to the whole school during assembly, never fazed her. She was normally so confident and laid-back, every-thing Poppy wasn't.

'What's up?'

Scarlett hugged herself. 'What if Jodie takes one look at me and decides she hates me? What if Red and I don't click? What if we fail the home check? So many things could go wrong.'

'It'll all be fine,' Poppy soothed.

Scarlett stared glumly ahead as the windscreen wipers whisked to and fro, and remained unusually quiet as they trundled through the lanes to Nethercote. Poppy chatted to Bill about the fete, although her mind was elsewhere. She hadn't made up her mind whether or not to tell Jodie that she knew she and Caitlyn had been friends. She wanted to know if Jodie had ever made the European Championships in Sweden. According to the newspaper cutting she was a promising young rider. So why was she working her fingers to the bone at a small, local horse rescue centre in the middle of Dartmoor and not competing for glory on the national showjumping circuit? Poppy remembered a throwaway remark Jodie had made during their visit. She'd said the horse sanctuary was her dad's dream, not hers. Had her dream been to be a professional showjumper? If so, why had she thrown it all away to look after the rescue horses? And where was her dad in all of this? It didn't make sense.

Bill turned off the main road and the Land Rover lurched along the long and windy track to Nethercote. Poppy jumped out and pointed to the side of the house. 'It's this way.'

Scarlett and Bill followed her to the two long rows of whitewashed stables. A familiar spotted head appeared over the door of the nearest stable.

'Hello Biscuit.' Poppy felt in her pocket for some pony nuts and offered them to the appaloosa. 'He was rescued from a high rise block of flats,' she told Scarlett, who was looking decidedly green.

But Scarlett wasn't listening. Her eyes were tracking back and forth across the yard. 'Is there a loo?'

Poppy spied Jodie leading Red out of the paddock. The chestnut gelding walked obediently by her side. It wasn't until the pair reached them that Poppy realised he wasn't wearing a headcollar.

Jodie read her mind. 'I don't bother with one. He's always followed me around like a shadow. It's because I hand-reared him.'

Scarlett gazed at Red, her expression a jumble of longing and fear.

She held out her hand tentatively and the gelding stretched his neck and blew gently into her palm. Scarlett scratched his poll and beamed at them. 'He's the most beautiful horse I have ever seen in my life.'

'I wouldn't go that far, but yes, he's not a bad sort,' said Jodie.

Jodie tacked Red up and led him to the mounting block.

'He was only backed in the spring and is still very green, but he's a fast learner,' she said, holding the gelding while Scarlett swung deftly into the saddle. Her hazel eyes were sparkling as she followed Jodie into a small, empty paddock.

'Have a walk and trot and see how he feels.'

Poppy, Bill and Jodie leant on the post and rail fence and watched Scarlett and Red as they walked around the field.

'You're right, she's a nice little rider,' Jodie said.

'Aye,' said Bill. 'She learnt as soon as she could walk and hasn't stopped since. It's broken her heart that she's almost outgrown Blaze, especially as we couldn't afford to buy her another horse, but she's never once complained. She's a good girl, is our Scarlett, and she'll look after your Red, I promise you that.'

There was a catch in Bill's normally gruff voice. Poppy caught Jodie's eye and was surprised to see her face darken.

'She's lucky to have a dad like you.'

Red trotted past, his chestnut ears pricked. Jodie gave a brief smile. 'I'll need to do a home visit of course, but I think we can safely say these two were a match made in heaven. The adoption forms are in the house. I'll go and find one.'

Scarlett jumped off Red and smothered him with kisses. 'I'm in love,' she declared, and then clutched Poppy's arm. 'Do you think I did OK?'

'More than OK. Jodie said you two were a match made in heaven. She's just gone to get the paperwork.'

Scarlett flung her arms around the chestnut gelding's neck. Red seemed to be enjoying the attention. Poppy loosened his girth and ran up his stirrup leathers.

Bill checked his watch. 'We'd better make a move. Baxters' are delivering the pig feed in half an hour.'

'Do you think we should turn Red out?' Scarlett asked.

'I don't know. I'll go and find Jodie.' Poppy ran past the stables to the house. As she drew near to the open back door the sound of raised voices and the angry clatter of saucepans stopped her in her tracks.

A woman's voice, high-pitched, verging on hysterical, rang out. 'I don't care what your father says. I don't want you to do it!'

'But it's not about what you or I want, is it? It never has been,' Jodie hissed back.

'We'll manage somehow. I'll ask for some more shifts at the pub.'

'A few extra hours' pulling pints won't feed this lot, Mum. You know that. I can make more in one night than you earn in a year.'

'I'll sell my wedding ring. That'll give us a bit of breathing space while we work something out.'

'Don't be ridiculous. It's the only piece of jewellery you have left.'

'Do you think I care more about a band of gold than I care about you?' The woman's voice softened, and Poppy had to strain to hear her. 'I worry, Jodie love. What happens if you get caught?'

Jodie laughed mirthlessly. 'We'll end up with two black sheep in the family, won't we? But don't worry, it'll be fine. I've gone over it a million times. Nothing can go wrong.'

Poppy darted back into the stable yard. She was scratching Biscuit's ear in what she hoped was a nonchalant manner when Jodie stalked out of the house, the adoption papers in one hand and a biro in the other.

'I see you've found a friend,' Jodie remarked, pausing to stroke the appaloosa's speckled forehead.

Poppy reddened, even though there was no way Jodie could have known she'd eavesdropped. 'We weren't sure what you wanted us to do with Red,' she mumbled.

'We'll put him back in the field.'

Poppy stole a look at the older girl as they walked across to Scarlett and Bill. There was a fierce expression on her face and a resolute set to her shoulders. Jodie caught her staring and raised her eyebrows.

'Anything wrong?' she asked.

I should be the one asking that, Poppy thought. Why was Jodie's mum so worried? What was it she didn't want Jodie to do? Instead she shook her head and smiled brightly.

'No. Everything is absolutely fine.'

7

The hands of Poppy's battered Mickey Mouse alarm clock had barely crawled around to seven o'clock the next morning when Charlie bounded into her bedroom.

'Don't forget our picnic! I've already planned our route and made some sandwiches. I just need to do drinks and some cake. It's going to be epic.' Charlie bounced back out of the room. Poppy groaned. She'd planned to spend the day helping Scarlett clear out the old stable Bill had earmarked for Red. She'd forgotten she'd promised her brother that they'd spend the day on the moor. She couldn't pull out. She'd never hear the end of it. Sighing, she threw back the duvet, waking Magpie, the McKeevers' cat, who had been snoring softly at the end of her bed. He narrowed his emerald green eyes at her before tucking his head between his paws and going back to sleep. Poppy reached for her mobile and texted Scarlett to say she would try and pop round before dinner.

Downstairs, Charlie was carefully cutting squares of lemon drizzle cake and wrapping them in cling film.

'I've cut up some carrots for Cloud. I even peeled them for him,' he said. Caroline had only recently let Charlie start using the sharp kitchen knives. Personally Poppy thought it was asking for trouble and quite expected to find pieces of chopped finger in her food, but by some small miracle he had so far managed to keep all his digits intact.

'Where d'you want to go?' she asked.

'I thought we'd try somewhere new.'

Poppy was surprised. Usually they picnicked in the Riverdale wood, on the small sandy strip of beach where they'd first seen Cloud. And then the penny dropped.

'Are we going to the old cottage by any chance?'

'What old cottage?' said Caroline, walking into the kitchen with a basket of dirty laundry balanced on her hip.

Charlie held his finger to his lips and Poppy nodded. She was as keen to go back to the old croft as her brother but knew that Caroline would worry if she knew. Deep water and derelict buildings seemed to freak adults out.

'Charlie wants to head down the bridleway that goes past the thatched cottage by the church,' Poppy said, crossing her fingers behind her back.

'Sounds lovely. I wish I could come too, but I must do some gardening. Make sure you've got your phone with you, and be back by four at the latest. Otherwise I'll send out a search party.'

'And we don't want that happening again, do we?' said Poppy, remembering the day she and Charlie had had to be rescued from the moor the first summer they'd moved to Riverdale.

'We certainly don't!' Caroline said, giving her a hug.

POPPY SPLIT their picnic into the two small saddle bags resting on Cloud's dappled grey flanks and tightened his girth. Smelling the carrots, the Connemara nibbled the hem of her checked shirt. She blew into his nose and he blew softly back.

'Ready?' she called to Charlie, who was wheeling his bike out of the barn. He was wearing a cycling helmet, a pair of their dad's old aviator sunglasses and his school rucksack.

'You bet!'

Poppy jumped into the saddle. 'Come on then, let's have ourselves an adventure!'

The August sun was high in the sky as they let themselves out of the gate that led to the moor. Puffs of candyfloss cloud wafted by and in the distance three crows shamelessly mobbed a buzzard. Soon they had left Waterby behind and were climbing steadily towards Princetown. The wind ruffled Cloud's mane as he tossed his head and snatched at the bit.

'OK for a canter?' she asked. Charlie nodded. He crouched low over the handlebars and started pedalling furiously, his elbows jutting out like chicken wings. Poppy kicked Cloud on, keeping pace with her brother until she could see he was beginning to tire.

Before long the dark green belt of conifers appeared on the horizon.

'Those trees are the perfect camouflage, hiding Witch Cottage from prying eyes and nosy parkers,' Charlie said.

'I'd never have found it if it wasn't for Cloud,' Poppy agreed.

'Do you think he'd been there before?'

Poppy pictured Caitlyn's diary, hidden in the bottom of her sock drawer. 'Maybe,' she hedged, as they wound their way through the evergreens.

Charlie flung his bike and rucksack on the grass and raced over to the tumbledown building. Poppy watched him pull open the front door and disappear inside. Seconds later a startled pigeon flew out of the hole in the roof in a blur of feathers and affront. Poppy jumped off Cloud and led him over to the banks of the tarn. She stared at their reflections as he drank, remembering Scarlett's ghost stories about the old woman and her son and the superstition that claimed anyone gazing into the still waters on Midsummer's Eve would see a reflection of the next person in the parish to die.

'Utter rubbish,' Poppy told her undulating reflection. A second face appeared at her side and she shrieked.

'Charlie! Don't creep up on me like that! You nearly gave me a heart attack!'

'Thought you didn't believe in ghosts,' he grinned.

'I don't, you twit. You made me jump, that's all.'

'If you say so,' Charlie said, undoing the saddle bags. Poppy ran up her stirrups and loosened Cloud's girth. Looping his reins over the crook of her arm she sat cross-legged at the water's edge and caught the crumpled bag of crisps Charlie lobbed her way.

'Chocolate spread and cheese?' he asked, holding out a squashed-looking sandwich.

'Don't you mean chocolate spread *or* cheese?'

Charlie shook his head. 'Nope. Chocolate spread *and* cheese. I was going to make jam and ham, it had a nice ring to it, but I thought it might be a bit *out there* for you.' He gave her a faintly patronising look, as if she was an aged auntie.

'So you thought you'd go for the more traditional chocolate spread and cheese option,' Poppy grimaced, taking the sandwich, which was wrapped in enough cling film to keep the entire contents of their fridge fresh.

'You can be very narrow-minded sometimes, Poppy. You really need to broaden your horizons.'

She gave him a withering smile. 'Thanks for the advice, little brother.' Peeling back the sandwich, she sniffed it cautiously. 'Gross,' she grumbled, nibbling a corner. It was surprisingly tasty. Who knew?

'It's not as bad as it sounds,' she conceded, taking a huge bite.

Charlie smirked. 'Told you so.'

AFTER THEIR PICNIC Poppy followed Charlie into the cottage. She left him poking around in the kitchen and headed up the rickety staircase. She was keen to see if Caitlyn had left anything else under the floorboards. Ducking her head, she entered the larger of the two bedrooms. She paused. Was it her imagination or did the room feel different somehow? She narrowed her eyes and tried to remember how it had looked on their last visit. The old hessian sack was still in the corner next to the broken floorboard Charlie had put his foot through. He had piled the two wooden crates on top of each other in front of the window. Poppy checked to see if the baby swallows were still in their nest in the eaves and smiled as she counted four orange beaks.

'Should have saved you some of Charlie's sandwiches,' she told them.

She kneeled on the floor, carefully prised open the broken floorboard and peered inside. A black beetle scuttled away, its antennae waving furiously. As it disappeared under a joist Poppy noticed a glint of metal. She reached in and pulled out a silver trophy. The silver had tarnished in places, but it was easy enough to read the inscription. *South Devon Open Showjumping Competition. 1st place: Jodie Morgan and Nethercote Nero.*

CHARLIE WAS OUTSIDE with Cloud by the time Poppy had hidden the trophy under the floorboards and gone back downstairs. She tightened Cloud's girth, ran down his stirrups and swung into the saddle. She stared at the grimy bedroom window. Something about the room was niggling her.

'Why did you move the crates?' she asked Charlie finally.

He looked at her in confusion. 'I didn't. I thought you must have.'

'How could I? I went up after you.' Poppy gave an involuntary shiver. 'If I didn't move them, and you didn't move them, who did?'

8

P oppy and Charlie had emerged from the dark canopy of conifers when Charlie stopped pedalling and pointed straight ahead.

'Someone's coming.'

Poppy halted Cloud and squinted into the sun. She could just about make out a chestnut-coloured blob in the distance. 'It's only a Dartmoor pony.'

'You need to get your eyes tested.' Charlie reached in his pocket for his small birdwatching binoculars. 'It's someone riding. Look.'

He handed the binoculars to Poppy. Charlie was right. A horse and rider were cantering towards them. The horse had four white socks and a flaxen mane and tail.

'It's Red!' Poppy exclaimed.

'I thought you horsey people called it chestnut, like white is always grey?' said Charlie.

'No, you twit. It's Red. Scarlett's new horse. But what's he doing here?' She trained the binoculars on the slim girl riding the chestnut gelding. She would have recognised the determined set of her shoulders a mile off. 'And Jodie,' she said, handing the binoculars back to Charlie.

'Let's go and say hello.'

'OK. But don't mention we've been to Witch Cottage,' Poppy told him.

'Er, why would I? It's our secret place.'

Red's flanks were dark with sweat as Jodie pulled him up a few metres from them.

'What are you two doing here?' she said warily.

'Just out for a hack,' said Poppy. 'We took a picnic,' she said, pointing to the saddlebags.

Jodie's face cleared. 'It's a lovely day for it. I decided to make time for one last ride before Red goes to Scarlett's in the morning.'

'She's beyond excited. She's spent hours getting everything ready for him. He's going to be treated like royalty,' Poppy told her.

Jodie ran her hand down the gelding's neck. 'King Red. It suits him.'

'Are you heading back? We could ride with you some of the way.'

Red stretched his neck towards Cloud and gave a low whinny. The Connemara pricked his ears and whickered back. Jodie glanced briefly towards the belt of conifers and checked her watch.

'Sure. Why not? I've got to get back for evening stables anyway. It'll give the boys a chance to get to know each other.'

Poppy smiled as Cloud and Red's noses touched. 'I think they're going to get along just fine.'

THAT EVENING, after checking her dad, Caroline and Charlie were safely downstairs engrossed in an episode of Dr Who, Poppy closed her bedroom door, reached in her sock drawer and pulled out Caitlyn's diary. She sat on her wicker chair with a cushion on her lap and turned to the last entry.

I am sitting on the banks of the tarn as I write this, dangling my feet in the icy water. Cloud keeps trying to nibble my pen. Nero is dozing next to him and Jodie is watching the swallows feeding their babies in the nest in the eaves.

So now I've set the scene.

I feel both happy and sad. Is that even possible? Happy because Jodie and I have had a brilliant summer, riding, competing and just hanging out here at 'our' cottage together with the ponies away from the Annoying Parents. Sad because it's the last day of the summer holidays and this time on Monday I won't be daydreaming here by the tarn, I'll be sitting in a stuffy classroom bored out of my mind. Riding will have to fit in around school and homework and when I can persuade Mum to give me a lift up to Gran's. It sucks. The only thing I've got to look forward to is the hunter trial at Widecombe. Jodie's not doing it - it's showjumping or nothing for her - but she's promised to come and be my groom for the day.

Back to today. Jodie and I wanted to mark the cottage as our territory. Tigers wee or scratch the bark of trees. Not us! We decided to each leave something of ours here, to lay claim to it. So I'm going to leave my diary and Jodie's going to leave the trophy she won at the South Devon show. We've found a loose floorboard in the big bedroom and we're going to hide them under it. I wonder if anyone will ever find them??

So I'm signing off now. I was getting too old for diaries anyway. If I need to offload I tell Cloud. He's the official Keeper of my Secrets. LOVE that pony!!

It's so long from me. See ya on the other side! :)

Poppy stared at the smiley face until her vision blurred with tears. Caitlyn had been so excited about the hunter trial at Widecombe. She'd had no idea that catastrophic disaster lay around the corner. All it took was a slippery drop fence and a moment's loss of concentration and her fate was sealed. What if Cloud hadn't been spooked by the crowds? What if she hadn't decided to compete? What if it hadn't rained?

Poppy knew that worrying about the what ifs got you precisely nowhere, but even so. Caitlyn would be the same age as Jodie now, and Cloud would still be hers, not Poppy's. She hid the diary back in her sock drawer and peered out of the window. Cloud and Chester were standing nose to tail by the gate, their tails swishing lazily. As if he had a sixth sense, Cloud lifted his head, saw her watching and whickered. Poppy brushed the tears from her cheeks. Did it matter that he'd been Caitlyn's first? For the first time in her life she realised she hadn't felt the usual dart of jealousy at the thought of Caitlyn and Cloud together. All she felt was intense sadness that Cait's future had been wrenched from her so cruelly.

Had Jodie acted as Caitlyn's groom that fateful day? Poppy pictured the brusque blonde girl standing with Tory and Cait's mum Jo on the sidelines, her hands full of grooming kit and bandages as she cheered horse and rider on as they'd galloped up to the drop fence, her eyes widening in horror as Cloud twisted in mid-air, lost his footing and somersaulted over, throwing Cait underneath him.

Poppy tried to imagine how she would feel if it was Scarlett tumbling to the muddy ground in a tangle of flailing limbs. It didn't bear thinking about. The image was so vivid she could almost hear the gasps of shock and the wail of sirens. She shivered. Poor Jodie. And poor Caitlyn.

Thoughts of the accident consumed Poppy's thoughts for the rest of the evening. It wasn't until she was lying in bed, staring at the ceiling, that she remembered the wooden crates. Caitlyn and Jodie may have marked the cottage as their territory. But someone else had now muscled in.

9

'So, what d'you think?' Scarlett asked, chewing her bottom lip. 'Is it good enough?'

Poppy surveyed the stable next to Blaze's. Up until a couple of days ago it had been used to store farm machinery and spare feed troughs. Every inch had been scrubbed and swept. Scarlett had laid a thick bed of straw and filled the hay rack with new hay. Two water-filled buckets stood in old rubber tyres. There was even a mineral lick attached to the ring by the door. Scarlett was hopping from one foot to the other. Poppy had never seen her look so nervous.

'It looks awesome!' she said. 'You've done a brilliant job. Jodie's going to be super impressed and Red's going to love it.'

'Are you sure?'

''Course I'm sure. What time are they due?'

'Ten o'clock. What time is it now?'

Poppy checked her watch. 'Quarter to.'

Scarlett groaned. 'Fifteen whole minutes! That's *ages*.'

'Come on, let's groom Blaze and Flynn. It'll pass the time.'

At ten past ten they heard the rattle of Jodie's Land Rover and trailer as it negotiated the potholed farm drive. Scarlett dropped the body brush and curry comb she'd been holding and clutched Blaze's neck in excitement.

'Oh my God, they're here! I must go and tell Mum.'

Poppy smiled indulgently as her best friend sprinted towards the back door. Jodie parked the Land Rover and jumped out.

'All ready for King Red?' she asked.

Poppy grinned, curtseyed and gestured to the immaculate stable. 'His palace awaits, ma'am. I'm surprised Scarlett didn't manage to find a roll of red carpet for his majesty.'

Jodie glanced inside and raised her eyebrows. 'I see what you mean. I think we can safely say Scarlett's passed the home visit. It puts Nethercote to shame. Red won't know he's born.'

Scarlett appeared, followed closely by Pat, who was carrying a tray laden with mugs of tea and a chocolate cake.

'Hello Jodie love. I thought I'd bake a cake to celebrate Red's arrival,' Pat said, setting the tray on the bonnet of the Land Rover. Jodie pulled down the ramp of the trailer, unloaded Red and handed Scarlett his lead rope.

The chestnut gelding's head was high and his nostrils flared as he took in his new surroundings.

'Red, I'd like to introduce you to Flynn,' said Scarlett. Flynn turned his head briefly and returned to his haynet, unimpressed by the new arrival. 'And this is Blaze.' Blaze and Red blew into each other's nostrils, their ears pricked. Blaze squealed loudly, throwing one hoof in the air. 'Be nice!' Scarlett scolded her.

'It's probably a good idea not to turn them out together for a couple of days. Let them get used to each other,' said Jodie.

She and Scarlett settled Red into his pristine stable while Pat cut generous slices of cake.

Jodie poked her head over the stable door. 'Poppy, can you get the adoption certificate? It's on the passenger seat.'

Poppy heaved open the heavy door of the Land Rover. The seat was covered in sweet wrappers, loops of baler twine, empty wormer packets and unopened envelopes that looked suspiciously like bills. She rummaged through the detritus, finding what she was looking for at the bottom. As she tugged on the sheet of white card bearing the Nethercote logo and the words *Certificate of Adoption* she dislodged Jodie's iPhone and it slid into a gap between the seat and the gearstick.

Sighing, Poppy stretched her arm into the gap and grabbed the phone. It beeped. She dropped it in surprise and it slithered right under the seat.

'Damn,' she muttered, tucking her hair behind her ears and feeling for the phone again. This time she pulled it out and without thinking scanned the text on the home screen.

Delivery tonight. Leave cash as agreed. Used notes or deal's off. You have been warned.

A voice behind Poppy made her start.

'Did you find it?'

Poppy shoved the phone back under the envelopes and sweet wrappers and smiled brightly at Jodie.

'Here it is!'

'Great. Let's celebrate with a slice of cake and then I must be off. There's somewhere I need to be.'

CHARLIE WAS SMACKING a golf ball around the garden with one of their dad's old five irons when Poppy arrived home.

'Guess what?' he said, his tongue between his teeth as he flexed his knees and lined up for a shot.

'Tiger Woods has asked you to take his place in next year's Open Championship?'

'Ha ha, very funny.' Charlie lifted the club and swung at the ball. Shielding his eyes, he scanned the sky. 'Where did it go?' he asked, puzzled.

'It's still there.' Poppy pointed at his feet.

He stared at the pitted white ball nestling in the grass. 'Oh.' He took another swipe. They both watched as the ball sailed in a graceful arc, smashing the glass on one of Caroline's cold frames. Charlie's face paled.

'You are going to be in *so* much trouble,' Poppy told him.

He thought for a moment, worry lines creasing his forehead. Then his face cleared. 'I know! I'll mend it with Dad's Super Glue.'

'I'm not sure that's going to work. Anyway, what were you going to tell me?'

Charlie pointed the club at the sky.

Poppy sighed. 'What exactly am I supposed to be looking at?'

'The moon,' said Charlie. 'The *full* moon,' he added dramatically.

Poppy looked again. There, peeping behind a cloud almost apologetically, as if it had turned up to a party uninvited, was the muted, perfectly spherical face of the moon.

'And?' said Poppy, bemused.

Charlie looked left and right to check no-one was in earshot, then whispered furtively, 'We can go to Witch Cottage and see if the legend is true.'

'What, Scarlett's supernatural claptrap about the old crone and Marmalade and the burning cloak?' Poppy scoffed. 'Of course it's not true!'

'It's Marmaduke actually, and how can you be so sure?'

'Because there are no such things as ghosts or witches, Charlie. It's an old wives' tale, I promise you.'

Charlie nodded to himself. 'I might have known.'

'Might have known what?' she said sharply.

'That you'd claim it was rubbish because really you were too frightened to go.'

Poppy bristled. 'I am not! Alright then, if it means that much to you we'll go. We'll wait until Dad and Caroline are asleep and ride Cloud over together. Happy now?'

Charlie whooped and sprinted towards the house, the golf club and shattered cold frame forgotten. As she watched him go, Poppy had the distinct impression she had been played like the proverbial fiddle by a master manipulator.

10

The sky was a deep indigo as Poppy and Charlie crept out of the house and headed for the stables. After waiting so patiently the moon had taken centre stage and was glowing with pearlescent luminosity, encircled by a smattering of glittering stars.

Cloud was dozing at the back of the stable he shared with Chester, but lifted his head and whickered when he heard the bolt slide open. Poppy offered them a handful of pony nuts, slipped on Cloud's bridle and led him into the yard. Charlie handed Poppy her riding hat and fastened up the straps of his cycling helmet.

'You'll be fine as long as you hold on tight,' she whispered, leading Cloud over to the low stone wall she used as a mounting block. 'I'll get on first.'

Once she was satisfied Charlie was safely on and his arms were wrapped around her waist, she clicked her tongue and turned Cloud towards the moor.

The Connemara was as excited as Charlie about their night-time adventure and jogged up the track towards the Riverdale tor. Poppy could feel her brother's warm breath on the back of her neck as she eased her pony back into a walk.

'You OK?' she asked.

'You bet!' he cried. 'This is awesome!'

Charlie had brought his digital camera, convinced he was going to snap a shot of the old witch as she glided around the banks of the tarn. Poppy had slipped her mobile in her back pocket, just in case. Adventures with her brother often ended up with a trip to accident and emergency. She wanted to be prepared.

Cloud's mane was burnished silver in the moonlight and his neck was arched. All he needed were wings and he could be Pegasus.

'Do you think you'll be alright to go a bit faster, if we take it steady?' Poppy called.

'Uh huh,' Charlie said, tightening his grip.

Poppy squeezed her legs and Cloud broke into a canter. He was as surefooted as the black-faced sheep that every so often loomed out of the darkness, the glow of their eyes just visible in the inky light. It was exhilarating, racing across the wide, open moor in the dead of night, and a smile crept across Poppy's face. Charlie clung on like a limpet.

'I thought riding was for girls and sissies but this is brilliant! When we get home can you teach me?'

"Course I can. We'll ask Scarlett to lend us Flynn.'

Ahead Poppy could just make out the shadowy strip of conifers that hid Witch Cottage from view. 'Nearly there,' she whispered.

Cloud slowed to a walk. The squelch of his hooves as he crossed the peaty ground sounded unnaturally loud in the still night air. He plunged into the darkness of the trees without hesitation. The conifers towered over them, their branches like twisted limbs, and Poppy felt her pulse quicken. She checked the luminous hands of her watch. Five to midnight. Ghosts or no ghosts, this was seriously spooky.

Cloud shifted and swerved through the trees. Eventually they reached the edge of the narrow forest. Poppy asked the Connemara to halt and he stood quietly as she peered into the gloom. The silhouette of Witch Cottage was as elusive and unformed as the first strokes of a watercolour painting.

'Now what?' she whispered.

'We should stay hidden in the trees, just in case,' said Charlie, slithering to the ground.

'In case of what?' Poppy jumped off, too, and held Cloud's reins tightly.

'Old crones and ginger cats, of course.' Charlie's grinning teeth gleamed in the moonlight.

They stood in silence either side of Cloud. Charlie fiddled with his camera. Poppy scuffed the ground with the toe of her jodhpur boot. She felt as conspicuous as an angel perched atop a Christmas tree, and not a little foolish. She stifled a yawn. Why on earth had she agreed to let Charlie drag her into the middle of nowhere in the middle of the night on such a crazy adventure?

After ten minutes in the dank shadows Poppy was starting to feel the cold. She turned to her brother. 'Come on, Charlie. Let's go home. There's patently no-one here. Not even a ghost is silly enough to be out at this time of night.'

'Five more minutes?' he pleaded.

Poppy hugged herself and exhaled loudly. 'Alright then. But I am never, ever coming on one of your stupid adventures again. Got it?'

'Thanks, sis.' Charlie ducked under Cloud's neck. Soon he was twiddling with his camera again, pointing it at the cottage and zooming the lens in and out.

Poppy was stifling another yawn when he clutched her arm and whispered urgently, 'There's a light in the cottage.'

'Absolutely Hilarious with a capital H,' Poppy whispered back, rolling her eyes.

'No, really Poppy, there is. Look!'

The tremor in his voice made Poppy grab the camera. She pointed it at the cottage. At first she thought the glow in the upstairs bedroom was moonlight reflecting off the window.

'Is it the old crone's burning cloak?' stammered Charlie. 'I knew Scarlett was telling the truth.'

Poppy shook her head. The beam of light was moving, as if a powerful torch was being waved around. Cloud had stiffened, his head high as he stared intently ahead. Charlie gripped her arm even tighter.

'Look at that!'

Poppy followed his gaze and gasped. A pick-up truck was rolling silently down the hill towards the cottage. They watched, transfixed, as two burly-looking men let themselves out, pulled an old tarpaulin off the back of the beaten-up truck and started unloading wooden crates.

'What are they *doing*?' breathed Charlie.

Poppy held her finger to her lips. The men were talking to each other in low voices, pointing to the light in the window. One took a mobile out of his pocket and started tapping furiously. The other picked up a crate, ducked under the low door frame and disappeared into the cottage.

Cloud shifted uneasily. Poppy rubbed his forehead and willed him to stay quiet. The man with the phone hefted a crate onto his hip. Once he was inside the cottage Poppy turned to her brother. 'I don't like this. We should go.'

'But -'

'No buts, Charlie. I don't know what those men are up to, but I don't think we should hang around to find out. They don't look the type to be messed with.'

Not giving him the chance to argue, she led Cloud over to a fallen tree and vaulted on, holding her hand out for Charlie to follow suit. He clambered on, looking wistfully over his shoulder as she turned Cloud for home.

Once clear of the conifers Poppy pushed Cloud into a canter, keen to put as much distance as she could between them and the two shadowy men.

'You look washed out. Are you feeling OK?' Caroline looked at Poppy in concern as she nibbled on a piece of toast the next morning.

'I'm fine.' Poppy smiled briefly at her stepmother and took a slurp of orange juice. The truth was she was shattered. After they'd slunk back into the house she'd been so wired sleep had been impossible. She'd lain in bed, her imagination working overtime as she'd wondered about the men at Witch Cottage and, more importantly, the crates they'd been carrying.

A text from Scarlett was a welcome distraction.

Are we riding this morning or what??!! I have a new pony to try out you know!!

Poppy took a final swig of juice and tapped a message back.

'Course we're riding :) I'll be over in 20 mins x

RED'S CHESTNUT coat shone and his four socks were dazzlingly white. Scarlett had even pulled his mane and oiled his hooves.

'Blimey, you must have been up at the crack of dawn,' said Poppy.

Cloud, who had grass stains on his hocks and a tangled mane and tail, looked positively scruffy in comparison.

'I woke up at four I was so excited,' Scarlett said. 'I've been getting him ready since six. He's even had a bath. With warm water, of course.'

'Of course,' said Poppy. Scarlett used the hose on Blaze and Flynn.

'Where shall we go?' said Scarlett.

'I want to head over towards Witch Cottage.'

'Not *again*. You and Charlie are obsessed with that place.'

'Ah, but wait until you hear this.' Poppy told her best friend about their nocturnal visit and the men they'd seen. Scarlett's jaw hit the floor.

'I can't believe I missed it. I wish you'd told me you were going.'

'You won't even go near the place in the middle of the day. Would you have really wanted to come on Charlie's ghost hunt at midnight?'

'Probably not,' Scarlett admitted. 'Do you think you should call the police?'

'What would I tell them? It was too dark to get proper descriptions or see their number plate. I don't even know if they were doing anything illegal. That's why I want to see what's in those crates they delivered.'

'I'd forgotten how close it is to the prison,' said Poppy, gazing at the granite walls of HMP Dartmoor, the two ponies walking side-by-side.

'We went to the museum there last summer,' said Scarlett.

Poppy raised her eyebrows. 'There's a museum at the prison?'

Scarlett nodded. 'You should go. Charlie would love it. They've got all the weapons the warders used to use on the prisoners, like strait-jackets, manacles and cat o'nine tails, and the knuckledusters and other weapons the convicts made. It's really interesting.'

Poppy pictured the two thickset men she and Charlie had seen the night before and her heart missed a beat. 'Do prisoners still escape?'

'They used to, in the olden days,' said Scarlett. 'It's only a Category

177

C prison now. The prisoners are low risk. They make gnomes and toadstools to sell as garden ornaments, can you believe? Mum bought one for her rose garden.'

Poppy couldn't imagine the two men they'd seen the night before painting red hats and impish grins onto stone gnomes. The fact that Witch Cottage was so close to the prison was a coincidence, she told herself.

Scarlett elected to hold the ponies while Poppy scooted across to the dilapidated stone building. The minute she walked through the door it felt different. The air, which had smelt so fusty the first time she'd explored the cottage, was alive with static. She ran lightly up the stairs to the first bedroom, expecting to find it piled high with crates. But the room was empty apart from the two wooden boxes still stacked by the window. Were they the same as the ones the men had unloaded from the pick-up? Poppy inspected the room, her eyes narrowed, searching for any clue. There were marks on the floor. Had they been there before? And had the doorframe always been cracked? She couldn't remember.

Frustrated, she walked around the room a second time, examining every inch. Her attention was caught by the hum of a mosquito. She watched it as it spiralled up towards the ceiling and landed on the loft hatch.

'Poppy!' Everything OK?'

Poppy yanked open the ancient window and stuck her head out. Scarlett was sitting on the old stone wall with Cloud and Red grazing next to her.

'Just coming,' Poppy shouted back.

Halfway down the stairs she stopped, shook her head at her own foolishness, and sprinted back up. The ceiling was so low in the tiny bedroom that she could almost touch it if she stood on her toes. She pulled one of the boxes into the centre of the room, climbed onto it and gave the loft hatch a tentative shove. It lifted easily. Poppy poked her head into the roof space. Expecting darkness she was surprised to see a patch of blue sky in the corner, then remembered the hole in the catslide roof.

She jumped off the box, carried the second one over and stacked them on top of each other. Now the ceiling was level with her shoulders and Poppy was sure she would be able to climb in. Testing her weight on the frame of the hatch, she looked around, taking in the shafts of sunlight, the swirling particles of decades-old dust, long-abandoned swallows' nests and the smell of dead mouse.

In the middle of the attic was the brick chimney breast. Behind it flapped the corner of a green tarpaulin. Her heart hammering, Poppy hauled herself through the hatch. A rusty nail caught her shin and she yelped in pain. The roof of the attic was so low she had to bend double. She crabbed sideways along one of the worm-ridden beams and peered around the chimney breast.

Hidden under the green tarpaulin were around a dozen wooden crates. Poppy pulled the closest one towards her and prised open the lid.

'MOBILE PHONES?' said Scarlett, her face perplexed.

Poppy nodded. 'Dozens of smartphones of all different makes. They were still in their boxes with the Cellophane on and everything.'

'And nothing else?'

'Nope.'

Scarlett looked around her fearfully, as if she was being watched. 'I knew this place was cursed. It was a mistake to come back.' She swung into the saddle and turned Red for home.

The chestnut gelding disappeared into the trees and Poppy had to trot to catch up. 'What are they doing there, that's what I want to know.'

'I don't know and I don't care. We should let the police deal with it, Poppy. Go and see that inspector you saw before.'

Poppy thought of the wide-girthed Inspector Bill Pearson and his penchant for digestive biscuits. Perhaps she should phone the police but a niggling voice in the back of her head told her she'd be wasting their time. 'Maybe.'

Seeing the worry on Scarlett's face she changed the subject. 'How's Red? Are you pleased with your new pony?'

'Pleased?' Scarlett reached down and patted the chestnut gelding's neck. 'I am beyond happy. He is the most gorgeous, lovely, brilliant horse in the world.'

'Apart from Cloud,' Poppy corrected her.

Scarlett laughed, the mobile phones pushed to the back of her mind, and she spent the rest of the ride home extolling Red's countless virtues. Poppy smiled and agreed in all the right places, but her thoughts were in a tiny attic under a catslide roof, where dust motes danced and faceless men stashed their ill-gotten gains under slippery green tarpaulins.

12

A t breakfast the following morning Caroline announced a shopping trip to Plymouth. Poppy's shoulders slumped.

'Torture,' muttered Charlie into his Shreddies.

'You've grown so much this summer your trousers could pass as shorts. We'll have to either stop feeding you or start balancing books on your head,' Caroline told him. 'Poppy, you need a new blazer and school skirt. And you both need new school shoes. It's not long until the start of term.'

'Don't remind us,' grumbled Poppy. Although she couldn't say she actually hated school, she had so many more interesting things she could be doing than learning about poems and probability. And the prospect of standing in a manically busy shoe shop holding a ticket in her hand waiting to have her feet measured on a sweaty measuring machine while dozens of out-of-control toddlers weaved around her legs did not appeal.

'We'll pop into Baxters' on the way home if you like?'

Slightly mollified, Poppy nodded. She never passed up an opportunity to spend half an hour looking around the leather-scented tack and feed store on the Tavistock road.

Their shopping expedition was as torturous as Charlie had

predicted, the only highlight being a bowl of pasta in a little Italian restaurant on the Barbican. Poppy drooled over the black leather jumping saddles and matching bridles in Baxters' and treated Cloud and Chester to a new lead rope each. On their way home Caroline remembered they needed eggs and pulled in outside Waterby Post Office and Stores.

'Hey, isn't that Scarlett?' Charlie said.

Through the glass window, which was pebble-dashed with posters advertising choral events, coffee mornings and rams for sale, Poppy saw her best friend ringing up someone's shopping on the till, watched by the twinkly-eyed shopkeeper Barney Broomfield.

'I'd forgotten it was her first shift at the shop this afternoon.'

Poppy waited until Scarlett had rung up an elderly lady's copy of the Radio Times and a tin of pitted prunes and asked, 'How's it going?'

'OK, I think,' said Scarlett, looking slightly flustered. 'Barney says it'll be brilliant for my mental arithmetic but I'm not so sure.' She sniffed her fingers and pulled a face. 'And my hands smell of money.'

Charlie jiggled coins in his shorts pocket. 'Can I have forty five pence worth of rhubarb and custards, please Scarlett.'

'Sure.' As Scarlett lifted the jar of sweets from a shelf she mouthed to Poppy, 'Look at the front page of the Herald!'

There was a pile of Tavistock Heralds by the front door. Poppy sidled over. The headline was like a punch in the solar plexus.

Exclusive: Police launch investigation after daring theft of mobile phones
By Stanley Smith

Blood pounding in her ears, Poppy picked up the top copy and scanned the article.

```
Police   have  launched  an  investigation  after
mobile  phones  worth  £20,000  were  stolen
during a daring raid on a Plymouth warehouse.
    The   thieves   disabled   CCTV   cameras   and
```

locked the security guard in his office before helping themselves to dozens of top-of-the-range Apple, Samsung and Sony smartphones.

'The phones were taken overnight on 15 August, and we are appealing for anyone who has information about the burglary to contact us,' said a police spokesman.

'Do you want to know a secret?' whispered a voice in her ear. Poppy jumped like a scalded cat, but it was only Charlie, brandishing a small paper bag of rhubarb and custards. 'Scarlett gave me an extra one for luck! You can have it if you like.'

POPPY CHANGED into jodhpurs and a tee-shirt the minute they arrived home. Hoping a ride on the moor might clear her head, she caught Cloud, gave him a cursory groom and tacked him up. Soon they were cantering towards the Riverdale tor. At the top Poppy slid to the ground, sat cross-legged on a flat granite boulder and shared an apple with her pony as she gazed at the sweeping panorama. Directly ahead, sandwiched between their two paddocks, was the slate roof of Riverdale. Poppy could just make out a Chester-shaped brown blob by the water trough. The McKeevers' gravel drive ran parallel to the track to Ashworthy. Scarlett's home was an archetypical working farm. An old, slightly shabby farmhouse surrounded by a jumble of barns, stables and outhouses. Scarlett loved houses with clean modern lines, all glass and steel, but Poppy adored Ashworthy's low ceilings and mullioned windows.

She couldn't see Witch Cottage from here. Even the chimneys of Dartmoor Prison were hidden behind a distant tor.

'What should I do, Cloud?'

The Connemara rubbed his head on her tee-shirt, leaving a layer of short, white hairs on the navy brushed cotton.

'Tell the police, tell Dad and Caroline, or try to find out who stole the mobiles myself?'

Telling the police or her parents was the obvious, sensible thing to do, Poppy knew that. But that would mean admitting she had lied *and* that she had dragged Charlie to a crime scene in the middle of the night. She had a feeling they wouldn't be impressed.

'I wonder what Caitlyn would have done if she were me,' she pondered. Cloud pricked his ears at the sound of Cait's name, as he always did. But Poppy no longer felt resentful. She wished Cait was still alive. She felt sure they'd have been friends if things had been different.

Cait wasn't around to ask, but Jodie was. Jodie knew Witch Cottage. She was both smart and tough. Poppy had a feeling Jodie wouldn't judge her for not phoning the police. She made up her mind.

Tomorrow she would cycle over to Nethercote.

Jodie would know what to do.

13

Nethercote's tall chimneys cast shadows at her feet as Poppy pushed her bike up the drive. It was late afternoon and the sun burned orange in the sky. She'd told Caroline she was cycling to Scarlett's, but instead she'd turned in the opposite direction and had followed the narrow lanes to the horse rescue sanctuary.

Poppy walked past the ivy-clad farmhouse to the stables. The yard was quiet save for the reassuringly familiar sound of horses chomping their suppers, and they lifted their heads to watch her from their stable doors as she passed.

There was no sign of Jodie.

Poppy rang the bell outside the feed room but it failed to summon the older girl. Poppy dithered, not wanting to knock on the door of the house. She sidled over to Biscuit's stable and stroked the appaloosa's spotted face.

'Where's Jodie?' she asked the rescue pony. 'I need to talk to her.'

'I'm here.'

Poppy spun around. Jodie was behind her, a water bucket in each hand.

'What did you want to talk to me about?'

Poppy didn't know where to start. 'It's a long story. Is there some-where we can sit down?'

'Sure. Follow me.' Jodie set the buckets down, splashing water over her boots. She led Poppy through the feed room to a tack room beyond. One wall was lined with saddle racks. Bridles hung from hooks on another. The only light came from a tiny, grimy window on the back wall. The old stone walls had leached any warmth from the room. Poppy shivered.

Jodie flicked a switch. A strip light flickered and died. 'Bloody light. Yet another thing that needs fixing.' She waved Poppy to a shabby tub chair in front of an ancient electric fire. 'What's up? It's not Red, is it?'

'Red's fine. He seems to have settled in and Scarlett's still treating him like royalty. We hacked out yesterday and he was as good as gold. Nothing to worry about there.' Poppy realised she was gabbling.

Jodie raised her eyebrows. 'So what's the problem?'

'You and Caitlyn were best friends, weren't you?'

Jodie fiddled with a loose strand of cotton on the arm of her chair. Her fingers were trembling. 'Did Tory tell you?'

'I haven't seen Tory for ages. I found an old newspaper clipping. You competed in the South Devon Open Showjumping Competition together. You won it.'

'And Caitlyn was second. Boy was she sore about that.'

'Why didn't you say anything when you recognised Cloud at the fete?'

'Seeing him brought it all back. I've spent the last seven years trying to forget what happened,' said Jodie.

'I'm sorry.'

'Why should you be? It wasn't your fault. It wasn't anyone's fault. It was one of those things. He's a lovely pony. I'm glad he's found a good home.'

'Do you still have Nero?' Poppy asked.

Jodie's features darkened. 'He went when Dad went...*away*. If that's it I'd better get on. There are a hundred and one things I should be doing.'

'There was something else,' Poppy said. 'It's about Witch Cottage.'

Jodie was still for a second, then shrugged. 'Never heard of it.'

'The old cottage on the moor towards Princetown that's supposed to be haunted. Where the wild swimmer drowned.'

Jodie shook her head. 'Sorry, I don't know what you're talking about.'

'But you do!' Poppy cried. 'I know you and Cait used to hang out there. I found her diary and your trophy under the floorboards. Exactly where you'd left them.' Poppy took Jodie's silence as an invitation to continue. 'I've found something else in the cottage. Something that shouldn't be there. And I don't know what to do.'

'What have you found?' Jodie asked sharply.

The palms of Poppy's hands felt sticky. She wiped them on her jodhpurs. 'Mobile phones. Dozens of them. All brand new. They're hidden under a tarpaulin in the attic.'

'What's that got to do with me?'

'I don't know what to do about them,' said Poppy.

'Have you told anyone else?'

'Only Scarlett. She says I should call the police.'

Jodie wound the cotton around her index finger and gave it a sharp tug. The thread snapped. She met Poppy's eyes. 'And will you?'

'Will I what?'

'Call the police?'

'I don't know. That's why I wanted to talk to you.'

'I'm all ears,' said Jodie, flicking the cotton onto the floor.

'I think the phones are the ones that were stolen from the warehouse in Plymouth. There was a story about it in this week's Herald.'

Jodie stared at the tack room's pitted ceiling. 'So what if they were? I still don't get what this has got to do with me.'

'You know what I'm talking about,' said Poppy.

Jodie stiffened. 'What did you say?'

'I don't mean you know about the phones. You know about the cottage. I wanted to talk it through with someone who understood.'

Jodie exhaled slowly. 'I understand alright.'

'So you'll help?' Poppy felt giddy with relief.

Jodie jumped to her feet and grabbed the Land Rover keys from a hook by the door. Her mouth had tightened into a hard, thin line. 'I think you'd better show me.'

~

JODIE WAS silent as the Land Rover bumped along the stony track towards the cottage. Poppy stared out of the window. There were a hundred questions she wanted to ask. Top of the list was why Jodie was claiming to have never heard of the cottage when she and Cait had practically spent their last summer together there. But one glance at Jodie's granite-like profile was enough to make her bite her tongue.

They rounded a bend and the cottage came into view. From this distance you couldn't see the hole in the roof and the rotting windows. Poppy imagined smoke curling from the chimney and a white-haired man with stooped shoulders tending a vegetable patch, watched by an elderly border collie.

Jodie pulled in alongside the tarn, braking so sharply that Poppy's seatbelt bit into her shoulder. The older girl sat for a while, her hands clutching the steering wheel. Somewhere in the Land Rover a mobile phone pinged with a new text message, but Jodie continued staring blankly ahead. Poppy found her stillness unnerving. Surreptitiously she felt her back pocket for her own mobile. It wasn't there. She'd meant to pick it up from the worktop in the kitchen where she'd left it charging but had been in such a hurry to leave that she'd clean forgotten.

When Jodie turned to face Poppy, her face was expressionless. 'Let's go.'

'The mobiles are in the attic. I can show you, if you like. There are a couple of wooden boxes you can stand on so you're high enough to see. There's a hole in the roof but there's a tarpaulin over them to keep them dry. Whoever hid them here planned it properly,' Poppy said, climbing the stairs. She knew she was babbling again but she couldn't help herself.

'Oh, it was planned alright,' Jodie said, following Poppy into the biggest bedroom. She pointed to the two boxes. 'Sit down.'

'Don't you want me to show you where they are?'

Jodie shook her head. 'Sit down,' she repeated.

Poppy did as she was told. Jodie walked to the window. She glanced over her shoulder at Poppy. 'I already know where they are.'

'I don't understand.'

'I know where they are because I put them there.'

14

P oppy gaped at Jodie. Sunlight streamed through the window but the older girl's profile was in shadow.

'What do you mean, you put them there?'

'I told you my dad deals in mobile phones.'

Poppy cast her mind back to the day they'd first visited Nethercote and Jodie had mentioned her dad ran an import business. But this was all wrong. Questions bubbled up inside her.

'But why is he storing them in a tumbledown cottage in the middle of nowhere? Is it because they were stolen from the warehouse in Plymouth? Where exactly *is* your dad, Jodie?'

'He's precisely two and a half miles north of here, staying full board at Her Majesty's pleasure.'

'What do you mean?'

Jodie gave an impatient shake of her head, as if she couldn't believe Poppy's naivety.

'He's in the slammer. The clink. He's a guest of HMP Dartmoor. He's in *prison*, Poppy. My dad the convict is serving time.'

Poppy swallowed. 'What did he do?'

'He didn't kill anyone or anything like that. He fiddled the books at the building company he worked for.'

'Fiddled the books? What do you mean?'

'It's easy for finance directors to steal a little bit here and there without anyone noticing, apparently. Only he got greedy. And careless. The other directors were suspicious and called in the police. Dad was convicted five years ago.'

'When you were still at school?'

Jodie laughed hollowly. 'He was sent to prison a week before my GCSEs. I bombed the lot.'

'I'm sorry.'

'You keep apologising, don't you Poppy? Even when it's not your fault. You need to toughen up, kid. Else people will trample all over you.'

Poppy recoiled at the bitterness in Jodie's voice. 'I'm... I mean, why did he do it?'

'He set up the sanctuary with the money my grandparents left him when they died, figuring that he'd be able to raise enough money to pay for the running costs. Of course he couldn't. Any idiot could have told him that. But then Dad's a dreamer, always has been.'

'So he used the money he'd stolen to pay for the horses?' Poppy said.

Jodie nodded. 'He wanted me to follow my dream, too, so he bought Nero and a top-of-the range horsebox so we could compete all over the South West. Mum turned a blind eye to his thieving and I never knew until the morning the police turned up at the house and arrested him.'

'What happened to Nero?'

'The police took everything of value because they said it was proceeds of crime, including Nero. I'll never forgive Dad for that.'

'So you had to give it all up?'

'He left me with twenty four rescue horses to look after. I couldn't ride professionally any more.'

'But you've managed to keep Nethercote going while he's been in prison,' Poppy said.

'Only just. And now the money's all gone.' Jodie stared out of the window. The silence in the tiny attic bedroom was stifling. Suddenly everything fell into place. The mysterious text message on Jodie's phone. Her dad's import business. The hidden mobiles. The towering granite walls of Dartmoor prison just a couple of miles away.

'You're going to try to smuggle those phones into the prison,' Poppy whispered.

Jodie balled her hands into fists and Poppy felt her stomach clench. But the older girl didn't move.

'It was his idea. He can sell a mobile phone for a flippin' fortune inside.'

'But how are you planning to -'

'Get them in? The wing Dad's in is nearest the perimeter wall. Two cells have windows looking out onto the moor. One on the fourth floor and the other directly above it. Dad's cell.'

Jodie left the window and sat on the box next to Poppy.

'The prison's a listed building so his window hasn't got a grating over it. He's spent the last couple of days making a rope from bedding and is going to lower it out of the window and over the wall. I'll be at the bottom, waiting.' She smiled mirthlessly. 'I'll tie the bag of phones to his rope and he'll haul them up. We'll make enough money in one night to keep the horses fed for a year.'

'Did you steal the phones from the warehouse?' Poppy asked.

Jodie bristled. 'I am not a thief. Not like *him*. He organised it all. I just met the men when they delivered the phones and hid them in the attic.'

Without thinking Poppy said, 'We didn't see you.'

Jodie looked at her in astonishment. '*What?*'

Poppy glanced out of the window towards the conifers. 'Charlie and I were watching from the trees.'

'What the hell were you doing here?'

Poppy rubbed her hand across her forehead. It was all too much to take in. 'Charlie wanted to see if the place was really haunted. We rode over on Cloud,' she muttered.

'What if they'd seen you? Those men aren't the kind of people to mess with,' Jodie said roughly.

Poppy had been through a whole gamut of emotions in the last half an hour. Shock. Anxiety. Fear. Incredulity. Suddenly anger superseded it all. 'What if *we'd* been seen? What about you? If you get caught you'll go to jail! Who'll look after the rescue horses then?' she cried.

'Don't you understand? I have to do this. I have no choice.'

Poppy shook her head in disbelief. 'So why've you told me all this?'

Jodie stood up and stalked over to the window again. 'I couldn't tell you at home because if my mum even gets a whiff that someone is onto us she'll go straight to the prison governor and incriminate Dad. She's already terrified I'll get caught. I couldn't risk you going to the police and reporting the phones. I had to stop you.'

'Of course I've got to tell the police! Have you gone crazy?'

Jodie feigned surprise. 'Well, well. Mild-mannered, quiet little Poppy actually has a backbone. Who'd have thought it?'

It was Poppy's turn to bristle. 'I'm phoning them as soon as I get home.'

Jodie's lips thinned again. 'You can't. I'll be sent to jail and you're right, there is no-one else to look after the horses. They'll have to be put down and it'll be your fault. Percy, Mr Darcy. Even Biscuit. Can you live with that on your conscience?'

Jodie was bluffing, Poppy was sure of it. 'Nethercote isn't the only horse rescue centre in Devon. There are dozens of them! Someone else will take them in.'

'Are you willing to risk it? Anyway, you're implicated now. You lifted the tarpaulin to have a look at the phones, right?'

Poppy nodded, unsure where this was heading.

'Your prints will be all over it. All over the cottage, in fact. I'll tell the police I recruited you and your brother to act as scouts.'

Poppy felt the blood drain from her face. 'You wouldn't!'

'Needs must,' Jodie said grimly. 'It'll be your word against mine. And let me warn you, I'm a very good liar. I'll take you down with me, for the sake of the horses. For the sake of Nethercote.'

15

Poppy slumped onto the box again, her head in her hands. What if Jodie was telling the truth, that she really was prepared to incriminate her? She couldn't believe the police would actually think she'd been involved, but you read about miscarriages of justice in the papers all the time. And if they heard that the son and daughter of a BBC war correspondent had been questioned about a prison smuggling ring the tabloids would have a field day. Her dad would probably lose his job and they'd have to move. Suddenly she was struck by a thought so terrible it pierced her heart. Without Riverdale she'd have to sell Cloud and Chester. That's if she wasn't already doing time in a Young Offender's Institute.

'It's not nice, being forced into something you don't want to do because you have no choice, is it?' said Jodie. 'Now you know how I feel. I don't want to break the law, but Dad gave me no alternative.'

'When are you doing it?' Poppy asked dully.

'Tonight at eleven. The sooner the better as far as I'm concerned.'

'He'll make you do it again, you know that, don't you?'

For the first time Poppy saw a flicker of doubt cross Jodie's face. The older girl shook her head.

'I've told him it's a one-off.'

'And you believe him, do you?'

Jodie gave an imperceptible nod.

'He probably even believes it himself,' Poppy said. 'When he decided to steal money from his company he probably told himself it would be the first and last time. But people get greedy. You said it yourself.'

Jodie exhaled loudly and stalked out of the room. 'It's happening tonight. End of.'

THEY DROVE BACK to Nethercote in silence. As Jodie pulled into the drive Poppy made a last ditch attempt to change her mind.

'There must be other ways to raise the money. Scarlett and I will help you.'

Jodie gave a short bark of laughter. 'Two gormless thirteen-year-olds? I don't think so. It costs thousands of pounds a year to run this place. Where are you going to find that kind of money? In your piggy banks? Down the back of the sofa? I promise you, this is the only way.'

'At least let us try.'

Jodie grabbed her arm. 'Haven't you been listening to anything I've said?' Her voice was thick with menace. Or was it unshed tears? Poppy couldn't be sure.

A door slammed. 'There you are! I made bacon butties for tea but you'd disappeared,' said Jodie's mum, appearing from the house.

Jodie let go of Poppy's arm, leaving a red hand-shaped imprint.

'I had a call about a mare that had been left tethered to a tree on the Tavistock road without food or water. Poppy and I drove over to have a look but we couldn't find her, could we, Poppy?'

Shocked at how smoothly Jodie had lied, Poppy said nothing.

Jodie's mum seemed oblivious to the undercurrents and smiled brightly. 'Would you like a bacon butty, love? There's plenty to go around.'

Poppy shook her head. 'No thanks. I've lost my appetite. Anyway, I need to get going. My stepmum will be wondering where I am.'

Poppy retrieved her bike but as she was about to pedal off, Jodie blocked her way.

'I'm not doing this for me or my dad. I'm doing it for the horses. So please, *please* don't tell anyone. You'll ruin everything.'

Poppy rushed past, too appalled to reply. Unshed tears burned her throat and anxiety knotted her stomach. Jodie went to grab her handlebar but Poppy swerved out of the way. The bike almost lost traction on the gravel but Poppy stamped on the pedals and brought it back under control. Once on the main road she put her head down and cycled as fast as she could towards Riverdale, relishing the burning pain in her thigh muscles as she attacked each hill because it took her mind off everything else. She wished she could turn back the clock. She wished she'd never asked Jodie for advice, never found the mobile phones, never let Charlie talk her into going looking for his stupid ghosts. She longed for blissful ignorance. But deep in her heart she knew it was too late for that.

The question was, what could she do to make things right?

POPPY FLUNG her bike on the grass and vaulted the gate to Cloud and Chester's paddock. The Connemara was dozing by the far hedge but opened his eyes and whickered with pleasure when Poppy called him. She threw her arms around him, breathing in lungfuls of his pure, horsey smell, imagining how awful it would be if they had to sell up and move away. She felt a sob rising in her throat at the thought of him being driven away in someone else's horsebox to a yard who knew where. The prospect was too terrible to bear and she collapsed onto the ground, tears streaming down her cheeks. When Cloud nuzzled her neck and blew softly into her ear she wailed even harder. She stayed like that, hugging her knees, with Cloud watching over her, until she was all cried out.

It was Chester who dragged her from her misery. The old donkey wandered over and gave her a determined nudge. As she gazed into his chocolate brown eyes she felt her resolve strengthen.

'I know, I'm being wet and pathetic,' she said in a quavering voice. 'What would Tory say? That every problem has a solution, that's what.'

She wiped her nose on the bottom of her tee-shirt and climbed stiffly to her feet. 'I just need to work out what it is.'

Her dad was in the lounge watching cricket, with Magpie on his lap looking daggers at Freddie, who was lying at his feet, his raspberry-pink tongue lolling.

'Hello, daughter of mine.' Mike McKeever patted the seat beside him.

Poppy sat down and tickled Magpie's chin. The cat gave Freddie a supercilious look and began purring loudly.

'Why the sad face?' her dad asked.

Poppy shrugged.

'You never have time to talk to me these days,' he said. 'You're always too busy with the other men in your life.'

Poppy looked quizzically at him until the penny dropped. 'You mean Cloud and Chester?'

Mike McKeever stuck out his bottom lip and nodded sorrowfully. He looked so like Charlie that she had to giggle.

'You twit,' she said fondly. 'It's because I love them more.'

'Fair enough. I know when I'm beaten. So I'm presuming that you've come to find me because you want something. A new Australian rug or some of those padded socks Cloud wears when he goes in Bill's trailer?'

'You mean a New Zealand rug, Dad. And they're not padded socks, they're travel boots. No, I don't want anything like that. I need some advice.'

Her dad muted the TV. 'Fire away.'

'If you had to raise a huge amount of money for a horse sanctuary, what would you do?'

'How much are we talking?'

'Thousands. And it needs to be raised quickly.'

'Is this for that place Scarlett got her new pony from?'

Poppy nodded. 'Nethercote'll have to close if Jodie can't find a way to raise enough money. She's getting desperate.' That was the understatement of the year, Poppy thought to herself.

Her dad rested his chin on steepled fingers. 'Britain is a country of animal lovers. If people knew her horses were under threat they'd dig deep into their pockets, I'm sure.'

'That's the problem. People don't know.'

'Well then, she must find a way to tell them.'

'But how?'

'She needs publicity and she must think big. She needs to tell her story to the TV and newspapers. The money'll come rolling in, I guarantee it.'

'But no-one's going to be interested in a tiny horse rescue place in Devon, Dad.'

'That's where you've got to think smart. Jodie needs a hook to draw the journalists in. An animal with a tragic back story that'll grab the headlines.'

Poppy pictured the real-life magazines her old friend Tory enjoyed with a cup of tea and a slice of Battenberg. There was no doubt Jodie could make a few quid selling her story. *How I smuggled stolen phones into prison to save my horses.* But Poppy didn't think any public relations guru worth their salt would recommend resorting to that particular course of action.

'Every horse at Nethercote has a tragic back story, Dad. That's why they're there.'

'Point taken. A tragic *out-of-the-ordinary* back story. You'll think of something, Poppy. You've lived with your old dad long enough to know what makes the news.'

It was true, Poppy thought. But her dad was a war correspondent. He covered conflicts in the Middle East. Proper weighty crises and catastrophes in which lives were lost and worlds turned upside down. Stories that newsreaders read with solemn voices, not the light and fluffy news items which ended the bulletins, leaving viewers with a happy heart, their faith in humankind restored.

'So if I do find a tragic, *out-of-the-ordinary* back story, can you help me?'

Her dad ruffled her hair. "Course I can, sweetheart. I went to journalism college with the producer of Spotlight. I'm sure I can pull in a favour or two. But the story needs to stand up.'

Poppy gave Magpie a last chuck under his chin. 'Fair enough. Better get started then, hadn't I?'

unched over the laptop at the kitchen table with a notepad
and pen beside her, Poppy called up the Nethercote Horse
Rescue website and clicked on a tab that said *Our horses*.
Jodie had reproduced the photos that she'd used on the display panels
at the fete. Kirsty, Mr Darcy and Percy were all there. Poppy even
spotted the four white socks and white-splodged nose of Red as a foal,
being bottle-fed by a much younger-looking Jodie. Poppy skim-read
their stories, looking for a hook that would entice the local television
station to send a camera crew to Nethercote. Each one was a litany of
human cruelty, neglect and ignorance. But although they made Poppy
feel sick to the stomach she knew such back stories were universal the
world over. Nothing out of the ordinary there.

Sighing, Poppy flipped the laptop closed and stared out of the
window, hoping for an epiphany. But the harder she tried to think, the
emptier her mind became. Caroline came in from the garden and
began washing lettuce for their dinner. Her dad wandered by in
search of his reading glasses. Magpie rubbed against her legs before
settling into Freddie's bed by the range, the feline equivalent of a self-
satisfied smirk on his whiskered face. Still Poppy's mind remained
stubbornly blank.

Her reverie was broken when Charlie bowled in like a mini hurricane.

'Can I have a biscuit, Mum?' he called, his hand already in the tin.

'Just one. Dinner won't be long,' said Caroline, taking a quiche out of the oven.

Biscuit. The word reverberated around Poppy's head like one of those tiny silver orbs in a pinball machine. Charlie rammed a ginger biscuit in his mouth and crunched noisily. Biscuit. Poppy clapped her hand to her head and Charlie and Caroline looked at her inquiringly.

'I'm so stupid! The answer's been there all along!' Poppy flung her chair back and hugged her brother. 'You're a genius, Charlie. An absolute, utter genius!'

Charlie's eyes widened in surprise. 'Usually you think I'm an annoying idiot.'

'Not today, little brother. Today you are the cleverest person I know. A proper mastermind. Right, I need to see Dad.'

He was in the lounge reading the paper. He peered over his glasses as she plonked herself on the sofa.

'I've found an *out-of-the-ordinary* back story,' she announced. 'What if there was a pony at Nethercote who'd been airlifted by helicopter from the top of a tower block where he'd been kept alive on vegetable peelings, scraps of bread and rainwater?'

Her dad folded the newspaper. 'I'd say that was pretty *out-of-the-ordinary.*'

'Caroline said this pony had even been on the news when he was rescued. So if his new home was under threat because of a lack of money, that might make headlines, right?'

'I'd say so,' said her dad. 'And this pony actually exists, does it?'

Poppy pictured Biscuit, the white spots on his chestnut coat like snowflakes as he snoozed in the daisies. His story wasn't on the Nethercote website, and in her desperation she'd completely forgotten him. 'Yes, he definitely exists. So will you phone your friend at Spotlight?'

Her dad was already reaching for his mobile. Poppy chewed a nail as she listened to the one-sided conversation. After what seemed like an age he hung up.

'You're lucky - it's the silly season and they're scratching around for news. They're sending a crew around first thing in the morning. Unless something else breaks it'll be top item on tomorrow's programme. With a fair wind and a bit of luck it'll be picked up by the nationals and those donations will come flooding in.'

Poppy hugged her dad. 'Thank you, thank you, thank you,' she gabbled into his lambswool sweater. 'You don't know how much this means.'

'No problem, sweetheart. You'd better go and tell Jodie the good news.'

POPPY GRABBED a slice of quiche and went to catch Cloud. If she cut across the moor it was only about three miles to Nethercote. The Spotlight reporter was due at half nine the following morning. She had to convince Jodie that the interview was the right thing to do. That the publicity it would attract would raise enough money to keep the rescue centre afloat. But, most importantly, Poppy had to talk Jodie out of her plan to smuggle the mobile phones into the prison. Poppy had a feeling that would be the hardest task.

Cloud cantered across the moor, jumping a low stone wall with ease and flying over a small stream. Emotions churned in Poppy's stomach like a witch's potion in a steaming cauldron. Love for her pony. Terror she could lose him. Anxiety about the conversation that lay ahead. And a glimmer of hope that if she could change Jodie's mind, she stood a chance of making everything alright.

Cloud looked around with interest as they walked up the Nethercote drive.

'This is where your new buddy Red used to live,' Poppy told him, trying to keep her tone light and her breathing steady. But the waver in her voice gave away her nerves.

Jodie's Land Rover wasn't parked in its usual place. Poppy rang the bell by the tack room but no-one came. Perhaps Jodie was in one of the paddocks. Poppy led Cloud past the stables. His eyes rolled and his nostrils flared in mock horror as the rescue horses watched them walk by.

'It's alright, silly,' Poppy said, stroking his neck. 'They won't hurt you.'

Jodie wasn't in the paddocks either. Poppy checked her watch. Half past six. Time was running out. She knocked at the back door. Inside a radio was playing pop music. She knocked again, harder this time. A door slammed and heels clicked on a stone floor. Jodie's mum appeared, a lipstick in one hand and a handbag in the other. Bracelets jangled on her wrists and her hair had been newly blow dried.

Poppy took a deep breath. 'Sorry to bother you but is Jodie in?'

'She isn't, I'm afraid. Disappeared about an hour ago. Didn't even stay for her dinner, the little minx.' Her voice was indignant.

'Do you know where she's gone? I really need to speak to her.'

Jodie's mum looked cagey. 'No idea.'

'When will she be back?'

'I don't know, love. I'm not her keeper. Look, I'm late for work. Can I leave her a message?'

Poppy dithered. Could she confide in Jodie's mum? Cloud shifted his weight and nudged Poppy in the back. Jodie's mum looked at her watch and frowned.

Poppy made a snap decision she hoped she wouldn't live to regret.

17

The air was close and alive with the hum of a million biting insects and the sun was disappearing over the horizon as they arrived home. Poppy untacked Cloud and sponged the sweaty patch under his saddle. Once she'd turned him out with Chester she mindlessly swept the yard until her back ached and sweat trickled down her forehead and between her shoulder blades.

When she could sweep no more she leant on the gate and watched the pony and donkey doze. Every now and then one of them would twitch and shift their weight. Poppy was always dreaming about them. Did they ever dream of her? More likely their dreams were filled with newly-cut hay, sweet spring grass and carrots. Lots of carrots.

She blew them a kiss and headed indoors, where her dad and Caroline were in the lounge watching television. Poppy slumped on the sofa.

'OK sweetheart? Was Jodie pleased?' said Caroline.

'Yes,' Poppy said. She kept her eyes glued to the screen so Caroline couldn't read her face.

'Where's Charlie?'

'Just gone up to bed. He's desperate to come over to Nethercote and watch the filming tomorrow. He's hoping they'll interview him as a concerned animal lover. D'you think Jodie would mind?'

Poppy shrugged. 'Probably not.'

Her mobile beeped. She checked the message.

I've made the call. It's over to you.

'Scarlett?' Caroline asked.

Poppy nodded. Did it count as a lie if she didn't actually articulate it? 'She wants me to go over and watch a film. Is that OK?'

'As long as you're back by ten. And make sure you take your phone.'

Poppy tapped out a reply and shoved the phone back in her pocket. For better or worse, the first part of her hastily-devised plan was in place.

POPPY'S BIKE was leaning up against the old stone wall around Caroline's vegetable garden, but she walked straight past it and headed for the tack room. Pedal power was no match for horse power in situations like this. She fixed her dad's head torch to her hat and grabbed Cloud's saddle and bridle.

The Connemara showed no surprise when she let herself into the paddock, as if night-time hacks were an everyday occurrence. Poppy glanced nervously towards the house as the gate clicked shut behind her, but the blind in the kitchen was drawn. As long as she was back by ten her parents would be none the wiser.

Something dark swooped in front of her face and she flinched, but it was only one of the bats that had made a home in the rafters of the barn. She led Cloud through the gate and jumped into the saddle.

The setting sun had turned the rippled mass of altocumulus cloud such a vivid shade of fiery orange that it resembled molten lava. Beneath the sky the moss-green moor stretched before them unremittingly, the vast expanse broken only by rocky granite outcrops and the occasional sheep.

Behind her, Riverdale was bathed in tangerine light. Poppy

pictured her brother, tucked up in bed, his thumb in his mouth and Magpie curled in a ball by his feet, snoring gently; the television turned down low as her dad and Caroline chatted about their day; Freddie, fast asleep in his basket by the range, his beetle-black nose twitching as he dreamed his doggy dreams. The urge to turn back and join them was so strong Poppy almost succumbed to it. This was Jodie's mess. Why should it be up to her to sort it out? Jodie had made her bed. Let her lie in it.

But Poppy knew it was too late. She'd set off a chain of events and had no choice but to see it through. She had to do right by the Nethercote horses. She just hoped her plan worked. And if it didn't....

Anxiety gnawing at her insides, Poppy clicked her tongue and asked for a canter. Cloud needed no encouragement and sprang forwards. He was fizzing with nervous energy, his neck arched and his tail high. Poppy licked her lips and tried to slow her racing heartbeat. The last thing she wanted was for her pony to pick up on her tension. The Connemara lengthened his stride until he was galloping flat out. She sighed. It seemed he already had.

'Hey boy, not so fast. There's a long way to go,' she soothed. She tried checking him but the reins slipped through her clammy fingers. A dark stain of sweat was spreading across his neck and shoulders and his head was tucked into his chest. Poppy sat down in the saddle, kept her legs firmly against Cloud's sides and gave a firm, even pull with both reins.

'Whoa,' she murmured. Cloud flicked back his ears and finally slowed his stride. Poppy checked him again and he broke into a fast, unbalanced trot.

'Steady,' she said, sitting for a few uncomfortable strides until she was able to ease him into a walk. She bent down and stroked his neck.

Poppy loosened the reins, relieved to have brought him back under control. He had never taken off like that before. She kept up a stream of chatter as they crossed the moor, hoping her voice would keep him calm. The sun was sinking below the horizon and the sky had darkened to the grey of a stormy sea. By Poppy's reckoning they were over halfway. With any luck they'd reach the cottage before darkness fell. She'd hoped for a clear night but no such luck. She'd have to rely on her pony's instinct and the beam of the head torch to guide them home.

They passed a small herd of Dartmoor ponies grazing by the side of a stream. A roan mare with a bay foal at foot lifted her head and whinnied. Cloud skittered to the left and Poppy clamped her legs to his sides and tightened her reins.

After a mile or so Cloud finally began to settle. Poppy let the reins slip through her fingers so he could stretch his neck. As she relaxed into his long, loping walk her mind began to wander. Humming tunelessly, she scratched a mosquito bite on her arm and played with a hank of the Connemara's mane. She was so preoccupied she didn't see the flash of iridescent green until too late. As they approached a clump of gorse bushes a male pheasant squawked in alarm and swooped in front of them, its speckled conker and black wings outstretched. Cloud boggled and leapt about three feet into the air, throwing Poppy out of the saddle. For a split second, as she teetered on the brink, she thought she might save herself. But the saddle slipped and with it went her balance. The ground rushed towards her as fast as a fairground helter-skelter and Poppy landed heavily, her right leg buckling underneath her. She gasped as she felt her ankle pop. Intense pain shot up her leg. And then everything went black.

18

Roused from semi-consciousness by a draught of warm air, Poppy reached for the alarm clock on her bedside table. When her hand came into contact with wiry grass and a small slab of cold granite her eyes snapped open. Cloud's nose was a few inches from her own. He blew softly into her face, as if he was trying to wake her. That explained the warm air at least.

Totally disorientated, Poppy looked around her, wondering if she'd fallen asleep in the paddock again. She sat up groggily and winced at the stabbing pain in her leg. Cloud whickered and nuzzled her neck, his liquid brown eyes dark with concern. She tried to piece together what had happened. Bit by bit she remembered: the text, the made-up visit to see Scarlett, the dash across the moor to the tumbledown cottage, the pheasant...

'Pesky pheasant!' Poppy muttered, attempting to stand. But the searing pain took her breath away and she collapsed on the grass again. Gingerly, she peeled down her sock. Her ankle had ballooned in size, the skin around it stretched and puffy. Her heart sank. How was she ever going to reach Witch Cottage now?

As if sensing her thoughts Cloud gave her a gentle nudge. Poppy swallowed back tears. 'I can't ride you, Cloud. There's no way I can stand to get on. And I can't walk a single step. I'll have to call Caroline and Dad. I have no other choice.'

She slid her phone out of her back pocket and groaned. No signal. Not even one measly bar. She threw it onto the grass in frustration. Cloud sniffed it cautiously, his nostrils flared, and took a step back.

'Don't leave me!' Poppy cried, the gravity of her situation beginning to sink in. It was almost nine o'clock at night, she was in the middle of the moor with a useless leg and an equally useless phone. Jodie was about to throw her life away and there was nothing Poppy could do to stop her. Her shoulders sagged in defeat.

Cloud must have registered the desperation in her voice, because he walked forward and rubbed his head against her, as if to say *Don't worry, I'll stick around.* She pressed her face against his warm cheek.

'I can do this,' she told him. Heaving herself upright she gathered Cloud's reins, rested her left hand on his withers and grabbed the stirrup. But her right ankle was too feeble and she crumpled to the ground. 'Oh Cloud, what am I going to do?'

The Connemara pawed the ground and sank to his knees with a grunt.

'Don't roll, you'll squash your saddle!'

But Cloud didn't roll. He lay down beside her and nudged her hip.

Was he lying down in sympathy? Poppy knew horses were empathetic but this was ridiculous. Maybe he'd twisted his leg when he'd spooked, too.

'Have you hurt yourself?' she cried.

Cloud nudged her again. Poppy leant against him, reassured by his solid bulk. She often lay down with him in the stable. She'd once read that if a horse even let someone near them while they were lying down it was a sign of trust. It had made her feel slightly superior that Cloud was so relaxed with her that he sometimes dozed off with his head in her lap. She'd watched videos on YouTube of horses who'd been trained to lie down on command. Some even lay down so their riders could mount them from their wheelchairs.

Suddenly a thought popped into her head. She knew from Caitlyn's diary that she'd started teaching Cloud tricks. Had she taught him to lie down so she could get on from the ground? It seemed unbelievable but it was worth a try. There were no other options.

Poppy shuffled on her bottom to Cloud's saddle, gathered the reins again and grabbed a handful of mane.

'Are you OK with this?' she asked him. He looked completely at ease. She took a deep breath, put her weight on her left knee and hauled her right leg over. Once she was sitting in the saddle she touched his withers and held on tightly as he scrambled to his feet.

Poppy threw her arms around his neck. 'You clever, clever boy!'

Leaving her swollen foot dangling she crossed the right stirrup over the saddle so it didn't bump against his side and clicked her tongue, her optimism restored.

'Come on Cloud. We have a disaster to avert!'

Poppy saw the headlights of Jodie's Land Rover before they left the inky blackness of the conifers. It looked as though they had arrived in the nick of time. Jodie, wearing a dark baseball cap and riding gloves, was cramming dozens of phones into a large black holdall.

'Jodie! It's me, Poppy.'

Jodie spun around. Her face, caught in the beam of Poppy's head torch, was twisted with fury and fear.

'What the hell are you doing here?'

'I've come to stop you.'

'Too late.'

'It isn't! You don't have to do this!'

'I do,' Jodie said grimly.

'But I've found another way to raise the money!'

'Yeah, right.'

'I really have. The BBC is sending a camera crew to Nethercote in the morning.'

'*What?*'

'They're going to do a story on your appeal.'

'There is no appeal.'

'There will be by the morning,' Poppy said. 'You're going to set one up on your website tonight.'

Jodie turned back to the holdall. 'It'd be a complete waste of time. There are too many animal sanctuaries out there asking for money. I've already told you that.'

'None of the others will be top item on tomorrow's news. My dad's had a word with the producer. She loves Biscuit's story. She's going to use old footage of him being carried down by the helicopter, and they're going to interview you about him and the appeal. Once people see the great work you're doing the donations will come flooding in!'

Jodie tucked a loose strand of hair behind her ear. Poppy noticed the slightest tremor in her fingers.

'Didn't it occur to you to ask me first?' Jodie said coldly.

Poppy was silent.

'No, I didn't think so. I'm not doing it. I don't need to. By this time tomorrow I'll have enough in the bank to keep Nethercote running for a year.'

'But it's all organised!'

Jodie shoved the last few phones into the bag and yanked the zip closed. 'Well, you've wasted your time. Now beggar off and leave me to it.'

'You'll get caught,' Poppy said.

'You sound like my mother. How many times do I have to say it? I will not get caught. Everything is planned. So if you'll excuse me, there's somewhere I need to be.'

'Your dad won't be there.'

Jodie flung the holdall in the back of the Land Rover and slammed the door. 'What are you wittering about?'

Poppy took a deep breath. 'He won't be lowering the rope. He's in solitary confinement.'

'*What?*' Jodie said again.

'The Governor knows what your dad's planning. He had a tip off. There are four prison officers in his cell and police on the ground waiting for the phones to arrive.'

'You've grassed us up?' Jodie hissed.

'Not me. It was your mum. But no-one knows it's you bringing the phones. She told them it was some lowlife your dad met in prison.'

'And that makes it alright does it?'

'She reckons he'll end up serving extra time. But that it's a small price to pay in the circumstances.'

Poppy thought it wise not repeat Jodie's mum's actual words, that he could go to hell for all she cared. Instead she said, 'Your mum said he'd be happy as long as you and the horses were OK.'

Jodie leant against the Land Rover, her head bowed. 'If that's true, what am I going to do with the phones?'

Poppy glanced at the cottage. 'Put them back in the attic. I'll call the police in a couple of days and say I've found them. It won't matter if my fingerprints are all over them. There'll be nothing to link them to you.'

'What about the gang who stole them. They know who I am,' Jodie said.

'But they're hardly going to hand themselves in, are they?'

Sensing Jodie waver Poppy pressed home her advantage. 'What would Cait tell you to do, if she was here? Would she want her best friend to break the law and risk going to prison? It's the last thing she'd want.'

Jodie was silent. After what seemed like an eternity she edged over to Cloud and stroked his head. Poppy felt a pounding in her chest and realised she'd stopped breathing.

'She'd tell me I was nuts to even consider it,' said Jodie finally.

Poppy sent a silent missive of thanks to Caitlyn.

'So you'll do it? The interview and everything?'

'You really think it'll work?'

The beam of the head torch bobbed like a yo-yo as Poppy nodded. 'It'll work. I promise.'

19

'So, are you going to give me a hand with these phones or what?' said Jodie.

Poppy reddened. 'I can't get off. I fell off Cloud and busted my ankle on the way over.'

Jodie raised her eyebrows. 'Is it broken?'

'I don't think so. I can still wiggle my toes, although it really hurts. I think it's just a sprain.'

'How did you get back on?'

'Well, that's the funny thing,' said Poppy. 'Did you and Caitlyn teach Cloud and Nero tricks that last summer?'

Jodie hooted with laughter. 'I tried to. Nero was hopeless. But Cloud was a quick learner, weren't you boy? Cait taught him to give her a kiss and take a bow, that kind of thing.'

'Did she teach him to lie down?'

Jodie's forehead creased. 'Not that I remember. But it was so long ago. D'you want me to go home and get the trailer?'

'No, we'll take it easy. We'll be fine. But will you be OK to put the phones back in the attic?'

'Do I have an option?' Jodie's tone was sardonic, but she dragged the hold-all out of the back of the Land Rover and hefted it onto her shoulder.

'I'll see you tomorrow,' Poppy said.

Jodie held her hand in a mock salute. As Cloud plunged back into the conifers Poppy glanced back. In the beam of the Land Rover's headlights she could just make out the older girl disappearing through the door of the cottage. Poppy ran her hand along Cloud's neck and allowed herself a smile.

'D'you know, Cloud? I think it's going to be alright.'

It was only when they were almost home that she realised she had overlooked one small but crucial problem. How on earth was she going to explain her sprained ankle to her parents?

'So you decided to ride Cloud to Scarlett's - even though it was pitch dark - and fell off on the way home when he shied at a sheep?' Caroline asked, her eyebrows raised.

'Er, yes. That's right.' Poppy hopped over to the gate and rested her bad ankle on the bottom bar. Her nose would be as long as Pinocchio's if she carried on lying like this.

'We'd better take you to minor injuries first thing to check it's not a fracture,' said her dad.

'I can't miss the filming!' Poppy cried. 'I've promised Jodie I'll be there. Honestly, I'm fine. The swelling's gone down already.' She rotated her ankle, hiding her grimace behind her long fringe. 'See?'

Caroline sighed. 'Alright. But you won't be able to ride. I'll drive you.'

Poppy hopped over to her stepmum and gave her a hug. Caroline ruffled her hair.

'Come on, Hopalong Cassidy. It's getting late and you should be in bed.'

Poppy screwed up her face. 'What did you call me?'

'Hopalong Cassidy. He was a cowboy in the old Western films my grandad used to love. Hopalong had a grey horse, too, though he was called Topper, if my memory serves me right.'

Lying in bed, her ankle resting on two pillows and Magpie nestled in the crook of her arm, Poppy Googled Hopalong Cassidy.

'Wikipedia says he was often called upon to intercede when dishonest characters took advantage of honest citizens,' she told the cat, who yawned widely, showing two rows of tiny incisors.

Poppy turned off the iPad and tickled Magpie's chin. 'We've more in common than a gammy leg.'

OVER BREAKFAST POPPY checked Nethercote's website. Jodie had been busy. On the home page was a huge banner urging people to support the rescue centre's new appeal. Under a photo of Jodie with her arm around Biscuit's neck was an open letter. Poppy's toast grew cold on her plate as she read:

'Hi, I'm Jodie Morgan, and I run Nethercote Horse Rescue.

I want to take this opportunity to tell you a little bit about us and the work we do.

Nethercote was founded by my dad, Alan Morgan, ten years ago. Dad always loved horses and opening a rescue centre was his life's dream.

Dad never once turned a horse away. He gave them all a second chance.

Horses like Biscuit, our most famous resident here at Nethercote, who was rescued by helicopter from the roof of a high rise block of flats. We try and rehome as many horses as possible, but I have promised Biscuit that he has a home here for the rest of his days.

Five years ago Dad left the running of Nethercote to me. I was fifteen and still at school. Running a rescue centre wasn't my dream - I wanted to be a famous showjumper - but I owed it to the horses to carry on.

A job like this is a vocation. Seeing a pony that arrived skinny and terrified go off to his new home sleek and confident makes all the hard work worthwhile.

But the last few years have been tough. Really tough. Money has been *tight and fundraising takes up precious time better spent rescuing, rehabilitating and rehoming our horses and ponies.*

This summer we reached crisis point at Nethercote. Costs for hay and feed have soared and donations have plummeted. Without financial help we won't be able to pay the winter feed bill, let alone meet ongoing veterinary and farrier costs. What will happen to the horses, you may well ask. The truth is, I don't know.

So we have launched Biscuit's Appeal, to raise enough money to enable us to carry on caring for the horses other people have forgotten. If you are able to help, please donate using the link below.

Every penny counts: £5 will buy a bale of hay, £10 will buy a sack of food, £20 will pay for the farrier to trim a pony's feet and £80 will buy him a new set of shoes.

So, you see, your help really can make all the difference to Biscuit and his friends here at Nethercote. Thank you for listening in our hour of need.

Yours, Jodie

Poppy swallowed. Jodie's letter was heartfelt and emotive and, as if that wasn't enough to get people reaching for their chequebooks, there was a blurry photo in the bottom right hand corner of Biscuit being winched to safety from the tower block in the Midlands. The appaloosa was a bag of skin and bones, a far cry from the plump, contented pony he was now.

Charlie bounded in, his hair as tousled as a bird's nest, Freddie hot on his heels. He skidded to a halt when he saw Poppy.

'No tablets at the breakfast table!'

'I'm not playing games, I'm reading. The BBC film crew is coming today and I need to check the website so I can give Jodie some advice on handling the media, if you must know,' Poppy told him officiously.

'Doesn't look like she needs it,' said Caroline, reading over Poppy's shoulder. 'I'd say she was pretty much on message already.'

'Yes, well, I did brief her last night. I mean, yesterday afternoon.' Poppy felt her cheeks redden. Hoping Caroline hadn't noticed, she picked up her plate and hobbled over to the sink. The swelling in her ankle had gone down overnight but it was still too tender to take her full weight.

'What time do we need to go?' Caroline asked.

'They're coming at half past nine so if we leave at eight thirty I can make sure Jodie's ready.'

'Can me and Freddie come? They might want to do a vod pod,' said Charlie.

Poppy gazed at him in exasperation. 'A *what?*'

'You know, when they ask members of the public what they think about something. They might do a vod pod about how important it is to save the ponies.'

Caroline laughed. 'He means vox pop. I suppose it wouldn't do any harm. As long as you promise not to get under everybody's feet. You don't mind, do you Poppy?'

'I won't be annoying, I promise.' Charlie smiled beseechingly at his sister.

'Oh alright, if you must. But if you ruin everything by messing up a shot or something I will have no option but to kill you.'

'I understand,' he nodded earnestly, before giving a fist pump and bowling back out of the kitchen, Freddie still at his feet.

Poppy sighed. Brothers!

20

J odie looked as if she'd only managed to snatch a couple of hours' sleep. Purple shadows darkened her eyes like shading on a pencil portrait and her face was pale. But she greeted the McKeevers with a cheerful smile and made a great fuss of Freddie, who promptly rolled on the ground with his legs in the air offering his belly to be tickled.

'Is there anything we can do?' Caroline asked.

'I've just got the yard to sweep and Biscuit to groom. I wanted him looking his best,' said Jodie.

'Poppy can take care of Biscuit and I'll sweep the yard. You go and get yourself ready.'

Jodie smiled gratefully and disappeared inside. Poppy tied Biscuit outside his stable and set to work with a body brush. The appaloosa was already beginning to lose his summer coat and Poppy sneezed violently as she was enveloped in a cloud of horse hair. Catching a whiff of the Polos in her back pocket, Biscuit nibbled at her jeans until Poppy relented. He wolfed two from her open palm as if he hadn't been fed for a week, which, Poppy reflected, had probably been the case when he'd been tethered at the top of the high rise. It was little wonder he was a guzzle guts when a decent meal back then would have been a pile of potato scrapings and a couple of slices of mouldy bread. Poppy shuddered, then peeled another couple of mints from the pack.

She was brushing out the tangles in the appaloosa's tail when Jodie's mum tottered across the yard in the highest wedge shoes Poppy had ever seen. She laid a hand on Poppy's arm.

'Thank you for everything you did yesterday, Poppy. You don't know how grateful I am. I've got my old Jodie back.'

'I was glad to help. I don't think deep down she wanted to do it, she just felt she had no option.'

Jodie's mum's lips thinned. 'Her father should never have put her in that position. What was he thinking?'

Poppy considered this. She would lay down her life for Cloud. She could understand why Alan Morgan had been prepared to take such a risk. But it didn't make it right.

The back door banged shut and Jodie appeared, wearing a clean, if a little creased, red Nethercote tee-shirt, navy jodhpurs and black riding boots. Despite her wan face she looked upbeat, as though a great weight had been lifted from her shoulders.

'Are you ready for your moment of fame?' Caroline asked.

Jodie grimaced. 'My stomach's churning, my mouth is as dry as sandpaper and I've absolutely no idea what I'm going to say. But otherwise, yes, bring it on.'

'We can have a run-through if you like,' Poppy said shyly. 'I can pretend I'm the reporter and ask you some questions.'

'And I'll be the cameraman,' said Charlie, sticking an imaginary camera in Jodie's face.

'Anything that'll help.'

Poppy and Charlie had watched their dad on the news enough times to know how to conduct a television interview and they spent the next ten minutes grilling Jodie until she was word perfect. They had hardly drawn breath when a spotless black BMW pulled up at the gate.

'Oh God, they're here!' Jodie cried, smoothing her hair self-consciously.

'You'll be fine,' Caroline told her. 'Forget the camera's there and just be yourself.'

A man in his thirties dressed in a cream linen suit and reeking of a spicy, pungent aftershave introduced himself as reporter Ben Byrne. He shook everyone's hand and gave Biscuit a tentative pat while his cameraman, a smiley girl called Pippa, fiddled with her camera.

'We'll do the interview first, then Pippa will get some general shots of the yard and we'll finish with a piece to camera,' Ben told them.

Biscuit watched with interest as Ben held out a microphone and said, 'Can you give us your name for the level?'

Jodie cleared her throat. 'Um. Jodie Morgan.'

'Great. And can you spell your name for the tape?'

'J-O-I-D. Sorry,' she said, shaking her head and shooting a desperate look at the others. Poppy gave her an encouraging smile and Caroline mouthed, 'You'll be fine.'

'J-O-D-I-E-M-O-R-G-A-N.'

'Wonderful. Let's get started.'

After the first couple of questions Jodie's nerves vanished and she talked animatedly about the rescue horses. Ben asked her about Biscuit and his condition when he'd arrived at Nethercote.

'The vet said he'd never make it. But Biscuit's a fighter. In fact he's as stubborn as I am. He refused to give up.' Jodie scratched the pony's forehead and he gave her an affectionate nudge. 'I promised him that if he pulled through he would never have to leave. And now I'm not sure I'll be able to keep that promise,' she said, her voice thick with emotion.

Poppy, who was standing behind the camera, could see that Pippa had zoomed in on Jodie's face, catching the single tear that slid down her cheek.

Interview over, they took Pippa on a tour of the rescue centre so she could get shots of horses grazing contentedly in the paddocks and looking over their stable doors.

'Jodie can send you some of the before pictures,' said Poppy, thinking of the photos of horses with matted coats, hollow necks, overgrown hooves and bony rumps that had had such an impact on her at the summer fete.

When Pippa had finished they returned to the yard.

'We don't need you for this bit, Jodie. I'm going to do a piece to camera telling everyone about the appeal,' said Ben.

'Why don't you hold Biscuit while you're doing it?' Pippa suggested.

Poppy untied the appaloosa and handed his lead rope to Ben, who took it gingerly.

'It's alright. He won't bite,' Jodie laughed.

Poppy darted forwards and brushed the reporter's linen jacket. He looked at her in bemusement.

'Just a bit of fluff,' she said, retreating to where Caroline, Charlie and Freddie were watching the proceedings.

Ben smoothed down his hair, glanced at his notebook and switched on his mike. Pippa squinted through the eyepiece of her camera and gave him the thumbs up. He gripped Biscuit's lead rope tightly and gave the camera a dazzling smile.

'Biscuit and his equine friends here at Nethercote Horse Rescue have been given a second chance by Jodie Morgan. But unless the rescue centre can raise more funds their future is uncertain...'

While everyone else was watching the reporter, Poppy's eyes were trained on Biscuit. *Come on*, she willed him silently. *You can do it*.

Ben was wrapping up his piece to camera when the gelding suddenly raised his head and sniffed the wind. He gave a comedy snort and turned towards the reporter. There was a glint in his eye as he gave Ben a purposeful nudge and started nibbling at his jacket. Momentarily thrown, Ben raised his eyebrows and shrugged theatrically. Biscuit, still picking at Ben's jacket, breathed in a lungful of the reporter's tangy aftershave, turned to face the camera and curled his top lip as if he was laughing his speckled head off.

Poppy held her breath as she watched Pippa focus on the appaloosa's yellow teeth. Beside her Charlie stifled a giggle. Poppy elbowed him in the ribs and held her finger to her lips. This was television gold. They'd never re-create it if they had to do a second take.

Ben had thrown his head back and was also roaring with laughter. 'And with that, it's back to you in the studio,' he spluttered, as Biscuit rolled his eyes at the camera and sneezed explosively all over the reporter's cream linen suit.

~

'THAT HORSE IS A COMIC GENIUS. You ought to get him an agent,' said Ben, as he helped Pippa heft the camera into the boot of the BMW.

'Comic genius? A total delinquent more like. I'm sorry about your jacket,' Jodie said for the umpteenth time.

'No worries. I'll get it dry cleaned on expenses.'

'What time will Jodie be on the news?' asked Charlie.

Ben checked his watch. 'Half past one and again at six thirty.'

'And you'll include the link so people can donate if they want to?' Poppy checked.

He nodded. 'I think people will be falling over themselves to help once they see Biscuit in action. He's a star in the making. I was well and truly upstaged,' he said ruefully.

~

'I BET I look like a complete and utter loser,' grumbled Jodie, as they settled in Nethercote's living room to watch the lunchtime bulletin.

'You don't need to worry. People'll be more interested in Biscuit than you,' said Charlie kindly.

'Thanks - I think.'

Poppy felt a flutter of nerves as the titles came up and the familiar soundtrack began to play. She was the one who had convinced Jodie this would work. What if it didn't? If no-one supported Biscuit's Appeal Jodie would be right back at square one. Actually worse than that. Poppy had already scuppered her money-making plan to smuggle phones into Dartmoor prison.

A willowy presenter with an improbably unlined forehead and immaculately coiffured hair swept into a chignon was sitting on a red sofa. She shuffled some papers on her lap and looked up as the titles ended. Poppy's mind wandered as the presenter read the headlines with a practised smile.

'- but first we go to a Devon horse sanctuary that needs your help. Ben Byrne reports.'

The camera cut to the main paddock where the plump, sleek Nethercote horses grazed serenely under a canopy of ancient oak trees, and then cut again to Ben's interview with Jodie, which was peppered with some of the less graphic photographs of the rescue horses. Jodie scowled when the camera zoomed in on the tear rolling down her cheek.

'Why did they have to show that?'

'It makes great television,' said Caroline.

Poppy's phone buzzed with a text from Scarlett.

OMG Poppy, you need to turn on the telly like NOW!! Jodie's on Spotlight!

I know, Poppy tapped back. *I fixed it.*

I'm recording it so I can show Red later.

You're nuts. He's not a human you know.

Yes he is!! Hey wait a minute, what d'you mean you fixed it?

Poppy grinned to herself. *It's a long story,* she tapped back. *Tell you later.*

Ben was now with Biscuit, doing his piece to camera.

'What I don't get is why he started eating Ben's jacket,' said Jodie.

Poppy absentmindedly fingered the packet of Polos in her jeans. She'd slipped one into the reporter's pocket when she'd pretended to dust off the piece of fluff, hoping that Biscuit would sniff it out. What she hadn't bargained for was the potency of Ben's aftershave, which had prompted the gelding to flash his teeth to the world.

'I never knew horses could laugh until Biscuit did that,' said Charlie.

'He's not laughing. It's called the flehmen response. I read it in my pony magazine,' Poppy said. 'When horses smell something they're not sure about they curl back their upper lips and breathe in with their nostrils closed. It must have been Ben's aftershave.'

'I'm not surprised Biscuit didn't like it. It was totally yuck,' Charlie said.

The appaloosa's reaction to the reporter looked even funnier on television. Even the presenter was hooting with laughter by the time Ben handed back to the studio.

'And they've remembered to include the link to the website,' said Caroline. 'I'd say that was a job well done.'

21

Slivers of sunlight stole through a gap in Poppy's curtains and danced on her closed eyelids with dogged determination, willing her to wake up. She yawned, stretched her arms above her head and rotated her bad ankle. Relieved to discover it was well and truly on the mend, she reached for her phone and tried to open the Nethercote website.

Large red letters told her the server application was unavailable. She hit refresh but the page failed to load. Poppy stabbed at the refresh button a couple more times before texting Jodie.

What's happened to the website? It won't load.

Her phone beeped within seconds.

Damn thing's crashed. No idea why.

A smile crept across Poppy's face. She had a sneaking suspicion. And if she was right it could only be good news for Nethercote. She Googled the rescue centre and half a dozen stories appeared. Biscuit had made headlines in the Daily Mail, the Daily Mirror and even a couple of the broadsheets. A clip of Spotlight's news item on YouTube had been viewed just over nine thousand times. Poppy checked the Daily Mail's Facebook page. The story had been shared by almost three hundred people. She typed #Biscuit into Google. Dozens more tweets, posts and Instagram tags popped up. She sighed with satisfaction. Her plan had worked. She was a public relations genius. Biscuit the Laughing Horse had gone viral.

~

POPPY CANTERED Cloud across the field to Ashworthy, humming happily to herself. Caroline had taken a bit of convincing that her ankle was OK to ride but had finally relented when Poppy had promised she'd hack out with Scarlett and Red. Soon the two girls were heading out across the moor.

'The YouTube views went up by almost fifteen hundred in the time it took me to eat my breakfast,' Poppy told Scarlett.

'That's amazing. But no-one will be able to donate if the website's crashed.'

'It's back up and running now. Jodie said donations have already reached twenty eight thousand but they're still pouring in. Channel 5 is sending a reporter over this afternoon and ITN is doing an outside broadcast from Nethercote this evening.'

'Better tell Jodie to wear lots of perfume,' Scarlett said.

'I can't imagine her smothering herself in Christian Dior, can you? She's more like us. Prefers Eau de Horse,' Poppy giggled.

Scarlett ran her hand along Red's neck. The gelding's chestnut coat gleamed.

'Did you give him another bath this morning?'

'Just a quick one to get rid of his stable stains. It's quite exhausting, keeping him spotless,' Scarlett admitted.

Poppy looked down at the grass stains on Cloud's front legs. 'Why don't you chill out? A few stable stains aren't going to kill him.'

'I know.' Scarlett was silent for a while. Then, as they skirted the base of the Riverdale tor, she said, 'Where are we going to go?'

'We need to ride to Witch Cottage. There's something I need to do.'

Scarlett groaned. 'But I hate it there, you know that.'

'It's just a derelict old cottage, Scar. Stones and mortar. There are no ghosts.'

'So why are we going?'

Poppy wondered where to start. She had a feeling that, in her excitement over Red, Scarlett had all but forgotten the existence of the phones Poppy had discovered hidden under the green tarpaulin in the croft's tiny attic. She may have realised that they were the ones stolen from the warehouse in Plymouth. But Poppy knew for certain that she had no clue they had been destined for the prison, and that Jodie had been pivotal in the whole shady enterprise.

Poppy and Scarlett now had to accidentally stumble across the cache of phones, paste on innocent faces and report their find to the police, as Poppy had promised Jodie she would.

'Poppy,' Scarlett repeated. 'Why do we need to go to Witch Cottage?'

'I'll tell you when we get there.'

The warm summer breeze tickled Cloud's silver mane and he snatched at the bit. His excitement was infectious. Poppy felt giddy with relief. As though it was seven o'clock on Christmas morning. Or the first day of the summer holidays. Everything had worked out just fine. Better than fine. Absolutely gobsmackingly brilliantly. And who could have guessed, a week ago, that Nethercote would be saved by an amazing, courageous, laughing horse?

The wiry moorland grass felt springy and perfect for a canter. Poppy kicked Cloud on. Red caught up with the Connemara in a couple of strides and soon the two ponies, one dappled grey, the other the colour of butterscotch, were galloping neck and neck towards Witch Cottage.

As they raced across the moor, their ponies' tails streaming like banners behind them, Poppy imagined Caitlyn and Jodie making the same journey on a warm summer's morning just like this one, their destination a tumbledown cottage with a teardrop-shaped tarn, a catslide roof and secrets woven into its granite walls.

Poppy glanced at her best friend. Scarlett must have sensed her gaze as she turned her head. Her hazel eyes sparkled.

'It feels like we're off on an adventure!' she cried.

Poppy, who was crouching low over Cloud's neck as he covered the ground in long, easy strides, couldn't help but agree. One adventure was over, but she was pretty sure there was another waiting for them, just beyond the vast Dartmoor horizon. And she couldn't wait.

MISSING ON THE MOOR

1

Poppy McKeever stared into the bathroom mirror and a ghost girl stared back. A ghost girl with an ashen face and hollow eyes, tinged with pink, like an albino rat in an animal testing laboratory. She grimaced as she registered the dark purple shadows under her bloodshot eyes and her straggly, dull brown hair, scraped back into an untidy ponytail. A wave of nausea rolled over her and she clung onto the rim of the basin until it passed.

'You look *terrible*,' piped a voice behind her.

Poppy turned to see her brother on the landing.

'I love you, too,' Poppy said, but her sarcasm was lost on eight-year-old Charlie, who was staring at her in fascination. She ran a flannel under the cold tap and pressed it to her face.

'You look like a zombie. One of those scary undead people who go around terrifying everyone. But Halloween was ages ago. Oh, wait, it's not a getup, it's really you,' he smirked.

Poppy shook the flannel in Charlie's direction but he ducked out of the way.

'Only joking, sis. You don't really look like a zombie. Shall I get Mum?'

The queasiness returned and Poppy held her hand over her mouth.

Charlie, who despite his daredevil attitude to life was as squeamish as a sissy, backed down the landing with a look of horror on his face. Soon he was crashing down the stairs three at a time, yelling for Caroline.

Her stepmum ran upstairs with a roll of kitchen towel, an orange bucket and a concerned expression on her face.

'Are you poorly, today of all days? What bad luck.'

Poppy nodded mutely. Caroline felt her forehead and frowned. 'You don't have a temperature. Come and sit down and tell me your symptoms.'

She led Poppy into her room and they perched together on the bed, the bucket on the floor between them.

'I couldn't sleep last night. I was awake for hours just staring at the ceiling. And then when I got up my heart was racing and my hands were shaking. Look!' Poppy held out her hands to show Caroline her trembling fingers. 'Charlie says I look like the walking dead. And I feel really sick. My tummy's turning somersaults. I think I've got gastric flu.'

A look of understanding flitted across Caroline's face. She took Poppy's hands in hers. 'Have a shower and get dressed. You'll be absolutely fine once you get going.'

'Are you mad? I can't go to Claydon Manor like this. I'm on death's door!' Poppy shrieked.

Caroline patted Poppy's thigh and stood up.

'I was exactly the same on the morning of my first show. It's not gastric flu, sweetheart. It's nerves.'

POPPY PULLED on her thickest fleece, filled a bucket with warm water and let herself out of the back door. A blast of cold air hit her in the face and she breathed deeply, as Caroline had instructed her to do whenever she felt anxiety begin to worm its way back into her stomach. She felt a bit sheepish that she'd let her nerves get such a grip and she marched over to the stables, determined not to let them ruin her big day.

Cloud and Chester watched from their stable as she set the bucket down and kissed them both on their peachy-soft muzzles. Cloud blew warm air into her face and Chester banged his leg against the door, impatient for his breakfast.

Poppy gave the donkey's ear an affectionate tug and disappeared into the tack room to mix their feeds. While they ate she filled two haynets and studied the list she'd written the evening before.

'Feed by seven at the latest,' she read, checking her watch. It was five to. She was on schedule. 'Fill haynets. Groom and plait. Pack grooming kit and tack. Don't forget water bucket. Put on travel rug and boots.'

'I don't think they'll fit you,' said an amused voice, making her jump.

'Tory!' cried Poppy.

Her old friend was in the doorway, leaning on her crutches. Poppy hugged her. Tory smelt of lavender and toast, as she always did.

'You said you were meeting us there!'

'I thought you might like some moral support. How are the nerves?'

Poppy gave the glimmer of a smile. 'The nerves are doing just great. It's me I'm worried about.'

'You'll be fine,' said Tory, making herself comfortable on an old wooden bench. 'Which class have you entered?'

'The novice jumping. It's two foot three!' Poppy felt another flutter of anxiety and took two deep breaths.

'You've been jumping courses much bigger than that with Bella, haven't you?' said Tory.

Poppy nodded.

'Well then, it'll be an absolute breeze, won't it Cloud?'

Hearing his name the Connemara poked his handsome head over the stable door and whickered. Poppy put his headcollar on and led him out of the stable. She'd groomed him until he'd shone the evening before but wanted to rinse off the stable stains on his legs and give him one final brush over before she tackled his mane.

'What time's Bill due?' Tory asked.

'Eight o'clock. I expect Scarlett's been up for hours getting Red ready.' Poppy knew her best friend wanted the former rescue pony looking his absolute best for their first show together. 'She texted me this morning in a panic because Jodie's announced she's coming to watch.'

Jodie Morgan owned Nethercote Horse Rescue, Red's old home. Forthright and not one to suffer fools gladly, Jodie had turned her back on her own showjumping dreams to run the horse sanctuary single-handedly. No wonder Scarlett was nervous at the prospect of jumping in front of her.

Poppy divided Cloud's mane into sections and secured them with elastic bands. She tapped each one, counting them in her head. 'Thirteen!' she cried.

'I thought Scarlett was the superstitious one,' said Tory.

'You're right, she is,' Poppy admitted. 'I'm being an idiot. It's only a number.' She began plaiting the sections as neatly as she could.

Charlie appeared with two mugs of tea and sat down next to Tory.

'I've got some news for you both,' Tory announced. 'You know the Christmas Eve Nativity service at St Mary's?'

The two children nodded. A team of volunteers worked for days creating a Bethlehem-like stable at the front of the church and real animals were drafted in to make the Nativity scene as authentic as possible.

'Rusty, the old donkey who's been appearing since before I can remember, has officially retired, so Reverend Kirton has decided to hold open auditions to find a new star for this year's service.'

Charlie leant forward, his eyes shining. 'Donkey auditions?'

'That's right,' said Tory. 'They're being held at the church after the service next Sunday. I thought you might want to take Chester.'

'You bet we would!' said Charlie. 'He'd be perfect. He's always really calm and he loves attention. And he wouldn't go to the toilet just when the Wise Men arrived like Rusty did last year.'

Tory took a sip of her tea. 'Good. I told Annette you'd bring him. She was delighted.'

Charlie screwed his face up. 'Wait a minute. Did you say Reverend Kirton's name was Annette?'

'Yes, why?'

A grin spread across his face. 'Annette Kirton,' he sniggered.

Tory and Poppy looked at him blankly.

Charlie was laughing hard. 'Come on, you two. Don't you get it? Annette *Kirton*.'

'Yes, very funny. But don't go taking the mickey out of her name at the audition. You'll ruin Chester's chances,' said Poppy.

'You're no fun,' he said, heading back indoors humming *Away in a Manger*.

Poppy curled up the final plait and wound the last elastic band around it several times to secure it. After oiling Cloud's hooves she gave him a quick blast of shine spray and stood back to admire her handiwork.

'You've done a beautiful job,' said Tory. 'Seeing him all plaited and gleaming takes me right back.'

Poppy thought she could detect a catch in Tory's voice. Small wonder. It must have been a morning just like this that had ended in disaster when Cloud had fallen at a drop fence during a hunter trial in Widecombe, throwing Tory's granddaughter Caitlyn beneath him.

An unwelcome thought occurred to her. 'This is his first proper competition since Widecombe, isn't it?'

'I suppose it is,' said Tory.

Poppy licked her lips. 'D'you think he'll be OK?'

Tory patted the seat beside her. 'I'm sure he will. He used to love competing. They both did.'

Poppy leant against Tory and gazed at her pony, trying to see him through a stranger's eyes. Cloud's dappled grey coat shone and he was muscled and fit. He looked every inch the superstar pony he was. They'd purposefully picked a novice class even though Cloud could have jumped it in his sleep. And she knew he'd look after her - he always did.

Poppy stretched out her fingers. They weren't trembling any more. And the butterflies had disappeared. Her phone beeped with a text from Scarlett.

'They're on their way,' she said.

Tory heaved herself to her feet. 'All set?' she asked.

Poppy felt a flutter in her stomach. But it was excitement, not nerves. She grinned.

'You bet. We can do this, can't we Cloud? Today Claydon Manor, tomorrow the world!'

2

_____

Poppy felt her nerves resurface as Scarlett's dad steered the Land Rover through Claydon Manor's imposing wrought iron gates.

'I suppose Georgia will be lording it over everyone as usual,' grumbled Scarlett, who was studying the schedule. 'How come they're holding unaffiliated and affiliated classes at the same show, anyway?'

'It's a trial, to see if it works. That's what Bella said.'

'And why's she not holding it at Redhall?'

'Because she's got builders in repairing the roof of the indoor school,' Poppy reminded her.

Scarlett tutted. 'I'm surprised the Cannings are letting the hoi polloi in, what with all the security there usually is around here.'

Poppy glanced at the beautiful grey stone Georgian manor house in the distance and the immaculate paddocks on either side of its sweeping gravelled drive.

'How on earth do they manage to keep their fields looking so perfect?' she wondered. 'Ours are a quagmire. I lost my welly in the mud yesterday.'

'It's because they have the money to throw at it, of course,' said Scarlett darkly.

Poppy sighed inwardly. She loved her best friend to bits, but there was no stopping her once she got started on the unfairness of the fact that Georgia Canning's parents had won the lottery and hers hadn't.

'What time's Sam's class?' Poppy asked her, hoping to change the subject.

'Eleven o'clock.' Scarlett gave Poppy a sidelong look. 'Why, d'you want to stay and watch?'

Poppy felt her face grow hot. She shrugged. 'I guess we might as well, as we're here.'

'Georgia'll be jumping in the same class on her ten thousand pound pony, no doubt,' said Scarlett.

'Give it a rest, Scar,' said Poppy, winding down the window and fanning the cool air into her face.

But Scarlett was still bellyaching about the Cannings when they pulled in next to a compact red horsebox on an expanse of hardstanding beside Claydon's huge wooden-slatted indoor arena.

Poppy had only been to one horse show before, and that was at Redhall Manor Equestrian Centre, where she and Scarlett had their weekly lessons with Redhall's indomitable owner, Bella Thompson. She'd only gone to watch and she still remembered how in awe she'd felt of the competitors as they'd stalked around in their bone white jodhpurs and midnight blue show jackets, laughing and chatting to each other like they were members of some exclusive club the rest of the population could only dream of joining. Poppy had stood on the sidelines, drinking it all in and wondering if she'd ever be included.

Now she had her own navy jacket, which was in the back of the Land Rover with her new white jodhpurs. OK, so they were both second-hand - Poppy preferred to call them *pre-loved* - but every time she'd tried them on in front of the mirror with her polished jodhpur boots she'd felt a step closer to joining the select few.

She surreptitiously practised the graceful smile she'd give as she bowed and accepted a red rosette from the judge before kicking Cloud into a canter and flying around the ring. There would be cheers from the spectators and approving nods from her fellow competitors.

With a win at her first ever show she might finally stop feeling inferior to Caitlyn.

Scarlett elbowed her in the ribs, bringing her back to earth with a bump.

'Stop daydreaming, Poppy. We need to get the ponies sorted and go and walk the course.'

~

CLAYDON MANOR WAS BUZZING. Everywhere Poppy looked riders were giving their ponies a final brush, tacking up or pinning numbers to their jackets. The place was ringing with noisy chatter and the occasional whinny. Poppy caught a whiff of hot dogs and fried onions and her stomach rumbled loudly.

Cloud stopped halfway down the ramp of the trailer, his head high and his nostrils flared. Poppy gave the lead rope a gentle tug and clicked her tongue. 'Come on baby, it's just a show. There's nothing to worry about.'

He lowered his head and gave her a nudge.

'I know. I should take my own advice,' Poppy said, tying him up next to Red.

Satisfied their ponies were happy munching their haynets the two girls headed for the indoor arena. They were just passing the outdoor school, which was being used as the warm-up area, when they almost walked into Georgia Canning.

Already in her white jodhpurs and show jacket and staring disdainfully at the anaemic-looking hot dog she was holding, Georgia looked them up and down.

'I thought you might be here,' she said, addressing Poppy. 'Are you jumping in the novice class?'

Poppy, who could feel Scarlett bristling beside her, nodded. She smiled, feeling the need to overcompensate for her best friend's obvious hostility. The show would have been cancelled if the Cannings hadn't offered the use of their yard, after all. 'It's my first show. Do you have any insider information?'

'I certainly do. Don't go near the hot dog stand. I swear this thing's raw.' Georgia held the sad-looking sausage and its doughy coffin at arm's length. 'The couple running it were completely clueless. I shall probably go down with food poisoning.'

'She meant insider information about the *course*, not the *food*,' Scarlett said scathingly.

Georgia fixed her cornflower-blue eyes on Scarlett, looked over her shoulder and leaned in conspiratorially. 'Ah, you want insider information on the *course*. Silly me. Well, it's about so high,' she held out the hot dog just below waist height. 'It starts with the first fence and ends with the last and there are a few more in between.'

With that she tossed her hot dog over her shoulder and stalked off towards the stables.

'Flippin' hilarious,' growled Scarlett. 'Who the hell does she think she is?'

Poppy tugged her best friend's arm. 'Ignore her, she was just winding you up. Come on, let's go and walk this course.'

POPPY TOOK one look at the brightly painted showjumps in Claydon Manor's imposing indoor arena and froze.

'I can't do it!' she hissed. 'They're enormous!'

Scarlett peered into the arena. 'They're two foot three,' she said patiently. 'You've been jumping three foot three in our lessons. You'll be fine. Just take a deep breath, put on your game face and come and walk the course. You'll see they're not so bad.'

'It's alright for you. You've done loads of shows.'

'I might have, but this is Red's first time, remember. I know it's your first show, but Cloud is an old pro. That makes us even.'

'But -'

'Poppy, you've been working towards this for weeks. You can't wimp out now,' Scarlett said firmly. She looked over Poppy's shoulder and began waving frantically. 'Thank goodness. Bella's here. She might be able to talk some sense into you.'

Poppy turned to see her riding instructor bearing down on them. Bella was in her trademark wax jacket, tweed skirt and wellies, topped off with a headscarf. This one, Poppy noticed, was decorated with eggbutt snaffles.

'How does the course look?' Bella bellowed.

'I wouldn't know. Poppy's refusing to walk it,' said Scarlett.

Bella raised her eyebrows. 'What do you mean?'

Poppy looked beseechingly at her. 'I don't think I can do it.'

'Nonsense! Of course you can. Come on, I'll walk it with you,' she said, steering Poppy into the arena before she had a chance to protest.

Poppy practised her deep breathing as she followed Bella and Scarlett around the course. The first jump was a red and white upright. Poppy had to admit that it looked straightforward enough. A right turn to another upright followed by a small oxer, then right again to a set of planks and a brush and rails.

Jump six was the first double. Poppy followed Scarlett and Bella's lead and counted the strides between the two fences. Eight of her strides. Was that one or two of Cloud's? She racked her brain but for the life of her couldn't remember. It was as if her head had been tipped on one side and every single brain cell had fallen out of her ear.

Fortunately Scarlett saved her. 'That's good. It's a perfect single stride for our boys,' she said.

They turned left to a wall followed by an upright. Two girls with ringing public school voices and an air of self-assurance Poppy could only dream of breezed past them to jump nine, a parallel bar painted in sky blue and primrose yellow. They were exactly the kind of girls Poppy had felt so in awe of at the Redhall show. Girls who had been given their first ponies before they were two and had probably hunted before they started at their expensive prep schools. She knew she shouldn't feel inferior. She just couldn't help herself.

Distracted by their casual confidence, she stopped looking where she was going and cannoned into the wing of the blue and yellow jump, knocking it flying.

'Sorry sorry sorry,' she gabbled as an irritable-looking show steward bustled over and began replacing the fallen poles. Poppy blushed at her ineptitude. But if she was worried what the two girls might think she needn't have bothered - they were so deep in conversation they didn't even look in her direction.

'Come on, clumsy,' said Scarlett, linking arms with her and leading her to the next jump, a frighteningly solid-looking gate. Poppy was about to give it a rattle in its cups but stopped herself just in time. Knowing her luck she'd send it flying, too.

'You need to change reins for the last three,' said Bella, marching over to a blue and white upright that was followed by the second double of the course. Poppy counted her strides. 'Eight for me, one for Cloud,' she muttered.

'Don't forget to wait for the starting bell otherwise you'll be eliminated,' Bella continued. 'And remember to go through the finish line. So, have you any questions?'

'Can I go home now, please?' said Poppy, worried she'd already forgotten the course.

Bella tutted. 'There's no need to be nervous. Angela has done a good job. It's a lovely inviting course with nice easy turns. Just remember not to rush the planks and keep nice and balanced for the two combinations. Why don't you girls go and find your ponies? I'll ask Sam to put up a couple of practice jumps for you if you like.'

The ritual of tacking up, putting on her hat, tightening Cloud's girth and running the stirrups down helped damp down Poppy's anxiety and she felt even better once she was in the saddle. Cloud felt solid and familiar. She was also relieved that he seemed to be taking everything in his stride, whereas Red, normally so laid-back, was fizzing like a bath bomb and had already worked himself into a sweat. Scarlett was struggling to keep the rangy chestnut calm as they walked over to the outdoor school.

'There's Sam,' Poppy said, spotting Bella's grandson's blond head by the entrance. He was watching one of the posh girls cantering her dark bay mare around the school. Poppy hadn't seen Sam for a couple of months. She was taken aback to see that he seemed to have grown half a foot in that time. His face was different, too. More angular, less boyish. But when he saw them he grinned like a loon and loped over. Poppy found herself smiling back, despite her somersaulting stomach.

'Hey, you two,' he said. 'Gran's sent me over to sort you out. We'll start with some circles in trot and canter, shall we?'

As Poppy asked Cloud for a trot, she heard Scarlett muttering, 'What's your name, Bella Thompson?' and then cursing loudly as Red shied at the red wing of one of the practice fences.

With half a dozen other riders all warming up in the same school Poppy knew she needed to blank everyone else out. They circled on both reins until Cloud was listening to her aids and working in a nice outline. Poppy sat deeply in the saddle for a couple of strides and squeezed him into a canter.

'I'll put up a cross-pole,' called Sam. Poppy checked Cloud and he popped over the little jump with ease. Red crabbed up to the fence and, at the last minute, sprang forwards and leapt over it with feet to spare. The chestnut gelding gave a joyful buck. Scarlett, to her credit, hardly moved in the saddle.

By the time they'd both jumped a small upright on each leg Bella had reappeared.

'I've just been over to the collecting ring. The class is about to start. Scarlett, you're fifth to jump and Poppy, you're seventh. Walk them on a long rein for five minutes to give them a breather and then you'd better make your way over.'

Sam ran his hand down Cloud's neck and the Connemara nibbled the pockets of his jeans. 'Still nervous?' he asked Poppy.

'Utterly terrified,' she admitted.

He brushed a fleck of mud from her jodhpurs. 'You've really no need to be, Poppy. You're a great rider. We all think so. It's a shame you're the only one who can't see it.'

3

Buoyed by Sam's words, Poppy headed for the collecting ring. *You're a great rider*, he'd said. Did he mean it, or was he just being kind, trying to boost her confidence before she went into the ring? True, he'd let her ride Star, his prizewinning jumping pony, on more than one occasion. And he'd made it clear he didn't let just anyone ride her. He'd once described Poppy as a quiet rider. She hadn't known if that was good or bad. Surely quiet riders were feeble and ineffectual? But Bella had told her it was a compliment.

Cloud broke into a jog and Poppy tightened her reins. The last thing she needed was to fall off in front of everyone because she wasn't concentrating. She checked the Connemara, who snatched at the bit, impatient to jump.

'There you are,' said Caroline, appearing from behind a horse trailer. 'I've been looking for you everywhere. I've left Charlie and Tory in the spectators' gallery. Your class has just started.' She looked around. 'Where's Scarlett?'

'Gone to get her gloves. She won't be a minute.'

Caroline regarded her, her hands on her hips. 'You and Cloud look amazing. Like you've been competing together all your lives.'

Poppy gave her stepmum a grateful smile. She always knew exactly the right thing to say.

'Break a leg,' Caroline added. Then she clutched her head and grimaced. 'What a crazy thing to say. *Don't* break a leg. In fact, don't break anything. Go out there and jump your hearts out, both of you.'

Poppy was giggling despite her nerves. 'OK boss, we will.'

THERE WERE ELEVEN in the novice class, which was for ponies up to 148cm, or 14.2hh in old money, as Tory was fond of saying.

The first pair to jump, a skinny girl with a long, blonde plait and an excitable dun pony, whizzed around the course but in their haste knocked down both the planks and the gate.

'That's the trouble when you let your pony flatten,' said Bella in a voice loud enough to be heard in Tavistock. A woman clasping a sweat rug gave her a filthy look and Poppy could see Sam cringing. Bella had many attributes. Diplomacy was not one of them.

The second rider was a girl in Poppy and Scarlett's year at school. Her skewbald gelding looked balanced and focused as they trotted calmly into the ring.

'Good luck,' Scarlett called.

'I don't think she's going to need it,' said Poppy. And she was right. The skewbald jumped a faultless clear round.

'That's the one to beat,' bellowed Bella.

Two more riders had four faults apiece and then it was Scarlett's turn to jump. Poppy gave her the thumbs up and Bella gave Red such a hearty pat on the rump that he shot into the ring like a stone in one of Charlie's homemade catapults.

'I'm not going to put any pressure on him. I want him to enjoy today,' Scarlett had told Poppy as they'd tacked up. Poppy noticed how her best friend let the chestnut gelding have a good look at the fillers as she trotted him around the ring, waiting for the starting bell to sound.

When it did Scarlett squeezed Red into a canter and turned him towards the first fence. His chestnut ears were pricked as he leapt over it. He took off on the wrong leg but it didn't faze Scarlett, who slowed him to a trot and then asked him to canter on the right leg. Red popped over the second and third fences like an old pro but hesitated at the planks, which were painted in a garish green and red.

'Come on, kiddo,' said Scarlett and he made an enormous cat-leap over the jump to the amusement of the spectators. Scarlett checked him and he jumped the brush and rails neatly, his white socks tucked into his chest.

Poppy realised she was holding her breath as Red cantered towards the double. She could see he was getting strong. Scarlett did her best to bring him back on the bit but he misjudged his stride and knocked down the first part of the double.

'That's a shame. They were doing so well,' said a familiar voice. Jodie Morgan had slipped into the collecting ring to watch Red's round.

'How's Biscuit?' Poppy asked, her eyes still on Scarlett and Red as they popped over the wall. Biscuit was an adorable appaloosa pony who'd helped save Jodie's horse rescue centre from bankruptcy that summer when he was filmed by the local television station and his story went viral.

'The Mail on Sunday is sending Liz Jones over next week to write a feature on him. "A day in the life of Nethercote's famous laughing horse",' said Jodie, her gloved hands sketching apostrophes in the air.

'Don't knock it. All publicity is good publicity,' Poppy reminded her. 'Think of your winter food bill.'

They groaned as Red knocked down the second part of the final double. But Scarlett was beaming as she cantered out of the ring.

'Eight faults in his first ever class! He's such a clever boy,' she said. Even Jodie, who rarely showed her feelings, was smiling.

'Number forty-seven!' shouted the collecting ring steward and the posh girl on the dark bay gelding trotted past them into the ring. Poppy walked Cloud around in circles, trying to steady her racing pulse.

'And that's four faults for Fiona Cavanagh-Smythe,' announced the

Tannoy what seemed like seconds later. 'And next to jump we have number thirty-two, Poppy McKeever riding Cloud Nine!'

Poppy looked around her in horror. After all the hard work, the endless jumping lessons, the books on riding techniques she'd pored over and the hours spent getting ready, and her worst nightmare had come true.

She looked at Scarlett in horror.

'I've forgotten the course!'

4

———————

Scarlett rode Red alongside Cloud and gave Poppy's arm a gentle squeeze.

'No, you haven't. Picture us walking it together. It'll come back to you once you start, I promise. And forget all about the people watching. It's just you and Cloud out there, OK? You can do it, Poppy.'

Poppy rammed her hat down low on her forehead and took a deep breath. Scarlett was right. She could do this. She kicked Cloud into a canter, nearly knocking the collecting ring steward flying. The lights in the arena seemed bright after the murky December weather outside and it took a moment for Poppy's eyes to adjust. She slowed Cloud to a trot and dipped her head at the judge, as she'd seen the other riders do. Her eyes scoured the arena for the first jump, the red and white upright. But which jump was next? Poppy forced herself to concentrate. Scarlett had held out her right arm as she'd measured the related distance to the green and white upright. Of course. And then the spread and a right turn to the planks. She could remember after all!

Poppy sat tall in the saddle and fixed her eyes on the first fence, as Bella had taught her to do. The starting bell sounded and she asked Cloud for a canter. His ears pricked, he met the upright perfectly. He landed neatly and Poppy turned him towards the green and white upright and the spread.

'Steady,' Poppy murmured as they approached the planks. But she needn't have worried. Cloud flew over with inches to spare. Mid-air, Poppy remembered they were changing direction and squeezed her left rein. The Connemara landed on the left leg and popped over the brush and rails as if it was a fallen log on the moor.

Four strides to the double, which Cloud cleared easily, and then a left turn to the wall. Poppy folded forwards, allowing her hands to go with him as he stretched over the jump.

For a second, as they landed, Poppy couldn't remember which jump was next, the white upright with the red fillers or the blue and white upright three strides before the double. Just in time she remembered and pointed Cloud at the white jump. Three long strides or four short ones to the blue and yellow parallel bar. Poppy opted for three and pushed Cloud on. He took off early and Poppy held her breath as his back legs rattled the pole in the cups. But it was their lucky day. The pole stayed where it was.

Jump ten was the solid-looking gate. Poppy pretended it was the small wattle gate she'd set up in Cloud and Chester's field as part of her homemade cross country course. Cloud jumped it easily. And then another left turn to the final three jumps, set up like a line of gridwork. Poppy remembered not to look down as Cloud jumped the first. Once he'd landed she sat down in the saddle and used her seat to push him forwards and he soared over the double.

Poppy shook her head in amazement as they cantered through the finish line. A clear round at their first show together! Her heart bursting with pride, she jumped off Cloud the minute they left the ring and threw her arms around him. Her legs felt as wobbly as pipe cleaners as the adrenalin flooded out of her system and she clung to her pony for support as first Bella and then Caroline, Scarlett, Sam, Tory, Charlie and Jodie all came up and clapped her on the shoulder and told her what a brilliant round it had been.

Poppy could have stayed where she was for several days, basking in all the attention, but the harassed-looking collecting ring steward marched over and asked them to move out of the way. Poppy ran up her stirrups and loosened Cloud's girth.

'I'll walk him around for you so you can go with Gran to look at the jump-off course,' said Sam, appearing by her side.

Poppy stared at him, wide-eyed. In her excitement she'd clean forgotten she would be jumping again, this time against the clock. She gave Cloud one last hug and watched Sam lead him away before following Bella and Scarlett to the spectators' gallery.

'There are only four clear rounds,' said Bella, as they leant on the rails and watched the stewards raise some fences and dismantle others. 'You jump the first then gallop to the third. The fourth and fifth are as before then it's a tight turn to the ninth.'

'Which one's that?' said Poppy, who was finding it hard to follow where Bella was pointing.

'The blue and yellow parallel bar that you demolished earlier,' said Scarlett helpfully.

'You can really make up some time with a tight turn to the gate, then it's a gallop down to the last two jumps. But don't let him flatten, whatever you do,' said Bella.

Poppy imagined she was riding the course. Ten fences. Nine if you were being pedantic. They all looked enormous.

'They've put them up at least four holes,' she groaned.

'They just look big because you're at ground level. Once you're in the saddle they'll look positively tiny,' said Scarlett.

Poppy was unconvinced.

'You're second to jump,' Bella announced. 'You'd better go and find your pony.'

ONCE AGAIN POPPY waited in the collecting ring, trying to contain her nerves. The girl on the skewbald cantered out to a round of applause.

'And a second clear round from Lucy White and Patchwork in a time of fifty-nine seconds,' announced the Tannoy.

'Good luck!' called Lucy as she passed.

Poppy smiled her thanks and clicked her tongue. Cloud trotted merrily into the ring. He was so obviously enjoying himself that Poppy felt her nerves melt away.

The bell went and they cantered towards the first jump. Safely over it, Cloud lengthened his stride to the third. Poppy checked him so he was back on his hocks in time to jump the planks. Four strides to the brush and rails and then the Connemara turned on a sixpence to jump the blue and yellow parallel bar. Poppy sat back in the saddle and pulled him sharply to the left. Too late she realised she'd set him an impossible task. The angle they were approaching the gate was too tight. She half expected him to run out. But Cloud had the heart of a lion and he took off so close to the wing that Poppy clipped it with her boot.

It was enough to send the gate crashing to the ground. Poppy resisted the urge to look back and instead focused on maintaining her contact and looking for the next jump. They met the blue and white upright perfectly and flew over the double.

'Four faults for Poppy McKeever and Cloud Nine in an impressive time of fifty-two seconds,' crackled the Tannoy. Euphoria swept through Poppy as they cantered out of the ring.

Sam and Scarlett were waiting for her in the collecting ring.

'Bad luck,' commiserated Scarlett.

'Never mind,' said Sam, feeling in his pocket for a handful of pony nuts.

'Never mind?' said Poppy, her face flushed. 'That was brilliant! The gate was totally my fault but Cloud jumped like an angel. We made the jump-off. Who cares if we had four faults. I feel like a proper rider at last.'

Realising her voice had gone all squeaky, she slithered off Cloud and buried her face in his neck, drinking in the heady smell of sweaty horse. Scarlett watched in astonishment as she took off her hat and ran up her stirrups.

'What on earth are you doing?'

'Taking Cloud back to the trailer, what else?' said Poppy.

'You twit! You're going to come at least fourth. And by the sound of that,' - they listened to the thud of crashing poles echoing around the indoor arena - 'probably third. Get back on and go and get your first rosette.'

'Alright, bossy knickers,' countered Poppy. But a big grin had spread across her face and she rammed on her hat and jumped back into the saddle without another word.

Bella appeared beside them.

'There were two clear rounds in the end, and someone else had four faults too. But yours was the fastest time by seven seconds. Well done, Poppy. You came third.'

5

Poppy knew she would remember cantering around the indoor arena for her first ever lap of honour for the rest of her life. Even if she lived to one hundred and two. In fact she would bore the other residents at her old people's home silly with stories of the day she came home with a rosette from her first ever show.

Once she was satisfied that Cloud was settled, Poppy went in search of the others. She found them in the spectators' gallery, watching the stewards build the course for the open jumping. Angela Snell, Georgia's trainer and the Claydon livery yard manager, stood in the middle of the arena, consulting a clipboard and barking instructions.

'You think I'm bossy,' said Scarlett, pointing her thumb at Angela. The woman's hair was pulled back in a severe bun and the tight set of her shoulders and her thin-lipped expression spoke of imperious impatience.

'Crikey, Sam. I thought our jumps were big, but these are enormous,' said Poppy, as the course took shape.

But Sam wasn't looking. Instead he was staring at a man with salt and pepper hair and a matching handlebar moustache who was sitting four rows behind them.

Poppy nudged him. 'Who's that?'

'Peter Frampton,' he whispered. His face had frozen. Whether it was through fear or awe, Poppy couldn't be sure.

'Who's Peter Frampton?' she whispered back.

'Only the guy who runs the British Showjumping Pony European Championships squad.' The words fell over themselves in a jumble. Sam rocked back on his seat and stared at the ceiling. 'What's he doing here?'

'Come to watch you and Georgia, I expect,' said Jodie. 'I heard on the grapevine that one of his team had moved to seniors, so he must have a space to fill.'

'Wait, that was the team you were picked for, wasn't it?' Poppy asked Jodie. 'You were going to represent Britain at the championships in Sweden.'

Jodie scowled. 'Until my dad decided to fiddle the books at work and the police seized Nero as proceeds of crime. He was my jumping pony,' she explained to Sam. 'At least you won't have to worry about that when you get picked.'

'*If* I get picked.' Sam risked another glance over his shoulder. Peter Frampton was making notes in a small, leather-bound notebook. 'Georgia's pony Barley has been jumping out of his skin all winter. They've beaten us at the last two indoor shows.'

Scarlett gave a derisive snort.

Poppy punched Sam lightly on the shoulder and stood up. 'And people tell me I'm a pessimist. Come on, we'll keep you company while you walk the course.'

~

SAM NEEDN'T HAVE WORRIED. He and Star pulled off a flawless round, flying over the enormous fences as if they were cavalettis in a pony paddock. They were the epitome of grace and style, thought Poppy, as the black Connemara mare cantered out of the ring to rapturous applause.

'When's Georgia due to jump?' Jodie asked.

'Last, I believe,' said Bella, who, like the others, was on the edge of her plastic seat.

'Typical. I bet she bribed the show organisers,' said Scarlett, loudly enough for Peter Frampton's head to jerk up.

'Scarlett!' said Poppy, shocked. 'That's not fair.'

Scarlett's hazel eyes blazed dangerously. 'Why are you sticking up for the moody madam all of a sudden?'

'You're virtually accusing her of cheating without one iota of evidence. You can't do that.'

'Why are you so bothered? She's a spoilt little rich girl who'll do anything to win.'

Keen not to ruin her perfect day with an argument with her best friend, Poppy decided to humour her. 'I'm not bothered at all,' she shrugged.

They sat and watched half a dozen more rounds in silence. Two more riders jumped clear, but neither showed Sam's flair. Charlie announced he was bored and talked Caroline into giving him money for a hot dog. Tory showed Poppy and Scarlett her sleek new mobile.

'It's a clever phone,' the old woman whispered proudly. 'My nephew gave it to me in case of emergencies.'

'Clever phone?' said Scarlett, frowning.

'It's ingenious. It has the internet and emails and everything.'

'You mean smart phone,' giggled Poppy.

'Yes, that's what I said. I just wish I could remember how to switch the damn thing on.'

POPPY WAS ATTEMPTING to show Tory how to send a text when the Tannoy echoed around the cavernous arena, 'And the last to jump is number one, Georgia Canning on her pony Pearl Barley.'

There was a faint ripple of applause and Poppy stole a look behind her. Peter Frampton was drumming his fingers on his thigh, an unreadable expression on his face.

'Trust her to be number one,' Scarlett muttered.

Poppy felt her patience snap. 'For God's sake, Scarlett, will you give it a rest? You're doing my head in. Can we please just watch the jumping?'

Scarlett's eyebrows shot upwards. 'Alright, keep your hair on. I was just saying.'

'Well, don't.'

'Where is she, anyway?'

'How would I know?' Poppy craned her neck towards the entrance, but there was no sign of Georgia or her palomino gelding. People in the spectators' gallery were beginning to fidget.

'Calling number one, Georgia Canning on Pearl Barley,' blared the Tannoy. 'This is your final call.'

'They'll be eliminated at this rate,' remarked Bella with satisfaction. They watched the collecting ring steward scuttle over to the judge and whisper urgently into his ear. The judge nodded, wrote something on his clipboard and beckoned over the other stewards who began building the jump-off course.

'I bet she heard the European squad man's here and chickened out,' said Scarlett.

'Maybe,' said Poppy. But she didn't believe it. Georgia Canning was the most competitive rider she had ever met. Her blatant desire to win radiated off her in waves. She wouldn't be put off by the fact that Peter Frampton was here. Far from it. She'd be doing everything in her power to impress him.

So where was she?

Poppy and Scarlett bumped into Charlie as they made their way back to the trailer. He was holding Freddie's lead in one hand and a triple cone ice cream in the other.

'I thought you were getting a hot dog,' said Poppy.

'The stall had gone.' Charlie took a huge mouthful of ice cream and juddered. 'Urgh. Brain freeze. How did Sam do?'

Poppy smiled. 'He walked it.'

'Someone needs to tell him he's never going to win like that.'

'You are an idiot sometimes. It means he won. Really easily. Georgia Canning was a no show.'

Charlie took another slurp of his ice cream. 'Perhaps she got food poisoning from her dodgy hot dog after all.'

6

———————

Poppy woke on the morning of the donkey auditions to a heavy hoar frost. Feathery wisps of ice like spun candyfloss clung to fences and branches and the grass was crunchy underfoot. She watched her breath unfurl like smoke from a chimney as she crossed the yard to the stables.

Charlie was already there, dressed in his pyjamas, wellies and Poppy's old parka. He had a bulging carrier bag beside him.

'What are you doing out here?' said Poppy suspiciously.

'Making Chester nice and festive for the auditions,' said Charlie, as though it was blindingly obvious.

Poppy let herself into the stable. Charlie pulled a length of silver tinsel from the bag. 'I thought this'd look nice in his mane. And I was going to try to hang a bauble from the top of his tail.'

'You're joking, right? He's not a flippin' Christmas tree,' said Poppy, rubbing the old donkey's ear.

Charlie's face fell. 'I know. I just wanted to make him stand out.'

Poppy knew how excited he was about the auditions. He had talked about little else all week.

'I don't think they had tinsel in those days, Charlie. But I tell you what, we can thread some of the tinsel around his headcollar and lead rope. How would that be?'

'That would be good,' said her brother. He eyed her hopefully. 'And maybe a couple of paperchains around his neck?'

Poppy rolled her eyes. 'Don't push your luck.'

THE AUDITIONS WERE BEING HELD in St Mary's Church after the Sunday morning service. Terrified about being late, Charlie had insisted they left Riverdale in plenty of time. As a result, the congregation was still singing a hymn as they rounded the lane to the tiny 12th century church.

Charlie let Chester graze on the verge opposite the entrance while they waited for the service to finish. He looked as pale as Poppy had on the morning of the show.

'I wonder what the competition will be like,' he said, hopping from one foot to the other.

'I can't think of any other donkeys in Waterby,' said Poppy.

'But the village website said 'Waterby *and surrounding villages*',' he fretted. 'There might be hundreds in the surrounding villages for all we know.'

'I don't suppose there are,' soothed Caroline.

'Look, here comes one,' said Poppy, pointing up the lane that led to the village shop.

Caroline and Charlie followed her gaze.

'That's not a donkey, it's a Shetland pony!' said Charlie, outraged.

'Maybe he's a method actor,' Poppy giggled. Charlie shot her a filthy look.

'Sorry Charlie. Oh look, here comes another one.'

They watched, speechless, as what was clearly two people in a slightly moth-eaten pantomime donkey suit lurched up the lane, fore and hind legs completely out of sync.

'He looks as though he's been at the Christmas sherry,' said Caroline finally. Poppy snorted loudly, causing the pantomime donkey to stand stock still and waggle his head at her.

Even Charlie was laughing when the donkey walked up to Caroline and offered her a hoof to shake.

Poppy was stroking the pantomime donkey's neck when she heard a muffled but familiar voice from inside the costume.

'My back's killing me, Scott. I need to stand up or I'll never walk upright again.'

'Sam, is that you in there?'

The donkey broke in two to reveal Sam in the hind legs and Bella's godson Scott at the front.

Sam grimaced as he stretched his back. 'Meet Delilah. As you can imagine, she was Scott's idea. Gran had the costume up in the attic. I think the last time she had an outing was before the war.'

'Hi Poppy, how's things?' said Scott, running his hands through his hair. 'And you must be Caroline and Charlie,' he said, flashing them a disarming smile.

Charlie seemed as immune to Scott's charms as Poppy had always been.

'You're here under false pretences. That's not a real donkey,' he said, pointing to Delilah's head, which was hanging lifelessly from the crook of Scott's arm.

'The poster didn't actually specify that the donkeys had to be real,' Scott pointed out.

Charlie rose to his full height. 'But that's not fair on the real donkeys!'

Sam stepped forward. 'It's OK, Charlie. We just came 'cos Scott wanted to see if we could make the front page of the Herald. We're not bothered about being in the actual Nativity, are we, Scott?' He elbowed Bella's godson in the ribs.

'God, no. I've got a hot date that night. And sorry to disappoint you, Samantha, it's not with you.'

Poppy caught Sam's eye and they exchanged a wry smile. Scott hadn't changed, it seemed.

The heavily-studded church doors swung open with a loud creak and the congregation began filing out. The last few were followed by a slim, bright-eyed woman in black vestments and a dog collar. She saw the small group waiting by the entrance and scuttled over, her hands outstretched.

'Welcome to our donkey auditions! Marvellous! I'm so pleased you could make it! As you know, our incumbent, Rusty, has retired so we are looking for someone with star quality to step into his shoes, or should I say hooves!'

Poppy couldn't help warming to Reverend Annette Kirton. She was one of those endlessly enthusiastic people whose speech was littered with exclamation marks.

'So, who do we have here? My goodness! Three lovely auditionees!' she trilled.

'I'm not sure that's actually a word,' said Poppy. But Reverend Kirton didn't hear. She was too busy shepherding Chester, the Shetland and Delilah into the church.

A car drew up outside and two men let themselves out. One was tall and stooped, the other short and stout. Poppy recognised them immediately as Henry Blossom and Sniffer Smith, the photographer and reporter from the Tavistock Herald.

Sniffer did a double take when he saw the three McKeevers. 'Small world, eh?' he said, whipping a pen from behind his ear and jotting something down in his battered notebook. Poppy had a horrible feeling it was something to do with the time she and Charlie had seen the big cat on the moor the first summer they'd moved to Riverdale. The wily old hack never missed an opportunity to embellish a story if there was a chance of flogging it to the nationals.

Henry strode over and shook their hands. 'Good to see you again. And how's that wrist of yours?' he asked Caroline.

'As good as new,' she smiled. Sniffer may have been a scheming chancer, but Henry was a genuinely nice man.

Reverend Kirton clapped her hands. 'We're all here. Wonderful! We need to know that our four-legged star is happy walking down the aisle of a packed church to the stable in front of the altar. So, if everyone not leading an auditionee can pretend to be in the congregation we'll make a start!'

'Who's going to lead us?' said a muffled voice from inside Delilah.

Poppy sighed. 'I suppose I can.' Her heart sank as Henry rattled off a couple of pictures of her holding the thin leather strap. 'You two owe me,' she hissed into the pantomime donkey's threadbare ear.

The Shetland went first. Despite his owner's best efforts he tried to nibble the flower arrangements on the end of each pew and refused point blank to walk up the two steps to the area in front of the altar.

'Well done!' said Reverend Kirton. 'Chester next, I think.'

Charlie scratched the old donkey's poll and led him quietly and without incident up the aisle. Chester stood serenely in front of the altar as if he had been attending church every Sunday all his life.

'Bravo!' cried the vicar. 'And finally, our pantomime dame, the delightful Delilah!'

Poppy gave the leather strap a vicious tug, ignoring the indignant cry from inside the costume. Delilah sashayed up the aisle as if she was on the catwalk of a Milan fashion show and when she reached the altar danced a little jig before collapsing on the stone floor in a tangle of legs.

The tiny congregation was laughing so hard at Delilah's antics that no-one heard the click of a latch. Poppy was the first to see a grey-haired man in a flat cap and a shabby Barbour jacket shove open the doors of the church. He was holding a frayed black lead rope, on the end of which was a thin grey donkey with the saddest eyes Poppy had ever seen.

The man swore loudly as the donkey registered Delilah, who was now taking a bow, and froze. He yanked the lead rope. 'Gerrup you stupid mule!' he growled, flicking the end of the rope at the donkey's bony rump. The donkey skittered forwards. The congregation fell silent.

The vicar fixed a smile to her face. 'A fourth auditionee! What a wonderful surprise!' She clapped her hands again. The donkey started shaking. 'And who have we here?'

The man shrugged. 'She don't have a name. I only picked 'er up from the market yesterday.'

'Oh!' said Reverend Kirton, for once lost for words.

Poppy stepped forward and held out her hand to the donkey, who was still quivering by the man's side.

'Female donkeys are called jennys. You could call her that,' she said softly, offering her a Polo. The donkey stretched out her neck to sniff the mint, but before she could take it the man yanked her head back.

'Hey, why did you do that?' Poppy cried. Caroline slid out of the pew and stood beside her.

'She needs to be taught some manners,' the man growled, winding the lead rope around his hand and pulling the donkey towards him.

Ignoring his filthy look, Poppy bent down and stroked the donkey's neck. She could feel how thin she was under her thick winter coat. One of her eyes was red and inflamed. It looked as though she was weeping. Poppy felt tears prick her own eyes.

Reverend Kirton finally found her voice and began telling the man what she wanted him to do. While his attention was focused on the vicar Poppy sneaked Jenny the Polo. The donkey snuffled it from her hand so gently that Poppy felt her heart break.

As she watched Jenny being dragged towards the altar she realised there was something familiar about the man's puffed out chest and wheezy voice. A memory of a grey-haired man tugged at her subconscious. A man wearing corduroy trousers and a brown hacking jacket as he talked to Hope Taylor's mum, Shelley, at the Waterby dog show.

Poppy shivered. Jenny's new owner was the man who had bought Cloud from Tory after Caitlyn was killed. The same man who had beaten the Connemara half to death after he had been rounded up in the drift. A man whose stinginess was legendary and whose cruelty had given Poppy nightmares.

Jenny's new owner was George Blackstone.

7

P oppy wrapped her coat tightly around her and huddled into the hedge as she waited for the school bus to trundle into view. The sky was granite grey and a bitterly cold wind was systematically stripping the trees of their few remaining leaves, whipping them into eddies at her feet.

She checked the time on her phone. Ten to eight. The bus was due any minute and Scarlett was nowhere to be seen. She'd miss it at this rate. As if on cue, Poppy heard the unmistakable hiss of air breaks as the bus rounded the corner.

'No Scarlett today?' asked the bus driver, a cheery woman called Val who was also secretary of the local Women's Institute.

Poppy shook her head. 'I don't think she's sick. She would have told me otherwise.'

'We'll give her a couple of minutes,' Val said, letting the engine idle.

Poppy smiled gratefully and found a seat. The window was clouded with condensation and she wiped the glass with her sleeve so she could watch for her best friend. She couldn't imagine buses in Twickenham waiting for anyone. The slower pace of life was one of the things she loved about Devon.

'Here she is,' said Val, throwing the gearstick into first.

Scarlett jumped onto the bus, her face pink with exertion. 'Thanks for waiting, Val,' she panted. Spying Poppy, she slid into the seat beside her.

'You were cutting it a bit fine,' said Poppy.

'I've run all the way. I wanted to show you this,' Scarlett said, fishing about in her school bag. 'It's today's Herald. You're famous!'

Poppy grabbed the paper and stared at the front page photo. There she was, holding Delilah the pantomime donkey's lead rope. Standing either side of them were Chester, Jenny and the Shetland.

'Sniffer Smith made us all line up for a photo at the end of the audition,' she said gloomily. 'Everyone's going to be taking the mickey at school.'

'Never mind that! You know who that is, don't you?' said Scarlett, her finger jabbing the newspaper.

'The one and only George Blackstone. I remembered seeing him talking to Shelley Taylor at the dog show. Speaking of which, I had an email from Hope this morning. She's got a two-day-a-week share in a pony at a barn near her dad's. She's so excited.'

Poppy scrolled down her phone to find the pictures of the bay gelding Hope had sent her and showed them to Scarlett.

'I also had a text from Sam.'

'Did you now?' said Scarlett, raising her eyebrows.

Poppy elbowed her best friend. 'Stop stirring. He was just letting me know he has been picked as first reserve for the Pony European Championships squad. There are six in the squad so he'll only get to travel to Denmark if one of them is dropped.'

'That's a shame.'

'He doesn't seem to mind. I think he's just pleased to make it onto the team. And there's always next year.'

'Georgia missed out. I wonder if she's recovered from her food poisoning,' said Scarlett.

'I have no idea,' said Poppy mildly. 'All I know is that I'm going to have to ride over to Claydon on Saturday to get my new gloves. I must have left them in the arena when we were watching Sam jump.'

Scarlett, who had got out a pen and was drawing horns and a beard on the photo of George Blackstone, tutted.

'Well, don't think I'm coming with you. I have absolutely no desire to go there, thank you very much. You're on your own.'

By Saturday the bitter wind had blown itself out and the morning was mild and murky. The kind of damp, dank day that made your hair frizz like wire wool.

Poppy pulled on her best jodhpurs and gave her boots a quick polish before heading out to the stables. She'd turned Chester out after breakfast and the old donkey was grazing in the far corner of the field. Cloud, still in his stable, whinnied impatiently as she slammed the back door shut.

'I know. But you'd only have rolled in the muddiest mud you could find and I want you looking smart for our trip to Claydon,' Poppy said, offering him a carrot.

She undid his rug and set to work, humming to herself as she groomed him from head to foot. Jodie had brought her clippers to Ashworthy the previous month and given both Cloud and Red trace clips. Charlie called them their go faster stripes.

Poppy brushed the knots from Cloud's tail and gave his mane a quick pull. She scooted inside for a bucket of warm water and sponged his eyes and nostrils. Finally, she picked out his feet and oiled his hooves.

She wasn't really sure why she was making such an effort. She knew that having a grey pony meant it was pointless getting precious about yellow feathers or the odd stable stain. Sometimes Cloud was so filthy he could easily be mistaken for a skewbald. She was used to being covered in grey hairs and laughed hollowly when Scarlett complained about keeping Red's four white socks clean. She had long ago come to terms with the fact that she was never likely to win a best turned out class. But Georgia and her pony were always so immaculate they could have stepped out of the pages of a riding magazine, and they left Poppy feeling inadequate.

Not today, she thought with satisfaction as she tacked Cloud up and led him out of the stable. Today he looked a million dollars.

They set off through the gate that led to the moor. Cloud felt fresh and full of energy and once they'd left Riverdale behind she gave him his head, relishing the cold air on her cheeks as they galloped past black-faced sheep, huddles of Dartmoor ponies and one lone back-pack-clad rambler, trudging along a faraway ridge. By Poppy's reckoning Claydon Manor was almost an hour's ride away so they should make it there and back before lunch.

Her feet were numb with cold by the time they reached the imposing electronic gates at the end of Claydon Manor's long drive. They had been open the day of the show but today they were firmly closed. A CCTV camera sat atop one of the stone gate posts, staring at her with its unblinking eye. Poppy peered up at it, wondering who was watching her on the other end. Set into the stone post at shoulder height was a cast iron letterbox, painted black. A triangle of white caught her eye. It was the corner of an envelope, which was wedged in the flap like a minnow trapped in the jaws of a pike.

Poppy brought Cloud alongside the letterbox, held her reins in her left hand and gave the envelope a tug. The corner tore off in her hand.

'Whoops,' she said under her breath. She slipped her hand inside the letterbox and pulled the rest of it out. Grubby and creased, it was one of those envelopes with a see-through window. Expecting the usual typewritten address Poppy was surprised to see a lock of black hair. Scrawled above the window in almost undecipherable handwriting was one word. *Canning.*

'Bit weird,' she said, shoving the envelope in her pocket. Cloud shifted his weight onto his other foot and Poppy looked around for the keypad on a metal post she and Scarlett had seen on their first visit to Claydon Manor.

Cloud stood patiently while she leaned over and pressed the button on the keypad with the picture of a tiny bell on it. She patted his neck.

'You're such a good boy. You'd be a whizz at handy pony.'

She wriggled her toes and stared through the bars of the wrought iron gates as she waited to be let in. Claydon Manor, in all its extravagant Georgian grandeur, was straight out of a Jane Austen novel. Poppy quite expected to see a butler standing to attention outside, his hands clasped behind his back and a deferential expression on his face. She couldn't imagine what it must have been like to grow up in such a huge mansion. She had been dragged around enough National Trust properties to know that there would be dozens of bedrooms, vast reception rooms and green baize doors leading to poky servants' quarters in the attic.

It was unimaginable to think that the haughty Georgia with her plummy voice and easy arrogance hailed from much humbler beginnings. Until her parents came into money she'd lived in a modest three bedroomed semi. Her mum had been a checkout girl at the local supermarket and her dad had been a builder. And now, for the price of a lottery ticket and six lucky numbers, they had all this.

A crackle from the speaker on the keypad interrupted Poppy's thoughts. A high-pitched voice cried, 'Who is that?'

'Poppy McKeever. I left some black leather gloves when I came to the show here the other day. I've come to pick them up.'

Poppy cocked her head to listen. She thought she could hear urgent whispers, but it could have been static on the intercom.

Then the woman's disembodied voice cut through the background noise. 'You'd better come in.' And with a click the huge iron gates slowly began to swing open.

Poppy let her reins slide through her hands as Cloud walked up the gravel drive, his stride long and his eyes swivelling left and right at Claydon's sleek liveries grazing in the paddocks either side. They passed a blue van parked on the grass verge. Above a picture of an old-fashioned chimney sweep were the words *Bert's Clean Sweep*. It wasn't until they were alongside the driver's door that she realised a man in blue overalls was snoozing in the driver's seat, his blue beanie hat pulled down so low that the only part of his face that was visible was his double chin.

Poppy jumped off Cloud and led him over to the panelled front door. She was about to knock when she saw a wrought iron door pull to her right. She gave it a tug and heard an answering clang from somewhere deep inside the house.

A crunch of gravel behind them made Cloud start and Poppy turned to see Angela Snell just a few feet away. The livery yard manager was holding Poppy's gloves in one hand and a mobile phone in the other.

'Did you see anyone on your way in?' said Angela shortly, her eyes narrowed.

'Only the chimney sweep.'

'And no-one was watching you?'

'No.'

'Are you sure?'

Poppy frowned. 'I told you already. The only person I saw was the sweep. And he was fast asleep. Why?'

Ignoring her, Angela held out the gloves. 'Yours, I believe?'

'Thanks.' Poppy shoved them in her pocket. As she did she remembered the envelope. She pulled it from her pocket. 'Oh, and this was poking out of the letterbox.'

Angela stiffened and her eyes slid over to the chimney sweep's van.

'I thought I'd bring it over, save you the job,' said Poppy, holding out the envelope and wondering why the older woman was acting so strangely.

Angela looked at Poppy, who was wearing a pair of Caroline's red woolly gloves, and then at her own gloveless hands. 'Stay there,' she instructed, and turned on her heels and headed for the chimney sweep's van.

'Is it me, or is this all a bit *weird*?' Poppy whispered to Cloud. He snuffled her hand with his velvety nose. His head shot up as he heard the van door open.

Angela strode back over and held out her hand. 'I'll take him.'

Poppy took a step back until she was touching Cloud's shoulder and clutched his reins tightly. 'No, you won't.'

Angela exhaled loudly. 'It's OK. I'm just going to put him in the stable next to Barley while you speak to him.' She nodded to the middle-aged man climbing stiffly out of the van. His blue overalls strained across his sizeable midriff. An image of digestive biscuits popped, unbidden, into Poppy's head.

'I don't understand -' she said.

Angela took Cloud's reins. 'Don't worry. I'll put a rug on him and give him some hay.'

Poppy watched mutely as Angela led her pony away. A meaty hand in a white latex glove reached over her shoulder and plucked the envelope from her hands.

'I'll be having that, young lady.'

8

P oppy stared at Bert the chimney sweep. He looked uncannily like Inspector Bill Pearson, the digestive-loving police officer she'd spoken to the day she'd discovered Shelley Taylor was swindling people out of a small fortune by pretending her daughter Hope had cancer. Perhaps they were twins, Poppy wondered wildly. One caught criminals for a living, the other spent his days cleaning chimneys. Bert slipped the envelope into the deep pocket of his soot-covered overalls, peeled off his latex gloves and held out his hand.

'Hello again, Poppy,' he said, showing her his warrant card. Bert the chimney sweep was indeed Inspector Bill Pearson from Devon and Cornwall Police. 'I think it's time for a cuppa and a chat, don't you?'

Poppy's mind was working overtime as she followed him around the side of the house. She felt as though she'd stepped into a television drama without being given any lines. What was the portly inspector doing here, dressed as a chimney sweep? Were times so hard he'd had to find a second job? Why hadn't Angela just taken the letter and let Poppy go home? And why had she seemed so cagey? Nothing made sense.

'After you,' said Inspector Pearson, holding the back door open.

Poppy heeled off her jodhpur boots and stepped into a cluttered boot room. Coats in various shades of khaki and brown hung from hooks on one wall, and on the other was a huge butler's sink. Above it was a pinboard covered with rosettes. Most of them were red.

'We'll talk in the library,' said the inspector. Poppy scurried after him down a wide, shadowy corridor with closed doors leading off either side. She felt like Alice, following the White Rabbit into the rabbit-hole.

Inspector Pearson stopped outside one of the doors. 'Won't be a moment.'

As the door opened Poppy caught a glimpse of a cavernous kitchen as big as Riverdale's entire downstairs. Dominating the room was a vast oak table, at the centre of which was a vase of dead roses. It was all Poppy registered before the door swung shut.

She rocked back on her heels, unsure what to do. Behind the huge, painted pine door she could hear the low rumble of voices. A shaft of light pierced the gloomy hallway. It was coming from the keyhole. Without thinking, Poppy sank to her knees and pressed her face against it.

A well-built man with close-cropped hair and a thick neck was sitting at the head of the table, tapping furiously into his phone. Next to him a woman stared blankly out of the window as she wound a pink hairband round and round her fingers. She had fair skin, ash-blonde hair, pale blue eyes and colourless lips. She was wearing a beige cashmere jumper. Everything about her looked muted, as though she'd been edited with a sepia filter.

A younger woman with shoulder-length brown hair, wearing jeans and a Jack Wills hoodie, had her back to them as she filled the kettle at the kitchen sink.

Inspector Pearson was talking to the couple at the table, showing them the scruffy white envelope, which was now in a police evidence bag. Curiouser and curiouser, thought Poppy, as she pressed her face closer to the keyhole.

The man stopped texting and said something in a gruff voice.

Inspector Pearson nodded, pulled on his latex gloves and used a kitchen knife to carefully prise open the envelope. He pulled out a single sheet of white paper and read it with raised eyebrows. He peered into the envelope, turned it upside down and gave it a shake.

The woman took one look at the lock of black hair on the table, buried her head in her hands and began keening softly. The sound was so wretched it made the hairs on the back of Poppy's neck stand up. Inspector Pearson cleared his throat and started speaking.

Poppy held her breath, straining to hear what was being said. But she only caught random words. *Letterbox. Fingerprints. Precious. Police.* It didn't make sense.

The thickset man thumped his fist on the table, making Poppy jump. Inspector Pearson slid his chair back and she scrambled to her feet. By the time the policeman had joined her in the hallway she was inspecting an antique map of Devon hanging over a mahogany console table.

'Sorry about that,' he said. 'I just need to ask you a couple of questions and then you can go.'

He pushed another door open to reveal a square room, lined floor to ceiling with books. It was north-facing and bitterly cold. The inspector switched on an electric fire between two chintzy armchairs and motioned Poppy to sit down. He took out a pocket notebook, a black ballpoint pen and the letter, which was back in its plastic evidence bag.

'So, Poppy, how did you come to be in possession of this letter?'

'It was in the letterbox.'

Inspector Pearson narrowed his eyes. 'If it was in the letterbox, how did you know it was there?'

'Sorry, I meant it was half in and half out. I thought I'd save someone a job by taking it down to the house. As I was going anyway.'

'So, you pulled it out of the letterbox. Were you wearing gloves?'

Poppy nodded.

'But I thought the reason you'd ridden over today was to pick up your gloves?'

'I'd left my new riding gloves here.' Poppy pulled the gloves out of her pocket and showed him. 'I borrowed my stepmum's gloves today.'

The inspector scribbled something down in his notebook. 'And did you see anyone outside the gates? Anyone at all?'

Poppy shook her head.

'Think very carefully, Poppy. This is important.'

Poppy pictured the ride to Claydon. She didn't think a single car had passed them. The only things they'd seen were sheep, Dartmoor ponies and the occasional buzzard.

'No, we didn't see anyone.'

'We?' he queried.

'Me and Cloud. My pony.'

'Right. And I gather from the Cannings that you're not a friend of Georgia's. So how did you come to leave your gloves here?'

'I was at the show last weekend. I left them in the arena by accident. They were new, else I probably wouldn't have bothered riding over.'

'Ah. You were at the show. Have you ever met Georgia before?'

'A few times, yes. Why?'

'Did you see her at the show?'

'She was there when we arrived, yes.'

'What time was that?'

'Um, about half eight, I suppose. Our class started at nine.'

'Did you speak to her?'

'Briefly.'

The inspector was watching her intently. 'What about?'

Poppy thought back. 'I asked her about the course. To see if she had any tips. It was my first show, you see.'

'She seemed OK to you? Not worried about anything?'

Georgia had seemed her usual snooty self. 'No.'

'Did you notice anything out of ordinary at the show? Anyone who looked out of place? Hanging around, asking questions?'

'I don't think so,' Poppy said. 'But I was concentrating on the jumping. I'm probably not the best person to ask.'

Inspector Pearson sighed.

'Wait, there was someone,' said Poppy.

'At the show?'

'No, this morning. I saw a walker, up on Barrow Ridge.'

'Man or woman?' he asked.

Poppy screwed up her eyes. 'A man, I think. Wearing camouflage gear and one of those massive backpacks students use when they're on a gap year.'

'Did you see his face?'

'He was too far away. But he just looked like a rambler. Sorry.'

There was a rap at the door and the woman in the Jack Wills hoodie walked in with a mug of tea and a plate of digestive biscuits.

'Hello Poppy.'

Poppy felt a jolt of recognition. The last time she'd seen this woman she'd been in police uniform, leading a man away in handcuffs.

Poppy looked from Inspector Pearson to PC Claire Bodiam and back again.

'Why are you dressed as a chimney sweep? Has something happened to Georgia? Is *that* why you're here?'

9

I nspector Pearson took a digestive biscuit and dunked it in his tea.

'I'm afraid we're not at liberty to tell you that.'

'We all thought she had food poisoning.'

His hand stopped in mid-air. A soggy corner of the biscuit fell into his tea with a soft plop.

'Why did you think that?'

'She was complaining about her hot dog. Said it was virtually raw. We assumed it had given her a gyppy tummy and that's why she didn't jump.'

A phone rang somewhere deep in the house. The inspector jumped to his feet. He was surprisingly nimble for someone of his size.

'Stay here,' he told Poppy, disappearing through the door with PC Bodiam close behind him.

This was getting weirder and weirder, Poppy thought. She wiggled her toes and gazed around the room. Hundreds, no thousands, of antique, leather-bound books lined the shelves. She padded across the room and studied the spines. An array of Encyclopaedia Britannicas with navy leather covers and gold-leaf lettering caught her eye and she pulled one from the shelf. To her surprise it wasn't an antique book at all – it was a moulded book panel designed to look like one. Poppy tried more. Every single book was a fake. They were all there for show, never to be read.

She sat back down and switched on her mobile. No phone signal here, let alone 3G. The wifi signal was strong but she didn't know the Cannings' passcode and she could hardly interrupt them to ask. She sighed, wondering how long Inspector Pearson was likely to be. And then she noticed the plastic evidence bag, which had slipped down the side of the armchair in his haste to leave.

Poppy knew she shouldn't look at the letter. But she also knew it would probably explain why the police were here, and what had happened to Georgia. It was becoming increasingly obvious that her disappearance had nothing to do with a dodgy hot dog. Poppy grappled with her conscience for all of thirty seconds. Inevitably curiosity won out. She checked that the door was closed and reached for the evidence bag.

The scruffy, white paper was blank on one side. Poppy turned it over, her mouth dry. Her eyes slid over the untidy lines of handwriting, scrawled in ugly capital letters:

```
THESE   ARE   OUR   DEMANDS.   TWO   MILLION   IN
EXCHANGE  FOR  YOUR  PRECIOUS  DAUGHTER.  WE'VE
SENT  A  LITTLE  GIFT  TO  SHOW  WE  MEAN  BUSINESS.
IT'LL  BE  A  FINGER  NEXT  TIME.  AND  SHE'S  DEAD
IF  YOU  TELL  THE  POLICE.  WAIT  FOR  THE  NEXT
INSTRUCTION.
```

Poppy's eyes widened. Was this a *ransom* note? Had Georgia been *kidnapped*? Common sense said no. Things like that happened in books and films, not real life. Real people didn't get kidnapped. But the Cannings were loaded. And why else were the police here?

Before Poppy had a chance to marshal her thoughts she heard footsteps in the hallway. She shoved the evidence bag back down the side of the armchair. She was sitting with her hands clasped demurely on her lap when PC Bodiam appeared moments later.

'You've been very helpful, Poppy. We won't take up any more of your time.'

'So, can I go home?' Poppy asked. Her eyes slid involuntarily to the armchair where a corner of plastic peeked out. She didn't notice the PC follow her gaze.

'You can. But Poppy – and this is really, really important – you must not tell a soul what you've seen, or think you've seen, here today. Lives could be in danger if even a whisper gets out that there are police at Claydon Manor.' PC Bodiam's voice was gentle, but her expression was deadly serious.

'I haven't seen anything,' Poppy gabbled.

PC Bodiam stared at the letter and then at Poppy. 'Well, that's alright then. Come on, I'll show you out.'

As they walked into the yard Angela Snell was leading Cloud out of his borrowed stable. Poppy tightened his girth and pulled his stirrup leathers down. She was about to edge her toe into the stirrup when PC Bodiam laid a hand on her arm. 'Don't worry. We know what we're doing. But you must not tell anyone we were here, do you understand?'

Poppy didn't understand at all. But she nodded anyway. PC Bodiam smiled briefly.

'Thank you. Believe me, Georgia's life depends on it.'

ONCE THEY WERE on the moor Poppy kicked Cloud into a canter. She wanted to put as much distance as possible between them and the oppressive atmosphere that hung over the old Georgian manor house like smog. She wished she could turn back the clock. If only she'd hacked out with Scarlett and Red instead. What did a pair of gloves matter, in the grand scheme of things? If she hadn't ridden over to Claydon, hadn't let curiosity get the better of her, she'd be blissfully ignorant. She'd be looking forward to an afternoon in front of the fire, watching an old Christmas film with Caroline and Charlie.

Instead, her stomach churned with misgiving and her mind was whirring. Georgia had been kidnapped by goodness knows who. The police obviously had no clue, otherwise Inspector Pearson wouldn't have quizzed her at such length. Poppy pictured the scrawled note. The threat it contained was clear. What would happen to Georgia if her parents didn't hand over the two million pounds? Or if they discovered that the Cannings had called in the police? Organised criminals didn't make idle threats. PC Bodiam said Georgia's life was in danger. And she wouldn't say that unless it was true.

Poppy slowed Cloud to a walk and let him stretch his neck. His ears were pricked and he looked around the moor with interest, completely oblivious to the maelstrom of thoughts swirling in Poppy's head.

She had the horrible feeling that PC Bodiam knew she'd read the ransom note. Why else would the normally kindly PC have given her such a blunt warning to keep quiet? Poppy chastised herself for snooping. She should have minded her own business and she'd have been none the wiser. As it was she knew too much.

Would they kill Georgia? Surely not. She was worth more to them alive than dead. Alive, she was their only bargaining tool. Dead, she was a liability. Cutting off a lock of hair was an easy way to instil terror, and it had worked. The wretched look on the face of Georgia's mum was proof of that.

What if the kidnappers were watching the house and had seen Poppy arrive? Was she now in danger, too? Were they following her, to see where she lived? And what about Cloud? Chester? They were the two most important things in Poppy's life. What if the kidnappers hurt them to get at Poppy?

She halted the Connemara and wheeled him around, shielding her eyes from the low winter sun as she scoured the open moorland anxiously. A movement to her right caught her eye and her insides turned to ice. But it was only a solitary sheep, picking its way through a patch of boggy ground.

Cloud tossed his head with impatience. With a heavy heart, Poppy turned him towards home.

10

———

Charlie must have been watching for them from his bedroom window because she was still tying Cloud up outside his stable when he burst out of the kitchen door, his face flushed with excitement.

'Chester's been chosen for the Nativity! A pair of net curtains just phoned and told Mum!'

'Good,' said Poppy shortly, running up the stirrup leathers and loosening Cloud's girth.

'Good? Is that all you can say?' said Charlie. 'I thought you'd be as pleased as I was.'

Poppy glanced at her brother. If he suspected something was up she'd never hear the end of it. He was as tenacious as a terrier. He'd dig and probe until she gave in and told him about the kidnap. She had to pretend everything was fine. Even though it absolutely wasn't.

'Sorry Charlie, my feet are so cold I can't think properly. That's brilliant. Have you told him?'

Mollified, Charlie grinned. 'Of course! He was especially pleased to find out he'd beaten a pantomime donkey *and* a Shetland pony. But he said he wouldn't have minded if Jenny had been chosen. I think he quite liked her.'

'So did I. She's so sweet. But George Blackstone will be mad that she wasn't chosen. Scarlett says he hates to lose anything.'

The kitchen window opened, emitting a fug of steam. Caroline poked her head out. 'Good, you're back. Lunch will be five minutes. Did you get your gloves?'

Poppy felt in the pockets of her coat and groaned. What a numbskull. After all that she'd left them in the library at Claydon Manor.

THAT NIGHT POPPY dreamt about Witch Cottage, an abandoned croft deep on the moor towards Princetown that locals claimed was haunted. In her dream, someone had built an impenetrable barbed wire fence just inside the dry stone wall that circled the cottage, and had driven a dozen *No Trespassing* signs into the peaty ground.

Ignoring the signs, Poppy had reached in her pocket for the powerful wirecutters she had with her and had snip, snip, snipped away at the barbed wire until she'd made a gap big enough to slip through. She'd crept past the teardrop-shaped tarn to the croft's tiny front door. She heard voices inside, low and urgent. She knelt down and looked through the keyhole. A rheumy eye stared back at her. Stifling a scream, she scrabbled to her feet and sprinted for the fence. But the wire had grown back and the barbs tore at her clothes like the arms of a giant octopus. The harder she struggled, the tighter they held her. Behind her, the sound of heavy footsteps grew closer. She dared not look around. Desperate to reach the safety of the trees, she felt in her pocket for the wirecutters. But they had turned into a pair of nail scissors. Poppy opened her lungs and screamed.

She woke with a start, her heart pounding and her pillow damp. She rubbed her eyes and steadied her breathing. In through the nose, out through the mouth, concentrating on the feeling of her diaphragm slowly expanding and contracting, just as she had on the day of the show. Slowly the nightmare slipped back into her unconsciousness like a retreating tide.

But the picture of Witch Cottage stayed with her as she clumped downstairs in her pyjamas and fleece slipper boots. The old croft sat resolutely in her mind's eye as she poured milk over her cereals and sipped the mug of tea Caroline handed her. She stared vacantly into space, remembering the tiny attic under the catslide roof where pigeons nested and dust motes danced. It had been used to hide ill-gotten gains once before. Could someone be using it again?

'Earth to Poppy. Is anyone at home?' Caroline was standing in front of her, her hands on her hips.

Poppy brushed her fringe out of her eyes. 'Sorry, I was miles away. What is it?'

'I asked if you wanted another cup of tea.' Caroline sat down and fixed her cornflower-blue eyes on Poppy's. 'It was the third time I'd asked. Is everything OK?'

'Everything's fine.'

'Only you've seemed very preoccupied since you got back from Claydon Manor yesterday. You would tell me if anything was wrong, wouldn't you?'

Poppy wasn't normally secretive. Dad always said fondly that she wore her heart on her sleeve, just like Mum had. But lying by omission didn't really count, did it? She crossed her fingers under the table.

''Course I would. And, yes please. I'd love another cup of tea.'

CLOUD WHICKERED as she let herself out of the back door. Poppy ruffled his forelock and blew softly into his nose.

'Fancy a ride to Witch Cottage later?' she whispered. He rubbed against her, leaving a layer of white hairs on her coat. 'I'll see if Scarlett and Red can come too, shall I?'

But Scarlett was otherwise engaged. *Great Auntie Miriam's down from Bristol for the day. Mum said I've got to stay in and entertain her. It's so unfair! She talks to me like I'm five. AND she has more whiskers than a walrus!!! (Great Auntie Miriam, that is, not Mum. Although actually, come to mention it...)* read the gloomy reply when Poppy texted her.

She was pulling on an extra pair of thermal socks when Charlie burst into her room.

'Poppy, come and look at what I've made,' he said, tugging the sleeve of her fleece.

'If I must,' Poppy sighed, following him into his room. Lego was strewn all over the floor in a kaleidoscope of primary colours. She winced as she trod on a red brick. Charlie was pointing to a large construction on his chest of drawers.

Poppy peered over his shoulder at a tableau of Lego people and animals all gathered around a manger.

'It's a Nativity scene,' she said.

'Not any Nativity scene. It's the one at St Mary's. It's so I can practice what we're supposed to do. Like a dress rehearsal. Only in Lego.'

'It's very good. Although I'm not sure there were monkeys and baby elephants in the original Nativity,' said Poppy.

'They're all I had. I'm having to use a giraffe to play Chester. But I think a pair of net curtains will be impressed, don't you?'

'You can't keep calling her that,' said Poppy, her eyes falling on Charlie's binoculars, which were hanging from the door of his wardrobe. 'Mind if I borrow them?'

'What for?' said Charlie suspiciously.

Poppy looked around her breezily. 'A spot of bird-watching while I'm out riding,' she said.

'Since when have you been interested in bird-watching?'

Poppy swiped them from the door knob and flashed him an innocent smile. 'Since now.'

THE BINOCULARS safely stored in an old rucksack, Poppy and Cloud set off towards Witch Cottage. Poppy whistled tunelessly as her pony's long stride ate up the miles. A pale sun glimmered in the hazy winter sky and gulls swooped and soared overhead.

Eventually they reached the small band of evergreens that hid the cottage from view. Although Poppy had only discovered the old croft that summer, Cloud knew it of old, and she gave him his head so he could pick his own path through the trees.

As the gaps in the conifers widened and sunlight pierced the dark canopy once again, Poppy halted her pony.

'We need to be careful. Just in case,' she said, jumping to the ground and slipping the rucksack from her shoulders. As she undid the straps she realised her fingers were trembling.

Did she really think Georgia Canning was being held to ransom in the derelict cottage, watched over by a gang of faceless kidnappers? Despite all she'd seen at Claydon Manor it still seemed totally ridiculous that a fourteen-year-old girl could disappear without trace.

Poppy led Cloud to the edge of the trees and fiddled with the lens of the binoculars until the old stone building swam into focus. There was the teardrop-shaped tarn she and Charlie had picnicked by. Next to it was the dry stone wall that circled the cottage. Poppy tracked back and forth, taking in every detail. The front door was still hanging off its ancient hinges, although the battalion of nettles that had guarded it all summer had died down. The window frames were still rotting and the hole in the catslide roof was even bigger than she remembered.

Satisfied she had covered every foot of the cottage, Poppy shoved the binoculars back into her rucksack and pulled it on. There was no sign of Georgia, but she knew she had to check inside, just to be sure.

Glancing left and right, she led Cloud past the tarn and looped his reins over an old fence post. She pushed open the front door and stepped into the small, square room that must once have been the parlour. She was immediately transported back to the dramatic day Jodie had admitted she was planning to smuggle stolen mobile phones into Dartmoor Prison two and a half miles away.

Poppy still remembered the determined set of Jodie's jaw as she'd defended her decision, claiming it was the only way she could raise enough money to keep Nethercote open. Luckily Poppy had shown her another way and, with the help of Biscuit, the horse sanctuary's future was now secure.

Today the room was empty, apart from the decaying body of a

dead pigeon in the fireplace. Poppy shivered, hoping it wasn't an omen.

The kitchen was empty, too. Poppy crept up the narrow staircase to the two tiny rooms in the eaves. But she knew before she poked her head around each door that there was no-one in them.

There was no doubt the place was deserted. She was an idiot for even thinking she'd find Georgia. Who did she think she was – Sherlock flippin' Holmes? If Devon and Cornwall Police had no inkling where the girl was, why should she, Poppy McKeever?

She ran lightly down the stairs, eager to be outside. She fished in her pocket for a handful of pony nuts and gave them to Cloud. 'That's for being patient while I was playing detective.'

She was tightening his girth when he stiffened and sniffed the wind.

'There's no-one here, silly,' she said.

But Cloud's nostrils flared and he wheeled around, wrenching the reins from her hands. She watched in horror as he weaved through the trees, stirrups flapping and his tail high.

'Cloud, come back!' she called, trying to keep her voice steady. He slid to a halt and watched her. 'That's it, good boy. Stand still and I'll come and get you. There's nothing to be frightened of.'

And then she heard the crackle of footsteps on the forest floor. Cloud, who was gawping at something over her right shoulder, gave a high-pitch whinny, spun on his hocks and cantered deeper into the trees. Fear crept down Poppy's spine like a droplet of icy water.

Her hand flew to her mouth and her rucksack dropped to the floor like a stone. She'd thought Witch Cottage was deserted. How wrong she'd been.

A BEAR of a man in camouflage fatigues and a green balaclava was standing four paces away. Poppy took two steps back, colliding with the solid trunk of a conifer.

Her eyes darted nervously to the large metal contraption in his left hand and then over her shoulder to Cloud. The Connemara had stopped on the edge of the small forest and was watching them intently.

Poppy chanced another look at the man, who was pulling off the balaclava with his right hand. He shoved it in his pocket. He had a thatch of red hair and a nose that was squished to one side as though it had been broken and hadn't set straight. He was the walker she'd seen on Barrow Ridge, she was sure of it. The one Inspector Pearson had been so interested in.

'Sorry for frightening your pony,' he said in a growly voice. 'Do you need a hand catching him?'

He waved the metal contraption towards Cloud. Poppy flinched, and edged around the conifer.

The man ducked into a small, square green canvas tent, covered with conifer branches, that Poppy hadn't noticed. He reappeared seconds later with a neatly-quartered apple in his hand. 'Will this help?'

Never take sweets from strangers, Caroline used to drill into Poppy and Charlie when they were little. Poppy dithered. Catching Cloud would be easier with an apple, but this gruff man could have escaped from Dartmoor Prison for all she knew.

Not waiting for an answer, he thrust the pieces of apple into Poppy's hand. She jumped as if she'd been scalded, muttered her thanks and fled through the trees. Once there was a safe distance between them she chanced a look over her shoulder. The man had turned his back to her and was on his knees, fiddling with the metal contraption. It had three legs and a black handle on the top.

Cloud was still watching her, his ears pricked. As Poppy edged towards him she breathed deeply, trying not to let her anxiety transmit to her pony. She held out a quarter of the apple and he extended his neck towards her. She stood still, letting him come to her. He snaffled the apple, his whiskers tickling her palm. Relief flooded her system as her hands tightened around his reins.

'Good boy,' she said, springing into the saddle and turning him for home.

As they retraced their steps across the moor Poppy wondered about the burly camouflage-clad man and what he was doing, camped out in the woods in the middle of winter. It seemed unlikely he had anything to do with Georgia's disappearance. Perhaps he was a rough sleeper, seeking shelter in Witch Cottage. Perhaps he lived off the land, a wild man of the woods, and that contraption was a trap in which he caught rabbits.

At least she now knew that Georgia wasn't being kept in the old croft. So much for her theory that the abductors were using it as their base. She was right back at square one.

Little did she know that within twenty four short hours, Georgia's whereabouts would be the least of her worries.

11

The alarm on Poppy's phone woke her at half past six. She allowed herself two presses of the snooze button before she threw back the duvet and jumped out of bed. It wasn't until she'd started pulling on her leggings, ready to race out of the house to muck out, feed and turn out Cloud and Chester before breakfast and school, that she remembered it was the first day of the Christmas holidays. Bliss. Two whole weeks with nothing to do. Well, she had tons of coursework but that could wait until the New Year.

'Don't forget we're picking your dad up from Bristol airport today,' said Caroline, as Poppy wolfed down three slices of toast and raspberry jam. Charlie whooped and Poppy grinned. Once Dad was home Christmas could begin.

They sang along to the radio on the long drive to Bristol, stopping for hot chocolates at a motorway service station to break the journey. Dad's plane had not long landed as they walked into the arrivals lounge and soon he was enveloping them all in a big bear hug.

'So, tell me your news,' he said as they set off for home.

'Where do I start?' said Charlie.

'At the beginning?' he said.

'Well, first we had the donkey auditions for this year's Nativity, held by a pair of net curtains.'

'A pair of what?'

Caroline gave a wry smile. 'Charlie means Reverend *Annette* Kirton.'

'Obviously,' said Dad, his mouth twitching. 'And then what?'

'And then she only went and chose Chester for the starring role.'

'That's brilliant! And Poppy, what've you been up to?'

Poppy met her dad's eyes in the rear-view mirror. If only she could tell him what had really been happening. But she'd promised the police. She shrugged. 'Nothing much.'

Caroline turned around in her seat. 'Apart from coming third in your first ever show.'

'Oh yeah,' grinned Poppy. 'I forgot about that.'

Two hours later Mike McKeever pulled into the Riverdale drive. 'D'you remember the day we moved in?'

'It seems like yesterday, and in other ways I feel like we've lived here all our lives,' said Caroline.

'Magpie was sick in his basket, I remember that. And Poppy was really, really grumpy,' said Charlie.

'No, she wasn't,' said Caroline loyally.

'I was,' admitted Poppy. 'I thought I didn't want to live here. How stupid was I? I'd hate to live in Twickenham now.'

'And do you remember, Tory was here to welcome us to Riverdale?'

'She's like our pretend granny now, isn't she?' said Charlie.

'She certainly is,' said Dad.

'And I thought Chester was a pony,' said Poppy.

Dad laughed. 'So you did. What you didn't realise was that there was a pony for you after all. You were just looking in the wrong place.'

He parked the car and Poppy and Charlie helped him unload his cases from the boot. Caroline opened the front door and Freddie bounded out, his plumy tail wagging frantically as he welcomed them all in turn.

Cloud was lying by the water trough, dozing.

'Where's the panto star?' said Dad.

Poppy scanned the field for Chester's familiar brown shape. 'Probably down by the wood.'

'I'm starving. When's lunch?' said Charlie.

'Now,' said Caroline. 'You carry Dad's cases in and I'll heat up the soup.'

AFTER LUNCH DAD brought the big cardboard box of Christmas decorations down from the loft and Poppy and Charlie decorated the tree.

'Can we watch *Home Alone* after?' Charlie was standing on a chair, reaching over to dangle a bauble on one of the high branches.

'You've seen it a million times,' said Poppy.

'Who cares? It's the best Christmas film ever.'

'If we must. But I need to put Cloud and Chester away first. I'll be twenty minutes, OK?'

'I love that bit where Kevin heats up the doorknob and the burglar burns his hand.' Charlie chuckled to himself. 'And when he leaves the cars and stuff at the bottom of the stairs. Genius.'

An orange sun was sliding below the horizon as Poppy made her way across the field, Cloud's headcollar slung casually over her shoulder. She never brought one for Chester – the old donkey always followed them back to the yard.

Cloud was still snoozing, his ears floppy and his bottom lip drooping, when Poppy reached him.

'Hello, sleepyhead,' she said.

He opened one eye and regarded her blearily. Poppy slipped the noseband of his headcollar over his nose and buckled the strap, calling over her shoulder to Chester as she did so.

A couple of burrs were caught in Cloud's mane and she spent several minutes teasing them out. His head drooped again and his eyes closed.

She tutted fondly. 'What's wrong with you today? Late night last night, was it?'

Satisfied she had managed to pull out every last barb, she combed through his mane with her fingers. There was still no sign of Chester. Usually he'd have wandered over by now and would be nibbling her pockets, hoping for a Polo or a handful of pony nuts.

'Where *is* he?' Poppy squinted into the half-light, searching the field's dips and hollows, tracking slowly along the band of trees that marked the start of the Riverdale wood. There was no sign of the old donkey.

'I did let him out this morning, didn't I?' Occasionally, if the weather forecast was really bad, she would leave him in the stable with plenty of hay. He didn't have the luxury of a thick New Zealand rug like Cloud. But no, she remembered turning them both out. Chester had been impatient to be out and had trodden on her foot in his hurry to trot through the field gate.

'We'd better check the fencing hasn't got a hole in it.' Poppy pulled the lead rope gently but Cloud didn't move. She clicked her tongue. 'Come on, lazybones.' He took a half-hearted couple of steps forwards. 'That's it. Good boy,' she said as he followed her unenthusiastically around the perimeter of the field. The post and rail fencing was intact. Apart from a couple of rabbits, which bobbed off into the wood with a flash of white tail, the field was empty.

Poppy gazed around her, a feeling of unease settling on her shoulders like mist on a soggy autumn night. Chester could be mischievous at times and Poppy wouldn't put it past him to untie a gate or push through a gap in a fence if the grass looked greener on the other side. But the gate had been shut when she'd let herself in and there weren't any holes in the fence. Usually by now he'd be standing by the gate, ready for his tea. So, where was he?

Her sense of unease growing, Poppy coaxed Cloud back across the field. She turned on the yard lights, hoping to see the donkey's choco-late brown eyes gazing guiltily back at her from the hay barn or tack room. Both were empty. So was the stable he shared with Cloud. Poppy left Cloud in the stable and sprinted to the back door with a hammering heart.

1 2

'Chester's disappeared!' she yelled at the top of her voice. Caroline, who was peeling potatoes at the sink, raised her eyebrows.

'What do you mean, disappeared?'

'He's not in the field. He's not in the yard. He's vanished!' Poppy could hear her voice climbing an octave and she took a deep breath. 'I've looked everywhere. He's gone.'

Caroline dropped the peeler in the sink and dried her hands on a tea towel. 'Grab the torches. I'll go and get your dad and Charlie. We'll come and have another look.'

'He wouldn't have run away, would he?' said Charlie in a small voice. They were walking four abreast across the field, having already searched the outbuildings and small paddock with no luck.

'Of course he wouldn't, sweetheart. I'm sure he's here somewhere. Try not to worry,' said Caroline.

They were walking past the water trough when Poppy stood on something sharp. She shone her torch down. A white plastic syringe was lying in the mud. She bent down to pick it up.

'Sedalin Gel,' she said, showing the syringe to Caroline. 'What on earth is that?'

Her stepmum shrugged. 'No idea.'

The rest of the label was obscured by mud. Poppy slipped it into her pocket and trudged on, the beam of her torch sweeping to and fro like a searchlight. Her disquiet grew with every step.

'I told you he wasn't here,' she said fretfully, when they reached the far side of the field and there was still no sign of the old donkey.

'Where *is* he, then?' demanded Charlie with a catch in his voice. 'Chester! *Chester*! Where are you?' he shouted.

Poppy would have given anything to have heard Chester's familiar wheezy hee-haw, but the moor was quiet, save for the sound of the westerly wind whipping through the trees.

'And you're absolutely sure you shut the gate properly this morning?' said her dad.

'OF COURSE I'M SURE!' Poppy wanted to yell at the top of her voice. But she took another deep breath and answered as calmly as she could. 'It was definitely closed. Anyway, if I'd left it open Cloud would have escaped, too, wouldn't he?'

'It's OK, Poppy. I believe you,' he said. 'The first thing we need to do is ring round all the neighbours, in case they've seen him.'

'And if they haven't?' asked Caroline.

'Let's cross that bridge when we come to it.'

Poppy fed Cloud and changed his rugs on autopilot. Her mind was focused on Chester. Where on earth could he be? Common sense told her he'd just wandered off, and would clip-clop back into the yard at any moment. She tried and failed to dismiss the nagging doubts that whispered darker scenarios to her subconscious.

'Where is he, Cloud?' Poppy whispered, running a frozen hand along his velvety neck. Ignoring her, he guzzled his tea noisily. At least he finally seemed to have perked up, she thought, as she let herself out of the stable and tramped wearily back to the house.

Caroline was sitting at the kitchen table, the phone pressed against her ear.

'Thanks Pat. No, I understand. And yes, if you could keep an eye out for him that'd be great. Tell Scarlett not to worry. He'll turn up, I'm sure. Thanks again. You too.' She ended the call and placed the phone carefully on the table.

'Pat and Bill haven't seen him. Neither have the Jennings or the Coreys. Just the Samsons to try and that's everyone within a mile of Riverdale.'

Poppy remembered the syringe in her pocket. She rinsed off the mud under the hot tap. 'Acepromazine,' she read to herself. 'Sedative. Oral gel.'

Her heartbeat quickening, she reached for her mobile phone and Googled Sedalin Gel. *Used for the sedation of horses and ponies. Has a general tranquilizing effect which lasts for up to six or seven hours.* Fear squeezed Poppy's insides like a vice.

'He's been stolen,' she said loudly. Caroline, in the middle of leaving a message on the Samsons' answerphone, trailed off and stared at Poppy.

'How d'you know?' Charlie demanded.

'I found this in the field, near to where Cloud was standing. He seemed really sleepy earlier. I didn't think anything of it. But this is a sedative for horses. Someone's given him it so they could take Chester.'

'Are you sure?' said her dad.

'How else do you explain this?' Poppy said, holding out the syringe. 'Someone has stolen him. We need to call the police.'

No-one really wanted the pork chops and mash Caroline had made for dinner. They sat in silence around the table, each busy with their own thoughts. Caroline sprang to her feet with an audible sigh of relief when there was a rap at the front door.

'It'll be the police. Poppy, perhaps you could clear the table.'

Poppy was mindlessly scraping leftovers into the green food caddy when Caroline re-appeared with PC Claire Bodiam and a fresh-faced young officer she introduced as PC Gilligan. He looked as if he was straight out of training school.

Poppy met PC Bodiam's eye. It's alright, she wanted to say. I haven't told anyone about Georgia. PC Bodiam gave a tiny nod, as if she understood.

The two police officers sat down. 'We wouldn't normally attend a theft report but we were passing and it was a quiet shift. We thought we might as well look in,' said PC Bodiam. 'Just as a matter of interest, do you have a four by four?'

'No, we've just got the estate. Why?' asked Poppy's dad.

'There are some tyre tracks at the bottom of the drive. They look wider than a car's.'

'They must have belonged to the thieves!' cried Charlie, his face pale.

'Possibly,' said PC Bodiam.

'Are you going to send out the crime scene people, like you did at Redhall?' Poppy asked.

'Probably not. We don't even know he was definitely stolen yet.'

Poppy showed the two police officers the sedative.

'Whoever took him tranquilised Cloud so they could steal Chester,' she said.

'That's what I don't get,' PC Bodiam admitted. 'We do get the occasional horse theft, and sheep rustling is a fairly common problem out in the rural. We even had eight Limousin cattle stolen from a farm over Okehampton way the other week. But who would go out of their way to steal an elderly donkey? It doesn't make sense.'

13

Poppy was shaking fresh straw into the stable the next morning when she heard the clatter of hooves on concrete. Her heart leapt and she sprinted to the open door, hoping to see Chester's woolly face, but it was Scarlett on Red. Her best friend jumped off and led the chestnut gelding over.

'Any news?'

'No,' said Poppy glumly. 'PC Bodiam has told the Farm Watch people and Caroline's posted his photo on some local Facebook horse groups. It's had loads of shares, but no-one's seen him.'

'Let's go for a ride, see if we can find him.'

'I don't know, Scar. I don't really feel like it. Anyway, I should probably stay here. In case there's any news.'

Scarlett looked shocked. 'But what if he's on the moor? What if he's hurt himself and needs our help?'

Trying to ignore the burn of unshed tears, Poppy stared at her feet. 'Caroline phoned Tory this morning.'

'How did she take it?'

'She was OK. Worried, but OK. She's coming over this afternoon.'

'By then we might have found him! Come on, Poppy. Let's give it a try at least. It's got to be better than sitting waiting for the phone to ring.'

'WHERE DO WE START?' said Poppy helplessly, as they rode onto the moor. It was a clear day and Dartmoor lay before them in all its bleak winter glory.

'We'll ride around the Riverdale tor and then head south, along the other side of the Riverdale wood, just in case he's taken shelter there,' said Scarlett decisively.

Perhaps Cloud sensed Poppy's despair for he seemed subdued as he followed Red around the base of the tor. But he probably missed the old donkey even more than she did.

She said as much to Scarlett.

Scarlett shook her head. 'It's probably the after-effects of the sedative.'

But Poppy knew she was wrong and every time he stopped to sniff the wind and gave a plaintive whinny it broke her heart.

They scoured the horizon for Chester-shaped brown blobs. Once Scarlett shrieked with excitement, making Cloud and Red both jump.

'There he is!' she cried, pointing to the lower slopes of a far-off tor. Poppy followed her gaze.

'It's a stag. I can see the antlers from here,' she said flatly. 'This is useless. I'm going home.' She wheeled Cloud to the right and kicked him into a canter. He lengthened his stride until the wiry moorland grass blurred beneath his feet. Poppy leaned low over his neck and gripped the reins tightly as he galloped for home, not bothering to wipe the tears that poured down her cheeks.

TORY WAS SITTING in the armchair by the fire, her swollen knuckles pale as she gripped the head of her walking stick and stared into the flames that crackled and leapt in the hearth.

Poppy hesitated by the door. Caroline had told her not to worry, that Tory didn't blame her. But Poppy had promised she would look after Chester and she hadn't. Chester was goodness only knew where and Poppy had failed him, failed them both. Fresh tears trickled down her face and she wiped them away impatiently. Apologising to Tory was the least she could do. She straightened her shoulders and walked into the room.

'I'm so, so sorry.' She knelt at Tory's feet, feeling the heat of the fire scorch her wind-chapped cheek.

'Oh pet, you mustn't blame yourself. It's not your fault,' the old woman said firmly.

'But –'

'No buts, Poppy. No-one looked after Chester better than you. Someone had a reason to take him. We just need to work out why.'

Poppy remembered Georgia. 'You don't think he's been kidnapped, do you?'

'Kidnapped?' Tory said, bemused. 'Who would kidnap an old donkey?'

'Maybe they think because Dad's on the TV we're loaded. Like the Cannings.'

The wrinkles on Tory's forehead deepened. 'What have the Cannings got to do with anything?'

Poppy bit her lip. 'Nothing. Pets do get kidnapped, though. It happened in the book I just read. The kidnapper left ransom notes in an old churchyard.'

'That's fiction,' said Tory kindly. 'Things like that don't happen in real life.'

'They might,' said Poppy. She cocked her head. 'Was that the phone?'

'I didn't hear, pet.'

Poppy sprang to her feet. 'I'll go and check.'

Caroline was replacing the handset in its base when Poppy burst into the kitchen.

'Who was that?' she demanded.

'Reverend Kirton. I thought I'd better tell her she needed to find a new donkey. She was just phoning back.'

Poppy stared at her stepmother. 'Don't you think we'll have found him by then?'

Caroline smiled brightly. 'I'm sure we will have. But I needed to warn her. The Nativity's on Friday. She needs time to find a stand-in.'

Charlie appeared in the doorway, Freddie by his side. 'Find a stand-in for what?'

'For the Nativity donkey,' said Caroline. 'Reverend Kirton says she'll probably ask George Blackstone if Jenny can do it.'

'George Blackstone!' Poppy exploded.

'How could she?' cried Charlie, his face crumpling. 'That was Chester's job! He'll be back to do it, won't he?'

Caroline made to comfort him but Poppy beat her to it. She wrapped her arms around his skinny frame. 'He'll be back, Charlie,' she whispered into his tousled blond hair. He was getting so tall. 'I promise.'

Caroline had invited Tory to stay the night and Poppy carried her small suitcase up to the spare bedroom before dinner.

'Thank you,' said Tory. She sat down heavily on the bed. 'Charlie's upset, isn't he. I've never seen him so down.'

'He loves Chester to bits. We all do.' There was a catch in Poppy's throat. 'He was so looking forward to the Nativity. He'd even made a Lego model of the church. I'll show you later.'

'Annette hasn't given the job to Delilah, has she?' said Tory. She had hooted with laughter when Poppy had phoned to tell her about Sam and Scott's appearance at the donkey auditions.

'No, she's going to ask George Blackstone to bring his poor, skinny donkey, Jenny.'

'George Blackstone?' Tory asked sharply.

Poppy shrugged. 'Jenny was the vicar's second choice, apparently. That's what she told Caroline, anyway.'

'Who else did she tell?' Tory wondered aloud as she struggled to her feet.

'What do you mean?'

Ignoring her, Tory waggled her stick at her suitcase. 'Pass me my coat, please, Poppy. There's somewhere we need to go.'

14

The McKeevers' estate car snaked its way along the windy lanes towards the Blackstone farm. They reached a cross-roads. Poppy's dad looked at Tory, who was sitting in the passenger seat, her handbag clutched to her chest and a determined look on her face.

'Straight across,' she said. 'And then second left. The farm's down a track on the right.'

Charlie had been desperate to come but Dad had put his foot down. 'First, we don't want to go in mob-handed. And second, you're eight, Charlie. You should be in bed.'

Charlie had stormed up to his bedroom in tears of anger and frustration.

'I'd better see if he's OK,' said Caroline. 'Phone me as soon as you can. And please be careful. In fact, I've changed my mind. I don't think Poppy should go, either. What if he's got a gun? We should call the police. Let them sort it out.'

Dad gave her a brief hug. 'We don't even know if he's taken Chester. Imagine the fall-out if we're wrong.'

'We're not wrong,' said Poppy. 'And I am going. Sorry, Caroline. But I have to, don't you see?'

Poppy had grabbed her coat and disappeared out of the house before Caroline could stop her.

'But you stay in the car, OK?' her dad said now. 'I mean it, Poppy. Caroline's right. Leave it to me and Tory. We'll sort it out.'

They drove past the pair of semi-detached farm cottages that stood on the edge of the Blackstone farm. Poppy had ridden past them more times than she could remember. They were on the route of her and Scarlett's favourite ride. Jimmy Flynn, George Blackstone's farm hand, lived in Rose Cottage with his mum and dad. Flint Cottage had stood empty since Hope Taylor and her mum Shelley moved out.

Tory pursed her lips. 'Margaret was telling me that George has thrown the Flynns out of their cottage. Says he wants to do them both up to sell.'

'But Rose Cottage doesn't need doing up,' said Poppy, grateful for anything to take her mind off what lay ahead, even if it was boring talk about people she didn't know. 'It always looks so immaculate.'

'They've had to move in with Jimmy's Auntie Flo in Tavistock until they find a new place closer to Waterby.'

Poppy stared out of the window but the two cottages were in darkness. 'That's sad.'

'It's wicked, that's what it is,' said Tory. 'All that Blackstone man ever thinks about is money. Money, money, money! And at his age! It's not like you can take it with you. His mother would turn in her grave if she could see him now.'

'Here we are,' said Poppy's dad, indicating right and turning onto a roughshod farm track. The car bumped along for what seemed like miles, but was probably only a couple of hundred yards. He winced as they hit a deep pothole, scraping the underside of the car.

Eventually the headlights picked out a handful of ramshackle farm buildings and an old farmhouse. He switched off the engine and turned to them both with a wry smile.

'Welcome, travellers. We have reached our destination.'

'REMEMBER WHAT I SAID. You stay here,' said Dad. He held the door open for Tory, who heaved herself out, still gripping her handbag in front of her like a shield. The door closed with a soft clunk and Poppy scrambled into Tory's seat to get a better view.

The yard was in darkness, save for the pale yellow glow of a security light over the back door of the farmhouse. Two border collies had started a cacophony of barking the minute the car had turned into the yard, and they were now straining at their ropes in an excited frenzy. Poppy watched her dad approach them with an outstretched hand. She could see his lips moving and she wound down the window so she could hear what he was saying.

'That's it, take it easy my friends. We've just come to see a man about a donkey.'

The two dogs grovelled on the ground, their tails pumping as he rubbed their tummies. They may be good sheepdogs but as guard dogs they were about as much use as a chocolate teapot, Poppy reflected.

Tory, meanwhile, had hobbled across the farmyard and was rapping sharply on the back door with her stick. 'I know you're in there, George Blackstone! Open up. You and I need to talk!'

After an age the door swung inwards and Poppy saw the old farmer silhouetted in the doorway. She counted to ten and let herself silently out of the car. She slunk past the two collies, a finger pressed to her lips, but they were too busy whining at their master to pay her any attention.

She stole as close to the house as she dared, stopping in a pool of darkness by the side of a tumbledown barn.

George Blackstone was shouting, his raspy voice filled with malice. 'I haven't got your bliddy donkey! And I've a good mind to call the old bill, have you two done for trespass.'

'I think you'll find trespass is a civil, not a criminal matter,' said Poppy's dad in his smooth television correspondent's voice. 'But we're more than happy to get the police involved, aren't we, Tory?'

'We certainly are. Just tell me where Chester is, George.'

The wily old farmer glanced in Poppy's direction and she shrank further into the shadows. He turned back to Tory, pointing his finger at her aggressively.

'Now look here, you meddling old bat. You can stop sticking your nose in right now. I told you. I don't know where your donkey is and I don't care.'

'So, you won't mind if we have a quick look around?' said Poppy's dad cheerfully.

George Blackstone took two steps forward and prodded his chest with a nicotine-stained finger. 'I shan't say this again Mister Lah-di-dah McKeever. Oh yes, I see you on the telly all the time, all smarm and smiles. Well, you don't impress me. I haven't got your cretinous donkey, do you understand? I've got far bigger fish to fry.'

Poppy's dad held up his hands in a placatory manner. 'Calm down, there's no need to shout.'

But George Blackstone had a murderous look in his eyes. Spittle was gathering at the corners of his mouth and Poppy could see a vein throbbing in his temple. He rose to his full height, his bulbous red nose centimetres from her dad's face.

'Don't you patronise me, you arrogant fool. Clear off my land!'

Poppy's dad lay a hand on Tory's shoulder. 'Come on, Tory, we'd better do as the gentleman says. We can't search the place without his permission.'

Poppy frowned in the darkness. *Come on, Dad, stand up to him*, she willed him silently. But he and Tory were tramping back to the car. She looked back at George Blackstone. He was watching them go with a smirk.

Poppy clenched her fists, fighting the urge to cry. A warm nose nudged her leg. It was the older of the two collies. His coat was matted and his eyes were milky. Poppy knelt down and hugged him. 'Poor boy,' she whispered as his tail thumped against the ground. His master was a cruel and greedy man. She couldn't take a chance that Chester was somewhere on the Blackstone farm.

Her mind made up, she crept along the walls of the old barn looking for a way in. She found a pair of big double doors halfway down. A steel padlock glinted in the beam of the security light.

Without much hope, Poppy gave it a sharp tug. To her surprise, the shackle came away from the body of the padlock. It hadn't been locked properly. Poppy glanced over her shoulder. George Blackstone had disappeared inside the farmhouse. Her dad and Tory were whispering urgently a few feet from the car. She knew she had a matter of seconds before they realised she'd gone.

Her heart in her mouth, she pushed the door open and slipped inside.

15

It was as dark as a starless night inside the old haybarn. Poppy was transported back to her seventh birthday party, to a game of blindman's bluff in the lounge of their old home in Twickenham. Caroline had carefully tied a blindfold over her eyes and she'd had to feel her way around the room, trying to identify her friends through touch alone. She employed the same tactic now, cautiously inching forwards, her hands in front of her like a zombie.

She didn't see the old metal plough lying in her path and tripped right over it, landing face down in a heap of musty straw. Dust filled her nostrils and she pinched her nose in an attempt to stop an attack of the sneezes. But the tickle refused to go away. *Atishoo atishoo atishoo.* She scrabbled to her feet and listened carefully to see if anyone had heard her.

Nothing.

To her right, in the cavernous darkness of the barn, she heard a rustling sound. Hoping more than anything it wasn't rats, Poppy took a tentative step forwards. She sneezed again and stared into the velvet blackness.

At first, when Poppy heard the mournful hee-haw, she thought she was imagining it. That maybe her desire to hear Chester's call had somehow conjured the donkey out of the darkness. But when a second hee-haw sliced through the still air in the barn, she knew instinctively that it was him. She stumbled towards the sound.

'Chester!' she called. He hee-hawed back. Tripping over old farm machinery and colliding with milking pails, she headed deeper into the barn. 'Hey, boy, where are you?'

The answering hee-haw was so loud he could only be a few feet away. She remembered her phone, tucked in her back pocket.

'Idiot!' she told herself, turning on the phone's torch. Keeping the spindly beam low, she waved it around. There, to her right, were four hairy legs, the colour of milk chocolate. One leg was hobbled to one of the barn's woodworm-ridden oak pillars.

'Oh Chester,' Poppy cried, burying her face in his soft coat. He nibbled her pocket. 'Yes,' she said, half laughing, half crying. 'I've got some somewhere.'

As she offered him a Polo another nose appeared. This one was seal-grey. 'Jenny!' Poppy thumbed another Polo out of the packet and the donkey took it timidly.

'We need to get you two out of here,' she told them, ruffling Chester's bristly mane. She ran towards the barn doors and yelled as loudly as her lungs allowed, 'He's in here!'

POPPY and her dad untied the shackles and used the ropes to loop loosely around the necks of the two donkeys while Tory watched, a mixture of relief and fury on her face.

'Follow me,' she commanded. 'He's not going to get away with this.' She set off determinedly towards the open barn doors.

'I'd better take Jenny,' Poppy told her dad. She clicked her tongue and gave the rope a gentle pull. The grey donkey tottered after her.

Tory was already hammering her fist against the back door of the farmhouse when they emerged from the barn. The door swung open and the old farmer appeared, a pasty in one hand and a dollop of tomato ketchup on his chin.

'What the hell are you doing back?' he snarled.

'You're a liar, George Blackstone.' Tory stepped aside and Poppy and her dad led the two donkeys into the light.

Blackstone's rheumy eyes darted from Chester to Tory and back again. 'This is a set-up. You're trying to frame me for theft,' he blustered.

'Oh, come on, you really think we'd do that?' said Poppy's dad incredulously.

'Still want to call the police?' Tory said. 'Perhaps you'd like to explain to them how Chester came to be hidden in your barn.'

Like a cornered animal, Blackstone turned on her. 'Maybe I did take your precious donkey, but that makes us even, doesn't it? Don't think I don't know that you let that damn Connemara out of its stable all them years ago.' He laughed nastily. 'What comes around, goes around, old woman.'

'Is that why you took Chester, as revenge for something you think happened years ago?' said Poppy's dad, shaking his head in disbelief.

Blackstone wiped his chin on the sleeve of his filthy tweed jacket and hooted scornfully. 'I was never going to keep the mangy old nag. Like I need another mouth to feed.' He waved his hand at Jenny. 'I thought if she was in the Nativity I'd be able to sell her on for a bit of a profit. Then the vicar picks your donkey. Stupid woman. But if your donkey happened to disappear, she'd have to use mine, wouldn't she?'

Tory nodded. 'I thought as much. I know how your mind works, George Blackstone. It all boils down to money, doesn't it? Never a thought for anyone else. Your mother would turn in her grave if she could see you now, honestly she would.'

'Stop droning on, woman! You'd have got him back after Christmas, no harm done.'

Poppy's dad reached for his mobile.

For the first time Poppy saw a flicker of fear in George Blackstone's bloodshot eyes. 'Oi, you aren't phoning the cops, are you? I thought we'd sorted this out.'

'I probably should, but no, they've got better things to do with their time. I'm phoning Bill to ask him to drive over with the trailer so we can take Chester home.'

Poppy stepped forward. 'What about Jenny? We can't leave her with *him*,' she cried.

The old hill farmer stared at her with loathing. 'That's my donkey and I paid good money for her. You must be mad if you think she's going with you.'

'How much did you pay?' said Poppy, thinking of the balance in her building society account. She'd been saving for a jumping saddle for well over a year, but that could wait.

Blackstone paused. Poppy knew he was probably thinking of a number, doubling it and more than likely multiplying it by ten for good measure. She held her breath and waited.

'Three hundred,' he said eventually. 'Yes, that's what I paid.'

'I'll give you three hundred and fifty for her,' she said.

'Hold on, Poppy, we need to talk about this first,' said her dad.

Poppy looked beseechingly at him. 'Please Dad. Look at the state of her. She's half-starved to death. I've got the money in my savings. And we've got the room.'

Tory lay a hand on his arm. 'I'll pay for her keep, Mike. Poppy's right. We can't leave the poor thing here.'

Poppy's dad shook his head ruefully. 'Alright. If Mr Blackstone agrees, I'll write a cheque now and we'll take her with us.'

George Blackstone looked positively jubilant as Poppy loaded Jenny and Chester into the back of Bill's trailer less than half an hour later.

'I don't suppose he paid more than fifty pounds for that poor donkey,' said Tory, as they bumped back down the farm track towards home.

'No wonder he was looking so pleased with himself,' said Poppy's dad. 'I hope he doesn't renege on our deal and report us to the police for stealing her.'

'He won't,' said Poppy with conviction.

'How can you be so sure, pet? He's as slippery as they come,' said Tory.

Poppy held up her mobile. 'Because I recorded everything. Him admitting he took Chester, agreeing to sell Jenny. It's all on my phone. As a kind of insurance,' she added, beaming at them both.

Her dad grinned back. 'That'll teach him to mess with a McKeever. Atta girl, Poppy.'

Poppy was awake early the next day. She sat up in bed and consulted her long list of things to do. Caroline had promised to phone the vet first thing to see if she could pop over and check Jenny's eye, and Poppy wanted everything shipshape before she arrived.

They'd left Jenny in the small paddock with Chester the previous night, but Poppy's plan was to clear out the second stable so the two donkeys could share that. Cloud would stay in his own stable next door.

Poppy pulled on an old pair of jods and her thickest fleece and went downstairs in search of breakfast. Charlie was already dressed and was eating a bowl of cereal at the kitchen table. He'd been asleep when they'd finally arrived home but Poppy had crept into his room and woken him to tell him the good news.

He looked at her anxiously. 'It wasn't a dream, was it? Chester is definitely back? And poor Jenny, too?'

'They're here. And I have a heap of work to do. Fancy helping?'

He pushed his bowl away and stood up. 'Try and stop me.'

After she had fed Cloud she turned him out with the two donkeys.

She and Charlie watched from the gate as the Connemara walked over to Jenny, his ears pricked and his neck extended.

'I hope they get on alright,' she muttered. But she needn't have worried. They touched noses and the grey donkey hee-hawed softly. Within minutes they were all grazing peacefully.

'That's one hurdle crossed. Now for the stable,' said Poppy.

They spent the next couple of hours lugging piles of old flower pots, ancient paint tins and tools out of the second stable. Charlie brushed away cobwebs and Poppy checked the wooden kickboards for loose nails. Satisfied everything was in order she laid a thick bed of straw and filled two water buckets.

The vet arrived just before lunch. 'I hear you've rescued another waif and stray,' she remarked, reaching into the back of her mud-splattered Land Rover for her medicine bag.

Caroline rolled her eyes and Poppy and Charlie grinned at each other.

The vet gave Jenny's poll a friendly scratch and examined her swollen eye. 'It looks like a straightforward case of equine conjunctivitis. I'll wash it out with some saline solution now and give you some antibiotic ointment to use three times a day. It should be looking better in a couple of days but keep using the ointment for two days after it's back to normal.'

Poppy nodded and stroked Jenny's neck while the vet listened to her heart, felt her legs, checked her feet and examined her teeth.

'How old do you think she is?' Poppy asked.

The vet straightened her back. 'Only about three, I'd say. Apart from the eye infection, and the fact that she's underweight, she's in good health. And I know how brilliant you are at putting condition on your animals. Cloud's looking great, by the way.'

Poppy flushed with pleasure. The vet had been one of the first people to see the Connemara when he'd come off the moor. He'd been skin and bone, a shadow of himself. Coaxing him back to good health had taken months of hard work.

'So, poor Jenny's going to be alright?' Charlie asked.

The vet smiled at them all. 'Poor Jenny? I'd say she's pretty lucky myself. Yes, Jenny's going to be absolutely fine.'

POPPY LAUGHED at Scarlett as they rode along one of the old railway tracks high on the moor later that afternoon. Clouds scudded across the periwinkle-blue sky and a bitter wind numbed their fingers and feet.

'Your face is a picture,' she said.

Scarlett had looked more and more astonished as Poppy had related the events of the previous evening.

'So, what will you tell the police?' she asked finally.

'Dad phoned them this morning to say Chester had come home. They're closing the crime report. We've got Chester back. George Blackstone's got his money. Everyone's happy.'

'Including poor Jenny.'

'Especially poor Jenny,' said Poppy with feeling. 'She's such a sweet donkey. You didn't see how rough Blackstone was with her at the church. I couldn't bear the thought of leaving her. She and Chester are like an old married couple already. Charlie's hoping for the patter of tiny donkey hooves.'

'But Chester's a gelding,' giggled Scarlett.

'And Charlie's eight. You can give him a talk on the birds and the bees if you like, but I'd rather not, thanks all the same. Come on, let's have a canter,' Poppy said. She felt carefree, as though an exam she'd been dreading for months had suddenly been cancelled. Chester was home, they'd saved Jenny from Blackstone's evil clutches and, now the sedative had worn off, Cloud was back to his normal, bouncy self.

She gathered her reins and the Connemara danced on the spot. Red crabbed sideways up the track. The two ponies were like coiled springs, waiting to be released.

Poppy laughed and gave Cloud his head. 'Race you to the tor,' she cried. Cloud sprang into a canter, Red matching him stride for stride.

Soon both girls were crouched low over their ponies' necks as they galloped towards the rocky outcrop.

When the smooth grassy ride became peppered with scattered rocks they slowed to a walk and let their reins slip through their fingers so the ponies could stretch their necks. Poppy wiggled her toes.

'I can't feel my feet. Let's walk the last bit,' she said, jumping off Cloud. Scarlett followed suit, yelping as her frozen feet hit the ground. As they sidestepped granite boulders and dodged peaty puddles Poppy had never felt happier. They settled on a wide, basin-like rock at the top of the tor and let the ponies nibble at the wiry grass while they gazed across the moor.

'This is the life,' sighed Poppy contentedly. 'No school for almost a fortnight, Christmas in a few days' time. Chester back home. Perfect.'

'Isn't it just,' Scarlett agreed. 'Bet Princess Georgia never has this much fun on her posh showjumper.'

It was as if Scarlett had flipped a switch. At the mention of Georgia's name an anxious knot formed in Poppy's stomach. She had managed to push the kidnapping deep into her subconscious when Chester had gone missing. But it had popped up again, like an irksome jack-in-a-box.

She chewed a nail. The urge to tell Scarlett was overwhelming. She knew she could trust her best friend. And wasn't it true that a problem shared was a problem halved?

'Talking about Georgia, d'you think she's still sore that she wasn't picked for the showjumping team?' said Scarlett.

'I don't suppose it's the main thing on her mind right now.'

Scarlett looked puzzled. 'Why?'

Poppy clambered to her feet. 'Come on, let's go home. My backside's gone completely numb. I'll tell you why on the way.'

ONCE AGAIN SCARLETT'S face was a picture of disbelief as Poppy recounted her trip to Claydon Manor.

'Surely if her parents just hand over the two million quid they'll get her back?' she said.

But Poppy had thought long and hard about this. 'I don't think they can afford to, Scar. Think about it. Georgia had to sell most of her jumping ponies a while back, didn't she? Don't you remember Sam telling us that they'd spent their way through their lottery win and that's why they opened the livery yard? They had to start making the place pay. The house was absolutely freezing when I was there. And everything looked shabby. Not shabby chic, just shabby. They may live in that enormous house, but I think they're what you call property rich and cash poor.'

Scarlett raised her eyebrows. 'Are you saying the Cannings are skint? Crikey.'

'Try not to sound too pleased,' Poppy said reprovingly.

'Sorry.' Scarlett looked shamefaced. 'But there's nothing we can do, is there?'

'I rode over to Witch Cottage, to see if she was there.'

Scarlett was aghast. 'And what would you have done if she was? These are not the type of people to mess with, Poppy.'

'You're right,' Poppy sighed. 'I just can't help thinking that I've missed something. Something important.'

'Let the police deal with it,' her best friend said firmly. 'If they can't find Georgia no-one will.'

THEY RODE home past the Blackstone farm. Poppy hadn't wanted to – she would be happy never to clap eyes on the place again – but it was the most direct route back and the sun was beginning to sink below the horizon. It would be dark in half an hour.

'New people must have moved in,' said Scarlett, as they trotted past the two farm cottages. A beaten-up red pick-up truck was parked on the muddy track behind Flint Cottage.

'It probably belongs to the builders. Tory said George Blackstone's doing up both cottages to sell,' said Poppy absentmindedly.

Scarlett pulled a face. 'To more out-of-towners, I expect.'

'Like us, you mean?' joked Poppy. It wasn't so long ago that the McKeevers had made the move from London to Devon in search of a quieter life.

Scarlett grinned. 'I forgot you used to be a city girl. It feels like you've lived here forever.'

Poppy pretended to look affronted. 'In a good way, I hope?'

'Of course, you twit.'

Poppy smiled to herself. To be described as a local was a compliment indeed.

17

Poppy was in her bedroom wrapping presents the following morning when Caroline poked her head around the door. Poppy was surprised to see her normally calm stepmum looking harassed.

'What's up?' she said through a mouthful of sticky tape.

'The vicar's just called. She's holding a dress rehearsal for the Nativity and wants Chester there.'

'That's alright, isn't it?'

'It's this afternoon! We were supposed to be going to the supermarket. I haven't got any food in for Christmas yet!'

The thought of spending over an hour in a crowded supermarket a couple of days before Christmas did not sound much fun.

'That's OK. I'll walk Charlie and Chester down to the church. I'll see if Scarlett wants to come, too. It'll be fun,' said Poppy.

'But that's not all,' said Caroline. 'She's suddenly announced that she wants Charlie to dress as a shepherd. There's no way he's going to agree to that, you know what he's like. And, anyway, how on earth am I supposed to find a costume in the next two hours?'

'Leave it to me,' said Poppy firmly.

SHE FOUND Charlie in the lounge, watching television.

'It's a supermoon tonight,' he told her. 'Biggest one for nearly seventy years. It's going to be amazing.'

'No time for supermoons now,' she said, depositing the armful of items she had spent the last half an hour collecting on the sofa.

'What's all that?' he said suspiciously.

'Your costume.'

'I'm not wearing a tea towel on my head. I'll look like an idiot.'

'But you used to love dressing up,' said Poppy.

'That was when I was seven,' scoffed Charlie. 'I'm eight now. And eight-year-old boys do not like dressing up.'

'But shepherds are cool. At least you don't have to be Angel Gabriel and wear a white sheet and tinsel.'

'And a brown pillowcase is any better?' Charlie crossed his arms and gave her a mutinous look. Poppy realised that going to the super-market with Caroline might have been the easier option.

'I spent ages hunting through the airing cupboard looking for that,' she said, holding the offending pillowcase against her. 'I turned it into a tunic for you!'

'That is not a tunic. It's a pillowcase with holes cut out for my head and arms,' said Charlie.

'I thought you could wear it over your brown trousers and that khaki long-sleeved top Caroline got for you the other day. I've found some rope to tie around your waist and head. And I've made you a crook, look.'

Poppy was quite pleased with the hook she'd fashioned out of cardboard, painted brown and fixed to the end of an old curtain pole. But Charlie gave her a withering look and turned back to the television.

'I suppose I'd better wear it, then,' she said, pulling the pillowcase over her head and poking her arms through the holes. She tied the longer length of rope around her waist and smoothed the cotton underneath. 'Now for the headdress.' She tied the tea towel around her forehead with the rest of the rope and picked up the crook. 'There. Pretty authentic shepherd, huh?'

Charlie looked at her out of the corner of his eye and shrugged.

'It's a shame,' she continued.

'What's a shame?' he asked grumpily.

'That you won't be leading Chester in the Nativity. I thought you were looking forward to it.'

'Of course I'll be leading him! A pair of net curtains chose us.'

'The *Reverend Kirton* chose Chester, not you. And if you had read the small print in the contract you'd have seen that the chosen donkey's helper must wear a shepherd's costume.'

'What contract?' cried Charlie, the supermoon forgotten.

Poppy crossed her fingers. 'The one she gave to Caroline on the way out. You were talking to Sam at the time.'

'But that's not –'

'Fair?' said Poppy. 'Of course it's fair. But it's your decision. It's fine. I'm more than happy to do it instead. I think my costume is cool.' She pulled off the tea towel and pillowcase and folded them neatly on the floor beside Charlie. 'I'll go and get Chester ready and we'll leave in fifteen minutes, OK?'

Charlie muttered something under his breath.

'Sorry, I didn't quite catch that,' said Poppy.

'I said, alright, I'll wear your stupid shepherd's costume.'

'Ah, but will you wear it with good grace?' said Poppy, aware she was pushing her luck.

Charlie's expression was doubtful. 'Why, does it say that in the contract, too?'

'No, of course it doesn't. But if you march up the aisle with a face like thunder it's not exactly going to make the congregation feel Christmassy, is it?'

Charlie rolled his eyes. 'I promise to wear your stupid – sorry, *splendid* – shepherd's costume with good grace,' he intoned.

'Glad that's finally settled,' said Poppy. 'Be ready in fifteen minutes.'

Once she was safely in the hallway she fist-pumped the air. It wasn't often that she got the better of her eight-year-old brother. When she did, victory was sweet.

~

THE REVEREND KIRTON was in the church porch, welcoming the stars of the Nativity, both human and animal, as they arrived.

'Lovely! You made it!' she exclaimed as Poppy, Scarlett, Charlie and Chester made their way into the nave. 'And what a wonderful costume, Charlie!'

Relieved to see that he wasn't the only one dressed in tea towels and bed linen, Charlie gave her a gracious smile. 'Thanks. It's just something I threw together at the last minute,' he said, neatly side-stepping an elbow in the ribs from his sister.

They joined the rest of the cast at the back of the church. As well as Chester, there were a couple of goats, a sheep and an alpaca called Nelly.

'I don't remember alpacas being in the Nativity,' giggled Scarlett, as Nelly yawned, showing two rows of yellowing teeth.

'I don't think Baby Jesus wore dungarees either,' observed Poppy. The vicar had clearly been unable to find a baby for this year's performance.

'Do we have a volunteer to lead Daisy the sheep?' asked Reverend Kirton. 'I'm told she's very friendly.'

'Oo, yes, I'll do it,' said Scarlett. 'I'm good with sheep. On account of us having a sheep farm,' she added.

'Marvellous!' cried the vicar, clapping her hands in delight.

Poppy settled in a pew at the back of the church and watched the proceedings with amusement. The animals conducted themselves impeccably. It was the children who ignored Reverend Kirton's entreaties to behave.

'No Matthew, pulling hair is *not nice*,' she told the smallest of the Three Kings, who had just given Mary's ponytail a violent tug. 'And Jasper, please be quiet when the innkeeper is saying his line. It is a rather important one, after all.'

A dark-haired woman slipped into the pew beside Poppy. 'How's it going?' she whispered.

Poppy did a double take. It was PC Bodiam, wearing a grey duffle coat over her police uniform.

'Has something happened?' said Poppy, aghast.

'No. I'm here as a mum, not a police officer. My daughter Meg is one of the angels. I'm working on Christmas Eve and won't get a chance to see the actual Nativity. I promised her I'd come to the rehearsal. Luckily I'm not on duty until three. What about you?'

'I brought Chester and Charlie.'

'I heard Chester came back. He must have found a way out of his field after all. It did seem a bit far-fetched that he'd been stolen,' said PC Bodiam.

Poppy coloured. Fortunately the police officer was too busy watching her daughter to notice. Keen to change the subject, she said, 'Any news on you-know-what?'

PC Bodiam glanced over her shoulder to check no-one was in earshot. 'She's still missing, if that's what you mean. You haven't told your parents, have you?'

'No,' said Poppy truthfully. 'Did her mum and dad not pay the ransom?'

'Ah, well there's a problem there. They've got a bit of a cash flow problem.'

So, she had been right. The Cannings were clean broke. 'What happens now?'

'We are following a number of lines of enquiry.' PC Bodiam smiled wryly. 'Sorry, that sounds a bit official, doesn't it? We've had some intel that looks like it might have legs.'

'Intel?'

'Sorry, more police speak. Intelligence. It means information. According to one of our sources, two women at Eastwood Park were overheard talking about a wealthy family who lived near Tavistock. They described the family as an 'easy target'.' PC Bodiam drew inverted commas in the air.

She fell silent as the angels shuffled to their feet and began singing

While Shepherds Watched Their Flocks. Or, as Charlie preferred to call it, *While Shepherds Washed Their Socks.* A girl aged about six with a band of silver tinsel tied around her poker-straight blonde hair waved furtively in their direction. PC Bodiam waved back. 'That's Meg,' she said with barely-disguised pride.

The Three Kings walked solemnly up the aisle and deposited their gifts of gold, frankincense and myrrh unceremoniously at the toddler Jesus's trainer-clad feet.

An image of Georgia, locked in a dark room all on her own while the rest of the world opened presents and stuffed themselves with turkey and mince pies, crept into Poppy's head. She shivered.

'It's not going to be much of a Christmas for Georgia, is it?'

The police officer shook her head. 'But you mustn't worry. We're doing everything we can to find her.'

'D'you think she'll be alright?'

PC Bodiam smiled sadly. 'I hope so, Poppy, I really do.'

18

P oppy sat, cross-legged, on the end of her bed. Scarlett lay on the floor, teasing Magpie with a ball of screwed up wrapping paper. Every now and then the cat raised his paw and swatted the ball lazily.

'Tell me what she said again?'

Poppy tried to remember PC Bodiam's exact words. 'Two women in some park or other were talking about a family with loads of money who lived near Tavistock.'

'There are probably lots of families with loads of money who live near Tavistock.'

'I know. But it's a bit of a coincidence, isn't it?'

'Maybe,' said Scarlett. 'Which park was it?'

'I'd have thought that's neither here nor there,' said Poppy, parroting one of Tory's favourite expressions.

'You never know.' Scarlett tickled Magpie's enormous stomach and sat up. 'Try and remember, just in case.'

'Um.' Poppy shut her eyes. 'East something. Eastwell! I think that was it.'

'Google it,' ordered Scarlett, joining Poppy on her bed. Poppy reached for her phone and tapped in Eastwell Park. According to Wikipedia it was a country estate near a place called Ashford in Kent.

'But that's the other side of the country,' said Scarlett. 'Why would two women in a country park in Kent be talking about a rich family in Devon?'

'I have absolutely no idea.'

'Are you sure it was Eastwell?'

Poppy tapped her lips with her index finger. 'It could have been Eastwood. I'll try that.'

They watched the screen as the search engine listed dozens of hits.

'OMG,' said Scarlett.

The two girls looked at each other in disbelief. Eastwood Park was a women's prison in Gloucestershire.

Poppy clutched Scarlett's arm. 'That's the prison Shelley Taylor was sent to!'

'You don't think –'

'She pretended her own daughter had cancer so she could con people out of hundreds of pounds. I wouldn't put anything past her, would you?'

'Are you sure that's where she went?'

'One hundred per cent. It was a women's prison in Gloucester-shire. I remember thinking it was the same county as the Badminton Horse Trials.'

The two girls were silent. And then Poppy gasped. 'Do you know what I also remember? You know that day we took Hope to the show at Redhall? D'you remember how Shelley was quizzing you about the Cannings when we dropped Hope off?'

Scarlett's eyes widened. 'I told her they'd won the lottery and that their house was full of antiques!' The colour drained from her face so her freckles stood out more than ever. 'I told her Georgia's pony cost ten grand. I even told her the name of the house. Oh my God, Poppy. This is all my fault!'

'Scar, we don't even know if Shelley's behind it,' Poppy reasoned.

'It has to be her. We should phone the police right now.'

'Hold on, we can't prove anything. We don't even know if Shelley's still in prison.'

'How long did she get, can you remember?'

Poppy thought hard. 'Three and a half years, I think. But sometimes people get let out early for good behaviour, don't they? At least they do on the telly.'

Scarlett jumped to her feet. 'Let's phone the prison now and find out.'

'They won't tell us. Prisoner confidentiality and all that.'

Scarlett looked agonised. 'So how will we find out?'

'That's easy. We'll ask Hope.'

THEY DISCUSSED TELLING Hope their theory that her mum had masterminded a dastardly kidnap plot but decided against it.

'It's not fair on Hope,' Poppy said. 'Shelley Taylor has made her life miserable enough already. There's no point worrying her until we know for sure that she's behind all this, if she even is.'

Instead they sent an email full of stories about the Nativity, the ponies and the latest village gossip.

'Just ask her casually at the end whether she's still in touch with her mum,' said Scarlett, peering over Poppy's shoulder.

Poppy typed furiously, read the email through one last time and pressed send.

'What's the time difference between here and Toronto?'

'Um. I'll check.' Poppy's fringe fell over her face as she opened Google. 'We're five hours ahead. So, it's just after eleven in the morning over there.'

Scarlett hugged her knees. 'I hope she sees it soon. I promised Mum I'd be home by five.'

'I'm sure she will. She's usually really quick to reply,' soothed Poppy.

'And what if she says her mum has been let out of prison? What do we do then?'

'That,' said Poppy, 'is the million dollar question.'

～

BUT BY THE time Scarlett left at five, there was still no email from Hope.

'Text me if you hear. Promise,' Scarlett said, her hazel eyes serious. 'I'll never be able to sleep tonight, worrying it's all my fault.'

'Don't be silly. It wasn't you who kidnapped Georgia, was it?'

'Who's kidnapped who?' trilled a voice. Poppy's heart sank. Charlie was standing in the kitchen door watching Scarlett pull on her wellies.

'No-one has kidnapped anyone. We were just talking about a film we watched the other day, weren't we Scar?'

'Yep. It was about a boy called George who got kidnapped. We saw it at my house. It was really good.'

'You never asked me,' said Charlie, his bottom lip jutting out.

'We would have done, but it was a twelve certificate. And you're only eight.' Poppy smiled sweetly, ignoring the daggers look Charlie gave her. He stomped out of the room and Poppy exhaled slowly.

'That was a close shave. If Charlie finds out we're in serious trouble.'

～

POPPY FEIGNED a headache after dinner so she could stay in her bedroom, checking and re-checking her emails. At nine o'clock she gave up and got ready for bed.

'One last time,' she told herself, reaching for the laptop.

And there it was, sitting in her inbox. An email from Hope. She opened it and began to read.

Hi Poppy and Scarlett!

Great to hear from you! I'm glad the ponies (and Chester) are all well. I miss them heaps. It's been snowing for the last couple of days in Toronto so it feels really Christmassy. They have turkey for Christmas lunch over here, only they have it with mashed potatoes, not roast potatoes. And Dad says we'll probably go tobogganing on Christmas morning, which'll be really cool.

I love it here, but a little bit of me wishes I could come and watch Chester in the Nativity. It sounds fun! Maybe one day I can come over for a holiday? Or you both could come over to Canada. That would be awesome!

Mum's still in prison. Dad says she's got at least another year to go. She writes to me once a week. She's never actually said, but I think she's sorry about everything.

Anyway, write soon. Send me some pics of the Nativity.

And have a FANTASTIC Christmas!

Love,

Hope xx

Poppy closed the laptop, slipped under the duvet and lay staring at the ceiling, her mind racing. When they'd realised Eastwood Park was the very same prison Shelley Taylor had been sent to Poppy had been convinced she must be behind the kidnap. She knew about the Cannings and their lottery win. She certainly had no compunction when it came to conning people out of their hard-earned cash. She'd spun an elaborate web of deceit to dupe countless good-hearted people into handing over money once before. And then she'd squandered it all on designer clothes. It wasn't that great a leap from fraud to kidnap. Poppy remembered the bitterness in Shelley's voice when Scarlett had told her about Claydon Manor and its expensive antiques and works of art. It was too much of a coincidence to think she wasn't involved, wasn't it?

And yet, according to Hope, she was still in prison. Poppy had no reason to doubt her friend. Hope had been as much a victim of Shelley's greed as any of the people who had given money to her fictitious charity appeal, believing they were helping to send a girl with leukaemia to America for treatment.

Certain sleep was beyond her grasp, Poppy let her mind wander. She thought about her visit to Claydon Manor and how she'd stumbled on a real-life drama with the highest of stakes. She pictured

Georgia's heartbroken mum sitting at the kitchen table with her head in her hands. The gruff voice of Inspector Pearson as he questioned Poppy about the ransom note. The sad look on PC Claire Bodiam's face when Poppy had asked her if Georgia would be OK.

She remembered the last time she'd seen Georgia. She'd been her usual scornful self, griping about her underdone hot dog and winding Scarlett up. Perhaps she was ordering her captors around in her usual superior way. Poppy hoped so. But she had long suspected that beneath the veneer of superiority Georgia was as insecure as she was. Perhaps, more likely, she had fallen apart.

Poppy wondered if the police felt as powerless as she did. What could they do, other than wait for the Cannings to scrabble together enough money to satisfy the kidnappers' demands? Had they searched outbuildings, followed every lead? Poppy remembered her own hunch that Georgia was being kept at Witch Cottage. It seemed ludicrous now, just silly schoolgirl speculation.

A vision of Dartmoor Prison's high granite walls lurked on the edge of Poppy's consciousness. The prison dominated the skyline on that part of the moor, vast and impenetrable. Did Eastwood Park look like HMP Dartmoor? Could Shelley have escaped? And then realisation pinged in her brain and she wondered how she could have been so blind. She knew from bitter experience that criminals still planned crimes inside jail. Look at Jodie's dad. He'd directed a phone smuggling operation from his cell after he'd been jailed for fiddling the books at work. Just because Shelley was in prison didn't mean she had nothing to do with Georgia's disappearance.

She had the local knowledge and the motive. And, thanks to her time inside, she also had the criminal contacts.

Poppy sat up in bed, all thought of sleep forgotten. If she was right, and Shelley was behind Georgia's kidnap, where would she hide her?

19

Snippets of conversation floated around in Poppy's head. Tory telling her indignantly that Jimmy Flynn and his parents had been forced out of Rose Cottage. George Blackstone muttering he had bigger fish to fry. The old farmer was supposed to be doing up both cottages to sell. But did the beaten-up red truck parked behind Flint Cottage belong to the builders, or was there another, far more sinister reason for its presence?

She reached for her phone and texted Scarlett.

Are you still awake?

The phone pinged in seconds.

Yep. Can't sleep. Why?

Think I know where Georgia is.

You're kidding me. How?

Just put two and two together and came up with about forty-six.

Are you gonna call the police?

Poppy closed her eyes and deliberated. Should she head straight downstairs and tell her dad and Caroline her theory? Leave it to the police to sort out? That would be the sensible option. But what if the police didn't believe her? What if they did, and she was wrong? Poppy could imagine the toe-curling embarrassment if a fleet of patrol cars with their blue lights flashing screeched up to the place in the middle of the night only to find it glaringly empty. She needed hard evidence before she called them out on a wild goose chase.

No. I need to check I'm right first.

When're you going, tomorrow?

Poppy tapped without thinking.

Tonight.

But it's almost ten o'clock!

Poppy sprinted across her room to the window and peered outside. The stables and fields were bathed in the silver glow of an enormous moon. Of course, Charlie's supermoon! It was so bright Poppy could pick out every tree and boulder between the house and the Riverdale tor. She tapped out another text.

It'll be fine. It's as light as day out there. I'll wait until Dad and Caroline are asleep and take Cloud. He'll look after me.

Poppy grinned when she saw her best friend's reply.

You're not going without us, OK?

OK. We'll meet you by the gate to the moor in 40 mins.

Poppy dressed quickly and climbed back into bed. After twenty minutes she heard the lounge door click shut and the sound of her dad and Caroline climbing the stairs to bed. After another quarter of an hour she heard the familiar low rumble of her dad snoring.

Poppy padded across her bedroom, eased open the door and crept along the landing, tiptoeing to avoid the creaky floorboard outside her parents' room. In the kitchen she gave Freddie a treat, pulled on her coat, flicked off the security light and slipped out of the back door.

As Poppy crossed the yard Jenny's head appeared over her stable door and the donkey gave the softest hee-haw. Poppy rubbed her head and the donkey nibbled the sleeve of her coat. Chester, laying asleep in the straw, his legs tucked neatly beneath him, opened an eye, saw it was Poppy and went back to sleep.

Poppy could hear Cloud moving around in the stable next door. She grabbed his saddle and bridle from the tack room, shoved her hat on and let herself into his stable. He watched her calmly, as if nocturnal hacks were an everyday occurrence.

Once he was tacked up she led him out of the stable to the gate that led to the moor. Scarlett and Red were nowhere to be seen. Poppy tightened her girth a notch and swung into the saddle. She checked the time on her phone. It was a quarter to eleven. She hoped Scarlett hadn't got cold feet. Suddenly the idea of riding to George Blackstone's farm in the middle of the night seemed at best foolhardly, at worst downright dangerous. If the cantankerous old farmer caught them on his land there was no knowing what he might do.

Cloud's head shot up. He sniffed the air and gave a low whinny. Poppy ran a hand down his neck and peered into the gloom. In the distance she could just make out the shape of Scarlett and Red. The chestnut gelding skittered left and right but Scarlett sat calmly in the saddle. At four, Red was still a baby and could be nervous out hacking. Goodness only knew what he was making of their late night ride. Poppy could hear Scarlett talking to him in a low, soothing voice. He whinnied when he saw Cloud and the two ponies touched noses.

'He thinks I've totally lost the plot,' said Scarlett. She grinned at Poppy. 'And I think he's probably right. Why on earth couldn't this wait until the morning?'

Poppy wasn't sure herself. 'I suppose I thought it was best if we checked out the place under the cover of darkness. If there's no-one there, there's no harm done and we'll leave it to the police to find Georgia.'

'You still haven't told me where we're going.'

Cloud snatched at the bit and Poppy tightened her reins. He was as excited as Red to be out. She kicked him into a canter and called over her shoulder, 'Flint Cottage, of course. That's where we're going.'

IT WAS EXHILARATING to canter across the moonlit moor. Dartmoor ponies watched silently as they approached and sheep scattered like bowling pins. Now and then they heard the eerie screech of a barn owl. Once they saw the zebra-striped face of a badger peering out from a copse of trees. Poppy felt the thunder of their ponies' hooves in time with the blood pounding in her temples. What would they find when they reached the old farm cottage? She patted her pocket to reassure herself she had her mobile phone and made a silent pledge to call the police at the first sign of trouble.

When the ponies' flanks were steaming they pulled up and walked the last half a mile to the boundary of the Blackstone farm.

'What's the plan?' Scarlett whispered.

Poppy realised she didn't actually have one. She gave a helpless shrug. 'I guess we need to check if that truck's still parked there for starters.'

'We can't ride up the lane. They'll hear the hooves on the tarmac. We'll have to go around the back.'

'You're right.' Poppy wondered why she hadn't thought of that. 'So, which way should we go?'

Scarlett halted Red. The moonlight had turned the chestnut gelding the colour of burnished copper. He fidgeted while Scarlett found her bearings. 'I reckon if we follow that old stone wall it should bring us out at the back of the cottages, don't you?'

Poppy had no idea. 'Let's give it a go.'

Like everything on the Blackstone farm, the old dry stone wall had long fallen into disrepair and Cloud and Red were forced to pick their way carefully through fallen boulders that peppered the close-cropped grass. Scarlett was right. The wall led straight to the back of the two farm cottages. The two girls fell silent as they drew nearer.

The back garden of Rose Cottage was as neat as a pin. A rectangle of lawn was sandwiched between two long borders of winter-flowering pansies. Poppy felt her breathing quicken when she saw a shadowy shape in the middle of the lawn. She gripped Cloud's reins tightly and was about to call a warning to Scarlett when she realised it was only a washing line hiding inside a green plastic cover.

The back garden of Flint Cottage was a choking tangle of brambles and overgrown shrubs, edged by an ancient wire stock fence that sagged pathetically like an old string vest.

'Look!' hissed Scarlett, pointing to fresh tyre tracks that looped up to the back fence and stopped abruptly right in front of them.

Poppy halted Cloud, her eyes searching for the truck they'd seen parked behind the cottage the day before. Shapes shifted in the silver light. Two oil drums, rusty with age. A roll of roofing felt as black as bitumen, leaning against a towering pile of rubble. An antiquated lawnmower that looked as though it had spluttered and died decades before.

But no beaten-up red truck. Wherever it was, it wasn't here.

20

Moonlight glinted off the windows of the two farm cottages, but otherwise they were in darkness.

'What do we do now?' said Scarlett in a low voice.

'I'm going to take a closer look.' Poppy jumped out of the saddle and handed her reins to Scarlett.

'Be careful!' Scarlett's eyes were as round as orbs.

Poppy gave her a quick smile and headed for the back garden of Rose Cottage. She gave the wooden gate a tentative tug, exhaling softly as it swung open.

To her relief, the security light at the back of the house wasn't working and she slipped across the lawn like a sylph to the patio doors. Cupping her eyes, she stared into a long, thin room that stretched the length of the house. The Flynns had probably used it as a lounge diner but it was now completely empty. Poppy sidled along to the kitchen window and peered inside. There was no sign of life. The surfaces were clean but bare. The only sound came from the drip, drip, drip of the tap.

Poppy glanced at Scarlett. She had jumped off Red and was pointing to the back of Flint Cottage. Poppy ran over to her.

'There's no-one there, Scar. I'm going to check Hope's old house.'

'There's a hole in the back fence, look. We'll be waiting in the garden. Don't be long. I'm getting really creeped out.'

Poppy nodded and climbed over the fence dividing the two gardens. She remembered the first time she and Scarlett had visited Flint Cottage. They'd taken a tin of chocolate brownies, keen to welcome the newcomers to the village. Hope had soon become a friend, but Poppy had never trusted Shelley. And her instincts had proved right.

She forced her way through the waist-high weeds, tripping over an old milk crate, until she reached the kitchen window. To her frustration the blind was drawn. She crouched down and peeped through the microscopic gap between the window frame and the bottom of the blind. Unlike Rose Cottage, the work surfaces in Flint Cottage were strewn with empty food packets, old teabags and dirty mugs and plates. Poppy's breathing quickened. Had the builders left it like this? Or had someone else been here?

She edged along the back wall to the dining room window. The two rooms hadn't been knocked through like the ones in Rose Cottage. Poppy wasn't sure if she felt relieved or anxious when she realised the curtains were open. She took a deep breath and stared into the room. It was empty, save for a cheap dining room table and four chairs.

Poppy was so busy trying to see if she could peer into the hallway from the dining room window that she didn't hear Scarlett and the two ponies approach. The first she knew they behind her was when Cloud gave her a business-like nudge.

'Oh my God!' she shrieked, all thoughts of staying concealed forgotten. 'Why did you creep up on me like that?'

'Sorry,' said Scarlett defensively. 'And I wasn't creeping up on you. I was leading your pony over because I want to go home. My feet are frozen and I'm worried Red'll catch a chill and there's clearly no-one here. The place is deserted.'

'You're right,' Poppy sighed. 'Good job I didn't call the police, isn't it? I'd have looked a proper muppet. C'mon, let's go home.'

Poppy took Cloud's reins from Scarlett and was edging her toe into the stirrup when she froze.

'What's that noise?' she hissed.

'What noise?' said Scarlett impatiently. 'I can't hear a thing.'

'That noise. Listen!'

Poppy felt her insides turn to ice. From somewhere near her feet she could hear the unmistakable sound of someone's knuckles rapping against a window. She clutched Cloud's neck, shrinking into his solid bulk. Scarlett was hopping around on one foot while Red, terrified by the noise, spun round and round.

'Steady boy,' she coaxed, eventually managing to clamber on. 'Poppy, can we *please* go!'

But Poppy was leading Cloud towards the tapping sound. She couldn't leave until she knew what it was. It seemed to be coming from beneath her feet. And then she saw something she hadn't noticed before – a tiny window behind a metal grill a few inches from the ground.

'Did you know Flint Cottage had a cellar?' she asked Scarlett, who was still trying to calm Red.

She shook her head. 'Poppy –'

Ignoring her, Poppy bent down and reached through the grill. The wooden window frame was as rotten as old fruit. She ran her fingers under it and gave it a tug. It opened a fraction.

Poppy knelt on the ground. 'Georgia!' she whispered urgently. 'Is that you?'

21

For a moment, all Poppy could hear was the beating of her own heart. Then a croaky voice whispered back, 'Is that the police?'

'Er, not exactly. It's me, Poppy McKeever. And Scarlett,' she added.

'Brilliant,' muttered the voice. Poppy jumped as the window flapped open. And then her jaw dropped as she saw Georgia's face staring back at her through the bars of the grill. There were dark circles under her china-blue eyes and an angry red welt on her temple. Her normally glossy black hair was lank and greasy.

'Is it her?' called Scarlett.

'Of course it's me!' Georgia hissed. 'You need to get me out of here before they come back.'

Poppy found she was rooted to the spot. 'Before who comes back?'

'Ricky and Bev. They've gone to get a Chinese takeaway. I heard them talking about it. They've been gone ages. They could be back at any minute!'

'Meet me by the back door. I'll see if I can force it open,' said Poppy.

'I'm locked in the cellar, you idiot! Don't you think I might have tried to get out before now otherwise?'

It seemed that even being kidnapped hadn't rubbed away any of Georgia's prickliness. Poppy felt a fleeting sympathy for her captors. She scrambled to her feet and handed Scarlett her reins.

'Call the police, Scar, and I'll see if I can break in.'

The back door was half-glazed. Thanking her lucky stars it wasn't a new uPVC door with toughened glass, Poppy looked around frantically, pouncing on a broken brick laying half-hidden in the undergrowth. Turning her face away from the door, she smashed the brick against the glass. It shattered like ice, leaving a circle of jagged shards like the jaws of a great white shark.

'Be careful, Poppy!' Scarlett shouted. She had jumped off Red and was holding both ponies in one hand and her mobile in the other.

'Tell them it's an emergency,' Poppy panted, and turned back to the door. She used the brick to smash a bigger hole and felt inside for the door handle.

'Please let the key be in the lock,' she muttered. The fates were being kind. Her fingers closed around the key and she turned it carefully. The last thing she needed was for it to fall onto the floor out of reach. The door now unlocked, she pulled the handle and gave it a shove. It didn't budge.

Poppy shot an anxious look at Scarlett.

'It might be bolted,' Scarlett mouthed, pointing to the top of the door. Poppy groaned.

'Are you coming?' shouted Georgia. The supercilious tone had been replaced by one of rising panic.

Poppy ran back to the cellar window. 'Can you remember if the back door was bolted?'

Georgia was clutching the bars of the grill. Her knuckles were the same alabaster-white as her face. 'I don't know! They blindfolded me. Can't you kick it in?'

Poppy shook her head. 'I suppose I can try.'

She balanced on her left leg and jabbed with her right, but the door stayed stubbornly shut. This was useless. She needed to open the bolt.

She knocked the rest of the broken glass out of the window and stood on tiptoes, but the top of the door was tantalisingly out of reach. She remembered the milk crate. Huffing as she pulled it out of the brambles, she set it on its side against the back door, hopped onto it and scrabbled blindly for the bolt.

'Yesss!' said Poppy as the bolt slid open. She opened the door and ran into the house. 'Georgia!' she yelled. 'Where are you?'

Poppy couldn't ever remember seeing a cellar door in Flint Cottage. Where would it be? She ran into the kitchen and came face to face with a white painted door. She used two hands to haul it open. But it was a pantry, empty apart from an old kettle and a lonely tin of peaches.

She was on her way to the lounge when she noticed the cupboard under the stairs. It was bolted top and bottom. Her heart thumping in her chest, she slid the bolts across and wrenched open the door.

At once she was hit by a damp, musty smell and the welcome sight of steep brick steps leading down. Poppy took the steps two at a time. They led to a tiny cellar, no more than eight foot by six foot, lit by the single bar of an electric fire. Against one wall was a green camp bed. On the floor beside it was a half-empty two litre bottle of water and the remains of a microwave meal. Georgia was still gazing out of the tiny window, a cheap nylon sleeping bag around her shaking shoulders.

'Georgia?' said Poppy uncertainly. 'Are you OK?'

The older girl slowly turned to face Poppy. She was still wearing her show jacket and jodhpurs, although the once-white material was black with filth. Tears were coursing down her cheeks. 'I thought I was going to die in here. Ricky has a gun, you see. And he gets really angry.' She touched the mark on her temple and lowered her eyes.

'You're safe now,' Poppy said, with as much confidence as she could muster. 'Scarlett is on the phone to the police. They'll be here any minute. But we should get out of the cellar. Come on.'

Poppy was halfway up the steps when she heard the whine of an engine in the distance. Georgia cried out as if she'd been struck and cringed against the wall.

'They're back!' she whispered.

Her terror was infectious and Poppy's insides turned to liquid. But she couldn't afford to panic. 'Georgia! We've got to go!' she shouted.

They sprinted up the cellar steps towards the back door. Poppy doubled back and slid the bolts closed. As soon as they saw the smashed glass the kidnappers would know Georgia had gone, but anything that gave them even a few seconds' advantage was worth doing.

Scarlett flung Cloud's reins at Poppy and jumped on Red. 'I had no signal,' she shrieked. 'And I can see a car coming!'

Georgia was staring at the two ponies as if she was in a trance.

'I'll get on first, then you get on the back,' ordered Poppy. It was a good job Cloud was used to Charlie riding behind her, she thought, as she lowered a hand to Georgia and pulled her into the saddle.

Headlights snaked around the side of the house and Red whinnied in fear. Georgia's arms felt as tight as a seatbelt around Poppy's waist.

'OK?' she said.

'Please, just go,' Georgia begged.

Poppy kicked Cloud into a canter and he flew through the hole in the fence, Red on his tail.

As they fled down the dirt track behind the two cottages Poppy allowed herself to think for one foolish moment that they were safe.

Until the truck rounded the corner with a furious roar and the two fleeing ponies were caught in its headlights. The truck sped towards them, its engine whining under the strain. And she realised just how much danger they were in.

22

Poppy made a decision she hoped she wouldn't regret.

'We need to split up,' she shouted to Scarlett. 'You go straight to ours and call the police. We'll head for the Riverdale woods. They'll never get the truck in there.'

Scarlett was trying to control Red, who was plunging and leaping like a bucking bronco, the whites of his eyes showing. She nodded and gave the gelding his head. He galloped into the night, his flaxen tail streaming behind him like a wisp of smoke.

'Stay safe,' Poppy called, even though she knew Scarlett would never hear over the noise of the revving engine. She kicked Cloud into a canter.

Poppy had been grateful for the supermoon when they'd set off for Flint Cottage, but now she longed for cloudy skies. The moon shone with such luminosity the moor was bathed in silver light, and she felt as exposed as a field mouse being hunted by a kestrel. Behind them the truck's diesel engine whined and spluttered as the driver – Poppy assumed it was Ricky – floored the throttle.

'They're getting closer!' cried Georgia. Poppy crouched low over the saddle and Cloud lengthened his stride until he was galloping full pelt, his neck stretched in front of him like a racehorse.

She tried to remember the lie of the land. Was there a river they could cross to escape Georgia's kidnappers? A memory of Beau and their race through the night after the storm at Oaklands flickered on the edge of her consciousness. They had nearly drowned that night. Scrub the river idea, she thought wildly.

Georgia was clutching Poppy so tightly she felt as if all the air was being squeezed out of her lungs.

'Faster!' Georgia urged, her breath hot on Poppy's neck.

They were galloping alongside the old stone wall on the edge of the Blackstone farm. By Poppy's reckoning it petered out in half a mile or so, but if they veered sharp left and jumped it now they stood a chance of losing the truck and reaching the Riverdale wood and safety. Poppy knew Cloud could turn on a sixpence – hadn't he proved it in the jump-off at Claydon? – but could she ask him to jump a solid stone wall at a ridiculously-tight angle with two people on his back? Did she have any choice?

'Hold on tight,' she told Georgia. She sat down in the saddle and gave a half-halt. 'Steady boy,' she murmured. Cloud's ears flicked back and his pace slowed. 'Ready?' she asked. She felt the older girl nod. Poppy half-halted again and turned Cloud on his quarters. The wall loomed before them. He managed one short stride before tucking his legs under him and taking off. Poppy felt a whoosh of cold air as they flew over the wall. He landed neatly on the other side and picked up a canter. Georgia loosened her grip a fraction and Poppy sucked in air gratefully.

She held her reins in one hand and patted her pony's neck over and over. 'You clever, clever boy.'

It wasn't long before Poppy could see the dark outline of the Riverdale wood. Cloud was breathing hard and fast and she could tell he was beginning to tire. She chanced a look back. The headlights of the truck were half-hidden by the old stone wall.

'Nearly there,' she crooned to her pony. Still he thundered on. She stared at his pricked ears until they were blurry with tears. She had asked the impossible and he had willingly delivered. He always did.

He plunged into the darkness of the wood and Poppy slowed

him to a walk. It would be beyond foolhardy to try to canter through the trees at this time of night. Cloud shook his head and Poppy let her reins slide through her fingers. He was still blowing hard.

'We should get off, give him a breather,' she told Georgia.

'But what if they find us?'

'I think we've lost them. I can't see the headlights any more, can you?'

Poppy halted Cloud and both girls slid off. Poppy ran the stirrups up and loosened the girth a couple of notches. She looked around, trying to get her bearings. In the distance she could hear the unmistakable sound of running water. They must be close to the stream. Georgia was shivering. Poppy took off her coat and handed it to the older girl, who took it gratefully. Poppy gave her what she hoped was a reassuring smile. 'It's not far now.'

They walked in silence through the trees, one either side of Cloud. When they reached the stream they turned left and followed it as it curved and dipped through the trees.

'This is where I first saw Cloud,' said Poppy, when they reached a small beach.

'What do you mean?'

'He was running wild on the moor. Had been for years. He escaped from the Blackstone farm, too.'

Georgia shuddered. Poppy thought she heard a small sob, but it could have been the soughing of the wind in the trees.

'You OK?' she asked.

Georgia gave a tiny shrug. 'Not really. How did you know where I was?'

'I didn't know for sure. It was a lucky guess.'

'But how did you even know I had been kidnapped? I heard Ricky on the phone to my parents. He said if they told anyone I'd be –' she left the sentence hanging in the air.

'The police know. And Angela.' Georgia's face was stricken. 'But no-one else,' Poppy added hastily. 'Apart from Scarlett. And she'd never tell.'

'Why didn't they come for me?' Georgia's usually clipped voice was pitifully feeble.

'They had no idea where you were.' They reached a fallen tree trunk Poppy recognised. 'We need to cross the stream here,' she said. 'It's not deep.'

Georgia gasped as they plunged into the icy water. Cloud stopped in the middle and drank thirstily.

'Not too much,' said Poppy, who could no longer feel her feet. He lifted his head and nudged her gently.

They scrambled up the bank on the other side. Poppy wanted answers to the many questions buzzing around in her head.

'Did they take you at the show?'

'How did you know?'

'You're still in your riding gear.'

'Remember when I saw you, just before your class? I was eating a hot dog.'

'I remember. You said it was raw. We thought you'd got food poisoning and that's why you didn't jump.'

Georgia laughed bitterly. 'If only I had. It was so disgusting I went to demand my money back. The man told me to wait in the back of the van while he found some change. The minute I stepped inside someone covered my mouth and nose with a handkerchief. I must have passed out because the next thing I knew I was locked in the cellar.'

'They sedated you, like George Blackstone sedated Cloud,' said Poppy wonderingly.

'I woke up with a thumping headache. I was so angry. I knew I'd missed my class. Someone had tipped off Angela that Peter Frampton was going to be there. I wanted so badly to impress him. Who won?'

'The open jumping? Sam.'

'And I suppose he was picked for the team?'

'First reserve,' said Poppy.

Georgia gave a derisive snort.

Poppy raised her eyes to the sky. 'What happened then?'

'I banged and banged on the door of the cellar until this woman told me to belt up else Ricky would do his nut,' mimicked Georgia in perfect Estuary English.

'That was Bev?' Poppy asked.

Georgia nodded. 'She told me I'd be alright as long as my parents paid the two million ransom. Two million!' She laughed hollowly. 'They had no idea we're stony broke.'

There's stony broke and stony broke, thought Poppy drily. Not being able to afford to heat your mansion didn't exactly mean you were penniless.

'Bev was alright, actually,' Georgia continued. 'She made sure I had plenty to eat and drink. She even bought me a pack of cards so I could play Solitaire to pass the time. But Ricky, he was horrible. I think Bev was terrified of him, too. He was always having a go at her.'

Poppy laced her fingers in Cloud's mane. 'I thought Hope's mum had something to do with it. That's why we came to Flint Cottage. That's where Hope and Shelley used to live.'

Georgia wheeled around to face her. 'Did you say Shelley?'

'Yes. Why?'

'I heard Bev talking on her mobile one morning while Ricky was out. She said, 'It's all going to plan, Shell. We should have the dough any day now.'' Once again Georgia had the harsh tone and glottal stops of Bev's accent to a tee.

Something clicked in Poppy's brain and everything became clear. 'Do you think Bev has been inside?'

'Inside what?' said Georgia irritably.

Poppy rolled her eyes. Georgia really had led a cosseted, sheltered life.

'Inside prison. Because Shelley's in a women's prison in Gloucestershire. She knows your mum and dad won the lottery. How's she to know they've spent all their winnings? What if she met Bev there? They could have concocted the plan to kidnap you and put it into action once Bev was released. With a little help from Bev's shady boyfriend. And once your parents coughed up they probably planned to split the proceeds three ways. Shelley provided the insider information and the house. Bev and Ricky were the team on the ground. And I bet George Blackstone was in on it, too. You were the bigger fish he was planning to fry.'

The trees were thinning out and Cloud had quickened his stride, keen to be home after his late-night adventure.

'Almost there,' said Poppy, stifling a yawn.

'How did you do in the end? At the show?' said Georgia.

'We were third,' said Poppy proudly. 'We had the fastest round in the jump-off but we clipped a fence and had four faults.'

'That pony of yours jumps like a dream. How he cleared that wall with us both on his back. I don't suppose you want to sell him, do you?'

'Georgia!' shrieked Poppy, outraged. 'Honestly, you've got a nerve, you really have. No, you can't buy my pony. He's not for sale. He never will be.'

Georgia shrugged and said testily, 'There's no need to throw a hissy fit. You should be flattered that I'm even asking.'

Poppy was speechless. Perhaps there was a direct correlation between money and manners. The more you had of one, the less you had of the other. It was no wonder Georgia rubbed so many people up the wrong way.

Blind to Poppy's chagrin, Georgia carried on. 'Well, if you ever change your mind –'

Poppy realised she was grinding her teeth. 'Don't worry, I won't,' she said grimly.

23

Poppy felt a wave of tiredness sweep over her as they trudged across the field to the house. When she and Scarlett had set off for Flint Cottage, Riverdale had been in darkness, but now lights blazed from almost every window and a police patrol car was parked outside. It looked as though Scarlett had successfully raised the alarm.

A small delegation of people was heading in their direction, led by her dad. Caroline walked alongside him. A couple of paces behind them strode Inspector Pearson and PC Bodiam with serious expressions on their faces. The inspector was talking urgently into a police radio.

Cloud stopped, his eyes boggling. 'It's OK,' Poppy whispered. 'They're just checking we're alright.'

Poppy's dad clasped her shoulders and looked her sternly in the eye. 'Don't ever, *ever* disappear like that again, Poppy McKeever. Goodness only knows what could have happened!'

'Sorry, Dad,' she said in a small voice.

'Come here,' he commanded, wrapping his arms around her. 'We're just glad you're safe.'

'Is Scarlett OK?' she mumbled into his coat.

348

'She's absolutely fine. Bill's taken her home. You can see her in the morning.'

Poppy clung to her dad. He felt safe and familiar. She felt weak with relief. Despite all the odds, they'd rescued Georgia and made it home in one piece.

She could hear PC Bodiam telling Georgia that her parents were on their way.

'Have you caught them?' Poppy asked.

Inspector Pearson broke away from his radio conversation to give her a reassuring smile. 'We certainly have. Fortunately for us Ricky isn't the sharpest tool in the box. He drove his truck into a patch of boggy ground and was quite literally stuck in the mud when our patrols arrived. He's on his way to the cells at Plymouth as we speak.'

'What about Bev?' asked Georgia.

'Officers found her in the cottage trying to cover up their tracks. It turns out she's on licence from prison so she'll be back behind bars before she knows it.'

'Was she at Eastwood Park?' Poppy asked.

Inspector Pearson nodded, surprised. 'How did you know that?'

Poppy caught PC Bodiam's eye and a look of understanding passed between them. 'Just a lucky guess,' she said.

BY THE TIME Cloud was snug in his stable with a fresh bucket of water and a full haynet, Poppy was drooping with exhaustion. Caroline settled her at the kitchen table with a mug of hot chocolate and a shortbread biscuit as though she was six. But Poppy didn't mind. She wrapped her fingers around the mug and watched her stepmum fill her hot water bottle.

Georgia's parents had screeched up the drive in their Range Rover and had whisked their daughter home. Not before the older girl had sought Poppy out in the tack room and thanked her for rescuing her.

'God knows what would have happened if the police had left it to my parents to pay up. I'd have died in that cellar.' She said it lightly, but there was a lingering fear in her eyes. Poppy couldn't imagine how Georgia had survived such a terrifying ordeal and guessed that the scars would take a long time to fade.

The two police officers had also gone, telling the McKeevers that statements could wait until the next day. Inspector Pearson had agreed to bring forward PC Bodiam's shift to the morning, which meant she would be able to watch her daughter in the Nativity after all.

Charlie had slept through the whole thing.

'He'll be gutted when he discovers he's missed all the excitement,' said Poppy. To her embarrassment her voice was all shaky.

Caroline sat beside her and put her arm around her shoulder. 'Hey, are you OK?'

She stared into her hot chocolate. 'I'm glad Georgia's safe, of course I am. But I was stupid, putting everyone in danger. What if Cloud was killed?'

'Well, he wasn't, was he?'

'And Dad's mad at me.'

'He was worried, Poppy. We all were. The first thing we knew something was wrong was when Scarlett started banging on the door yelling something about kidnappers. Your dad was all set to race off in his pyjamas but I convinced him to call the police and let them deal with it.'

The image of her dad sprinting across the moor in his stripy jimjams was enough to tease a smile out of her.

'That's better,' said Caroline, patting her arm. 'Inspector Pearson said he was going to nominate you and Scarlett for a Chief Constable's award for bravery. Imagine that!'

Poppy groaned. 'I really hope he doesn't. Fame and fortune are over-rated. Look where it got Georgia Canning.'

24

The skies were heavy with the threat of snow when Poppy peered out of her bedroom window the next morning. Chester and Jenny were watching over their stable door, their long ears pricked and their eyes fixed firmly on the back door as they waited for her to arrive with their breakfast. Suddenly desperate to see her pony, Poppy eased the window open and whistled softly. Cloud appeared, looked up at her bedroom window and whinnied.

She was pulling on her jeans when Charlie flung open her bedroom door, his face a study of incredulity.

'Ever heard of knocking?' said Poppy pointedly.

Ignoring her, he sat on the end of the bed. 'Mum's just told me what happened last night. Why didn't you take me with you? I could have helped!'

Poppy grabbed her sweatshirt and made for the door, sighing inwardly as Charlie followed her.

She decided to appease him. 'I know. But there wasn't time to wake you. I will take you next time, I promise.'

'Oh, OK.' Charlie seemed to accept this. 'Don't forget what day it is.'

Poppy always lost track of the days during school holidays. 'Saturday?' she hazarded.

'I don't mean what day it is, I mean what *day* it is. It's Christmas Eve! It's *Nativity day*.'

So it was. Poppy had clean forgotten in all the excitement. 'Well, we'd better make sure Chester is looking his best, hadn't we?'

'And Jenny,' said Charlie. 'A pair of net curtains says she can come, too. The more the merrier, she told Mum.'

'Pity she didn't decide that after the donkey auditions. George Blackstone would have had no reason to take Chester.'

'But we'd have never got Jenny then, would we?' said Charlie, with the simple logic of an eight-year-old.

'True. But you really have got to stop calling her that.'

'Stop calling her Jenny?' said Charlie, his eyebrows knotted. 'But that's her name. It was your idea, remember.'

'No, you idiot. I mean the Reverend Curtains. I mean Kirton. See? You've got me doing it now!'

Charlie creased up laughing and Poppy batted him lightly on the arm. 'Come on, little brother. Let's go and groom those donkeys.'

THE NATIVITY WAS due to start at three o'clock and at half past two the McKeevers set off along the windy country lanes towards St Mary's Church with Chester and Jenny.

The two donkeys had stood patiently as Poppy and Charlie groomed them until their thick coats shone. Caroline had made Poppy a makeshift shepherd's costume to match Charlie's, which she was wearing over her black jeans and brown leather boots.

'Bill reckons it'll snow tonight,' said Poppy's dad, looking up at the leaden sky. 'I can almost smell it in the air, can't you?'

Caroline laughed. 'Crystallised water doesn't smell.'

'Yes, it does,' he said. 'What do you think, kids?'

Poppy breathed in deeply. The sharp, cold tang of snowflakes filled her nostrils. 'Definitely,' she said.

'Of course it does!' said Charlie.

Caroline made a show of sniffing and shaking her head. 'Nope, can't smell a thing.'

'What if we're snowed in for Christmas?' said Charlie.

'It won't be the first time, and I don't suppose it'll be the last. It'll be an adventure. We've enough food in to feed an army and I don't think a bit of snow will stop Father Christmas and his reindeer, do you?'

Charlie looked at his dad pityingly. 'He's not real, you know.'

But Mike McKeever was watching a burly man dressed in camouflage gear and carrying a video camera disappear into the church. 'I don't believe it!' he said, striding after the man and tapping him on the shoulder.

Poppy watched as the mysterious red-haired man she'd seen at Witch Cottage turned in surprise. His face split into a grin.

'Mike McKeever as I live and breathe! What are you doing here?' he said, pumping her dad's hand.

'I live up the road, old friend. The question is, what are *you* doing here?'

The man held up his camera. 'I bumped into the vicar in the pub yesterday and she asked if I could film the Nativity. She's planning to sell copies to raise money for the church roof appeal.'

Poppy's dad beckoned them over. 'Come and say hello to John. We worked together in the Middle East years ago. Until John decided that filming wild animals was more fun than filming war zones.'

Charlie was staring at the man slack-jawed. 'Are you John Dunne the wildlife cameraman?'

The bearlike man's eyes crinkled. 'The very same. And who are you, young man?'

'I'm your biggest fan,' said Charlie earnestly. 'I've watched your film on snow leopards like about a million times. And that's my sister, Poppy.'

Poppy gave the cameraman a quick smile. 'Actually, we've already met.'

John Dunne looked puzzled, and then his face cleared. 'The girl with the grey pony. Of course. I didn't recognise you without your hat.'

'You still haven't told us what you're doing here,' said Poppy's dad.

'I'm filming a pair of barn owls in an old croft near Princetown for a new documentary. I've been camped out for about a week, that's why I look a bit rough.' He scratched the stubble on his chin and grinned self-consciously. 'I think I probably gave Poppy a bit of a fright the other day, but she galloped off before I could tell her who I was.'

Poppy realised the three-legged contraption he'd been carrying in the woods must have been a tripod for his camera. Not a trap at all. She shook her head.

'No, you didn't scare me at all.'

SCARLETT WAS ALREADY at the back of the church with Daisy the sheep and the rest of the cast. They watched the congregation slowly file in. It seemed as though the whole village had turned out for the service. Even Barney Broomfield, who ran the village shop, was there in his trademark red sweater. With his white beard, twinkly blue eyes and generous stomach, he bore more than a passing resemblance to Father Christmas.

Poppy nudged her brother. 'Still think there's no such thing as Santa?'

Charlie grinned. 'Maybe I was wrong.'

'There's a first time for everything,' she said drily.

They waved to Bella, Tory and Sam. Poppy mouthed, 'Where's Delilah?'

'Back in the loft, thank God,' Sam mouthed back.

PC Bodiam, wearing a pretty teal dress, denim jacket and black leather boots, walked in hand-in-hand with her daughter Meg, who looked the picture of Christmas in her angel costume, albeit her tinsel halo was slightly askew. PC Bodiam straightened the halo and ushered her to the back of the church before sliding into a pew.

Poppy felt hot breath on the back of her neck.

'Charlie!' she admonished. But it was Nelly the alpaca nibbling her hood.

'Look, there's Georgia,' whispered Scarlett.

Sure enough, Georgia was stalking into the church with a man and woman flanking her like bodyguards protecting a film star. Poppy did a double take when she realised the smiley woman with rosy cheeks, bundled up in a damson-coloured quilted coat, was Georgia's mum. She bore no resemblance to the muted ghost of a woman Poppy had spied through the keyhole at Claydon Manor. Even Georgia's dad looked happy. Poppy was glad for them. It could have been such a different story.

Gradually the pews filled up and before long the church was packed to the rafters. The Reverend Kirton bustled over to see them.

'Everyone remember what to do?' They nodded. 'Marvellous! You are my Christmas stars, every one of you. Even you, Matthew,' she said, bestowing a benevolent smile on the smallest of the Three Kings, who was balancing a homemade gold ingot on his head.

The organ wheezed into life and the congregation shuffled to their feet as the first few bars of *O Little Town of Bethlehem* rang around the church.

Poppy glanced out of the small leaded window beside them and gasped. Snowflakes were falling, scurrying and whirling in the half-light of a late December afternoon.

'It's snowing!' she breathed. The gaggle of children stared out of the window, transfixed. They passed on the news in excited whispers. The words gained a momentum of their own and soon the entire congregation was laughing and smiling at the thought of a white Christmas.

Suddenly Poppy felt giddy with happiness. The horror of the last few days felt like a bad dream. Chester and Jenny were safe. Cloud was tucked up in his stable, waiting for her to come home. Tomorrow was Christmas. And Poppy had a feeling it was going be the best one ever.

AFTERWORD

Thank you for reading *The Riverdale Pony Stories*. If you enjoyed this book it would be great if you could spare a couple of minutes to write a quick review on Amazon. I'd love to hear your feedback!

THE HUNT FOR THE GOLDEN HORSE

Read on for the first chapter of The Hunt for the Golden Horse, the seventh book in the Riverdale Pony Stories.

The Hunt for the Golden Horse

1

Poppy McKeever woke with a start, her heart hammering. The nightmare was so vivid she could feel the roughness of the blanket that covered her mum's face and taste the seawater saltiness of unshed tears at the back of her throat. She sat up and drew her knees tightly to her chest. Magpie, curled in a ball at the foot of the bed, lifted his head and watched her with unblinking green eyes.

It was years since she'd dreamed about the accident. In the ten years since it happened time had blurred the edges of her grief. These days, if she ever forced herself to replay the events of that awful afternoon, it was as though she was watching a grainy black and white film, with actors playing the roles. It felt remote, detached from her. But the dream had thrown everything into three dimensional horror.

Poppy could see the wide eyes of the driver as he wrenched the steering wheel to the right, a second too late. She could feel the air being squeezed out of her lungs as Hannah's mum clutched her to her chest, shielding her from the sight of the ambulance as it drove off in silence. Poppy hadn't understood why the sirens had been switched off. It wasn't until much later that she realised why.

She hugged her knees, wondering what trick of her subconscious had made her relive that terrible afternoon. She checked the time on her mobile. Half-past four. Soon the sky would turn pink and the dawn chorus would begin, the start of another glorious late spring day on Dartmoor. But now her bedroom was still cocooned in velvety darkness. Poppy reached for Magpie. At the touch of her hand the old cat stood up, stretched, and lumbered up the bed, settling beside her. Poppy coiled herself around his warm bulk and steadied her breathing until her pulse stopped racing and her eyelids grew heavy. Sleep, when it finally returned, was deep and dreamless.

'Are you OK?' Caroline asked, as Poppy sat slumped at the kitchen table, nibbling unenthusiastically on a corner of toast.

'Didn't sleep very well.'

Her stepmum smiled indulgently. 'Excited about the holidays, I expect.'

Poppy pushed her plate away and stood up. 'Something like that.' She gave Caroline a quick smile. It wasn't her fault, after all. 'Better go and feed the neddies before they call out a search party.' Plucking the biggest carrot from the vegetable rack, Poppy headed for the back door just as the phone started ringing.

Cloud, Chester and Jenny were at the far side of the field, grazing side by side under the leafy green canopy of a vast oak tree. It was funny, thought Poppy. When she'd brought Jenny home she'd been worried that her arrival might cause friction between Cloud and Chester. Two's company and all that. Far from it. They rubbed along together just fine.

Cloud saw her and whinnied, his brown eyes fixed on hers as she tramped across the field. She ruffled his forelock and he nibbled the pocket of her shorts in search of the carrot.

'That's to share,' she scolded him gently, snapping it in three. Cloud and Chester crunched theirs noisily and wandered off. Jenny waited patiently for her turn, her lips as soft as a kiss as she snuffled the carrot from Poppy's palm.

Poppy ran her hand through the donkey's seal-grey coat. She was plump and content, unrecognisable as the skinny creature George Blackstone had dragged along to the donkey auditions the previous Christmas. Five months of five star care had seen to that.

The donkey's long ears snapped forward and she gave a low heehaw. Poppy was surprised to see Charlie sprinting across the field towards them, his face flushed.

'Guess what?' he panted, skidding to a halt in front of them.

'The real Charlie was kidnapped by aliens in the night and you are in fact an evil imposter?'

Charlie shook his head impatiently. 'You know your friend Hannah from Twickenham?'

'Of course I do. Why?'

'Her mum just rang. She's coming to stay!'

'Sarah's coming to stay?' said Poppy, bemused.

'No! *Hannah's* coming to stay. Her mum's got to have an operation and her dad's away on business. She's just asked Mum if Hannah can stay with us for half-term and Mum's said yes. She's arriving tomorrow morning!'

Poppy rested her hand on Jenny's wither. 'Cool.'

'You don't sound very excited,' said Charlie.

She gave a little shake of her head. 'Of course I am. It's just been a long time, that's all.'

Three years in fact. She'd kept in touch with Hannah by email when they'd first moved to Riverdale, but as the months passed the emails had grown fewer and farther in between, eventually drying up altogether. Poppy couldn't remember the last time she'd heard from Hannah. They'd been eleven when they last saw each other. Poppy had been mad about ponies. Hannah had wanted to be a famous pop star. Poppy read voraciously. Hannah was more interested in clothes and listening to music. Poppy was an introvert. Hannah was the total opposite, and yet their friendship had always worked. They'd known each other since pre-school and their mums had been close friends. They'd been inseparable until the McKeevers' move to Devon three years before.

Now they were fourteen. Poppy was still mad about ponies, although she wasn't as shy as she'd once been. Did Hannah still want to win X Factor? Poppy had no idea. Would they still get on? Poppy wasn't even sure she'd recognise Hannah if she passed her in the street.

As she followed Charlie back to the house, she mulled over the news. She hadn't thought about her old best friend for months and months, and in less than twenty four hours she would be here. Poppy couldn't decide if she was excited or terrified.

ABOUT THE AUTHOR

Amanda Wills is the Amazon bestselling author of The Riverdale Pony Stories, which follow the adventures of pony-mad Poppy McKeever and her beloved Connemara Cloud.

She is also the author of Flick Henderson and the Deadly Game, a fast-paced mystery about a super-cool new heroine who has her sights set on becoming an investigative journalist.

Amanda, a UK-based former journalist and police press officer, lives in Kent with her husband and fellow indie author Adrian Wills and their sons Oliver and Thomas.

Find out more at www.amandawills.co.uk or at www.facebook.com/riverdaleseries or follow amandawillsauthor on Instagram.

www.amandawills.co.uk
amanda@amandawills.co.uk

Printed in Great Britain
by Amazon

18587009R00215